Look at what leading researchers are saying about

Sales Psychology 101:

Katherine Peil, one of the world's leading emotions researchers:

"...Now comes Scott Syverson. A master himself – perhaps the master of *this century* - who offers something far, far, more powerful. A marketing savant, gifted with a prodigious comprehension of human dynamics, Syverson not only offers a profoundly new approach to persuasion, but reveals the personal insights to safeguard us against hucksters such as [Edward] Bernays. He liberates us from a gargantuan gap in our understanding of what it means to be human, a gap leaving us vulnerable to the external manipulators of our irrational "herd instincts" or "unconscious drives". Indeed, in Sales Psychology 101, he offers prescient insights about our internal biological control mechanisms and natural evaluations upon which our everyday decision-making processes rest. He opens our eyes to incredible human capacities long overlooked a collection of natural yet largely uncultivated assets that he calls Paradaptive Intelligence. Best of all, Syverson's system is founded upon good hard science; cutting-edge scientific facts that are only now coming to light for the social scientists themselves...I know this because it is my science upon which his model is based. It is a body of research some 30 years in the making..."

Richard Potts, Smithsonian Institution, Human Origins Program Anthropologist:

"...It is especially interesting to read how the melding between the business world and psychology also converges on the ideas I've put forth about our evolved adaptation in response to change. Emotional interpretations do indeed seem of paramount importance in how people respond to one another and to the volatile aspects of their surroundings. Your ideas make sense to me...it seems like you are on a useful path, and I appreciate the fact that you seek to build a bridge to the evolutionary sciences and an understanding of human evolution specifically."

Sales Psychology 101:

Paradaptive Intelligence ~
The Grand Unifying Theory of Adaptation, Consumer
Behavior
and Sales

Sales Psychology 101:

Paradaptive Intelligence ~
The Grand Unifying Theory of Adaptation, Consumer Behavior
and Sales

"The only Master intellect serves is adaptation."
Scott Syverson

SCOTT SYVERSON

Alpha Psi 1246 Publishing, Ltd.,
P.O. Box 9422, Greenville, SC 29605

Lulu Publishing Services rev. date: 03/06/2018

To mankind,

and to Rob who didn't make this journey with me,

but inspired the effort.

Contents

Table of Graphs

*= Courtesy of EFS International

Foreword

In the period of the 1840s, the science of biology was dominated by the identification and cataloguing of species. The driving force behind this was the belief that if enough species were assembled and described, that a pattern or formulation of order would appear. So the collective mind trust and thought leaders focused on identifying small groups of families and classes of animals based on physical characteristics. Everyone was focused on species, until Charles Darwin's 1859 book entitled The Origins of Species, which shifted the focus from species to speciation, or how different species came into being. The effect upon the science of biology was profound and still shapes its very core to this day, but is more refined as it uses DNA rather than morphology to tease out the secrets of speciation.

The world of commerce is very analogous to this same scenario. Business researchers for centuries have sought to formulate small theorems and postulates to describe observed business behavior. Everyone it seems, is focused on cataloguing business behavior. At the core of business is a transaction. The base unit of commerce, of business, is the exchange of money for a product or service. All businesses are built solely to capture as many profitable transactions as the skill and resources of the owners will allow. It's their sole purpose for being. Yet, with the some sixteen-hundred books written every year in America describing sales alone, I've chosen not to describe or catalogue sales, but to explain the origins of transactions. And just like Darwin before me, I discovered that adaptation was at the very core of commerce. HOWEVER, there is significant difference between Darwin and I. Darwin described Type I adaptation, when genetic reprogramming through mutations was selected by the environment. In other words - body form, physiology, and behavior were changed via DNA mutation to generally exploit and compete for energy sources or mates in the environment. Type II adaptation, described herein, is just the opposite of Type I adaptation. While derived from and still subject to Type I adaptation, rather than change body architecture to create competitive advantages, evolution has created Type II, which focuses on behavioral changes necessary to take advantage of any beneficial Type I mutation. This is carried to its fullest potential by humans who utilize a non-specific body plan that is highly flexible and relies upon behavioral programming that is flexible and capable of in-the-moment adaptation changes. Where Type I adaptation would take many, many generations to adapt a body form to dig to exploit a food source underground, like a gopher or badger, Type II adaptation can accomplish this in just a few minutes needed by a man to form a digging implement or shovel.

This new form of adaptation, Type II, is emergent and only seen primarily in hominids, of which Homo sapiens are the highest form of this new adaptive strategy in nature. But in order to fully understand adaptation in nature, both Type I and Type II adaptation have to be considered, which was not possible prior to this book.

After making these discoveries, I was confronted with a choice. I could either present the Theory of Paradaptive Intelligence as an abstract stand-alone theory and let readers work on their own to apply what was learned or to present the theory along with context so the reader could more easily see the model in action. I chose the route of context, which was much more arduous, but more gratifying in the end.

The quest for answers that resulted in this book started one night in a Washington State University M.B.A. class in the mid 1990's. The professor for that class, one of my advisors in the program, stated that the best model, the state-of-the-art of business science, could only predict 38% of consumer behavior. And that was using a multiple regression model using twelve variables. In other words, using a dozen variables such as age, sex, zip code, income, education, eye color, zodiac sign, hat size, and anything else that would fit in the kitchen sink, science could only account for and predict 38% of why consumers act the way they do. Astounded, I questioned him hard in an open class about the validity and nature of his statement and the research behind it. Well, he didn't take too kindly to my questions, and after the class asked for a private moment which he used to chew on my backside for what he thought was questioning his authority. For those of you who have never done a competitive entrance masters program, you stay in the program by the grace of the instructors. They can eject you at any point in time despite your grades, if they have reason to doubt your viability as a masters candidate. Questioning authority certainly fell into the category of questionable viability. It required a lot of fast talking in one part and enduring a cat-o-nine-tails tongue lashing of the second part to assuage his bruised ego and remain in the program. The funny part was, I wasn't and didn't intend to question his authority. My curiosity meter had been pegged by his statement, my intellect was fully aroused and wanted to know more. *"How could that be?"* I wondered. *"We've got to be looking in the wrong direction, with the wrong approach if all we can explain is 38%."* Despite the open wounds on my backside, a passion was lit that night that still burns even though the cat-o-nine-tails scars have long since disappeared. It's funny how sometimes one's life can be changed by a simple, seemingly innocuous statement — a power that teachers and professors sometimes forget they wield.

At that time in my career I had been doing a lot of new product development requiring marketing research and statistical modeling and I was astounded that the craft upon which I had been honing my skills could not be of more value in understanding consumer behavior. At that time, semi-fresh from a brief stint in another university's M.B.A. program and with a B.A. in Business Administration majoring in marketing in my back pocket, I believed that statistics could solve any problem. Even before graduating from WSU's M.B.A. program, I started researching various ways of examining and extending our understanding of consumer behavior. I felt that everyone was taking the wrong approach. The standard course of affairs was to observe behavior and figure out some way to quantify that behavior so as to be able to apply various statistical tools to tease out the strength of the relationship between reasonably related characteristics surrounding the event of study. But I felt this was backwards. Why not understand how the mind works first, and then work backwards towards consumer behavior and what was known within business science? A simple idea, right? Nonetheless, it was a totally novel concept. I started looking for models of how the mind worked and tried to work backwards towards consumer behavior. I tried to interest some of my professors in working with me on research, but they would have none of it. My concept was way outside the comfort zone of both tenured and untenured professors' protocol for research. Primarily, no business scientist had the expertise or credentials to risk delving into an area of research of the human psyche and its functionality in business. This was the domain of psychology and sociology. And conversely, no psychologist or sociologist had the chops to raid the turf of the business science community. The potential risk of exposure for working outside their expertise was just too great. Essentially, this idea was in a no man's land. Picture the trench warfare of World War I with two sides dug-in, unwilling to expose themselves, but more than willing to blast the crap out of anything that moved in front of them not from their camp. That will give you an idea of where this concept stood in the mid 1990's.

I continued to try to develop a model, drawing inspiration from whatever I could lay my hands on, but to no avail. My models were defective and lacked cohesiveness across the full range of observed business behaviors. That's just a fancy way of saying they were bad.

Then one day, by sheer chance, I met a bright, cheerful, and intelligent lady in the Yakima office of the Washington State Lottery Commission, where I worked at the time, by the name of Katherine Peil. She was there doing a special project for the governor of the State of Washington, the nature of which I've long forgotten. After executing whatever it was her mission required, we struck up a friendly conversation that quickly turned to both our passions, the human mind and a partnership of interest was struck. She soon related and shared her research, which I realized was the missing dimension for which I'd been searching. My efforts to develop my own model were not wasted, for it prepared me to see the right answer and recognize it when it was presented. Now, some twenty plus years later, the fruits of a pleasantly struck-up conversation await, ripened and ready for you to digest in the following pages.

That chance conversation also carries portent of a differing nature. The world of knowledge, best exemplified in academia, is split into two main categories: Liberal Arts and the Sciences. The foundational principle of the sciences is organization. Take math, for example. As one of the founding disciplines of the sciences, it seeks to organize numbers and their properties into orderly rules, principles, postulates, theorems, and branches. The aforementioned science of biology and Darwin's contribution are another. Physics exists to study and organize the attributes of matter at the atomic level, where geology seeks to organize the structure, material, formation, and evolving nature of the planet. Astronomy seeks to organize the nature of planetary bodies in relationship to one another and develop the principles for the formation of individual bodies as well as the aggregate of all heavenly bodies. I think you're starting to get the idea here.

Liberal Arts, on the other hand, are about the study of style. Whether it's literature, art, music, or the like, the focus is finding patterns that create a style and show the propagation of those styles through societies whether they are individual style, trends, sub-cultures, or movements. Which brings me to the business sciences. I'm the proud owner of several sheep's skins that hang upon the wall proclaiming my proficiency in the arts of business administration. That's right, business is an art. At least that's what the preponderance of universities and colleges believe. And to those of us who while away our lives seeking to express our style in business, it is a performing art. We perform our style, our interpretation, of how we think business should be executed, in public for anyone to see and we get paid for it. Aside from the tutu and tights, is that any different from a ballerina? As performers, we seek the highest billing our styles will allow, whether it is with one troupe or the next company…of performers.

And the reason for this is understandable and logical. Business has no foundational core upon which to organize. If you survey the landscape of the business "sciences," what you see is a landscape of statistical analysis that creates pockets of measurements between likely variables scattered around and floating on isolated puddles of unconnected theories and concepts that amounts to nothing more than detailed ignorance of what is actually happening in the human brain.

However, what is presented in this book will change that paradigm. Presented here are the organizing principles of how the mind works at adapting. This allows an unprecedented understanding of how business decisions are made, which are an extension of the adaptation process hardwired into every mind. By applying these principles, a pattern of organization appears and blows across the landscape pushing puddles of disparate theories and concepts together to form one pool of understanding of consumer behavior and sales, and thus the origins of transactions. *Sales Psychology 101* is the leading title of four books that will organize various areas of study once thought of as arts and worthy of only the study of style. With central organizing principles that will allow for quantification, repeatability, and predictability, the study of business has moved from an endeavor of style to one of organization.

There were many ways of introducing the Paradaptive Intelligence model to the world. I could have gone the route of introduction by way of an abstract, or attempt to publish the theory in a peer reviewed scientific publication. In either instance, the dry recitation of theory would have worked against understanding. The latter path is more problematic because of peer review. The greater rhetorical question is whether those imbued in the present models can free themselves of the prejudices their discipline's orientation produces in order to understand a new paradigm totally derived from alien concepts. This is a lesson learned in the 1990's. My aim is not to impugn, but to teach. The intent of this book is to create peers. A new model is best shown in context so that not only theory can be expressed, but also application and thus bring greater understanding more quickly to those availing themselves to the new concepts contained herein. This is why I chose the third method of introduction for the Paradaptive Intelligence model portrayed in this book — theory with application is always the best teacher. By going directly to those who will use the concepts by writing for the business practitioners, it reverses the trend of theoretician acceptance first followed by field application. I've calculated this path to be the shortest path to vetting the theory presented. It can (and will) take a decade or better for model presented herein to be the accepted model upon which all business behavior is measured against. The reason for this is rather straight forward. The business sciences are not organized around the elements unified in the Paradaptive Intelligence model. The model straddles the disciplines of the business sciences, psychology, economics, anthropology, and biology – as well as a few others to be covered in later volumes. There is no discipline in science anywhere in which these concepts are unified or studied in concert. This is also why this model had to come from a source outside the standard partitions of academics. The multi-discipline, bio-mechanism approach to business behavior is just not present in the current confines of academia. Nor can anyone academic discipline address the whole model. Can biologists speak to innovation adoption models? Can psychologists speak to evolution theory? Can anthropologists speak to emotion-based decision making algorithms? And so on. Which brings me around again to the method of introduction of the model of Paradaptive Intelligence. Perhaps now my choice of introduction methodology of writing for the end user is a little clearer.

Finally, no endeavor, such as that taken to prepare this book, is done in a vacuum. There were several hands that helped stir the pot and I would be remiss if their contributions were not recognized. I must first extend grateful appreciation to Katherine Peil, upon whose peer reviewed research and medical journal published theory serves as the foundation for the theory of Paradaptive Intelligence. Her mentoring over the years and patience in answering all my questions has allowed me to see and seek insights to applications that were beyond the model's initial aims. I must also recognize Katherine for her help in editing the earliest manuscripts for accuracy and application of her science. Without her help, assistance, and support, this book could not have been written. Secondly, I need to recognize my friend Rob Nielsen, a salesman's salesman and the person who inspired me to make this journey. In addition to his editing help, he was my leading proof against concept when it came to verifying how eagles really do work within the science presented. The other person who made this book possible is John Pierce. Without his encouragement, enthusiasm, and insight at every step, this book would have been impossible. He supported this book and effort in more ways than I can express. My technical support team also bears the need for kudos. There are always two voices in every book. The first voice is always that of the author, but a quieter second voice belongs to the editor. That quiet but firm voice belongs to my four editors Heather Burden, June Lordi, Sally Lauterio, and the vivacious Gayle Barnhouse. In addition, I need to recognize the creative brilliance of my graphics designer Ted Durham, who worked uncomplaining about the constant changes when normal individuals would have been reaching for a 2x4 or other blunt instruments of persuasion.

Scott Syverson

Preface

The most widespread species on planet earth is *Homo sapiens*. We have adapted to survive in every clime from the poles to the equator, from Eskimos in the Arctic to the tribes of the rain forest of Brazil or the desert Bedouin nomads that wander the Sahara of North Africa. But how is it that man, *Homo sapiens*, a member of the Great Apes, has achieved such environmental diversity when previous versions of man, such as *Homo neanderthal*, *Homo heidelbergenis*, or *Homo floresiensis* not only failed to achieve geographic and climatic diversity, but failed to survive as a species? Many of these predecessors had brain volumes equitable to ours or larger, so clearly a large brain was not necessarily the winning ticket in the evolutionary lottery. What is just as important as a large brain is the organization of that brain, which wouldn't necessarily show up directly in the fossil record that can only describe overall brain volumes. So where did man's adaptability come from?

And, what the heck does this have to do with a book on sales and consumer behavior?

The answer: Far more than you can guess.

Richard Potts, head of the Human Origins Department at the Smithsonian's Museum of Natural History recently introduced a theory based upon soil samples associated with the fossil record of archaic genus *Homo* remains. At the time when the remains were alive, many other hominid species were roaming the earth. The soil samples indicate that there were tremendous climatic swings happening contemporary to the remains. He proposes that rapidly changing climate shifts put selective evolutionary pressure on hominids, challenging different species of man to adapt. And the most adaptable proved to be us, *Homo sapiens*. But what exactly was the actual mechanism of that adaptability?

The old adage "The only constant is change" has yet to be proven wrong or irrelevant, a curious fact singularly missing from the premise of the Global Warming crowd. Nonetheless, in a world of complex systems both natural and man-made that are constantly in motion, it is logical that the creatures with the greatest adaptability would become the most successful and prevalent.

The success of man's ability to adapt lies with his emotion system. Emotions direct and motivate us to either change our behavior or our environment through innovation. Modifying our environment doesn't just mean bringing water to deserts for farming or clearing forest for cities; it can be as simple as making tools or clothing, both of which change our relationship with the environment in just the smallest of ways. It was *Homo sapiens'* superior emotion system that helped him to not only cope and adapt to rapid environmental changes, but also to conquer every terrestrial corner of the earth, and even the non-terrestrial such as the oceans and beyond the ionosphere.

Man has now mastered his environment in the industrial age by creating microenvironments within the larger macro environment, by surrounding himself with air-conditioning, central heating, and running water. But rapid environmental change is a relative term. Scientists measure it in units of centuries. In the modern, industrial society rapid environmental change now refers to the shift of walking from our air-conditioned and heated homes for a brief moment to get inside our equally ventilated motor vehicle on our way to our environmentally controlled places of work.

So what happened to our abilities to adapt? They manifest and reside in commerce. The business world of the free market is always changing and in a state of flux. The emotion system that equipped man for environmental changes is now harnessed for a different type of survival: hunting and gathering in an exchange-based society. The only thing that has changed from pre-historic man to today is the rate of change. Change that was once measured in centuries is now measured in months, days, or seconds, depending on the cyclic rate of a particular industry.

Salesmen fill the hunter role as they stalk parties willing to exchange their currency for his products or services. Because they are constantly working with new parties or old partners on new deals, their adaptation skills are challenged like no others. It is for this reason that this book strives to make clear to all those involved or dependent upon the sales profession just what the mechanisms of adaptation are and how adaptation presents itself in an exchanged based society as consumer behavior. Harnessing this understanding improves performance, thus survivability, and this starts with understanding the emotional system that is universal to all humans.

There has been a monumental shift in evolution research that seems to have gone unrecognized by the sciences. Business on the other hand, leads in this new science. The standard paradigm of evolution is hardware based. Environmental pressure selectively favored physical traits or behaviors in a gene pool, thus changing the *hardware*, the body and DNA, as a means of adaptation. Usually this generally occurred to confer some mechanical or behavioral advantage to a species to better compete for a food source, take advantage of a noncompetitive energy source in the environment, or create higher appeal in mating. The shift in evolution has been the introduction of *software* change. With improvements to *Homo sapiens'* emotion system, his flexible, bipedal, opposable thumb, evaporative cooled, omnivore chassis was "reprogrammed" to increase survivability and achieve greater environment habitation diversity. This new reprogramming not only changed *Homo sapiens* behavior, but it moved the future ability to make behavioral changes away from genetic coding to behavioral circuits genetically encoded in the brain that were capable of modifying behavior or environment on the fly, in the moment, which we call adaptability.

But, by controlling the micro-environment that surrounds him as well as an exchange based society that can deliver any food, substance, material, or item from any corner of the globe with just a phone call and a credit card, man has removed all traditional evolutionary pressures. These traditional evolutionary pressures have been replaced by those man has created in his exchange-based society. Now, those that are the quickest and the most adaptable in the business domain become evolutionary trend setters by the influence they wield upon others to change their behavior or environment.

If science is desirous of understanding this new paradigm, then they need to study business to understand man's adaptation skills. And because consumer behavior/sales is the prime manifestation of our adaptation hardwiring in an exchange-based society, there is no better candidate to study than that of the salesperson if one wants to understand adaptability.

1

INTRODUCTION TO THE GRAND UNIFYING THEORY OF ADAPTATION, CONSUMER BEHAVIOR AND SALES

YOU REALLY WON'T _KNOW_ WHAT YOU'RE DOING IN SALES, UNTIL YOU'VE READ THIS BOOK.

"Feelings are the fine instrument which shape decision-making in an animal cursed and blessed with intelligence, and the freedom which is its corollary. They are signals directing us towards goodness, safety, pleasure, and group survival."
Willard Gaylin

If you go to any bookstore or library and browse the self-help section for salespeople, usually a voluminous section, you find a myriad of approaches. But with all the volumes, why can no one explain what is really happening in the mind of the prospect or client? These books focus on telling the reader what to do and how to do it, but they can't explain the who, when, where and why. As you peruse the offerings, a pattern appears. Sales and selling books take on a vocabulary template of their own. They tend to speak in terms of actions of the salesman, reactions or objections of the prospective client, and strategies and practices to deal with them. While these are helpful from a distance, this approach appears to be superficial, taking the direction of dealing with the symptoms rather than the looking at the deeper underlying structures that control and influence the communications transactions. The boundary appears to be drawn at the edge of business related issues, but no one is willing, or able, to go beyond the realm of rational reasoning into the human dimension, which has been the domain of the science in the fields of psychology and human physiology.

1

The reason for this is understandable. Discussion of the human psyche has been messy, convoluted, complicated, and an enormous topic while being written in jargon incomprehensible and impenetrable to even the most learned businessman. Freud's, Jung's, Skinner's, and Gestalt models of the human psyche lent little of themselves in a way that was useful to anyone operating in the real world with real people. Thomas Henry Huxley, a contemporary biologist of and proponent for Charles Darwin wrote, "The great tragedy of science is the slaying of a beautiful hypothesis by an ugly fact." The ugly truth of the matter is that none of the current models in psychology can help the salesperson explain one whit of what they encounter on a daily basis. But the human dimension is the medium through which all commerce is built and transacted. What is missing in the field of psychology is a proper model of emotions that would allow the salesman and businessman to understand the unruly beast of human emotions they wrangle with on a daily basis. Emotions do not speak to us in articulated words and structured thoughts -- that is the domain of the rational mind. Rather, emotions come to us, influence, and control our behavior via fuzzy, unstructured urges. Because the nature of these urges are ill-defined and nebulous, they have presented an impenetrable fog for the businessman, politician, and scientist into understanding how the human mind makes decisions. This lack of penetration into emotional functionality has created a culture that is opinion driven in the business and political world about how people think.

The unspoken truth of sales is that the relationship between seller and buyer is laced with undercurrents and emotional urges. This is a black-box process in which everyone has a certain, intuitive level of understanding of what's going on but don't know what's actually happening in the black box of emotions. It's like driving a car. Almost every adult knows how to start a car and drive, but how many are mechanics that can tell you in detail what's going on in the rest of the car and how everything operates. The salesman knows how they feel — sort of — and usually can read the client's feelings — mostly. He or she may have a gut level idea or ingrained response of how to respond to the emotion proffered by prospective clients, but a clear cause and effect relationship is nowhere to be had.

In a complex sales environment, where multiple decision makers are required to sign-off, each participant brings a different emotional content to the table, creating an emotional matrix requiring multiple approaches by the salesman and his team. Some are better than others at reading and making the right response. But, all and all, this is a mysterious process that has been the domain of shamans, charlatans, con men, and people with letters after their names that don't have to sell to make a living. It makes little difference to them whether their explanations are of practical use.

Because this process has not been well understood, no one has ventured too close to the topic, choosing to skirt the "elephant in the living room" and speak in tongues of processes that get quantifiable results without quite knowing or being able to explain the mechanisms in play.

Until now.

Adaptation is the process in which humans adjust to meet the constantly changing environment that surrounds them. There are only two directions in which this adjustment can go: changing your behavior to fit the surroundings or changing the surroundings to fit your behavior. Humans are unsurpassed in their ability to do both. But in an exchanged based society, how is adaptation manifested? Specialization is necessary to increase efficiency and is required for communal living. Money is the medium of exchange in which knowledge and labor products can be converted for exchange of other knowledge and labor products. So rather than designing a tool or process for our every problem, we buy solutions from people who specialize in solving those issues. We call that process of buying solutions consumer behavior. And once you understand the rules and principles driving adaptation, and thus consumer behavior, then you will understand sales, which is the reciprocal of consumer behavior.

This book will bridge our understanding of adaptation and consumer behavior using the latest model of emotions emerging from researcher Katherine Peil called the Emotional Feedback System. The basis of the Emotional Feedback System (EFS), combined with other scientific gains, comprises the Paradaptive Intelligence Network which governs the everyday world of the sales professional, regardless of their language or society, because it is the apparatus of adaptation and source of consumer behavior that guides us in what to change: our behavior or surroundings.

The aim of this book is to blend science and practicality into a manual for the above average sales professional. Charles Brower, president of Batten, Barton, Durstine & Osborn, one of the world's oldest and most respected advertising agencies, once stated, "There is no such thing as a 'soft sell' or a 'hard sell.' There is only 'smart-sell' and 'stupid-sell'." Stupidity is the purposeful cultivation of ignorance. Or put another way, stupidity is the intentional absence of adaption, for both purposeful ignorance and non-adaptation describe two sides of the same coin. The intent of this book is to provide the mental architecture of human decision-making to dispel ignorance and facilitate adaptation. The main thrust, at its core, is the unique sales approach of not selling to get a yes, but to sell so they can't say no. This is done by disengaging the seller's defenses and managing prospective clients' emotions through question-based selling. Using the techniques and models presented in this book, you'll know why your clients and prospects are reacting the way they are long before they themselves know why, thereby giving you knowledge into how best to respond to whatever emotion is directed at you. *Sales Psychology 101* will go beyond the intuitive level and bring structure, principles, and techniques that will allow the sales professional to understand and manage the emotional transactions that occur in every sales cycle. Why is this important? Because as you will learn, *all* human endeavors, and especially sales, are based on human emotions. With the help of cutting edge science from the field of psychology, sociology, anthropology, and the business sciences, among others, *Sales Psychology 101* will help the reader to understand why many of the classical selling techniques and methodologies, dispensed with certainty, are absolutely wrong and detrimental to the sales process.

In any sales organization, there are always those salesmen that seem to outperform everyone else. People often refer to those salesmen in euphemisms such as "thinks outside the box" or "they don't make them like that anymore," or "they broke the mold when they made him." In fact, these salesmen have a developed high level of understanding of the workings of emotions, which guides them intuitively through the sales cycle and produce more sales. Yet, when asked how they do it, they are at a loss to explain just what it is they do, or when, or why they do it.

The sales self-help section of any bookstore is laced with books of two basic types: "mimic me" and empirical quantification. The "mimic me" books are generally written by great salesmen of the "they broke the mold when they made him" type. These books are full of useful and entertaining anecdotes and insights into specific sales formats where the reader can copy methods, phrases, or strategies if applicable to their realm of the sales kingdom. The entertainment value often overshadows the fact the authors really can't quite explain the fundamental communication transactions portrayed in the book or the emotions that drive them. Almost all of the material in these books has been recycled for each new generation of salespeople, updated for the times. And dutifully, each generation, like you, tries these new approaches only to find that they initially yield positive results before they fade or become erratic. The reason for the erratic performance is because the authors of these refurbished concepts did not know or understand the specific timing and application of their described techniques because they had no understanding, vocabulary, or model of the workings of the prospect's mind to guide their readers in application. So these "new" techniques were applied willy-nilly. Occasionally they would hit the proper timing, seeming to validate the concept by obtaining a sale. So if a little is good, then a lot more is better and sales people would initially increase the frequency, duration, and amplitude of their newfound tool, spraying it all over the sales process. And thus, the erratic performance would start. Because results become erratic, salespeople discontinue the new tools, reverting to their old habits, which produced just as erratic results, but whose processes are more comfortable.

The other type of self-help book is comprised of those that seek to quantify the sales activity. They seek to explore the relation between variables in a statistical manner. Examples such as "This type of question will yield this type of response X% of the time," or "Eighty percent of sales are closed on the fifth call or after the fifth closing attempt" abound in these books. While statistics are helpful in understanding the strength of relationship between two or more variables, it cannot explain the mechanisms or causation of that relationship. *Sales Psychology 101* looks to give its readers a bridge to understanding both types of sales books by peeling back the lid of the black box to expose the mechanism of emotions and their inner workings. Once the mechanisms are understood, then both anecdotes and statistics become clearer, allowing the reader to develop variations of their own to apply in their particular portion of the sales kingdom at the right time, in the right sequence.

In business, there are two broad marketing objectives: 1) Gain an ever-larger customer base, and 2) Retain market share from competitive loss. So there are two objectives, one offensive and one defensive. *Offensive Selling*, the classic approach to sales, focuses on selling or the acts of the salesperson rather than what is happening with the prospect. It also implies a converse: *Defensive Selling*. This is where the focus is put on the competition. The old adage of "there is no better defense than a good offense" has been the mantra of many good companies. But as in sports, you will not reach the pinnacle of performance without both an offensive and defensive element. There is great debate among sports fans and businessmen alike as to which is the most important. As for business, there is only one answer, which is best voiced in the old axiom, "It's cheaper to keep the customers you already have than to find new ones." Using the methods described *in Sales Psychology 101* includes both offensive and defensive selling. This is accomplished not by focusing on what the salesperson is doing or the competition. It focuses on what is happening inside the prospect. It is both a strategic philosophy as well as tactical application of principles and technique that will harden your customers against competitive Offensive Selling while building market share. With *Sales Psychology 101*, you'll learn building market share is derived from using the Innovation Emotional tonal algorithm pathway. Defensive selling is accomplished by utilizing the Relationship emotional tonal algorithm pathway. In classical offensive selling, you sell to obtain a yes. In defensive selling, you sell so the prospect or client won't say yes to the competition. The difference is that with *Sales Psychology 101* you will understand what mechanisms are in play and how to fine tune them. Finally, once you understand the emotional underpinnings of sales transactions, *Sales Psychology 101* will teach you strategies that will help frame your presentation in new ways aimed not at obtaining a yes, as in classical sales techniques, but how to frame your presentation so they can't say no.

Question-based selling has been around long enough to certify it as a reasonably effective means of sales activity, but does so without understanding the emotional mechanism questioning engages. Literature on question-based selling has extensively catalogued different types of questions. Different types of questions are statistically qualified as to their potential to get customers to identify "needs" or conclude in a sale. This system is numerically based and lacks the vocabulary to discuss the mechanisms beyond the questions it statistically analyzes. *Sales Psychology 101* will show how every question evokes an emotion, and every "need" is an emotion unspecified.

But there is more to selling than getting a client to sign a contract or write a check. And no salesman is an island. Rarely does the salesman's job or the sale end with signing a contract. *Sales Psychology 101* should be an enterprise-wide commitment. As we'll see later, every department not involved in a sale of the moment is involved with the sales in the future and why the emotions of a sales cycle do not stop with the commitment of a prospect to become your customer.

Additionally, through the model developed in this book, we will also see why outdated concepts, like buyer beware, which was based on partial understanding of the emotional requirements of buyers, have been pushed aside as the evolution of packaging and retailer environs have moved forward. Finally, we will explore, using our newfound understanding of the emotional system, proper management techniques and principles designed to improve the efficacy of the sales organization to create a world class sales force.

Sales Psychology 101 will give the readers detailed understanding of the emotion system of man, including its function and purpose. Chapters 2 – 9 will lay out the mental components, their function and operating principles that are the adaptive machinery. With that basic understanding, in Chapters 10 – 16 we'll introduce you to consumer behavior by examining the twelve emotional stages that are encountered in selling and their specific order so that you'll not only be able to understand prospects, but you'll be able to predict and repeat the process at will with an accuracy rate bordering on clairvoyant. This, combined with the twelve emotional stages of business relationships, will give the sales professional unprecedented control of the sales process. *Sales Psychology 101* will provide, for the first time, controllability of the sales process to the salesperson, but will also serve as the first practical model of consumer behavior. In Chapters 17 - 19, we'll look at ancillary topics such as manipulation (a no-no) and building world class sales organizations using the techniques described in the book.

Having a micro-level model of human actions that can be scaled to the macro level will be of great benefit, not only to the salespeople reading this book, but everyone in the allied field of sales, such as marketing, advertising, and marketing research, as well as the entire management structure who, by lack of understanding of the basic process between their firm (the salesperson) and the prospect, often enact policies detrimental to the firm's overall effort to sell their product and manage effectively.

But perhaps the most important aspect of this book is its ability to link all the life sciences to business, which heretofore was not possible, by using the Paradaptive Intelligence model. By laying down a common architecture of adaptive algorithms DNA encoded in the brains of mammal and our human antecedents our behavior can be examined to teased out and better understood in their baser influences as well as those higher functions which distances us from them. This will take us on a journey of evolutionary discovery within the business world. Just like nature selects for those organisms best suited for an environment, so too in business. By understanding the adaptation circuitry of man, we will be able to understand how the market place uses these algorithms to selects top performers in sales, and how it selects market leading firms by not only their ability to identify and recruit top notch sales talent, but to convert staff into top performers. Once you understand the basic adaptation circuitry, you will see how in man's modern jungle of commerce, the business world ruthlessly and efficiently culls those who don't use the full extent of their Paradaptive Intelligence.

8

SECTION I

Mechanisms of Adaption

Multi-cellular organisms initially needed little central nervous system control. Theirs was a world of random movement. They would move about randomly, colliding with food sources or into other multi-cellular critters that might find them delectable. This arrangement and dependence on the Theory of Chaos worked well and still does for many creatures, with examples such as amoebas to reptiles, which approach things of pleasure, like food and mating partners, and move away from things of potential pain and harm when encountered. This mental mechanism is called the reactor. But to change from a random movement in search of life's needed sustenance to a pattern of movement to be in positions of likely encounters with sustenance and safety required more sophistication of the central nervous system. To repeatedly place an organism at a location likely to encounter sustenance and mating partners, or avoid predators, required a separate mechanism capable of forethought to work alongside the mental mechanism that controlled random movement and the approach/avoid impulses. This mental mechanism is called the adaptor. But in order for forethought to be operative, something else is needed − foreknowledge. And thus, the need for a separate mechanism to store foreknowledge was needed. So forethought and foreknowledge go hand in hand. This ability to combine forethought and foreknowledge conferred powerful survival advantages to an organism. The initial protocol of learning was based on repeated occurrences before it was placed into memory. We call this conditioned learning and this occurs via the reactor. But, in order to accumulate foreknowledge faster and more accurately, a different process of placing useful information into storage and recall for later use was needed.

Whether through random genetic mutation or divine design, an arms race of sorts ensued as organisms competed for greater and greater forethought computational power and quicker learning to obtain the survival advantages they conferred. The history of this arms race is well documented in mammals. But the arms race continued unabated, especially in the primates and more specifically in hominids. When directly applicable pre-stored foreknowledge was unavailable, hominids developed inductive and deductive reasoning to apply portions of similar experiences to bridge the gaps of new and unknown scenarios. The lack of any similar experience to solve problems led to the development of another function – imagination. Memory and learning protocols continued development to keep pace with the growth of reasoning, moving from conditioned learning of the reactor where repetition events led to storage in memory to active learning where only one event was needed to learn from or, in some instances, failure was all that was needed. Using deductive and inductive reasoning based on other known similar circumstance found in memory, causes of failure could be imputed. Failing that, imagination could be used to impute the reasons of failure. The use of inductive and deductive reasoning along with the use of imagination is called active learning and works alongside conditioned learning. All this sophistication in learning and the needs for information for inductive and deductive reasoning along with imagination, necessitated the need for another mental mechanism to control the flow of information to and from memory into the forethought mechanism, the adaptor. This mechanism controlling information flow is called the ego. In order for survival advantages of forethought to be realized, the adaptor had to assume primacy over the reactor, but still needed to work with and through the reactor, which is still the workhorse and control center of the central nervous system.

With the ordering and propagation of all these mental mechanisms, another mechanism was needed to control and coordinate the interplay of all of them to accomplish aims and goals of the animal for survival. This is accomplished by the mental mechanism called the Human Action Cycle. The Human Action Cycle is the wellspring of human emotions that signal to us whether to change our behavior or our environment. All this computational mental ability combined with a communal living strategy required a few more refinements. To live cooperatively, hominids needed to communicate goals and aims to each other both verbally and nonverbally to ensure those goals and aims were to the benefit of not only the individual but also to the tribal community to which that person belonged. The mechanism that influences the adaptor to pursue goals and aims that benefit society as well as the individual and the balance between those two purposes is called the conductor, because it controls how we conduct ourselves with others of our species. People often refer to this as our "conscious." The mechanism that signals nonverbally our goals, aims, and emotions through facial expressions and body language to others in the society is called the Mirror Neuron System. All combined, the reactor, adaptor, conductor, ego, Human Action Cycle, and the Mirror Neuron System comprise the Paradaptive Intelligence Network and it is this that is the frame work of humans' unique and vast adaptive capabilities.

Competition caused an arms race of the central nervous system among mammals. It caused many of these mental mechanisms to appear in different and various combinations and varying capacities within the Mammalia class. Up to this time, mammals were still reactive to the environment, trying to gain the optimal survival advantage from what they encountered in their environment. But the central nervous system arms race for more computational power of the brain pushed members of the primate order to go one step forward by giving them, and a select few others in the subphylum Vertebrata and Mollusca, the ability to change their environment by making implements and tools. Up to this point, all Darwinian evolution was centered upon changing or modifying morphology to solve problems. Tool making required significant, additional changes to the central nervous center, specifically in the Paradaptive Intelligence Network. A complex system was developed that allowed members of the family of Hominoidea not only to create tools but to *evaluate* their effectiveness and devise means for improvement -- this is innovation. It is this improvement, the ability to evaluate and improve implements, which sets us, *Homo sapiens*, apart from all other tool makers. It is this ability to adapt tools when needed or change our behavior to fit the environment and the ability to discern when to do which that is the source of our adaptability.

In animals, lacking many of the mental mechanisms of man, changes in behavior are accomplished by DNA reprogramming of the reactor. Behaviors that are genetically encoded into DNA are called instincts. And man is susceptible to this sort of reprogramming by random genetic mutation. However, where man is markedly differentiated from animals is that he is endowed with the Paradaptive Intelligence Network that allows for behavioral and environmental changes without genetic reprogramming. This is the genesis of humans' vast adaptive abilities, which will be the focus of this section.

2

PARADAPTIVE INTELLIGENCE NETWORK

"Evidence is presented that the mass suppression of emotion throughout the civilized world has stifled our growth emotionally, leading us down a path of emotional ignorance."
Dr. Wayne Payne's Ph. D. dissertation
in which he coined the term "emotional intelligence."

The term "emotional intelligence" has been bandied about and proselytized by so many, that beyond its intuitive definition, what does it really mean? It's like using the word to define the same word, especially in light of the fact that emotions have been little studied and poorly understood, even within the field of psychology. So how is it we can have "emotional intelligence" about something (emotions) that science, through the work of Peil, is now only coming to grips with? The obvious answer is we can't.

Starting now, we'll let the pundits and profiteers continue to blather about "emotional intelligence" while the readers of this book will start a journey in a new direction, the direction of understanding. The primary function of emotions is to act as feedback and advisory signals to keep us on course to obtain and achieve goals set by the conscious mind. Just like the body has regulatory systems to control too little blood oxygenation– the Sympathetic System (increases heart rate and respiration), too much oxygenation – the Parasympathetic System (decreases heart rate and respiration), blood sugar-insulin of the endocrinal system, and dozens of other regulatory systems, the mind has a regulatory system to control behavior. The unique aspect of Peil's EFS theory was to approach emotions as a biological regulatory system, or more simply put, what is the biological purpose of emotions. The primary purpose of this regulatory system is adaptation. Adaptation can be defined as implementing changes to achieve beneficial goals and objectives serving as motivations in a shifting environment.

As we will learn, there is a simple, robust set of mechanisms networked in the mind that creates a system to help guide us to reach our motives. Emotions just so happen to be the currency, or the language, if you will, that one portion of the brain uses to speak to other portions of the brain. Just as electricity is used in a missile guidance system to provide information to a central processor on where the missile is going, emotions tell humans whether or not they're on track to meet a motive. The function of the missile guidance system is not to produce electricity, but to vary the quantity and type of electricity to communicate information gathered by sensors and report them to the processor as a means to guide the craft to a target, a goal. It only uses the electricity as a form of communication, which is what emotions do. What we'll learn is that all human actions are guided by emotions. And, more importantly we will learn that commerce is the quantification of emotions.

So what shall we call our understanding of how this system works now that we understand emotions are guiding us to get on, and stay on track to achieve goals set by the conscious mind? For the remainder of this book, we'll use the concept of **Paradaptive Intelligence** and its combined individual structures to form the **Paradaptive Intelligence Network** model. The meaning of *para* comes from the French form of "a thing that protects from," such as *para*chute, a device that protects us when departing from an aircraft before it's landed. Truncated from *adaptive*, –*daptive* also comes from the French form *apapier*, which means to be able to adapt – "to change (oneself) so that one's behavior, attitude, etc., will conform to new or changed circumstances." There is even a duality to the use of the word *intelligence* here. Intelligence can mean "the ability to learn facts and skills and apply them…" or "… information about secret plans or activities…" In this case, both apply, since the secrets of our emotion system have been hiding in plain sight since our creation, and we are going to expand our ability to use it. So literally, "**Paradaptive Intelligence Network**" translates into "**a set of subsystems using gathered, secret information about self-protective changes in attitude and behavior to conform to new or changed circumstance**." And that is exactly what this book is about.

SIX SUBSYSTEMS OF THE
PARADAPTIVE INTELLIGENCE NETWORK

The Paradaptive Intelligence Network is comprised of six subsystems within the brain, each serving a different function. The six subsystems are categorized by function:

1) **Reactor** – responsible for the body maintenance, survival, and protection; responsible for conditioned learning, metering corrective signals.

2) **Adaptor** – responsible for the conscious mind and adaptation
3) **Conductor** – responsible for our conduct, values and morals associated with communal living and maximizing survival; responsible for metering growth signals.
4) **Ego** – a mind and memory filter serving as gatekeeper to the adaptor and director of active learning.
5) **Human Action Cycle** – coordinates and facilitates communication and activities among the reactor, adaptor, and conductor to achieve a motive.
6) **Mirror Neuron System** – whose job is to communicate our emotions to others and interpret theirs through facial expressions and body language.

These are the mental mechanisms of adaptation. Of all the six subsystems, the adaptor has primacy. It is your conscious mind, the seat of your awareness of yourself and the world, the mechanism of forethought. The amount of information available to the adaptor from the body and memory is staggering, so it has an assistant, a gatekeeper (the *ego*) which decides what information is placed into or drawn from memory and what information is admitted to the adaptor. When the conscious mind determines it wants the body to perform some action in the world outside the mind, it must do so through the Human Action Cycle that works with and coordinates all the other subsystems. In addition to executing the requested action of the adaptor (a motive) the Human Action Cycle is also responsible for giving feedback to the adaptor, to encourage it to stay on course or to change it (adapt) to achieve the desired motivation. This signaling comes from the reactor, because the reactor is in charge of the body and therefore has control of the entire sensory suite of the body. It sees, smells, hears, feels (touch), and tastes all, 24/7, and therefore is the first to know what kind of results your actions are generating in the world. It communicates these results and suggests courses of action through the internal, inter-subsystem language of emotions. The conductor is also a subsystem that influences the motives of the adaptor. It influences the adaptor to pursue motives and create action plans in ways that maximize the results for the individual as well as society. Through emotions generated from the reactor, it signals whether our actions are acceptable outcomes to both the individual and society. A simple way of looking at the difference between the reactor and the conductor is to understand the reactor provides feedback to the adaptor and suggestion as to whether we're on course to achieve motives, and the conductor provides guidance as to how efficient and effective those actions were in accomplishing the activity of any given growth signal emotion. This information is combined into one form of communication, the language between the reactor and conductor to the adaptor, called emotions. These are signals telling you whether you're on target or you need to adjust or redirect some aspect of your actions and which direction to go.

The Paradaptive Intelligence model is a model that describes not only all human adaptation behavior but all adaptive behavior observed in the animal kingdom. It is the Paradaptive Intelligence Network that is at the core of all animal behavior. Adaptive behavior is dependent upon emotions that are created through DNA mutation (Type I Adaptation) to create on-the-fly behavioral Adaptation (Type II Adaptation) sequences of emotions called emotional algorithms that all creatures use to varying degrees based upon the number of emotions with which they are equipped by God, nature, or both. While humans have the greatest number of emotions and thus the greatest flexibility in adaptive behavior, all animals display adaptive behavior but to a lesser extent. These animal behaviors can be understood by walking back through the animal phylum and even the kingdom by pruning various emotions, Paradaptive Intelligence Network subsystems, and external signally (such as quorum signaling in single cell creatures) systems, all of which are feedback systems, to describe the lesser behavioral adaptive capabilities. This now adds another level of precision in understanding evolution through the development of emotions as a measure of organism capabilities to distinguish one species, genus, family, suborder, order, class, phylum, and kingdom from another.

Paradaptive Intelligence is a model that describes the adaptational mechanisms of the brain, which control all human behavior through emotions. Sales Psychology 101 is a book dedicated to describing for business and all sciences the application of this model in a business centric approach to understand and explain how and why transactions occur in a context based approach.

3

SENSORY COMMAND AND CONTROL
– THE REACTOR

"What can give us surer knowledge than our senses?
With what else can we better distinguish the true from the false?"
Lucretius

An old axiom claims that verbal communication only comprises five percent of what is communicated. While it is uncertain that what you say comprises precisely five percent of the communication package, there is certainly an element of truth in this notion. If you think about it, when talking to another, not only are your words evaluated, but the context, tone, rhythm, inflections, facial expressions, and body language are evaluated simultaneously to determine the subtext of your words. But those are not the only evaluations that are happening. In addition, your ears will be hearing and evaluating any background noise, your peripheral vision is being screened, your nose is passing information to the brain, as well as your sense of touch from your skin, taste…plus other body parts and bodily functions are all reporting in. All that vast information is being dumped continuously on the brain while you're having a conversation with a prospect or client.

The process of evaluating the constant and massive stream of information is done by the reactor. Its mission is to preserve and maintain the body, so it is constantly monitoring the environment for threats to the body and self. It maintains the body by performing all the routine bodily functions and activities. It is why you may become aware that you are thirsty in the middle of a conversation with a prospect or suddenly become aware of a spider scuttling across the floor. Both those signals indicate a possible threat to the body: dehydration or the requirement to determine if the spider is a Black Widow or Brown Recluse spider (though if you generally have a phobia towards spiders, it wouldn't really matter what type it was).

The reactor is command central for all sensory organs and is responsible for all your subconscious bodily actions and movement. The reactor joins body to mind – the

17

adaptor. Its focus is self-preservation. This is the same structure that animals use constantly to probe their environment for threats (pain) and pleasure (food, companionship, or the opposite sex). Your subconscious works every moment of the day and never turns off. This is why in the middle of a deep sleep you can be awakened instantly by a sound out of place in your home and know that it was a sound that has awoken you. In fact, Peil, originator of the EFS model, argues that the reactor is actually a sixth sense. This sixth sense can detect danger or threats to the body from the massive stream of sensory data washing through your central nervous system every instant.

REACTOR- COMMUNICATION DATA STREAM FILTER

In addition to all the common senses shared with animals, humans have additional demands put upon the reactor by the unique human trait of complex language. Communication in any language is fraught with unknowns. Words are vocal symbols or abstracts of some concept. Because each person's vocabulary and definition of abstracts is unique, the reactor must rely on sentence context, tone, facial expression, rhythm, pitch, body language, and gestures to determine what concepts one is conveying. Your reactor is charged with monitoring the above streams of data. If it determines some discordance between any of those variables, such as a facial expression incongruent with the other streams of information it is receiving, it will signal the adaptor with an emotion, usually a mild form of threat (negative emotion).

The reactor will determine whether the data stream is either positive or negative. If the attributes of the data stream are good for the body, it will direct you to move closer. It moves you towards pleasure. Examples of this are food tasting good, the building being clean, someone having a nice smile, a fragrance being enticing, someone having a great laugh or sense of humor, a person appearing attractive, or an area being well lit so it's safe to walk at night. Or the finding may be negative. The reactor moves you away from the threat of pain. Examples of this are a person lying, someone acting aggressively, an area being dark so you hesitate to walk that way, a person appearing unkempt, a building looking derelict and unsafe, a person having bad breath, someone who is loud and interruptive, or someone dominating you by not allowing you to speak. The reactor is constantly scanning for known threats or pleasures.

The reactor measures the potential for pain in a process that assesses risk. If pain is imminent, we reflexively dodge out of the way of a flying chair aimed at our head. There is a whole gradient of danger that the reactor informs the adaptor of, from mild to imminent. It might range from something like, "Something is not quite right about what he just said" to "He just told an out-and-out lie!" or "Careful where you put your foot while walking in the tall grass," to "Stop! Don't put your foot down on the rattlesnake!" High level threats trigger the reactor's Fight, Flight or Freeze response.

The reactor makes its presence known in the motive, outcome, and evaluation phases of the Human Action Cycle (Chapter 7). Technically speaking, the reactor is also present in the actions phase because all actions to speak or move must go through the central nervous system, which is commanded by the reactor.

PROTECT THE BODY AND SELF BIAS

All emotions originate in the subconscious in the mechanism called the reactor. The main directive of the reactor is to protect the body and self. It does this with a bias to approach what is positive, pleasurable, and move away from what is negative, harmful. It is because this function of the brain is shared with most of the animal kingdom that scientists did not consider it a part of the human consciousness and was considered a vestigial mental appendage. In the motives phase of the Human Action Cycle, the reactor will influence your thoughts to seek pleasure and avoid pain. The reactor is more concerned with the immediate, short-term cycle of events: it lives in the now, in the moment. It wants you to avoid pain and seek pleasure now!

It is for the reason this portion of your subconscious is named the reactor. Because of its two-state reaction, approach or repulsion, it will confer to the adaptor. And also like a nuclear reactor, if left unchecked by the adaptor, your reactor would run wild with "animal" instincts quickly and cause a tremendous amount of damage to you.

In sales, the prospective client's subconscious will produce an emotion based upon the adaptation plan (your product or service plus an implementation plan) being presented to his or her adaptor, which is the conscious part of the mind. The adaptor will recognize what emotion is emanating from the reactor and may choose to accept it and act upon it, ignore it, or worse, choose not to control the pleasure/pain impulses at all. Because of the reactor's ability to have such a powerful influence upon the conscious adaptor, it is imperative to understand its features. The subconscious mind has two critical features that every salesperson must know and understand intimately: the six universal needs that drive relationships and the structure of emotions the reactor produces.

SIX UNIVERAL NEEDS

The only needs that a person has are attached to innovating solutions and relationships in the subconscious. Peil lists and describes them in Figure 3.1. It is important to note that there is a hierarchy to these needs; they must be fulfilled in order. In order for the sixth need to be fulfilled, one through five must have been satisfied consecutively. Knowing and understanding these needs is essential to any salesperson because these are powerful appeals through which to communicate your products' attributes and features. The first need is that of freedom.

Freedom

Freedom is the ability to select your own path without constraints. Freedom is choice, and choice is another name for adaptation. So freedom is the potential to adapt. Every individual has his or her own unique set of skills and talents. And only he or she knows best how to use them to maximum extent. Rules, laws, policies, procedures, methodologies, etc., constrain us and prevent us from exercising judgment, which in turn minimizes our opportunity for success, and thus minimizes rather than expands the number and volume of sales. Yet, they're a part of business life. Having the freedom to apply your particular skills and talents in the best way ensures maximum sales volume. This is all true with your prospects, also. Their constraints tend to shape the dimensions of their imagination or contractual obligations, thus they may not be able to initially see the solution in the adaption plan presented by a salesman. But, with persistence and good communications you can prevail, describing your product in terms of giving the client the freedom to work more efficiently, profitably, or knowledgably. The adaptation plan you present gives your clients another degree of freedom that will allow them to bring forth and use skills and talents that may be constrained by their current methodologies or circumstances.

Power

Power is about the ability to make changes in one's environment. Knowing that there are constraints to one's freedom and having the authority or power to enact change are two different things. This is nothing new, salespeople have been doing this since the dawn of sales. It's called "qualifying the lead," and it involves determining whether the prospect you're talking to has the freedom to make buying decision and the power to make changes. Freedom within the sales domain refers to the lack of contractual obligations or other commitments and obligations that would prevent the consumer from buying your product. Power refers to the ability to command a change, the expenditure in company resources, to affect a purchase of your products or services.

Or, as sometimes happens, salespeople may stage a presentation to someone in the client's firm to make a "yes or 'know'" decision. 'Know' refers to educating a person who will decide whether to present it to the decisions maker. These people have freedom, but no power. In this way, an influencer or screener to the decision maker can make a determination to know whether your product is worthy and becomes your internal advocate to move it to the person with the power to make internal company environment changes.

If the adaptation plan you are presenting provides new or expanded information to the decision makers, you are providing them with an opportunity to exercise their power to make the right changes.

More correctly stated, when you are qualifying a lead to determine if you are talking to the decision maker, you're screening for both power and freedom. If they are constrained from making any changes to their business due to a prior contractual obligation, they will never be able to exercise their power.

Connection

The need to be connected to other people is a powerful motivator. This is why people follow fashions or conform to business or social practices. If opinion leaders, leading companies, or local businesses are adopting your products' benefits, you can use this need to help make that connection to your product.

This need also explains why you need to take time to cultivate a relationship with your clients and prospects. They have a need to establish a connection with you. While the discussion of your product may serve as the entry point in the relationship, they're subconsciously developing that relationship and will not make a purchasing decision until they are comfortable in their relationship relative to the significance of the purchase.

Esteem

The changes that your client will make with your product will raise their esteem, both in the eyes of colleagues and themselves. They will pride themselves on having recognized the problem (constraint to more freedom), acknowledging their ability to change it (power), and cultivating the right relationship with you (connection) to resolve issues. Remember, improved esteem can only come from change in relationships; it does not spring from holding the status quo. Your clients are pre-programmed to satisfy esteem needs by making changes in their environment. They have an internal need to be seen as important by others, and that can only be met by making changes/improvements (adaptation) in the workplace.

Creativity

By virtue that you are talking to a decision maker, be it owner or manager with the vested power to make changes, and they have already satisfied their need for freedom, power, connection and esteem, then they have cleared all the hurdles to satisfy their next need, creativity. Creativity can be collaborative or singular, but the need to express it is there. This is important for you as the salesperson to note, because it means you do not have to have all the answers. If your adaptation plan draws the interest of the prospect, simply asking something like "How can we make this work?" can unleash their creative need while supplying the finishing touches to the adaptation plan. Again, note that creativity is a change (adaptation) driven need.

Meaning

Having met the previous five needs, your clients and prospects are now in a position to assess their place in the world. For salespeople, this means helping their clients determine their place in the business world by helping them with adaptation plans. By removing the emotional barriers in their business environment by solving problems, clients will be able to determine if they have the talent, drive, and resources to grow their companies to another level or if they were meant to be the best local mom-and-pop organization. Additionally, your accepted adaptation plan will give them a better understanding of how their business works and how they fit in to their commerce world.

Knowing these six basic needs can help you frame the dialogue, questions, and presentations surrounding their product adaptation plan. Most, if not all, of your clients could not articulate these needs if their lives depended upon it. Yet now that you understand what drives them, you'll be able to give them the best adaptation plan you have to offer.

FIGURE 3.1

<u>The Universal Needs Of The Reactor</u>

The Reactor operates upon an innate, genetic value system which is communicated through feelings relating to six universal human needs. Together they drive us to meet all three human purposes of self-preservation, self-development, and self-actualization:

1. **The Need for Freedom:** Every human has the inner urge to be free in order to self-regulate. The need for freedom safeguards our self-directed movement and free will choice. It moves us to resist external controllers that interfere with our inner purposes. It gives us a sense of rightful privacy, liberation from judgments of our personal choices, and a sense of unlimited possibilities and life potentials. Physical, intellectual, and emotional freedom are crucial for self-preservation, and serve as facilitators for the higher purposes.

2. **The Need for Power**: Every human needs to be able to personally *create change* in order meet all needs and purposes. Inner empowerment fills us with the enthusiasm to make things happen. This need gives us a sense of integrity, fairness, and justice. Power is crucial for self-preservation, and provides the energized impetus for evolutionary change. Together, freedom and power *define* and *protect* the internal and external conditions necessary for self-regulation. They bring anger and conflict when efforts are hindered, boundaries are violated, and opportunities are limited.

3. **The Need for Connection**: Every human needs to interact and be connected with others. This need underlies all empathy, all trust, and all love. It moves us to procreate, cooperate, build families' and communities. The urge to commune, affiliate, to love and be loved, is most basic, but it will take the back seat if community takes away too much of our freedom or empowerment. The connection need ushers self-development and cooperation.

4. **The Need for Esteem:** Every human needs to feel worthy and good about themselves. It springs from the innate value potential, and drives active self-development and self-actualization. It is the basis of confidence, honor, remorse, and natural morality.

5. **The Need for Creativity:** All humans experience the urge to creatively express themselves. Whether through art, literature, dance, creative play, physical labor, or working at daily professional tasks, emotional fulfillment comes through active creation of that which we imagine. This need channels human power into our amazing cultural creations.

6. **The Need for Meaning:** All humans are born curious, seeking new experiences and taking delight in patterns that make sense of the wonders of our world. This inner urge to understand draws upon the analytical and rational capabilities of the brain and leads us to develop philosophy, science, meaningful worldviews, and long-term need-meeting strategies.

4

THE CONSCIOUS MIND – THE ADAPTOR

"Men are not prisoners of fate, but only prisoners of their own mind."
Franklin D. Roosevelt, 32nd President of the United States of America

"The human mind is not meant to be governed, certainly not by any book of rules yet written; it is supposed to run itself, and we are obliged to follow it along, trying to keep up with it as best we can."
Lewis Thomas

The adaptor, the primary part of your consciousness, is comprised of memories, imagination, abstract reasoning -- inductive and deductive, and logic. It originates your willful actions. Its mission is self-development. Its primary function is that of an adaptation engine by adapting to ever evolving circumstances in the environment. It has two modes of adaptation: innovation and relationships. For innovation it uses past experiences from memory to identify similar patterns and applicable situations to predict and generate outcomes in the present. It uses abstract reasoning to analyze and gauge the applicability of a memory to the moment's circumstances to generate outcomes based on a current motive or goal. It combines memory, analysis, and the input from the reactor and conductor which it uses to devise an adaptation strategy or action plan and implements it. If no such memory is present that can be related to present circumstances to obtain a desired outcome, imagination is used to create part or an entire action plan. If the reactor says "I want something – move closer," the adaptor may make a conscious decision to adapt that impulse request and devise an action plan to obtain what is being signaled by the reactor or to ignore the impulse. The adaptor uses relationships as a way of obtaining tools and innovation, resources, and adaptation plans from others. The primary mission of the adaptor of adaptation is accomplished by self-development (learning). The more self-development, i.e. knowledge, the conscious mind obtains, the more adaptable it will be, thus increasing survivability.

For example, the reactor informs you that you're hungry and you then spy an orange on the counter on the other side of the room. Your adaptor accepts the input from the reactor, devises an action plan to walk to the counter, peel and eat the orange. But on the way, you see a bunch of slimy goo on the floor that you have to pass through to get to the counter. At this point, your reactor is telling you there is a possible threat to the body in an unknown substance on the floor, and your ego searches memory, recalling similar substances that turned out to be slippery. The adaptor decides to forego the orange at this time.

And this all happens is the blink of an eye. For example, imagine walking into a store on a cold call. The proprietor is behind the counter. You introduce yourself and why you are there. The proprietor searches his memory and finds that most of the salesmen in his experience stay too long and interrupt his business activities. He makes an analysis that this probably applies to you. His reactor tells him that disrupting his business routine is bad for him because he has things to do in his environment and his ability to survive is tied to his gainful business activities. You represent an unknown, disruptive force. He combines those two elements and derives an action plan, with a beginning, middle, and end to get rid of you as soon as possible and says, "Thanks for coming by. Perhaps I could get your card and call you at a later time. This just isn't a good time for me." Or try this scenario: you're walking on a downtown street on a warm summer day and glance across the street to see someone emerging from an ice cream shop, licking a double scoop. Your reactor sees something that is cold and sweet, both pleasures, and issues a positive signal to the adaptor to move towards the ice cream parlor. You might even say to yourself, "That looks good! I should get one." That's your reactor at work. Left unchecked by the adaptor, you would immediately turn to the shop, step off the curb, cutting the traffic in the middle of the block, and walk straight to the store. In so doing, you fail to see the bus hurtling towards you that runs you over causing fatal injuries. Perhaps you've seen this very same behavior in a dog that walks right in front of you while you are driving. That is because the dog does not have abstract reasoning. It sees, it does. In this scenario, your adaptor devises an adaption plan to walk to the end of the block, wait for the light, look both ways before crossing the street and arrive safely at the ice cream shop. This type of interplay happens tens of thousands of times a day, continuously, but without your awareness.

The conscious mind is always learning, whether you are directing it or not. If the learning structures in your brain had a bumper stick, it might say: "$#@% (excrement) Happens, So Does Learning." This learning takes two forms:

conditioned and active. Conditioned learning is associated with lower animals, like Pavlov's dog, where if two things repeatedly happen in proximity to each other, an association will be formed. If you remember in Pavlov's famous experiment, before feeding his dog, he rang a bell. After a time, the dog associated the bell with food and would start salivating at the sound of the bell. In humans, we call that conditioned learning and that's how habits are formed. The smartest breed of dog, Border Collies, can learn a new command in less than five repetitions, so as a baseline a habit can be formed on more or less than five repetitions. This type of learning is associative, where active learning is relational. Keep in mind that conditional learning is not necessarily bad; without it you would not be able to mindlessly shave your face or put on make-up in the morning out of habit, doing something that you've done hundreds, thousands of times, without thinking.

In active learning, abstract reasoning is used to deduce or learn the relationship between elements so that learning can occur from just one instance, or it doesn't even have to occur. You can learn from mistakes. And this may occur without your awareness. For example, you're introduced to someone at a business conference who shakes your hand and gives you her name. A name is an abstract thought or concept that you link to a memory of what that person looked like, how firm his or her handshake was, what fragrance they were wearing, and any other information you may have gathered in that first impression. That is active learning. It doesn't take numerous, repeated introductions to learn their name as it would in conditional learning.

Your brain is constantly seeking relationships in your environment in order to adapt to it. This is a powerful fact that is best served by the following statement: The only master intellect serves is adaptation. Think about it—you're always learning. What you learn is stored in your memory. Your adaptor uses memory, abstract reasoning, and imagination to form adaptation strategies to adjust to the constantly changing world around you.

COOPERATION BIAS

The primary bias of the adaptor is cooperation. This is the source behind the phrase "power of suggestion" where by merely suggesting an action to someone unleashes powerful, deep-rooted mental mechanisms to comply. It is also the reason why you'll hear so much about adaptation plans throughout this book. Stating plans of actions to buy and implement your product of service to prospects and clients plays upon the built-in bias of cooperation present in all humans. Humans are social creatures, and as we'll find out in the next couple of chapters, there are built-in subsystems aimed at our social nature and cooperation. With social creatures, self-development can only occur with the cooperation of others. It is impossible to learn or use language without the cooperation of others to teach us language, likewise for customs, rites, rituals, and rules of the society that an individual occupies. These are the basic tools necessary for self-development. If an individual is deficient in these societal underpinnings, they will be cut-off and denied the opportunity for self-development. This makes sense if you view this from a biological standpoint. Culture and knowledge transmission occurs verbally and by example, thus creating the need for cooperation. Written language came later and is a creation of man. Written languages would not be viable unless everyone cooperated and agreed to the same symbols and rules of use of writing. Babies are a prime example—they learn to talk first, and later we teach them to link their new-found language to the symbols of the alphabet and rules of grammar. All the while they are learning to read, they are still absorbing the culture of their societies by watching and interacting with others. This is why humans are more comfortable with peace and serenity (cooperation—or in the business vernacular "professionalism") rather than conflict and confrontation, the latter being the domain of the reactor's bias to protect the body and obtain scarce resources for preservation.

The adaptor bias also looks to the future. Its primary mission is to gather and learn information for possible future scenarios of adaptation, which is why it is always learning. In contrast, the reactor looks to the past, seeking to obtain or avoid known pleasures or pains based on past experience.

5

THE CONDUCTOR

"Let a man's talents or virtues be what they may, we only feel satisfaction in his society as he is satisfied in himself."
William Hazlitt

"A man cannot be comfortable without his own approval."
Mark Twain

The conductor is the third regulating mechanism of the emotional apparatus. Its function is to ensure optimal, maximized adaptation solutions in tool making/innovation and greatest relationship development possible. Its focus is self-actualization. Its mission is to influence the adaptor to strive for self-actualization and satisfaction of the six universal needs, the latter of which are resident in the conductor. Self-actualization is described as a state where an individual reaches his or her fullest potential. The conductor provides this direction so that an individual will direct his or her activities, no matter what it is, to achieve the best possible results while maximizing relationships, thus securing the individual's survival by ensuring not only optimal results for their efforts, but also the best outcomes for their identified society and relationships. By providing betterment to society, or tribe, the individual promulgates the health and well-being of himself or herself as occupants of that society. By aiming for optimal results for themselves and others, individuals secure their position within their society by creating value, goods, and services that allow them to obtain their baser requirements like food, shelter, warmth, mobility, entertainment, etc., thus increasing their survival potential.

Its secondary function, and arguably its founding precept, is that it is the governor of relations with others of the same species. All animals, whether solitary hunters or social/ pack/herd animals, must interact with each other, if for nothing else than to

29

procreate and perpetuate the species. This function manifests itself in humans as the instinct to protect family and tribal members by providing aid and comfort.

Think of the conductor as a little angel sitting on your shoulder, encouraging you to do right for yourself and others. If the reactor is the body and the adaptor is the mind, then the conductor might be considered the soul. While it may be a simplistic metaphor, it should help give you a visualization of what this regulator's activities are. The configuration of our conductor is unique to humans. Other than a few great apes and possibly a few species of birds, no other animals have need for such a regulator, because they lack the conscious mind that we possess to innovate by changing our behavior or environment and measure those innovations against personal and tribal benefit. Without this very important regulator, you would have a highly rational mind capable of great adaptability guided and controlled by the impulses from the reactor. In short, it would be anarchy where everyone is out for themselves seeking personal pleasure. The conductor allows the rational mind, the adaptor, to sort out what impulses from reactor to adopt or ignore defined by whether it will be to the betterment of the individual, society, or both.

SELF-ACTUALIZATION BIAS

This propensity to maximize potential manifests itself in two forms. The first is to optimize your personal potential in all your activities. The second is maximizing the potential of your activities for tribal benefit. Carried to extremes, a person whose activities only optimize for themselves is called selfish, self-centered, a taker, or a narcissist. An extreme example of this would be a criminal. On the other extreme is a person called selfless, a giver, or philanthropist. An example of this type of person would be Nobel Prize winner Mother Theresa who cared nothing for herself but devoted all her activities to those around her in the slums of India.

These two biases, while similar, have separate aims and can come into conflict. Optimizing potential for yourself may not be in the best interest of society, while optimizing exclusively for society would have just as tragic consequences on your survivability. Imagine how difficult it would be to raise children if you didn't create results for your benefit that would allow you to provide for the needs of child rearing. Or imagine a world ruled by anarchy where no one conducted themselves in a way that benefited others. There would be no roads or societal infrastructure with very little regard for family, the basic unit of societies.

How this dilemma is resolved internally is one of the defining characteristics of personality.

PRIMACY

Having now seen and discussed the Reactor, Adaptor, Conductor and their primary missions and biases, it is now time to understand the relationship of these separate processing center of the brain. The reactor, adaptor, and conductor as processing centers roughly correlate to the reptilian, paleomammalian, and nonmammalian brain structures. Each of these structures have their own biases that influence the other brain structures in their processes. In addition, each has its own mission. Depending on circumstances in the external world, each of these processing centers will assert differing levels of control over the individual depending upon the degree to which the precedents of its primary mission are involved. This is called primacy. It is the measure of control of which that processing center is directing or controlling the activity of the individual. The Adaptor, in the brain's architecture, is designed to be the mechanism running operations the majority of time. The Reactor and Conductor only assert primacy based upon the degree to which their mission is involved and remain silent when the individual is engaged in activities not relevant to its mission.

The Adaptor has a control sharing arrangement with the Reactor and Conductor. The Reactor and Conductor are never active at the same time. So at any point in time only one or two processing centers will be active, the Adaptor and either the Conductor or Reactor. In circumstances of extreme, either the Reactor or Conductor may assume total control. This extreme circumstance with which the Reactor is totally in control is better understood as the Fight, Flight of Freeze response to a threat. The extreme circumstance in which the Conductor assumes total control is when an individual makes a sacrifice without thinking for and individual with whom they have the highest levels of relationship. The conductor only asserts primacy when a relationship is involved.

The best way to understand this relationship is to think of it in terms of in the percentage of time in which a particular processing center will direct the activities of the individual. For instance, in a situation where a mild threat in the external environment may be present, the Reactor may only have thirty percent control of the individual while the Adaptor retains seventy percent control. So an individual's actions will reflect a small element of threat mediation and much larger element of adaptive behavior. Let's say that mild threat was a spider crawling along a wall. The smaller Reactor activity would be to keep an eye on it and track the spider's movements periodically while continuing with whatever activities the Adaptor was involved with initially.

6

THE GATEKEEPER – EGO

"Everyone thinks that all the bells echo his own thoughts."
German Proverb

Egos – everyone has one, it seems. But what are we really talking about? There are tons of popular phrases about peoples' egos from abundance to the lack thereof. But like many things in our lives, the actual item itself and your ability to describe it is usually lost very early when linked to the popular lexicon. In its simplest form, ego is your sense of yourself, your earliest sense of personal self-identity or who you are. But, where it really gets interesting is when you ask yourself, what function does it serve?

The ego is the gatekeeper to the conscious mind. While Freud identified it, he really couldn't tell you what exactly it did. Peil describes it in this way: "The modern ego is the connective overlap between the body and mind, acting as a *doorway*, which *mediates the information flow* into and out of the mind." Unlike the unconscious mind, the Reactor, which can simultaneously filter through copious quantities of incoming data from all the body's senses, the conscious can only deal with one thing at a time, and it has two basic elements competing for eminence: the body and the world. The body is communicating information collected by the central nervous system and the Paradaptive Intelligence Network loop. The world is what is happening outside the body arriving to the mind via collection from our sensory organs. The ego selectively determines what enters the conscious mind from either the world or the body. Its goal is to keep our expectations and outcomes reasonably close to one another so that the mind's abilities to control can evolve at a stable pace. In short, it wants to put us in positions that are close enough to our skill level to grow, but not put us in situations that are well beyond our capabilities because that will end up badly for us, causing harm.

For example, if an ego lets a person believes that they can hit the fastball of a major league baseball pitcher (expectations) without ever having moved beyond playing T-ball in preschool, we would believe that person's outcome in trying to do so would not end well for them. It takes time and practice to develop the skills to hit a major league fastball, which is why baseball players go through so many levels of play, from T-ball and Little League to middle school, high school, college, farm teams, minor leagues, etc. At each level, the expectations and outcomes are reasonably close, creating an environment for the body to develop and control the development of desired skills of hitting progressively faster and faster fastballs and curvier and curvier curveballs at a stable pace. A dysfunctional ego may let you actually step into a batter's box against a pro with a flaming heater and get injured when you react instinctively (reactor) at something being thrown at you in a blur.

The ego acts as a gatekeeper by performing in two modes: security and maintenance. In the security mode, the ego controls the flow *into the consciousness*. The ego will decide whether incoming information streams are suitable for either the conscious or unconscious processing path, based on how threatening or affirming the incoming information is to the mind's subjective view of reality. If the incoming information is consistent with expectations, fear is low and the information will be admitted. Put simply, the ego determines what is important to your conscious mind and what it should be aware of at any point in time.

If the information is not consistent with expectations, the ego will reject or filter that information so as to conform to what you think is going on. In this way, the ego also filters the reactor for pain/pleasure information. If the ego gatekeeper fails to learn or recognize the reactor's signals, the individual would be in serious jeopardy. Let's take a "for instance" look at someone we all know, that person who has "a big ego." In this example, this person, a guy, has "a big ego" because he thinks he is God's gift to women, when in reality, every female he knows thinks he's a jerk. Yes, this is the ego at work. But remember, its job is to filter, and in this case, the ego filters out all the sneers, sideways looks, gestures, and jabs sent in the guy's direction from women who don't like him, which is just about everyone. Instead, his ego only filters in the courtesy smiles that he receives, or the fact that everyone seems to recognize him wherever he goes, which supports his belief that he's really good with the ladies. In addition, his ego filters out the jabs and snide intentions of the remarks coming in and confirms only that women speak to him often, again confirming to him that he's pretty special. It's not that he has a "big ego" but rather his ego is dysfunctional, filtering out essential information and he's not getting the whole picture. This is a prime example of the ego's protection mode. It is filtering out painful, disturbing, hurtful information that he's disliked, and only letting in information that confirms what he believes. In science, they call this confirmatory bias, and it happens to everyone, even scientists. Our ego filter is more likely to only let us see what we want to see because it wants to protect us from bad, negative information and for us to experience the happy, positive aspects of life. This is why scientists go to great lengths to set up and document how they will measure results in an experiment before they ever start or lift a beaker. By doing this, they won't fall victim to their ego's protective filtering mechanism. In a sense, the phrase "big ego" may actually be right. A "big ego" really means a big, overactive filter. It's not that people with "big egos" think they can do things that others can't; it's more the case that they just don't get the whole picture because their minds are holding back the truth for them.

This is important for business people to know, because egos may not be letting them see what exactly is going on in their business, filtering out problems, discord, and inefficiencies that others see. Salespeople are often in a better position to see what's going on in a business than the owners or managers, because owner egos may be filtering out negative information and not giving them the whole picture.

In the ego's maintenance mode, it acts as a filter for what is put *into memory*, which means that the ego controls active learning. By placing your performance, or what you learned about your abilities into memory, you could select in the future to participate in activities that are closely matched to your capabilities, leading to growth opportunities. For example, let's say that you try your hand at ballroom dancing and you are possessed of two left feet. You stagger about the dance floor, collide with other dancers, giving them bruised ribs while mangling your dance partner's toes before plowing into the band leader, giving him a fat lip. A functioning ego would place that nightmare into memory so that in the future, you would not put yourself in a position where your inability to dance would create mayhem for others. But a malfunctioning ego may not place this incident into memory. So the next time you're out with a new date and the band strikes up a tune, you may not remember the last time you took to the dance floor as you grab your date's hand and fly to the dance floor with the same, inevitable results.

Sound complicated? It's not really. Try this example: a new salesman three months on the job and fresh out of college lands an appointment with a major account that the company to date has been unable to penetrate. The new salesperson's sales manager knows that this is a big complex account and the new person is overmatched, lacking the experience, industry knowledge, and product knowledge to put it together. So he accompanies the new salesperson to his first presentation, hoping to mask over or smooth any mistakes the new salesperson might make. The new salesperson's ego thinks he's doing great; after all, he landed the appointment with the prospect where all others had failed. So during the presentation, his ego filters out that the customer rolled his eyes at some of the claims he made and that the smile he gave the salesman was not one of encouragement and agreement which his ego filters in to agree with his internal belief that he's doing a great job. But the smile was one of derision expressing his thoughts of "you've got to be kidding me, right?" The sales manager sees the customer's reactions and his ego allows him to see them for what they really are, which enables him to jump in and re-direct the prospect from some of the overly simplified remarks the salesperson made and acknowledge that the prospect's business is not so straight forward and "cookie cutter" as the salesperson described.

At the bottom of it all, the ego in security mode only lets in information to memory that confirms what you think is happening. The best way to prevent the ego from excluding or filtering needed information is not to have a preconception of events before you get there and focus on learning and asking questions such as what is going on in the business environment of your prospects and clients. Preconceived ideas are directives to the ego's filtering system. Moving from a preconceived idea of how you're doing to a point of asking how you're actually doing will open the ego filters, letting in information that you will need to conclude a sales call successfully.

The maintenance mode also controls the exit gate of the mind on what is learned and placed in memory. This function controls our self-growth, updating our expectations of what we can and can't do. If the ego fails to recognize our failures, no learning occurs, the wrong information is placed into memory (such as 'that client was an idiot, and it wasn't my fault) and no new adaptation strategy is developed for future use in a similar situation. In short, you won't learn from your mistakes if you avoid seeing your mistakes or remembering them. You need to explore your complex feelings after a sales call, good or bad, and ask such simple questions as, 'Was my reactor telling me to move away from a line of approach or presentation and did I ignore it?" and "Did this help or hinder the sales process?" This line of inquiry will help you recognize when your reactor is trying to help you, and insure that helpful, self-development memories will be recorded to memory by your ego to help you in future similar business and sales situations.

7

HUMAN ACTION CYCLE

"…all cultures have in common a small number of emotions or emotion words, but that every culture has multiple ways of nuancing them…"
Dr. Robert W. Schrauf

One of the great mysteries of science has been man's emotions and the purpose they serve. There have been several models of their purpose and function, but all were wide of the mark and did not accurately describe real life interactions. And most certainly none of the models could predict behavior, a major scientific requirement for a model to be accepted within the realm of science. In fact, science has viewed man's emotional responses as a vestigial leftover of man's evolution from our common ancestry with lower forms of life and nothing more than a mental appendix. As such, little or no effort went into emotional systems research because of its relegated status as an evolutionary leftover that had to be endured. This stance of dealing with and enduring it is something that all salespeople can relate to. But like the appendix, which research has now shown to have a useful, purposeful function as a reservoir for necessary microbial fauna that populates our digestive tract, emotions now have been found to have a useful, purposeful, central function in the way the mind is structured, operates, and adapts.

If humans were computers, the operating system would be whatever spoken language they use. Language is the lens through which humans see and interpret the objects that populate their world. And just like computers, humans also have a machine language, a language that actually pushes the levers and operates internal mechanisms just like the computer does to make calculations, read and store data, and create output to peripherals like a display, printer, or modem. In humans, this machine language is emotions.

In the 1980's, Katherine Peil started research in this long-neglected area of the human psyche, and brain structures, at the University of Washington in Seattle where she developed an organizing theory called the Emotional Feedback System. Peil continued that research through the years, at Northwestern and most recently at Harvard, refining the theory to its present form, of which a streamlined, simplified version is herein presented. The reader should note that while the Emotional Feedback System Theory is elegant and robust, it was designed to explain a much wider range of human activities than just sales. While Peil's theory is worthy of its own book, this book has attempted to reduce it down and include only those elements necessary to explain behavior as it pertains to adaptation, consumer behavior, and the endeavors of the salesperson. For a more complete viewing of Peil's theory, further information will be listed in the appendix of this book, where more detailed descriptions can be found.

The best way to understand the application of the emotional system to sales is to understand it from an internal perspective: how, what, and why this system does what it does. We will describe how the theory and its elements relate to the reader with the belief that if you know yourself, you will be able to translate that into how clients and prospects will respond and act.

HUMAN ACTION CYCLE – THE CORE PROCESS

At the core of the human psyche is the Human Action Cycle (HAC). Your conscious mind, the adaptor, after being influenced by both reactor and conductor, and fed information by the ego, has decided upon a goal. The adaptor must work through this system, the HAC, to accomplish anything it devises. The reason for this is the adaptor does not control the human body. It can't move arms, speak words, control facial expressions, etc. That is all controlled by the reactor. It is in charge of the central nervous system to perform its prime directive — protect the body — which in turn links it to every sensory organ and motor control neuron. This is a prime solution to the reactor's prime directive of protecting the body: put a system in place that has all the information from the sensory organs and all the muscle motor control neurons and can operate autonomously, when needed, to protect the body. And this is why you can duck from something being thrown at your head without thinking. So a system is needed, the HAC, to translate adaptor orders into action by working through the reactor. Think of the HAC as an order fulfillment system. Emotions are produced in the process of order fulfillment as feedback on how things are progressing in the real world outside the body. This is necessary because there are several types of errors that can occur. For example, bad design and bad execution are just a couple of types of errors that can occur. With bad design, what seemed like a good idea in your mind may turn out to be a bad idea once put into motion in the real world. Something like unconsidered reaction from a device, machine, or person may occur because you lacked information about it, or them to illuminate the bad design. Bad execution is another. You have a good idea, but may lack the skill, talent, coordination, resources, or to properly plan to actually carry it off. You need a system that lets you know how things are going in the real world as your plan unfolds. Emotions perform this feedback function as part of the order fulfillment process, so that the adaptor can adjust and adapt to what it's doing in the real world. These feedback signals, emotions, are produced in the reactor for one simple reason, the ego.

As you recall, the ego's job is to act as a filter due to the tremendous amount of information available at any moment on the body's central nervous system that could paralyze the adaptor with information overload if all was allowed in. Because the reactor is monitoring the entire central nervous system simultaneously, it has all the facts. It is also aware of what the adaptor is trying to accomplish: after all, it's being directed to move the body, speak works, and so on, to accomplish the adaptor's goal. It takes all the facts pulled from all the live feeds of the central nervous system, compares them to what is desired by the adaptor and issues a progress report all tied up into a nice little bundle, a bundle we call an emotion. The reason why this bundling occurs is because the ego would never allow in all the data streams the reactor is using to make its determination. It will only let in the executive summary – the emotion – to enter the mind. After the emotion is received, and if the adaptor is interested, the ego may select one of the live feeds from the central nervous system to concentrate on, if it's still occurring, so the adaptor can focus on what's going on outside the body to get a better idea of what or how to adapt.

By definition, a feedback system is designed to home in on its target. To do that, it must be able to give varying levels of feedback to let you know when you're getting closer and when you're moving in the wrong direction, when you're getting warmer and when you're getting colder. For example, a metal detector chirps louder and longer the closer you get to a metal source, helping to locate an object. So, a proper feedback system must be able to communicate both intensity and proximity, and the Emotional Feedback System does just this. What we'll discover is there is only a half dozen emotions. What we have thought of as separate, distinct emotions turns out to be members of the six different categories of emotions expressing varying intensity levels, telling us we're on the right track or wrong track, getting warmer or colder. So, a proper feedback system must constantly change its signal based upon the actions of the operator. This helps us put into perspective why our emotions are constantly changing. Our emotional feedback system in the HAC will constantly be varying emotions to move us towards our desired objectives and away from harmful things.

A CLOSER LOOK AT THE HAC

Now that we have a better idea of what's happening with the HAC, let's break it down further into detail. As a feedback system, the HAC is comprised of five basic steps: 1) Motives, 2) Actions, 3) Outcomes, 4) Evaluations, and 5) Corrections. The cycle can be seen in Figure 7.1. There are three structures of the emotion system that shape, monitor, and control the Human Action Cycle: the reactor, the adaptor, and the conductor discussed in previous chapters. Because this is the basic model of how the mind relates to the external world and the internal self, it is also the model of how the mind relates to the business world externally and internally.

It is important to note the Human Action Cycle is only concerned with actions, not thought. Actions in the real world are the wellspring of emotions; without actions, there can be no emotion attached. It's important to note that the conscious decision to take no action is an action because conscious inaction can manipulate results in the real world, thereby creating outcomes. Sales is a process based solely on actions. As a thought experiment to make the point, think of the way that you would commit a crime, like the perfect bank robbery. As you scheme, you will generate no emotions because it's all inside your head, even though it breaks every rule of society. You have not interacted with the world. But the second you start to put that plan into action in the real world, you'll develop an emotion that tells you how the execution is going and feelings that you shouldn't be doing it (hopefully).

Human Action Cycles can last seconds or decades. They can be both tactical and strategic. It is the tool with which the mind executes any plan or motive, in the case of this book, those associated with business or commerce motives. For example, you could have a long term ten-year plan or even a simple vision (i.e. motive or goal) of yourself in business in the future. Human Action Cycles can be paused in the actions phase and stored while material or other elements necessary to the execution are gathered or the appropriate time for actions is at hand. Making an appointment with a client next week is an example. There is nothing for you to do until you meet with the client, so you pause whatever you have planned, and do other things, other HACs. Or they can be but brief interludes that cycle within other HACs. Stopping in the middle of a presentation to deal with a client's "objection" within the flow of a presentation is another example. You pause the presentation, execute a HAC to deal with the issue brought up, then resume your previously paused presentation HAC.

However, there are some fundamentals to HAC. You may have hundreds or thousands on pause, but your mind can only entertain and execute one HAC at any moment in time. However, different HACs can be rapidly paused, un-paused, and cycled to the forefront. This happens without your notice or consent. It is why you can "multi-task" and appear to be able to do several things at once when, in fact, you're just rapidly cycling through different HACs. Not all minds are created equal, and like everything else in the human condition, the ability to pause, un-pause, and recall HACs and the rate at which this can be done will vary from person to person. Some people will be better at handling many HACs more rapidly than others.

Quick Look at the Cycle in Action

Motives are consciously formed as an expectation of a desirable outcome. To obtain an outcome requires an action plan be built as to how exactly one will obtain their goal. A Motive with an Action Plan creates a MAP of where you're going and how you're going to get there. Action plans come in two forms: internal (change our behavior) or external (change the environment).

Implementation of the action plan within the world constitutes actions. Our actions create outcomes. Outcomes are observed and interpreted in the best possible terms. An evaluation of the outcome is performed, and the findings are issued in the form of an emotion which is the correction phase of the Human Action Cycle. The conscious mind will make corrections by ignoring or accepting the emotional signal. If it accepts the emotion it will modify or create a new action plan to the MAP. And the whole process will start over based upon the new correction action created by the adaptor.

A DETAILED EXAMINATION OF THE HUMAN ACTION CYCLE

The components of the Human Action Cycle, according to the EFS Model, consist of the following: motives, actions, outcomes, evaluations and corrections and are described by Peil in this way:

Motives: the conscious expectations of desirable outcomes based upon sound knowledge, sense of time, cause and effect, awareness, and acceptance of bodily needs, and predictive, creative plans and strategies, and to meet them on a long-term basis. Motives are closely associated with *freedom* of the six universal needs discussed in Chapter 3. You have to have freedom in order to pursue motives.

Figure 7.1

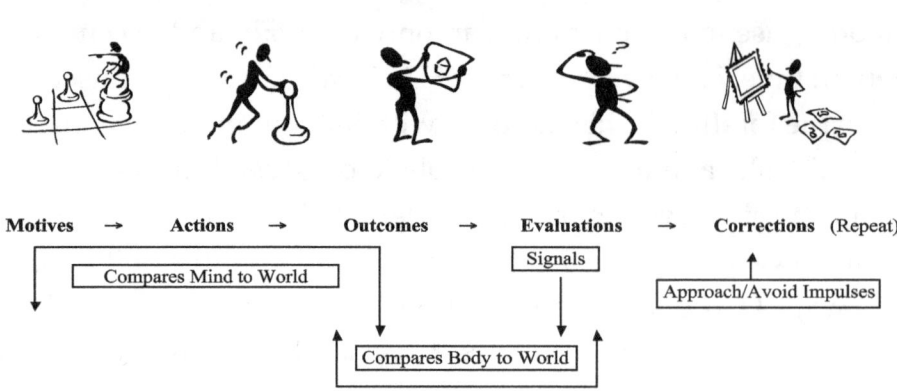

Actions: the full flexibility of choice and volition to act in any way we choose to resolve a challenge, and be effective in a wide variety of environments. Actions are closely associated with power of the six universal needs discussed in Chapter 3. You have to have the power to make change in order to create some sort of action in the world exterior to the body.

Outcomes: the subjective, mental interpretation of incoming information, sifted through knowledge, beliefs, and attitudes to draw the most optimistic yet realistic conclusion about what effect the action had upon the world.

Evaluations: where the body validates or negates the minds of interpretation by Feeling Tones which draw upon <u>additional subconscious</u> information the mind has not considered including both infinite genetic wisdom and emotional baggage left over from any conditional learning that has slipped past the consciousness.

Corrections: where the mind *internally adapts* its knowledge (it learns and grows) according to the feeling messages, then acts upon the improved motives with *external adaptations*— further communications and actions. The mind consciously averts conditioned learning and all instinctive reactor responses that are now disempowering of the self.

FEEDBACK CYCLE

While all this may sound complicated, it doesn't really have to be. It's actually as simple as this:

1) We want something to happen. (motives)
2) So we take actions to make it happen. (actions)
3) Those actions have outcomes –good, bad, or unintended. (outcomes)

4) We observe and catalogue the outcomes of those actions. We then evaluate the outcomes in the rosiest, most realistic way and attach an emotion to it. (evaluation)

5) We then learn from our mistakes on what didn't work and change our actions, or determine what was working well for us and keep doing it (corrections), before repeating the cycle by changing our actions to fully achieve our motives.

This should come instinctively for every salesperson because this is done on a daily basis. We want to make sales, because sales lead us to money. Money makes you happy and secure, which are both pleasurable (think of the reactor at work here seeking pleasure). This motivates you to do what is necessary to be prepared to call on clients and then actually visiting them (think of your adaptor). While you are interacting and presenting to your prospective client, your reactor is monitoring your effect upon the client and giving feedback to the adaptor, which is taking mental notes on when the prospective is pleased, confused, uninterested, or otherwise (this is the feedback cycle between reactor and adaptor at work here). Both during your interaction with your prospects and clients and after you have concluded your interactions with them, you will be evaluating what resonated with the client or not; you'll then generate an emotional tone within your consciousness as to how you're doing — "I'm nailing it!", "I'm blowing it!" or, most likely, something in between. You'll take corrective actions to maximize what is resonating with the client (approach) and switch to a different tack in areas that weren't working to achieve your motivational aims (get the sale). This is the approach (pleasure) or repulsed (move away) response coming from your reactor as it guides you away from things that are not helping you obtain your motive aims, or provides pleasure to keep you doing the same. Afterwards, you'll review what worked well and commit that to memory as active learning for future calls as well as what didn't work so you don't go down that unproductive path again.

Remember, all the while this is happening within you, the same is occurring in your client or prospect, which will be guiding the way they interact with you.

One of the most important things to draw from the Human Action Cycle is the evaluation stage and the emotional signals. This will be discussed later on in much greater detail as it pertains to your prospect or client's internal state as the bedrock of all sales.

Finally, it should be noted that not all actions originate in the subconscious, like ducking from a thrown chair. That is a reaction to something potentially painful to the body in the environment. Motives are formed and expressed consciously without your subconscious being involved as anything other than the interface between body and mind executing the speech, motion, and physical actions the adaptor is calling for and observing the results via the sensory systems of the body. These conscious motives may be influenced by input from the reactor to seek pleasure outcomes and not painful outcomes, as well as the conductor to seek the best results for you and your tribe, and the feedback you get along the way as you implement them. An active adaptor can and will come up with an adaptation strategy as a basis of achieving a motive. Remember, motives are the conscious expectations of desirable outcomes. For example, consciously, you can decide, starting right now, that you're going to become a better salesperson. As the action plan of your MAP, you decide that you will start searching for ways to improve your presales activities, presentation skills, and sales techniques. Your motive to become a better salesperson is influenced by your reactor to seek pleasure. Pleasure is derived from improving your security and lifestyle via the adaptation strategy of skill improvement. Your expectations are based on experience, and buttressed by abstract reasoning that such schemes in other endeavors you've partaken and observed in others will apply to this situation as well, that improved skills should yield more sales and provide pleasure.

The beauty of the HAC is its simplicity. It is a simple five-step process that creates a vast array of corrective and growth signals (emotions) from a simple pallet of six basic emotions, accompanied by intensity signaling from the agitation expression and complex emotion. It is fractal in its design and execution, a simple algorithm, expressed repeatedly with minor variations that can create a seemingly endless design of ways to accomplish motives. What makes it all feel like one big, seamless experience is the speed and rapidity with which the mind can shift from one HAC to the next.

The following are some simple examples so you can get an idea of how emotions are dependent upon the evaluation of accomplishing a motive.

PLEASURE (JOY)

Joy Example # 1

You drive past a boat dealership and see the boat of your dreams parked prominently out front. A boat is a pleasure craft. Your reactor is seeking pleasure in the environment and heavily signals the adaptor of imminent pleasure. If the adaptor is not engaged, you'll swerve across three lanes, pull into the dealership in a screech of tire smoke, parking across three parking spots, leaving the car running as you walk in and write the salesperson a fat check, draining your savings account and leaving you financially vulnerable should a disruption in your income occur. Additionally, because of your impulsiveness, you did not consider insurance, towing, docking, and the operating cost of running a boat. Your cash flow can't handle the additional burdens of being a boat owner, and so it sits unused. You now feel financially vulnerable, or resent the boat because you no longer have any disposable income for entertainment; you may blame the salesman for conning you into the purchase and plot revenge on the dealership by gossiping about what crooks they are. You knew that you could not afford the purchase of the boat when you saw it, but you did it anyway. Your reactor was in charge and without control from the adaptor, so you are now experiencing a series of responses to your unchecked actions. What you are now feeling are negative emotions that are designed for you to correct your actions. The HAC you had developed and implemented to save cash for a rainy day to survive any cash flow interruptions is now dashed. This is the source of your emotions; it's telling you how you're doing on your plan to have a financial buffer.

Joy Example #2

Same scenario as #1, but this time you look at your watch and see you have a half-hour window until your next appointment, so you carefully go around the block, pull into the parking lot and find a parking spot in the shade. You examine the boat, talk to the salesman, get pricing information and leave with the boat model's literature. That night, you review all the information and come up with a plan to generate a way to obtain the money necessary to buy and operate the boat by working an extra job during the evenings. After eighteen months, you are able to walk into the dealership, put down a sizable chunk of cash that allows you to put the rest of purchase on a very small contract that does not strain your cash flow and allows you to operate the boat without significant impact on your disposable cash. Because of your controlled, planned approach when you looked at the boat you feel pride, contentment, and happiness, plus you made a friend of the salesman that sold you the boat. In this scenario, the adaptor noted the reactors finding of pleasure in the environment but kept it in check by coming up with a MAP to obtain that pleasure and executing it. The emotions you are feeling are designed to encourage continued behavior of this nature, doing well on the execution of a HAC controlled by the adaptor.

Joy Example #3: The Twist

Now take Examples 1 and 2 and put this modifier on them. You are a millionaire, and the cost of the boat was insignificant to you, having set aside funds for its purchase. You have been looking for a new boat to replace the one docked at your house on the lake, and this boat is perfect. You safely circle the block, pull in and buy it. You're happy to find out it is even at a special price. When it arrives, it looks great at your dock, and does everything you need it to do in the style you wanted. You feel lucky because you were in the right place at the right time and took decisive action. This action led you to getting the boat you wanted at a much-reduced price. You feel happy and content at your quick action. Because you already had an action plan in progress with money set aside, when you saw the boat you wanted, acting impulsively did not lead to a negative outcome but a positive one. You're happy, getting positive emotions from your reactor telling you that you did well on executing the HAC to replace your old boat.

Joy Example #4: And Yet Another Twist

Same scenario as #3, but this time after seeing boat, you constrain yourself, telling yourself that you didn't get where you did by making impulsive, rash decisions. You go about your business and plan to come back the next day. The next day, you go to the boat dealership and talk to the salesman, only to find out that the boat you wanted was sold the day before near closing time. A new line of boats is coming in and they had priced that boat to move to make way for the new season's offerings, which won't be in for couple of weeks. The style of boat that caught your eye is discontinued. You are unhappy with yourself for not acting when you saw it, as was your impulse and let your rigid processes control you, giving you a sense of loss of freedom. You're angry at letting it slip through your grasp and go into denial that it really wasn't that good of a deal. You later see the boat go by your house on the lake and you resent the person who bought it out from under you. This is your Paradaptive Intelligence Network telling you that you did poorly on the HAC to replace your boat by letting the perfect boat slip through your fingers when you had the money and time. You're also disgusted with yourself for letting the desire to adhere to a stupid process, such as not making impulse buys, get in the way of obtaining the perfect boat. Now your poor choice of behavior is going to cost you more for something less satisfying.

THREAT/FEAR (PAIN)

Pain Example #1

You're preparing a business proposal for a client that contains a complicated financing arrangement to make the deal work. A co-worker familiar with the client offers you a simpler financing option. Immediately, you see that this a superior approach than the one you've structured. However, the person proposing the option is a business rival, or threat, to you; both of you are vying for the same promotion. Your initial impulse is to take the rival's suggestion, but if you do, he could take credit for saving the deal and put you at a disadvantage for the promotion. So you ignore his input, present the proposal, and lose the bid to a rival supplier, who offered a simpler approach to financing, which is what the deal came down to between bidders. You become angry with yourself for not doing what was right; instead you opted to play head games because of a rival and now you've not only lost the deal but also your promotion chances are dimmed because you couldn't land the customer. You're angry with yourself for not listening to what your gut (reactor) was telling you; you're frustrated that things aren't going right on the road to the promotion; this isn't the first time you've made this type of mistake. And your fears come true when your rival is promoted. You resent his promotion and plan your revenge by undercutting his leadership at your firm. These are painful experiences that are telling you that you did poorly on your HAC to get promoted and that you need to change your methodology.

Pain Example #2

Same scenario as above, but this time, you take his advice with a positive outcome, winning the bid. Your promotional chances are improved. In addition, you find out that your rival is not such a bad guy, and you appreciate his creativity and collaboration, giving you confidence that you can work with him in any capacity in the future. Winning the bid gives you a sense of esteem and lifts your morale, which in turn lifts people around you with whom you work. However, your competitor's contribution to the sale is discovered and he gets the promotion. You feel that even though you did the right thing for the client and the firm, you were punished for being a stand-up guy. This is your Paradaptive Intelligence Network telling you that you did not do well on the HAC to get promoted this time. Those emotions are telling you that you need to change your attitude (behavior) because your reactor is seeing all the positive impact your actions had on people around you, and you were not being punished. Instead you were given a growth opportunity, which you took and learned from, but now your ego is preventing you from placing this incident in your memory as a method to garner the respect and admiration of those who work with you.

Pain Example #3: The Twist

Same scenario as in #1, but this time, unbeknownst to you, the exchange between you and your rival is witnessed by your boss. While he wants to win the business deal, he values the ability to make decisions in the absence of perfect information.

He sees decision making as a manager's most valuable asset. You are aware of your boss's value system and stick with your original idea of financing the deal. You still lose the deal, but the boss comes by to console you on the loss and encourages you to stick to your guns. You have made marks with the boss and learned a new financing option from your rival to boot, having improved your prospects on two fronts. You feel happy and satisfied; your esteem is improved by your boss's pep talk, which improves your morale, even though you're still unhappy about not getting the deal. This is your Paradaptive Intelligence Network signaling you that while you did not succeed at your HAC to obtain the sale, you did learn that your methodology in many respects to getting the promotion was correct and you need to repeat that action as you continue to seek the promotion.

Pain Example #4: And Yet Another Twist

Using the same scenario as in #3, this time you choose to take your rival's advice and win the bid. However, the boss's opinion of you changes relative to that of your rival and promotes him. When you ask for feedback about the promotion, your boss reiterates his philosophy on leadership and tells you that you need to work on this area of your professional skill set and gain some seasoning and experience. You realize that changing your bid at the last second for a concept that you weren't quite as familiar with was a very risky move and you were lucky to pull it off. Your gut (reactor) told you it was more risky to make a move so late in the game, especially after you had originally signaled something else to the client. Now you're confused as to what to do in the future. This confusion leads you to feel that you were manipulated in some way. You blame your rival for this setback and seek to undercut his newfound success by gossiping about him. This is your Paradaptive Intelligence Network telling you that you should feel good about the HAC for getting the sale because you were successful, but the HAC for promotion failed and you need to change your methods.

Pain Example # 5: Another Quick Example

A co-worker is hurt and requires immediate medical attention. You are in a rural area and the co-worker doesn't have the time, due to blood loss, to wait for an ambulance, so you choose to drive him to the hospital. You speed, ignoring your reactor, which is telling you to slow down because the excessive speed could end up killing you. You rush to the hospital, saving the co-worker from an even direr outcome. While speeding to the hospital, you ignored your reactor. The feedback it was giving to your adaptor became more and more urgent because of the imminent threat posed by the high speeds involved, yet you fought off the fear driving your urge (reactor) to slow down. The same can be said about pleasure:

the more imminent the pleasure, the more tempted (reactor) you will become to fulfill that desire.

As you can see from the examples above, no action is either good or bad. It only becomes good (positive) or bad (negative) relative only to what your motive is. These examples demonstrate that emotions tell you where and how to change your behaviors and actions to help you achieve your aims.

CONCLUSION

We've talked about and described all the micro-elements, now it's time to put all the ingredients together into one graphic, (Figures 7.2 and 7.3) to see how it all flows and works seamlessly together to help us perform our sales activities. While a HAC can be long and complex, unfolding over weeks, months, years, or happen in just seconds, the process is constant. The duration of the cycle is dependent on the situation, allowing potentially for many short-term cycles to occur within medium and long-term cycles.

The novel elements that should be taken away as a salesperson is to recognize how the Paradaptive Intelligence Network through the reactor, adaptor, conductor, and ego and their participation in a HAC contribute to the generation of emotions in our clients, whether they want something (attracted to/pleasure) or are being told to move away (repulsion/pain) from something in their business surroundings or processes. How they respond to these reactor inputs will dictate their emotions they have towards their business. And it also allows us to see also how their personal life emotions can bleed over to their professional activities, interrupting and influencing their performance in the business arena.

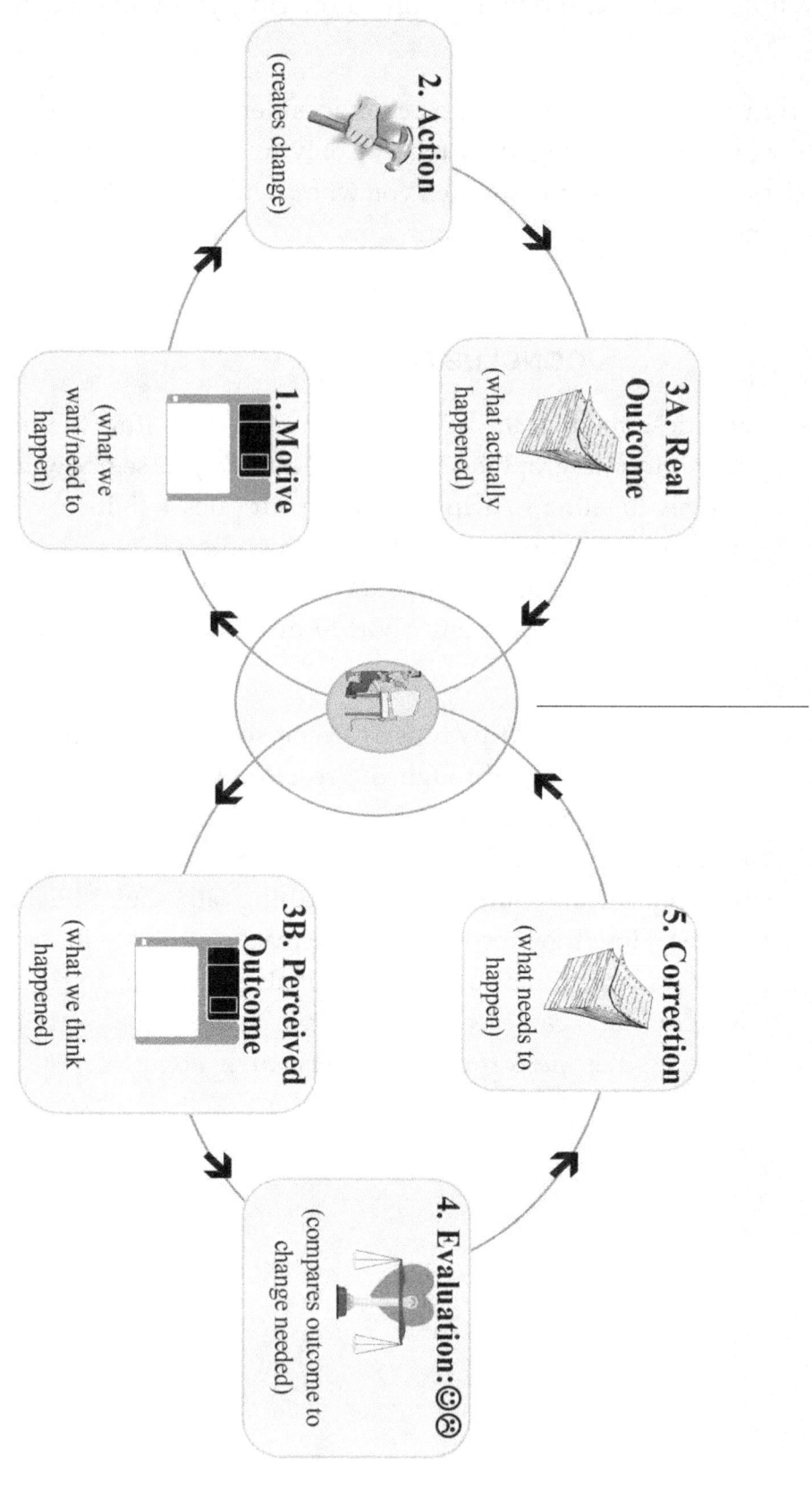

FIGURE 7.2

Brain Processing Center

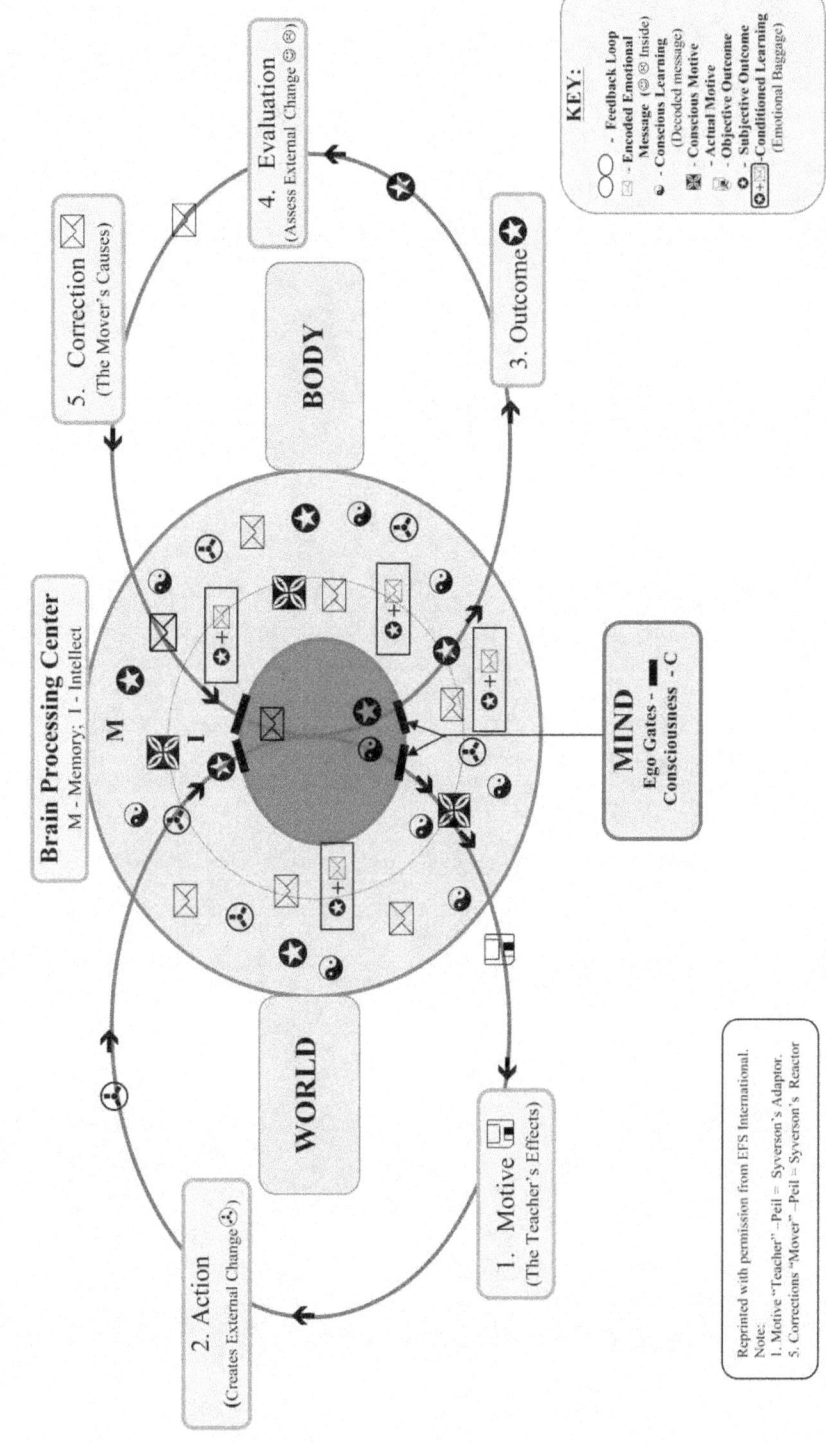

The Emotional Feedback System™

FIGURE 7.3

Summary Reference Chart: The Human Body-Mind As Master Information Processor

(Note: Since "body" and "mind" are rather arbitrary conceptual self-distinctions, intellect and memory functions overlap both.)

Scott Syverson

EMOTIONS –
THE LANGUAGE OF FEEDBACK

"The only living language is the language in which we think and have our being."
Antonio Machado

It is the interplay between the reactor, conductor, and adaptor that dictates your emotional state. We have discussed all the separate elements, so it's time to see the interplay between them. The Human Action Cycle is the core of all human actions, which starts with a motive, a goal. With a goal set, an action plan is needed to bring forth the desired, positive outcome of the motive (M). Your adaptor accesses memory that is filled by what the ego deposited here to see if there are exemplars that can be applied to the motive, along with imagination, if necessary, to invent an action plan (AP). With your MAP (M + AP) in place, you set the plan into motion through actions with the real world. Just like Newton's Third Law of Motion — for every action, there is an equal and opposite reaction — your actions collide and interact with things in the physical world. As you interact with the world, you'll get outcomes. These outcomes need to be evaluated, or put another way: "How am I doing?" This evaluation is the reactor's job because it noted and compared all the data streams as they were coming in from all your senses. It is the only mechanism in the Paradaptive Intelligence Network that has all the facts about the impact of your actions out in the real world. It will interpret these outcomes in the best possible light. Why? Because if it didn't, the mind would not get the full extract out of what your actions (may have) caused. The reactor lacks deductive and inductive reasoning tools; that's the adaptor's job. So it assumes that all aspects of the outcome are attributed to your actions. (This can lead to some goofy results – it's not a perfect system. Like the football fan in the end zone, no shirt on, painted blue for his favorite team that eats a hotdog in one mouthful and his team scores on the next play. His reactor is interpreting that rosy outcome to his hotdog gulping.) Otherwise, the adaptor might leave out important information in its evaluation and render an inaccurate evaluation. This evaluation is sent to the adaptor in the form of an emotion. The emotion is designed to help the adaptor make a correction to the action plan. The adaptor will make a correction, an adaptation, either choosing to accept and act on the emotion and take another course or to ignore it.

TRI-VALENCE STRUCTURE OF EMOTIONS

Emotions contain multiple encoded signals from the reactor. An emotion is comprised of three elements or tri-valances. The first valance is the agitation expression. The second valance of the tri-level signal is the basic emotion, which identifies it as one of the six universal basic emotions. The third level of the tri-level signal is called the complex emotion and indicates the degree or proximity to how close or far you are from achieving your aims, or may be a blend of two corrective emotions to give you better information of the corrections you need to make.

AGITATION EXPRESSION

The first level of the tri-valance of an emotion contains the agitation expression. The agitation expression is binary in nature, coming in two forms: positive (+) and negative (-). The agitation expression signals the adaptor with either a positive (+) expression to approach, move towards, repeat or a negative (-) expression to move away from, avoid, repulsion to the object of the emotion, be it behavior, person, place or thing. The negative form is the emotional, mental equivalent of physical pain. The strength of this agitation expression can vary from weak to overwhelming, depending on the emotion. If you've ever watched a scary movie at home and found yourself edging for the door or had a sudden urge to find a snack in the kitchen, or go to the toilet at the scariest part, you just experienced a strong negative agitation expression. An extreme example of a negative agitation expression can be found when something frightens you so badly that it triggers the Fight, Flight, or Freeze response. This call to action, the Fight, Flight or Freeze response, is the reason that it is listed as an action point in Figure 8.5. If you just did something that was so much fun that you want to do it again, like when you get off a roller coaster, you just experienced a strong positive agitation expression. An extreme example of positive agitation expression is love, which is one of the purest, strongest concentrations of positive agitation.

Agitation expression is the portion of the emotional signal that tells you whether you're on the right track or wrong track to obtaining the designs of the motivation.

It's the reactor telling you whether you're on the warmer or colder path to obtaining what the adaptor desires.

SIX UNIVERSAL BASIC EMOTIONS

When observing human emotional behavior, one sees six basic types of emotions: joy, fear, anger, sadness, disgust, and surprise. (See Figure 8.2) This signal is contained in the second valance of the emotional signal. These represent the entire universe of emotions that you will deal with as a salesperson. Further, these six basic emotions can be grouped into three categories: growth, corrective, and surprise. Knowing how to identify them and what causes them will put you miles ahead in the sales game as well as your personal life. Each of these basic patterns has variations of emotions based on intensity with one exception, surprise. The six basic emotions can be described as the following:

Joy – Joy tells us *good things* have happened to us. It moves us to make this happen again. Contentment is a form of joy with lower intensity (agitation expression) although its facial expression is considered universal.

Fear – Fear tells us of *threatening* situations and moves us to avoid them.

Anger – Anger tells us of *obstacles* and *violated <u>non-negotiable</u> boundaries* interfering with our purposeful actions. It moves us to push back and fight in self-preservation defense.

Sadness – Sadness tells us of significant *losses* and moves us to find replacements.

Disgust – Disgust tells us that certain things are *unwholesome* and are to be avoided. This moves us away from contact with things that are deleterious to the body or self.

Surprise – Surprise tells us that something completely *unexpected* has happened. It calls for investigation.

GROWTH SIGNALS (JOY)

Joy signals success. It is pleasure. We experience it when we close a sale. The receipt of remuneration when the sale is turned in and converted into money is a secondary moment of joy, and one could argue that when it is put to use by either spending it or saving it in some form, there is another moment of joy. This means that each sale has three opportunities to create moments of joy in your life, which reinforces the desire to repeat these moments of joy by making more sales. This is the only affirming, do-it-again emotion that humans have in their repertoire. Joy comes in various intensities. Each intensity has a label or name that we are all familiar with; some of the most intense are listed in Figure 8.1. These are all growth signals telling you that repeated pursuit will bring good things to the body or self, which will help it grow and protect it, improving your survival chances. Increased sales get you a better lifestyle, guarantees your career in the company, earns you friends via your business associations, banishes worry (a corrective signal itself), gives you confidence, and so on.

CORRECTIVE SIGNAL

You've probably labeled fear, anger, disgust, and sadness as negative emotions. You need to change your way of thinking, starting now. While it is true that all corrective signals contain a negative (-) signal on the agitation expression level, these are not negative emotions — they are a corrective signal. Corrective signals direct you to stop what you're doing and try a different approach. Many of these corrective signals linger because your adaptor may not be able to come up with an action plan based upon resources at hand. Most importantly of all, you need to know that the mechanism by which you are motivated by the subconscious is pain, psychic pain, generated by a negative agitation expression. While this may not be physical pain, such as your flesh being rendered in some manner, it is a pain nonetheless unique to the mind. This pain is why these four emotion types have been labeled as negative — they hurt. Most times it hurts you and sometime makes you hurt others, and your ego gate (if functioning properly) will place that pain into memory to prevent repeat episodes in the future.

All humans are pain averse and want to shed it. Business owners and managers want to relieve themselves of their psychic pain, and it is your job as a salesperson to help them with this by providing an adaptation plan which is your product or service plus an implementation plan. The human brain is not wired for anything else. Keep this in mind as we move forward, because this understanding of psychic pain will help you understand your role as a salesperson.

Fear

Fear signals us that something is threatening our body or self. This may not be a physical threat. Your subconscious can't distinguish between threats to your body and anything else that has the potential to impact your survival or motives you're pursuing. This includes relationships with people and issues of work. So if there is

FIGURE 8.1

Nature's Most Desirous Feeling Tones

The inner compass leads us in the directions that nature intended---with the highest feelings connoting both *internal mental states* and *external expressive actions*. The highest feeling tones are all positive, pleasurable feelings—evolved outgrowths of joy—resonating with universal validity:

Exuberance - A divine feeling of passion for spontaneous life experience. *

Awe - A divine sense of inspired wonder at the majesty, mystery, and beauty of nature.

Love (squared) - A divine sense of joyous acceptance of and connection to an intimate other.

Justice - A divine sense of balanced, free-flowing, and equitable empowerment.

Mirth - A sublime transcendent humor and ironic delight in life's pitfalls and challenges.

Faith - A divine sense that all events are meaningful and purposeful. *

Compassion - A divine sense of empathic understanding and acceptance of others.

Respect - A divine sense of honorable acceptance of the value of one's self and others. *

Generosity - A divine sense of delight in giving and sharing one's resources.

Grace - A divine tolerance and forgiveness for the pitfalls of ignorance. *

Honor - A divine sense of purpose and accountability for its fulfillment.

Courage - A divine sense of confident empowerment to surmount any challenge. *

Gratitude - A divine sense of thankfulness for kindnesses received and for the gift of life itself.

Devotion - A divine sense of loyalty to loved ones, to humanity, and to the source of all life.

Universal Oneness - A divine sense that all life forms are connected. *

Transcendence - A divine sense of becoming one with the source of life.

*= Emotions seen in the domain of commerce.

something going wrong with any of your relationships or upsets in your work environment upon which your survival is predicated, you will experience some form of fear whether or not you're actually in the presence of that threat. The correct response to fear is to remove yourself from what is causing the fear to lessen its effect so that you may learn the exact nature of the threat and deal with that issue when it is prudent. Additionally, your ability to communicate that fear to others will help you find creative resolutions. This among all basic emotions is what salespersons deal with the most during a sales cycle for two reasons. First, a prospective client already knows or suspects that inefficiencies, problems, and current processes are costing them money which threatens (fear) their survival. Second, you and your products or services are unknowns to your prospective client, both of which may cause change and have the potential to cause upset (threat) in their workplace. They fear heaping more change and upset upon their business when it is already struggling with problems. This is such an important aspect to salespeople that we will deal with this exclusively in Chapter 10.

Again, fear has many intensities which are listed in Figure 8.2. If the emotion is strong enough, the subconscious will take control and invoke flight (panic) of the Fight, Flight, or Freeze response. Or a more appropriate name might be the rage and panic response. The Freeze occurs when both rage and panic occur simultaneously and offset each other, vying for supremacy and thus locking the body into stillness.

Just to show you how prevalent and misunderstood fear is in the workplace, just think of the word "stress" or the phrase "work stress." Just to be clear, it is important to know that stress is not an emotion and the body has no "stress" response. When we experience "stress" at work, our body is responding to the fear stemming from a threat. The "stress" that we are feeling is the body's response to a threat the subconscious mind has detected and is physiologically girding for fight/flight. Fear releases adrenaline, quickens the heart, and causes a myriad of other physiological responses. This mild to moderate fear response is what we think of as stress. So when you call on a client that is "stressed out," you know that they have an environment of threats, and hopefully, you have a product in your salesman's haversack that will be able to eliminate or reduce some of those threats.

Anger

Anger can signal two separate things, obstacles or boundary violations. Obstacles are barriers put in your way, preventing you from implementing your action plan and obtaining your desired outcome. Barriers tend to be put in our way by other individuals; even if they occur naturally or were unforeseen, we tend to think that

Figure 8.2
Universal Feelings & Their Learned Offshoots

GROWTH SIGNALS

Joy

(Success) ——————⟶ Attachment ⇒ Trust ⇒ Love ⇒ Curiosity ⇒ Confidence ⇒ Liberation ⇒ Friendship ⇒ Fairness ⇒ Accomplishment ⇒ Acceptance ⇒ Appreciation ⇒ Enthusiasm ⇒ Worthiness ⇒ Hope⇒ Camaraderie ⇒ Tolerance ⇒ Tenacity ⇒ Pride ⇒ *Loyalty* ⇒ *Faith* ⇒ *Awe* ⇒ *Justice* ⇒ *Mirth* ⇒ *Compassion* ⇒ *Honor* ⇒ *Courage* ⇒ *Gratitude* ⇒ *Grace* ⇒ *Devotion* ⇒ *Universal Oneness*

Invokes impulses of approach & exploration; Yields purposeful awareness, learning, & cooperative creative expression

CORRECTIVE SIGNALS

Fear

(Threat)——————⟶ Detachment ⇒ Anguish ⇒ Mistrust ⇒ Anxiety ⇒ Want ⇒ Doubt ⇒ Shame ⇒ Inferiority ⇒ Embarrassment ⇒ Worry ⇒

Paranoia (Add a dash of anger: Envy ⇒ Greed ⇒ Guilt)

Invokes impulsive "flight" responses (withdrawal, denial, hiding, isolation)
Right track responses: 1.Learn Learn Learn! (Get exposure!) 2. Communicate & Create

Anger

(Obstacles)——————⟶ Distress ⇒ Frustration ⇒ Betrayal ⇒ Intolerance ⇒ Resentment ⇒ Self-Righteousness ⇒ Superiority ⇒ Injustice ⇒ Vengeance ⇒ Contempt

(Add a dash of fear and disgust: ⇒ Hate)

(Add a hint of sexuality: Lust ⇒ Jealousy)

Invokes impulsive "fight" responses (aggression, blame, revenge)

Right track responses: 1.Learn Learn Learn! (Identify the injustice!) 2. Communicate & Create (Build justice); If 1&2 fail repeatedly; 3. Fight (nonviolently): and finally 4. Take flight from toxic situations

Sadness

(Losses)——————⟶ Loneliness ⇒ Boredom ⇒ Longing ⇒ Grief ⇒ Isolation ⇒ Despair ⇒ Depression

(Add a touch of compassion: Sympathy ⇒ Remorse)

Invokes impulsive flight responses, can drive self-destructive impulses
Right track responses: 1.Learn Learn Learn! 2. Communicate & Create (replacements)

Disgust

(Aversion)——————⟶ Unpleasantness ⇒ Disliking ⇒ Unwholesomeness

(Add a hint of fear and anger: ⇒ Resentment ⇒ Contempt ⇒ Hate)

Invokes impulses of fight or flight
Right track responses: 1.Learn Learn Learn! 2. Communicate & Create (wholesome adaptations)

someone has placed it there to test us or make us work harder. The other thing that it signals is that someone has violated a non-negotiable boundary with you.

Boundaries are not just things like property lines and personal space, but also include rules, laws, norms, practices, traditions, policies, and the like. Just a few examples of boundary violations are: someone has lied, cheated, stole from you, been disrespectful, or insulted you. There are many other boundaries that individuals set, and they are particular to each individual, such as customs or territory. But, as with obstacles, anger caused by boundary violations are aimed specifically at other individuals, provoking a fight response. Fighting is aimed at another person or creature; it is misplaced when attempting to fight an object, like a tree that is interfering with your view (however, it might move you as a motive to cut it down). There are numerous intensities of the fight responses that escalate (See Figure 8.2). The fight response is part of the rage mechanism necessary and triggered in the fight aspect of the Fight, Flight, or Freeze response. By triggering an anger response, the subconscious is signaling you to challenge something intrusive and reclaim control by use of aggression. By learning from an incident as to who was impinging upon you and what boundary violation or obstacle occurred, you can use that information to prevent future instances before they reach critical mass. Once deciphered, the next adaptive step is to communicate with whoever is creating the anger response and work creatively to resolve the obstacle or boundary infringement with a goal of creating justice, whether that is a simple apology and retraction, or some change in your relationship with the violator. If this yields no results, then you will fight more aggressively. This could be something like speaking to someone higher in the authority chain of the violator or bringing legal action. Finally, if no pain relief is found, you remove yourself from the situation by doing whatever is necessary to leave because the escalating urge to strike physically that is hardwired into our systems may become so overpowering that you do threaten or hurt someone, which most societies deem criminal, or say something you'll regret. This is the source of "crimes of passion."

There is a unique relationship in sales to anger. At some point, every salesperson runs into a situation where he or she is discussing the terms of a deal when the customer becomes angry. If you're unfamiliar with this phenomenon, you will believe the anger is aimed at you personally. It is not. Something in the terms you're discussing just became a barrier to your customer to closing the deal he or she wants. People associate obstacles with people, so even though you may be quoting a company policy, the prospect will become angry with you. Usually, it's price. Price is always an obstacle. This type of response is the most incandescent of all buying signals. They are clearly telling you they want to buy, and left to their own, they will find a way to surmount this obstacle. This is why there is a sales adage about never negotiating down your price. If the customer is motivated and demonstrates it by showing anger, you don't need to renegotiate unless you absolutely, positively need the sale for yourself at that moment.

Sadness

This corrective signal notifies us of significant loss and motivates us to seek replacement. This is not an emotion that is encountered in volume in sales unless you're in the mortuary or a related industry. But, from time to time, we all have customers that have encountered significant personal or professional loss. We may get a call that a client needs to replace our product due to theft, fire, or natural disaster. Or we may be demonstrating or doing a presentation for a prospect, and it triggers a personal response like, "Gee, I wish you were here five months ago when my wife was dying with cancer. Your product could have saved me a lot of time that I could have spent with her."

The salient issue is that mild to moderate sadness will trigger a response to seek replacement when the time is right. Significant loss will trigger the Fight, Flight, or Freeze response to produce a strong desire to flee as the usual manifestation. A significant business loss, such as a fire for example, can trigger both sadness and fear – fear that their livelihood, their survival, is threatened because their means to make money has been diminished and sadness that what they have built is gone and needs to be replaced.

Because all strong corrective signals can trigger the Fight, Flight, or Freeze response, even an emotion like sadness can produce unexpected actions in people. This is why people are so confused about emotions and don't like to mess with them. The Fight, Flight, or Freeze response when triggered by sadness can appear to produce "erratic" or unpredictable consequences. A strong sadness emotion may suddenly cause someone grieving to become combative for no reason, or those grieving many just run away, mindlessly, with no destination other than to not be where they are. At worse, they may become catatonic as a freeze response.

Disgust

This is another emotion that is not seen in abundance in business unless you are in the business of selling goods that can spoil, decay, or destabilize. This emotion is generally directed at the product and not you personally, unless there is a hygiene issue. This emotion alerts us to unwholesomeness in our environment. Some business practices may evoke this response (see Figure 8.2), so be mindful of what and how you present your business to all prospects. Trying to take advantage of certain situations with clients may create disgust in you and your tactic, which creates aversions in others to doing business with you. Begging is usually considered an unwholesome activity, so be wary of how you appear to ask for the sale. Discounting is another activity that some in the business world find disgusting. Needlessly discounting the price of a product or service signals that you don't think it's worth the price and you're falsely anchoring the higher price to gain leverage, which many people find a disgusting business practice.

SURPRISE

Surprise is an emotion that notifies us that something completely unexpected from our expectations has occurred, good, bad, or otherwise. Try as we might to gather information about our client's or prospect's business to give an informative, customized MAP and presentation of your product application to their unique circumstances, occasionally something completely unexpected happens. This is usually not a good event because it signals your action plan is now no longer applicable. More often than not, surprise occurs because your efforts to discover your prospective client's background, history, and circumstances were not thorough enough. Your best response is to learn as much as you can about the event or issue that interrupted the execution of your game plan, reschedule, and regroup.

According to Peil, surprise is unique in that it has no complex emotion valence attached to it. It exists in just the basic emotion form, which is why it is not listed in Figure 8.2.

COMPLEX EMOTIONS

Five of the six basic emotions joy, fear, anger, disgust, and sadness − have a component that signals the intensity or flavor of the emotion called complex emotions. This is the third component of every emotion. These are the emotions that we are more familiar with because they are the parts of our lexicon we use to describe what we are feeling. Complex emotions are where the strength, the intensity, the proximity of either growth or corrective signal is expressed. Varying intensity of a specific type of basic emotions implies that there are continuums of basic emotion from weak to strong, and that is exactly the case for corrective signals. Complex emotions have names that we've given them in each spoken language, yet no matter what the language, these labels universally express specific degrees of intensity of a specific basic emotion. These complex emotions (Figure 8.3 and 8.4) can arise as just an intensity variation of a basic emotion called a tone, or be formed by a combination of two basic emotions at varying intensities to create emotions called blends. In this way, the basic emotions can be blended like the primary colors on a painter's wheel to create a multitude of emotional hues. As for this book and its focus on adaptation, consumer behavior, and sales, we'll be dealing almost exclusively with emotional tones. Blended emotional tones are more regularly seen as feedback to actions being executed in HAC and are exclusively corrective signals. A blend can signal on two dimensions, or axes, what corrections need to occur.

Just like the colors on the painter's wheel and color progressions, emotions for the adaptation and relationships have progression, too. In Figure 8.3, you'll see progressions associated with different basic emotions. Please note that many emotions are rooted in past, while others are anchored in the present or the future. These progressions of emotional tones have one rule: you must flow from one adjacent emotional tone to the next – you cannot skip over one emotional tone to reach another when innovating or in relationships. Complex emotions algorithms are comprised of two segments: one that represents the past are corrective signals, and one that starts in the moment and moves to the future comprised of growth signals. The past portion represents our past failures and negative experiences held in memory. Just think of a two-year-old toddler that has just become really mobile. They explore their surroundings with abandon. They are fearless. Why? Because they have no experience in negative emotions and corrective signals in their memory. As they explore their world, they will experience bad things and bad outcomes. These bad experiences become points of intensities on their continuums of corrective emotions, coupled with words of their language associated with that corrective signal intensity. Take sadness, for example. As an infant, toddler, and then up through teen, they make numerous relationships, whether it's their pet turtle or other tykes and teens. Each relationship has varying degrees of attachment. So when that person leaves their life for whatever reason, the strength of that attachment is translated into strength of loss and becomes a point of intensity on the continuum of sadness and will become associated with a word in their language that closely gauges the level of loss intensity of the emotion they are feeling.

Now that we have an idea of how emotions work in general, it's time to look specifically at consumer behavior and how it relates to sales. Take a look at Figure 8.4. This is the emotional tonal algorithm that all innovation and must follow. This is DNA encoded into every human being and is the flow, the algorithm, of emotion

Figure 8.3

Time, The Evolution of Consciousness, & Feeling States

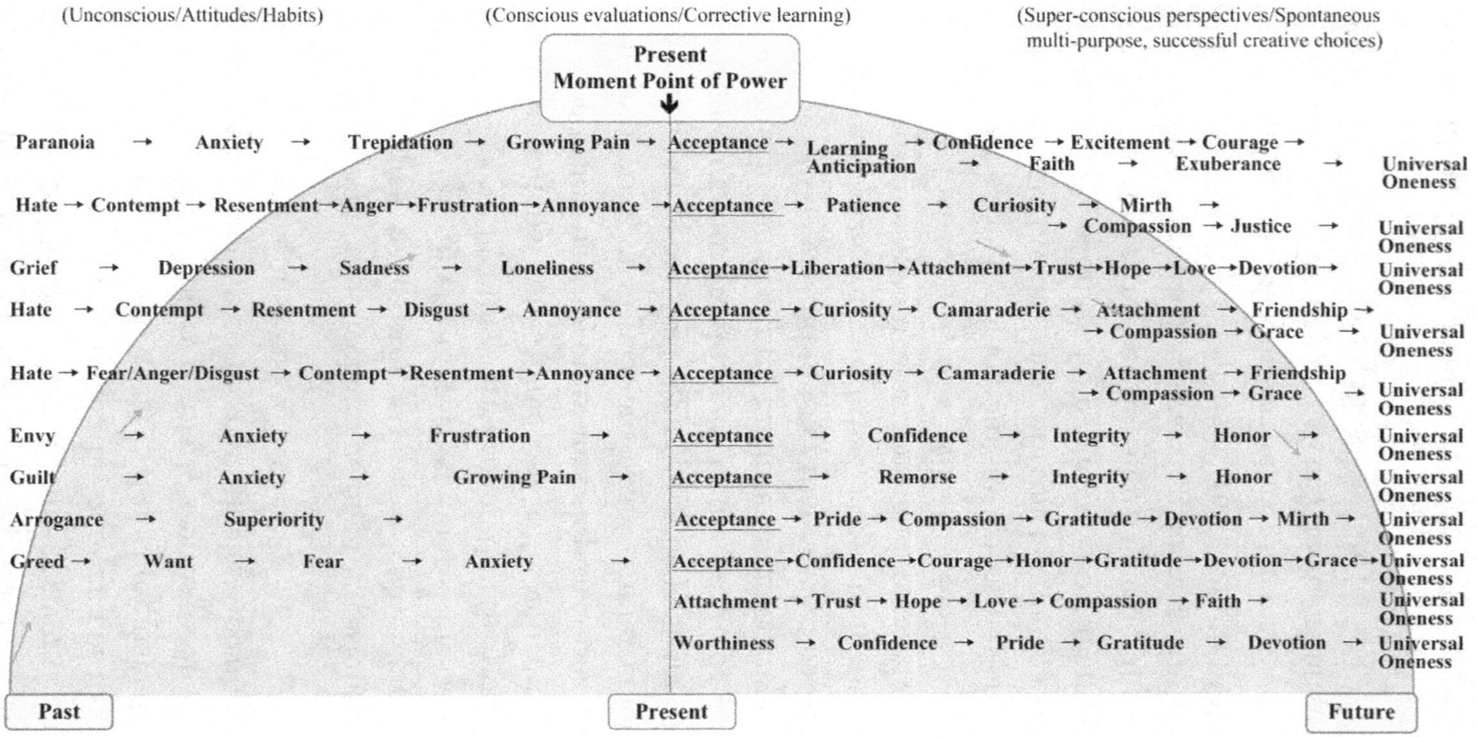

(Unconscious/Attitudes/Habits)

(Conscious evaluations/Corrective learning)

(Super-conscious perspectives/Spontaneous multi-purpose, successful creative choices)

Past | **Present** | **Future**

Present
Moment Point of Power

Paranoia → Anxiety → Trepidation → Growing Pain → Acceptance → Learning/Anticipation → Confidence → Excitement → Courage → Universal Oneness

Faith → Exuberance →

Hate → Contempt → Resentment→Anger→Frustration→Annoyance → Acceptance → Patience → Curiosity → Mirth → Justice → Universal Oneness

Compassion →

Grief → Depression → Sadness → Loneliness → Acceptance→Liberation→Attachment→Trust→Hope→Love→Devotion → Universal Oneness

Hate → Contempt → Resentment → Disgust → Annoyance → Acceptance → Curiosity → Camaraderie → Attachment → Compassion → Grace → Universal Oneness

Hate → Fear/Anger/Disgust → Contempt→Resentment→Annoyance → Acceptance → Curiosity → Camaraderie → Attachment → Friendship → Universal Oneness

Compassion → Grace →

Envy → Anxiety → Frustration → Acceptance → Confidence → Integrity → Honor → Universal Oneness

Guilt → Anxiety → Growing Pain → Acceptance → Remorse → Integrity → Honor → Universal Oneness

Arrogance → Superiority → Acceptance → Pride → Compassion → Gratitude → Devotion → Mirth → Universal Oneness

Greed → Want → Fear → Anxiety → Acceptance→Confidence→Courage→Honor→Gratitude→Devotion→Grace→Universal Oneness

Attachment → Trust → Hope → Love → Compassion → Faith → Universal Oneness

Worthiness → Confidence → Pride → Gratitude → Devotion → Universal Oneness tones that we call consumer behavior. This is the emotional pathway of adaptation. This is the same pathway that early Homo sapiens used to create or modify early stone tools, clothes, or any other implement formed by human hands. It represents a test of sorts, a test of emotional satisfaction, that each new tool or innovation must pass before its use is implemented. This series of emotions is now used in our exchange based society to form tools (products or services) that we sell to others or that we build for ourselves, just the same as earlier *Homo sapiens*. What is represented in Figure 8.4 is the most powerful information that a salesperson can have because *all sales transactions will traverse all or part of the Innovation emotional tonal algorithm.*

The Innovation complex emotional tonal algorithm used in Figure 8.4 is adapted from Figure 8.3, with self-actualization becoming synonymous with a satisfied customer. This is the complex emotional tonal algorithm that all humans use to evaluate inanimate objects as tools or use to change their behavior. This also includes services, which are nothing more than another form of a tool in the form of someone else to accomplish a motive.

A prospective client is defined as any person that you as a salesperson meet for business purposes who has not obtained the emotion courage. As salespeople, you will encounter people at every emotion listed on this continuum (Figure 8.5) below and including courage and their emotional state will be dependent upon their circumstances or actions prior to your introduction. Regardless of what emotional state you encounter them in, they are inherently programmed to move away from and eliminate the negative emotions, and to seek positive outcomes. The stronger the negative emotion, the corrective signal, the more they will be driven to move away from what they are doing. The stronger the positive emotions, the growth signal, the more they will be driven to seek, obtain, and implement solutions to nullify psychic pain and repeat the experience. The emotional tonal algorithm for Innovation starts with the strongest negative emotion, and an individual is rewarded with less psychic pain with each emotion stage they obtain as they move to the right. When the individual arrives at acceptance, rather than corrective signal – psychic pain – they are rewarded with growth signals of joy that increase in intensity as they move to the right of the graph.

A tool, product, or service can fail to move beyond any one of the emotional tones at any point for a myriad of reasons. When this occurs, the tool or innovation is simply abandoned, and the prospect searches for another tool that will relieve his or her psychic pain. In some cases, individuals may pause the HAC that is pursuing a specific innovation or tool, create a motive to modify some part of the current HAC,

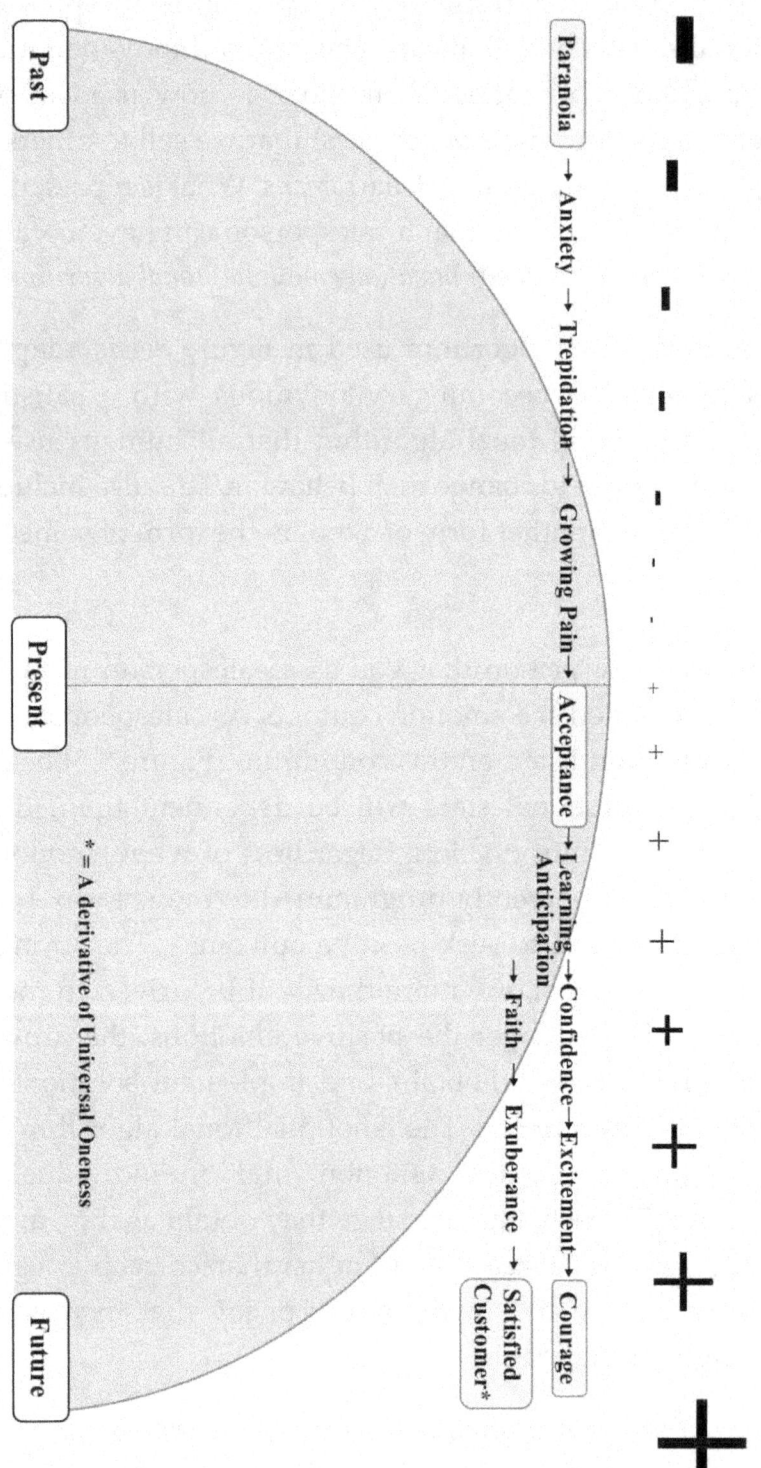

FIGURE 8.4

Emotional Tonal Algorithm
For Innovation/Tool Seeking

and execute the modification using the same emotional pathway. The resulting improvement to the original HAC is then implemented. Once the enhancement or modification is implemented to the original HAC, the vetting process of the tool or innovation picks up where it left off. An example of this is someone who wants to buy but can't afford the price upfront, so they pause the HAC to seek financing before coming back to the HAC to buy and conclude the purchase HAC.

The power of this model is that this book will teach you to how to look for and identify every complex emotion in the emotion tonal algorithm and what is required to satisfy that emotion so that a prospect can move on to the next emotion until a sale and customer satisfaction is achieved. In this way, you'll know what is needed in the moment and what is coming next, putting you, the salesperson, in charge of managing the sales process, helping the prospect satisfy the emotions he is hardwired to fulfill. By taking them down a pathway of growth signals, you will not only help the prospect rid them of their pain, you'll be taking them on a journey they are hardwired to enjoy. And this brings us to our first bit of unification. There have been many books that have claimed or stated the customers will sell themselves or want to be sold, and you just need to get out of the way. While these claims are close, because they lack the proper foundation, vocabulary, and construct to accurately reflect the actual mechanism in play, they do not paint the whole picture. Customers are not programmed to sell themselves. They are mentally rewarded with stronger and stronger pulses of joy, growth signals, for seeking solutions that will nullify their psychic pain. So as long as your product or service can demonstrate properties that will nullify their pain, they will be internally rewarded to seek them out and explore them for efficacy and other parameters. It doesn't guarantee a sale. Pointing out how lack of proper foundations, constructs, and vocabulary has led to a lot of half-truths and misunderstandings will be a common theme in this book. It will unify many, many concepts described in popular literature on the topic of sales into one coherent theory. While there are too many of the popular nuggets and tidbits of wisdom scattered throughout the public domain for this book to discuss and demonstrate unification for every single one of them, from time to time it will use an example to re-affirm the unifying power of the model presented herein.

Fear and anger are what drives your customers: fear of change, fear of disruption, fear that their business is not keeping up, fear that profits are not being maximized or are being constrained and thus so is their livelihood and survivability. Other fears such as that they will miss a deadline or a payment, or anger at the inefficiencies in

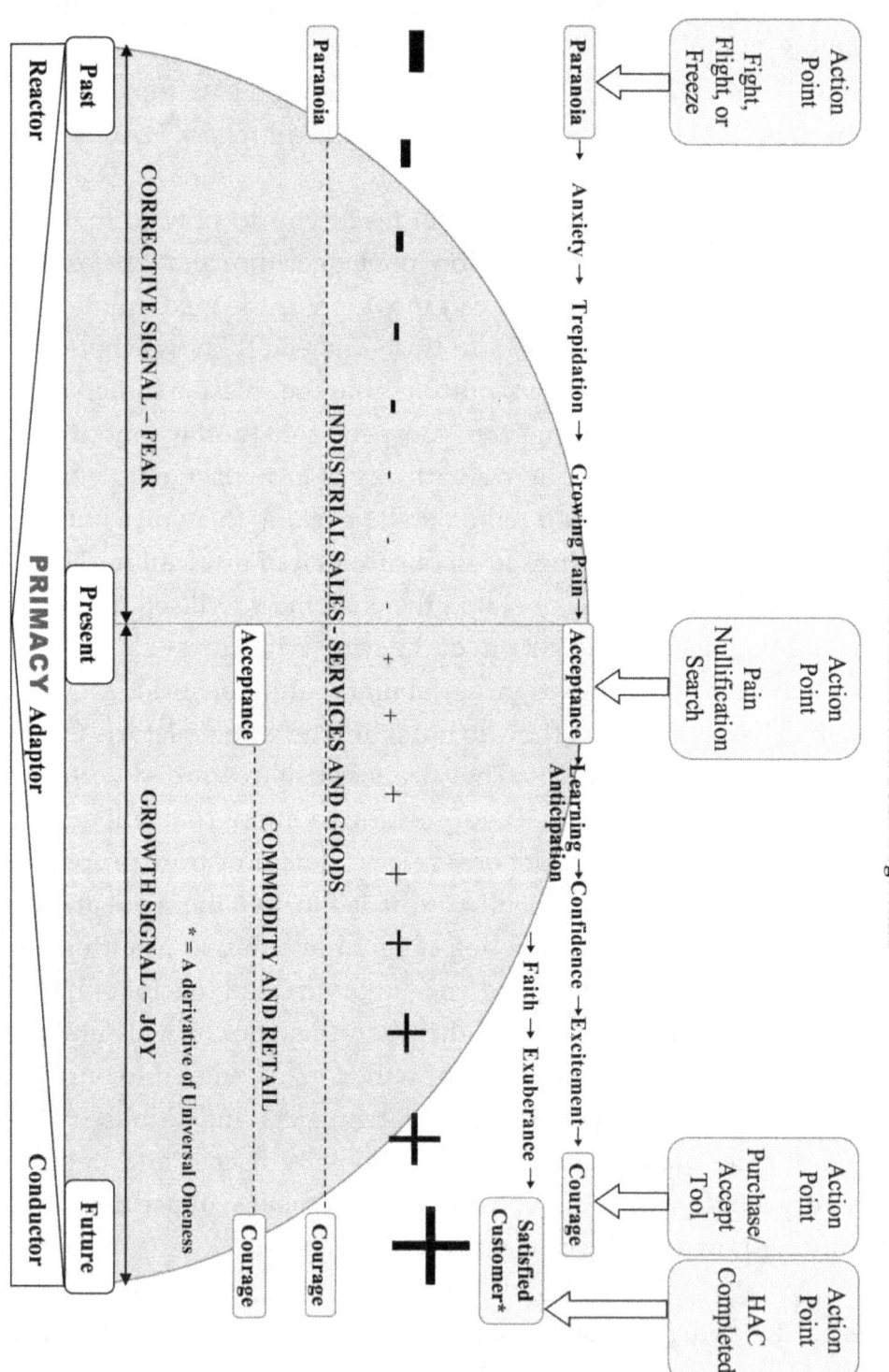

FIGURE 8.5

Innovation Emotional Tonal Algorithm™

their business and lack of control of critical variables, to mention just a few also dominate their motives. This will be covered in depth in Chapter 10.

This powerful tool, Figure 8.5, has several key milestones for the salesperson. First, clients or prospects will not fully accept appointments to demo or explore your product until they have reached the acceptance emotional tone. Acceptance is an action point on the Innovation complex emotion tonal algorithm that not only signals the shift from the past to the present, but also signals the internal shift to acknowledging the necessity of seeking a remedy to the psychic pain triggered by the corrective signals fear or anger in their business environment. Information about your adaptation plan has the potential to relieve their psychic pain. When coupled with the potential of pain relief or pain nullification, a prospect will be compelled to take a look at your product.

If you look at Figure 8.5, you'll see all the negative emotions of the Innovation complex emotion tonal algorithm are rooted in the past. Getting prospects into the present is done by de-escalating the negativity caused by psychic pain from the corrective signal fear or anger, which changes the line flow from psychic pain to the basic emotion joy, which in turn sends them stronger and stronger growth signals as they progress through the phase of fixing something that is threatening or angering them.

So if your prospect is still reluctant or displaying anxiety about some aspect of your product, it is pointless to schedule an appointment for demonstration. They are still living in the past and are relating some negative past event to some aspect of the adaptation plan you are attempting to discuss. You have to address their fears of past events and bridge the complex emotional tones of fear to get them into the present and show acceptance of the necessity to examine the known potential solution(s) presented in your adaptation plan. An example of this is if you sell computer products and you call upon a prospect that is still doing work by hand. When asked, the individual may tell you that they tried computers in the early eighties and it "didn't work out so well." That experience, rooted in fear and the past, is blinding that person from seeing what's happening today, how that's costing them money and creating stress because they are living with threats and inefficiencies. He or she is oblivious to what tomorrow could bring. Really, what is going on is that person may not necessarily be negative to new adaptation plans; it may just be that they're frightened of any adaptation plans involving computers. At this point in the sales cycle, you should be talking to him or her about their past and not your product, because if you don't put their past in the past, it will sabotage the sale you are attempting to make.

The second action point for salespeople to learn is the courage complex emotional tone. Courage is an action word. Courage is the emotion tone where the customer signs the contract, writes a check, or buys your product. Courage is the purchase point. Your goal as a salesperson is to get a prospect through the courage emotion. So you must move the client through five prior emotional tones from acceptance, learning anticipation, confidence, excitement, and at last, courage.

The third milestone is the satisfied customer. It is important to note that there are two other post-sales stages that must be traversed after the sale before getting to satisfied customer: faith and exuberance. How the supporting and ancillary functions of a salesperson's company impact the Innovation emotional tonal algorithm of a post sales cycle will be discussed in Chapter 15.

In looking at Graphs 8.3 and 8.4, and all subsequent graphs of this type, its design demonstrates the non-linear gradation of the complex emotion signal, whether it is a corrective signal or growth signal as emotions move along an algorithm. The half circle moves from the past in the left-hand corner, to the zenith in the present, to the future in the lower right hand corner. The area directly above or below an emotion on the algorithm covers a segment, or arc, of the semi-circle. The length of the arcs will be greatest at the emotions at both ends of the algorithm and shortest in the middle where the corrective and growth signals meet. This reflects that the emotional gradient of where psychic pain and pleasure is greatest on the points furthest from the middle and the middle emotions have the weakest gradients of stimuli. It also demonstrates why some algorithms second lines are placed to the right on the graph. These second line emotions of growth signal provide strong stimuli, and thus capture larger arcs on the graph.

MULTI-PERSON SIGNOFF DEALS

In many sales scenarios, a salesperson must successfully engineer situations where other parts of a company not directly involved with the sale of a product or service, but may be impacted by its implementation, must give their approval before the purchase can be consummated. For example, the marketing department wants to integrate a new product that combines sales leads, sales person reporting, contract signings, and commissions earned. This has the potential to impact the Information Technology department, Accounts Receivable, Operations, Accounts Payable, and

Marketing. Clearly, in this scenario, Sales would be driving this change internally, acting as a champion. The salesman of the product might be required to discuss and demo the technical requirements needed for integration with each impacted department or division. Such an endeavor usually requires those department and division heads to spend budgets in ways they had not planned for. In forming a strategy to overcome these obstacles, the salesperson can use the complex emotion tonal algorithm for the basic emotion fear or anger in Figure 8.5, depending upon whether the project threatens their budget or is an obstacle to them implementing their own objectives for their department in the manner or time frame they had planned.

In multi-person signoff deals, the two action points, acceptance and courage play slightly different. In this environment, getting someone to the acceptance emotional stage means that they will not interfere with the sale. They accept the necessity of making the improvement to the marketing department as being beneficial to the company overall. Taking them to the courage action point indicates that they will openly endorse the project, even if it means their division goals, budget, or operations may have detrimental impacts.

As a salesperson, having this information will do two things for you. First, you will be able to determine which impacted parties must have acceptance only, and which will need to be moved to courage emotion in order for the deal to go through. Secondly, by now having the precise vocabulary of the tonal algorithm, you can ask specific questions about their attitudinal level. Are they fearful? Full of anxiety? Do they believe it's a growing pain of the company, but not related to them? Are they experiencing learning anticipation on how this will benefit the company and how their department is crucial to the forward progress of the company? By being able to precisely determine their attitude and knowing to what level you must move them, you will no longer have to guess and can use your time and resources more prudently.

9

BECOME KNOWN...ANIMATE!

"ex·pres·sion, n,... 6. a showing of feeling, character, etc..."
Webster New World Dictionary, College Edition

There is an old adage in sales that people want to buy from people they know. And like most things of this sort, there is a kernel of truth to it, but where it strays from reality is in the interpretation of the definition of "know." The common usage of the word "know" in this instance implies that people only want to buy from people who they have previous buying experience with and "know" personal facts about such as their dog's name or their favorite pie. This could not be farther from the truth. In the world of commerce, people want to buy from people they "know" how to read. That is why people choose to do business with those whom they have previous commercial experience with, not only because they are familiar with the protocols of their transactions, but most importantly, they know how to read those individuals.

Knowing how to read the person across from you in a commercial transaction is the biggest factor in whether that transaction will occur. Even if all the numbers look good, people will refrain from doing the deal if they just don't feel good or have questions about the other party. They sense risk in not having a good read of the person they intend to partner with in commerce. Until they know how to read the person across the desk from them, or become synchronized with them, they will hold out until they can get a better understanding of vital parameters such as the truthfulness and accuracy of their words. If the eyes are the gateway to the soul, then expressions are the gateway to emotions.

Just like computers, when talking to each other, humans have a synchronization process. In computers, it goes something like this:

#1: Ready to send.
#2: Ready to receive.
#1: Sending timing ping.
#2: Received ping, synchronized.
#1: Ready to send data.
#2: Ready to receive data.
#1: Sending data packet.
#2: Received data packet.
#1: Check sum should equal 7.
#2: Check sum equals 8, resend data packet.

Et cetera, et cetera.

In humans, this synchronization process occurs through the facial expressions of emotion.

In commerce, as well as all other phases of life, you want to know that the person you are communicating with is not lying, but genuine, and just as important, that you understand exactly what they are saying by interpreting the verbal portion of their words supported by emotional context. This emotional context is conveyed mostly in the emotional facial expressions, with subsequent smaller portions coming from tone, inflection, body language, and gestures. But not all facial expressions are the same from person to person.

UNIVERSAL EXPRESSIONS

According to the work of anthropologist, Paul Ekman, there are only six universally understood facial emotional expressions:

* Anger
* Disgust
* Fear

* Joy
* Sadness
* Surprise

It is important to note that two separate researchers, Ekman and Peil, and others, researching in completely different areas of science, identified the same foundational basic emotions.

Additionally, there is an argument in the science literature as to whether contentment should be on this list. For the purposes of sales, generally, contentment should be included in this list for reasons that will follow.

All other expressions not universal vary from culture to culture, region to region, person to person. To put it another way, outside of the six universally known expressions, you're just guessing about what a stranger is feeling when talking to them, until you can synchronize with that individual. Most salespeople will be performing sales activities within their cultures, thus eliminating one of the variables of synchronization. Additionally, most sales activity occurs in the sales region where the salesperson is operating from or familiar with eliminating more variables of synchronization. It is for this reason that contentment should be put on the same list. Unless you are a salesman doing international sales or travels to a wide number of regions, you should feel confident about your ability to recognize contentment in the prospective client across from you. If you are a widely-traveled salesperson, the issue of contentment can be remedied by material that will be covered later in this book.

There are a large number of emotional expressions in between the six universal facial expressions (See Figure 9.1). It is these expressions that need to be catalogued and synchronized on the road to being "known." As a salesperson, you need to be able to understand the visual cues such as facial expressions that your client is giving you, to understand what a prospective client is going through. But more importantly, the client needs to understand the information you are communicating to them so that you can move them towards a sale. The only way for this to happen is for you to become "known" to them.

The system in your brain responsible for facial emotional cataloging and recognition is called the Mirror Neuron System. Its purpose is to signal your internal emotional state to others via facial expressions and interpreting others emotional states from their countenance. It is this system that is responsible for synchronization between individuals in face to face engagements and the root of becoming "known."

MIRROR NEURON SYSTEM

The Mirror Neuron System identifies the emotions of others by first imitating the other person's expression, via a micro expression, on your face. Once the other person's expression has been mimicked, the actual emotion associated with that expression is signaled from your reactor as an emotional sensation that is imposed briefly on your adaptor. Every time the person you are talking to changes their expression, the corresponding emotion it represents will be mimicked or "mirrored" and signaled to your conscious mind so that you will be better able to understand their actions and words. By matching words, body language, tone, and inflections to a facial expression, you will analyze and learn any facial expressions unique to that person. As this cataloguing continues, the clarity of their words' meaning will increase as well the efficiency of communication.

This system all makes sense when you remember from Chapter 2 that emotions spring from the reactor as a signaling mechanism for you to achieve your aims (motives) and that the reactor is responsible for muscle activity in its function of linking the mind to the body, as when one makes a facial expression. This pathway between facial muscles movement, emotion identification, and signaling then is all interrelated.

Perhaps the best, most simple example of the Mirror Neuron System in action is the yawn. You see someone else yawn, and you are compelled to mimic or mirror that yawn moments later, and even though you may not have been tired, now the yawn has washed a wave of tiredness over you. Keep this example in mind as you read on in this chapter.

This process of synchronization, as illustrated by the yawn example, is unconscious, and most likely, you won't even know it's happening because it is so fast and seamless. The existence of the Mirror Neuron System had long been suspected in humans, having been identified in animals much earlier, but it wasn't until 2009 its existence was proven in humans. The best way to understand the Mirror Neuron System is to think of it as a template library for matching facial expressions to emotions.

Oddly, one of the experiments used to verify existence of the Mirror Neuron System did so by deletion. Subjects of one of the experiments were shown a series of photographs of people with various expressions and asked to name the emotions those expressions conveyed. Most subjects scored high in accuracy, missing 20% or less. This was used as a baseline. Next, they were given a cork bit to put in their mouths and asked to bite down hard, immobilizing a good deal of their facial musculature. Then they were shown another series of photos of different people with the same facial expressions as the previous set and again asked to identify the emotions of the people in the pictures. The scores plummeted, with most of the subjects' scores down around 40% accuracy. By interfering with the body's ability to mimic facial expressions, the mind's ability to recognize emotions in others was manifestly curtailed.

This experiment also illustrates the need for synchronization. Looking at photos of an unknown person with no synchronization allowed for high, but not perfect scores. Such a high success rate can be associated to cultural and possibly regional correlations between subjects and the people in the photos, but it still shows that there is a significant error rate of 15-20% that can lead to miscommunication errors and misunderstandings that can be deadly to the aims of a salesperson.

Synchronization is a process by which, in the course of conversation, individuals in a communication transaction learn and identify many of the facial expressions unique to each other, thus filling the holes of emotional expression between the universal expressions. How many of these in-between (the universal expressions) need to be charted and understood before a person becomes known to the other person is unclear and may vary from person to person or situation. Clearly, there is an association between risk and the level of comfort of being a "known quantity." But as a salesperson, it is clear that the more synchronization you can accomplish, the less opportunity there will be for misunderstanding and miscommunication.

The Mirror Neuron System is thought to start development in infancy. While the construction of the Mirror Neuron System is embedded in the DNA of our cells, this genetic directive is for the construction of library only. It does not fill the library with facial models and matching emotions; these have to be learned, with the exception of the universal expressions. It's analogous to building a library with shelves, but the books (facial expression and corresponding emotions) must be accumulated by learning. The primary time for filling this library is thought to start in early infancy. Culturally, individuals in all societies hold their infants to their face and make expressions to their babies to entertain and soothe them. But what is also happening is that these infants are also learning facial expressions and associated emotions to fill their Mirror Neuron System's library shelves. There has been a long, heated debate about babies that do not get held enough in infancy that tend to grow up dysfunctional or with social issues, but the actual mechanism of this finding was not understood. With the emergence of the Mirror Neuron System, this mechanism, at least in part, is now understood. With diminished opportunities to fill their Mirror Neuron System library, these individuals can't understand other people because their facial expression quick reference list and library is incomplete, and thus they're mistrustful of others, lacking the ability to understand, sympathize, empathize, or communicate fully with others because they can't understand other's intentions based on facial expressions.

Another version of this is the Wolf Boy Syndrome. Occasionally, an individual is discovered that is raised in a high degree of isolation and dubbed a Wolf Boy, as in the urban myth of an abandoned infant boy raised by wolves. Despite therapists' best efforts, these individuals are usually never able to be fully integrated into society because the window for development of the Mirror Neuron System happens early in a child's upbringing, estimated to close at a time somewhere between the ages of three and five. It is theorized that it takes many exposures to each of the gradations of the non-universal expressions and associated emotions to learn and catalogue them. If the library is incomplete at the time the Mirror Neuron System is genetically encoded to cease development, there is no opportunity or ability to add to the library later on. To give a parallel example, autism is now being seen as a genetic inability to develop or fully develop the Mirror Neuron System, and individuals with this genetic disability are unable to synchronize with others with whom they engage in communication transactions. They have no way of identifying the emotional state or authenticating the contents of communications with others. Granted, autism is considered a spectrum disorder with many other variables, but the Mirror Neuron System is a large element to that disorder range. If the Mirror Neuron System had improper genetic coding for development, then there is high probability that the genetic coding deficit may be spread over to other neurological systems. Without the ability to develop a library of facial expressions due to isolation, the "wolf boy" is in fact a case of induced autism.

MICRO EXPRESSIONS

The process of synchronization occurs through facial mimicry know as a micro expression. Micro expressions happen subconsciously and may not ever register on either party in the conversation because they can happen so quickly and be lost in the movements of speech or transitions of facial expressions as topics and dialogue continue to flow. But high-speed cameras capture these micro expressions, even when one of the persons in the communications transaction is not present, like during a phone call. These micro expressions occur as your brain tries to sort the emotional content being sent over the phone or received by the eyes.

Sadly, many TV science dramas, and even experts on body language, misinterpret micro expressions as evidence of an internal state of the person giving the micro expression. In actuality, they are describing the mechanism of empathy. While it is true that once a person's unconscious Mirror Neuron System identifies the expression and corresponding emotional state by mimicry, that emotion will briefly be affected in the consciousness as empathy. These micro expressions are only for identification purpose of identifying someone else's emotions and is not evidence of the real emotional state of the receiver. Once identified, the receiver will resume the original emotional state he or she was experiencing prior to the Mirror Neuron

FIGURE 9.1

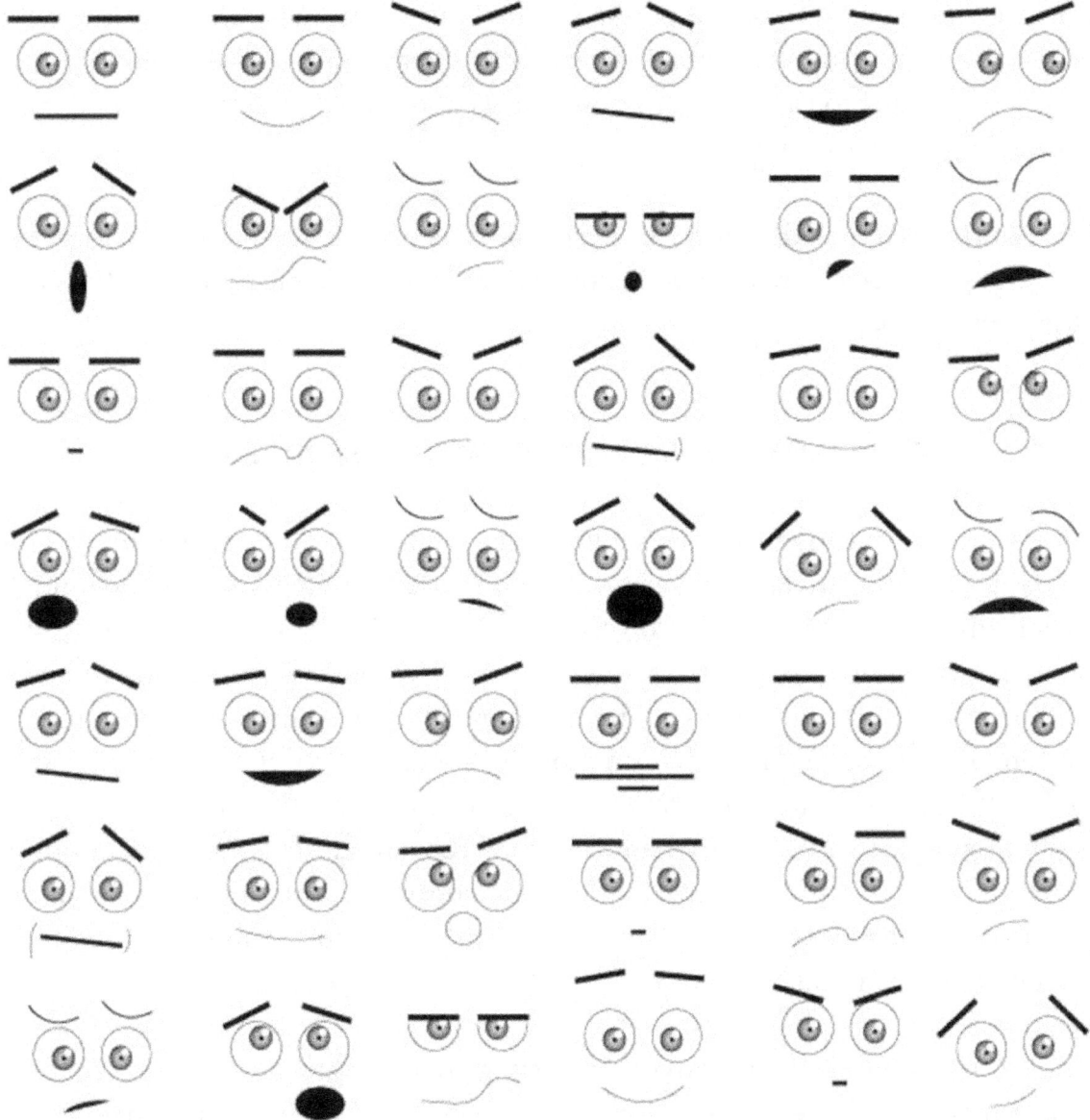

System's query. As a verification of this function for you, look again to babies. Those with infants are familiar with this phenomenon. Often a baby will cycle through a half-dozen or more emotions on his or her face. This occurs as you hold the baby up to your face. This is the Mirror Neuron System in development and on display as it searches for a matching expression. For those of you who have forgotten or do not have children, there are many amusing videos of babies cycling through expressions on the internet.

What is true, though, is that if an individual is trying to mask an emotional state by subduing his or her expression or supplanting an alternative one, an internal subconscious battle will occur and occasionally conscious control will lose out to the subconscious' drive to display the true emotional state and do so with a micro expression. Generally, these happen so fast that the conscious brain of a viewer does not register it, but the subconscious reactor is always engaged and will spot this sending a message to the viewer's conscious as a 'red flag', a discordance signaling the individual to move away.

While working knowledge of micro expressions is of little value to the salesperson, their impact can be of great value in communicating to clients and potential clients in the overall process.

FORCED FEEDBACK LOOP OF MICRO EXPRESSIONS

There is another old adage that says if you put a smile on your face, eventually you'll feel happy. Again, there is a kernel of truth to this when you understand the mechanisms of the Mirror Neuron System. Every time you consciously put an expression on your face, the Mirror Neuron System will inject the corresponding emotion into the consciousness of the adaptor, which will momentarily affect this emotion. If you are constantly consciously switching to the same expression, repeatedly forcing your conscious mind to affect that emotion, eventually, the conscious adaptor will be overwhelmed by the repeated affectations and adopt this new emotional state as a baseline. So if you do continually put a smile on your face, eventually the subconscious will be forced to adopt the emotion of happiness associated with smiling.

As noted in Chapter 2- Paradaptive Intelligence, there is a strong correlation between the six universal facial expressions and the six universal basic emotion patterns. So, as a salesperson, you can use this knowledge to craft the emotional state you wish to present to your potential clients and sales calls by choosing a game face that gets an attitude change.

Further anecdotal evidence of the forced feedback loop comes from another, totally unrelated, source – dentistry. Often times a patient has devices put in their mouths that force them to hold their mouth open. This forces the patient to assume the posture of a yawn which momentarily registers upon the adaptor as a moment of tiredness. Because the patient is forced to hold that facial expression of a yawn via the device, they become very, very tired and hence a large number fall asleep because the adaptor is overwhelmed by the repeated affectation of a yawn and the empathetic response of tiredness.

USING THE FORCED FEEDBACK LOOP TO INFLUENCE OTHERS

Everyone has the experience of "feeding off the energy of others." It really isn't energy that's being transferred. It is facial expressions and affectation of the subconscious by the reactor identifying emotional states to determine content meaning and intentions at play. If you are excited or enthusiastic about your product or some particular aspect or feature of it, you will constantly be putting an expression on your face to reflect your emotions. Just like the forced-feedback-loop discussed above, your client or prospect will be forced subconsciously to mimic and affect your emotional state as part of the subconscious' effort to understand your communications. Eventually, the subconscious reactor will overwhelm the adaptor and supplant that emotional state as the baseline in your prospect or client.

So, yes, it is true that a positive attitude, excitement, and enthusiasm are contagious, and now you know the mechanism at work. But there are limitations to this process due to factors discussed in the previous chapter, namely emotions being generated by other mind processes.

Just because you smile a lot or are cheerful does not mean that you can dictate the emotional state or change the reasoned decision of others. There is no way you can move a prospective client whose emotion towards computers is paranoia to the courage phase just by smiling and being enthusiastic. Additionally, someone adopting your emotional state does not mean they have changed their mind or emotional tone towards your product. Your clients can be happy, or any other projected attitude, and still be fearful of purchasing your product. But with a positive, happy attitude presented, you can make it easier to move the client one emotional tonal step from paranoia to trepidation by keeping the reactor engaged with happiness, signaling him to move towards you while letting substantive sales techniques and product information do the rest. You do this by displaying an expression that keeps the client positively engaged rather than expressing an emotion that has a negative element with an agitation element that encourages him to move away.

The underlying principle is that the emotions you display can be affected by prospective clients to keep them engaged with positive reactor messages. This compels them to approach you so that substantive sales techniques and product knowledge can change emotional tonal states via rational and cognitive reasoning in the adaptor.

ANIMATE !!!

The quickest way to conclude a sales cycle includes animating yourself. Remember, your objective is to synchronize your persona with the prospective client's Mirror Neuron System. The more of your emotional expressions you make available to your prospective clients, the quicker they can focus on communicating with you about their business issues rather than trying to figure out what exactly you're trying to communicate. A simple step you can take to speed this process up is animating your emotional states with exaggerated expressions. This makes it easy for them to figure out whether you have a very dry sense of humor, or some other personality trait, or are actually feeling what they think you are feeling. If an attribute of your product really helps clients and it makes you happy to show them how it will help, a pump of your fist and few "Wa-hoos!" makes it apparent where your verbal content, tone, body language, and intent is really coming from. It is perfectly okay to exaggerate your emotions a little for the purposes of becoming "known" to your perspective client as long as that emotion is genuine. Animating a false emotion will be caught by a viewer's reactor and send a strong signal to move away from you.

TODAY'S MEDIA ALTERNATIVES

The burgeoning application of internet media to the sales world has created a dilemma for the salesperson. In days of old, salespeople would board planes, trains, and automobiles to meet face-to-face with prospects in order to further the sale. But in today's internet savvy world, there are web meeting services galore to get you in front of prospects without physically making an appearance. As we have learned, the adaptor relies on the subconscious to monitor incoming streams of visual, tonal, and body language cues to help decipher the meaning of words in addition to facial expressions, only part of which internet meetings can readily communicate. This limited stream of data to the listener/viewer in an internet conference who is used to receiving far more data can have a negative impact on the sales process. With a reduced amount of personal data being conveyed to the prospect electronically, it is much easier for information to be misconstrued, lost, and misinterpreted.

Internet conferences do have their time and purpose in the salesperson's playbook, but it is important to know when and where to apply them. Sales by proxy via the internet is best served in clarifying meetings where plans and proposals are being discussed, *after* the synchronization between principals has occurred and an element of trust has developed. In the worst-case scenario where the salesperson is totally dependent upon video conferencing, he or she must be aware that the reduced stream of personal information flowing to the prospect will slow the overall process and offset the gain in time from not having travelled to a face-to-face meeting. Additionally, because it is impossible for teleconferencing to provide the same level of information to the sensory array of a prospect that a face-to-face meeting can, there is going to be a higher percentage of miscommunication to this form of media. This will require more documentation to be exchanged to get the same level and understanding, thus consuming more time and reducing the time savings of teleconferencing.

This type of sales conferencing usually commences due to long distances between salesman and prospect, which makes it cost prohibitive for regular face-to-face sales presentations. Yet, as mentioned earlier in this chapter, that very distance implies that there may be regional differences in facial expressions which require other input from the sensory array of the reactor to decipher meaning. This factor, too, also increases the chances for misunderstanding due to under-transmission of other interpretation cues.

Given all this, salespeople using this technological meeting platform must understand that they must compensate for the overall limited bandwidth communicated to a prospective client's reactor. That compensation must be in the form of increased animation of their personage to make it easier for the parties in the teleconference to gather the full meaning of what is trying to be communicated.

CONCLUSION

In conclusion, it is important to allow your clients, to the furthest extent possible, access to your emotions via facial expressions so that your clients can synchronize their Mirror Neuron System to you. Let your expressiveness work for you upon prospective clients so that their adaptors render a positive verdict of predictable communication. With a positive verdict, the client will "know" you. This is the foundation of trust that is needed so that you can use product information and techniques to be discussed in later chapters to help SPAN (Chapter 14) all the emotional tones necessary to get your client to the courage phase.

SALES MYTHS AND ADAGES

The Business Poker Face

This concept is probably the most destructive of all the business myths. In the unwritten lore of sales, there is the notion that proper business decorum is to be a smooth, steady, balanced, unflappable salesperson. Holding your countenance void and withholding emotional signals only slows the synchronization process. While being unflappable is great as a problem-solver in sales, essentially this sales myth promotes stripping yourself, as a salesman, of all but the blandest of expressions to be "professional." This book submits that being unflappable and being void of expression are two separate things. Reacting to both positive and negative developments is not unprofessional. The trick is not to let them unbalance you or disrupt your adaptive, cognitive self. By showing these reactions, you help your prospective and clients synchronize with you, which leads to trust. Trust is a necessary element if product information as a basis of adaptive behavior is to be accepted.

A corollary to demonstrate the destructiveness of this myth is coulrophobia, or the fear of clowns. *Nursing Standard* magazine interviewed 250 children, ages four to sixteen, and found clowns to be "universally scary." In another study, researcher Penny Curtis found some kids found clowns to be "quite frightening and unknowable." We now know why. The grease paint of the clown obscures the emotional signaling of the Mirror Neuron System, replacing it with a painted-on expression that is incongruent with the clown's actions. The clown has a painted smile yet strikes another clown with a boat oar, ladder, seltzer spray, etc. This dissonance between facial expression and action sets up negative, threat based signaling from the reactor, compelling children to move away from the threat – the clown. So, the business poker face is equivalent to that of a clown's. It both obscures emotional signaling and refutes the cooperation bias, forcing people to move away from you.

Sell Yourself First

The old sales adage is that the first thing you sell is yourself. Again, the lack of a proper vocabulary and understanding of mechanisms involved lead to the belief that you were actually selling yourself – you're actually synchronizing your Mirror Neuron System. However, this adage does validate the concept of synchronization, which salesmen have recognized for ages, albeit in a miss-categorized sense. What this illustrates is that, without proper understanding of the mechanisms in play, the human mind will concoct overly-broad definitions and meanings to describe a sense or feeling the subconscious is registering. The real mechanism in play is Mirror Neuron System and its demanded synchronization process.

The Icebreaker - Asking Questions About Something in The Prospect's Office

This venerable sales technique has utility long recognized, but misunderstood. Having a conversation centered on some other topic found in the office allows for a more unguarded conversation. When the topic of business and the reason for the appointment begins, both salesman and prospect slip into internally perceived roles. The client acts as interested skeptic and the salesman as, well, a salesman. At this time, the aforementioned business poker face usually rears its ugly head. The unguarded prior conversation on the nonbusiness topic let more emotional expressions be synchronized because there were no assigned roles and thus emotional and facial expressions were not as restricted by the poker business face myth. As a salesperson, you'll want to keep that animation going on your part which will utilize the force feedback loop of the Mirror Neuron System to goad the prospect's Mirror Neuron System to figure out your emotions for empathetic syncope, making them create micro expressions and forcing them out of the role they've been trained to assume. All of which will increase the communication, and that is always good for salespeople and client alike.

Speaking Engagements

Most salespeople will find themselves speaking to a large group of people at some point in time. Many salespeople are fearful of this scenario, and for good reason. Without experience, being in front a large group can be highly disruptive to the cognitive process of a presenter, creating confusion and anxiety over the effectiveness of the presentation and thus reflecting upon his or her business worthiness. The myth holds that if you picture the audience in their underwear (or nothing at all), you will relieve your anxiety by this visualization. It is not clear whether this remedy actually works or not, but what is clear is that we now have an understanding of the actual mechanism in play, which is the Mirror Neuron System. As discussed in the section on "Using the Force Feedback Loop to Influence Others," the reverse comes true to the speaker. As a speaker, if you go from face to face, focusing on the audience, your subconscious reactor will impose the identified emotions of each new audience member you view upon your subconscious. This stream of rapidly changing emotional recognitions will destabilize your internal emotional state until your conscious focus on your speaking is disrupted and your fears of low business worth are realized by poor execution. The only way to avoid this negative influence is to avoid looking at the audience's faces or learn to look but tune them out. A good speaker will look above heads of an audience, or if you're the President, you'll look at a teleprompter, thus avoiding the absorption of disruptive emotional states of individuals in the audience as your reactor empathizes with the emotions of the faces you encounter.

The Golf Course or Lunch Appointment

These venues are used to create more varied and unguarded moments to allow synchronization of the Mirror Neuron System. It's hard to shade or obscure your true emotional state when your facial muscles are engaged in the process of chewing or spilling something on your favorite tie. Additionally, the client gets to see your interactions with others, like your server. People may have the motive of sending false signals to prospects in order to gain a sale, but that motive doesn't carry over to third parties (like restaurant staff), so seeing how you interact with others gives a prospect a reference point to compare your expression to that you give others. Likewise, if you shank a ball from the tee box at the golf course, the change in venue inclines you to more varied expressions than just "Ooops!" Both these venues work to the salesperson's advantage because the whole intent is to present more expressions to your client so that he or can synchronize to you and may better understand your communications thereby trust and accept your adaptation solutions.

It is important to note that such engagements at offsite locations also serve another important purpose, which is to learn your pattern of reasoning and approach to issues. This serves the buyer's adaptor so that the client can learn to predict your actions. *Predictability is the main ingredient of trust.* Predictability has three states: always the right response, always the wrong response, or inconsistent. Clients and prospects value only one of these states. This must be looked upon from the client's perspective: they have a survival or adaptive problem, and you have a solution. They don't necessarily need to like you in order to do business with you: they only need to accept you in order to move forward. Liking you and having a personal relationship only comes into play as a tie breaker between you and your competitors when the client views your product as having little or no variation from the competition. And even then, they can like you and still consider you unpredictable. This need for predictability increases as the degree of risk to the client increases for selecting you as a vendor.

Off-site interactions give your prospective client a two-for-one experience in learning your thought processes and speeding up the communication process of synchronization governed by the Mirror Neuron System.

Celebrity

But perhaps the best way to illustrate the power of synchronization is to examine it in an extreme situation where content is missing. The best example of this is the arena of celebrity. Take actors, for example. They're trained to emote, portray emotions in furtherance of telling a story about someone they are not. The best actors are those that can totally eliminate their own characteristics from that of the character they are portraying. In viewing their work, you, as a viewer, synchronize with the actor via the content of the story, learning what the actor's expressions actually mean. Everybody in this electronic media age has a favorite actor or actress, or two. These are people who are now known to you, who you can easily read their facial expressions. Their manner of portrayal takes advantage of your reactor to render a positive verdict to direct you towards them so that you are drawn into the story. But this is like emotional Chinese food, satisfying, but not fulfilling. After the actor's portrayal is over, you're left with a person who is known to you, one whose emotions you can read because you have synchronized with him or her, but you know little to nothing about the actor as a person. The information obtained from their performance about their character has no bearing or relation to the real personality of the actor or actress. In the real course of life, as you are synchronizing with people, you obtain information about their reactions, tendencies, humor, values, likes and dislikes, how they think, etc. By the time that your synchronization is complete, you not only have mastered a wide enough swath of their inventory of facial expression to cross the threshold of being known, but you have also amassed significant personal information about them as well. But with actors, the reactor is satisfied having synchronized facial expression, but the corresponding conscious adaptor is left void, having learned nothing of the real person behind the character. And nature abhors a void. People feel compelled, without knowing why, to find out more about the actor or actress' personal life to balance that individual's portfolio in their conscious and memory, and thus creates a cult of celebrity. You may feel a desire to peruse the tabloids, entertainment magazines, or the visual versions on television as a way of filling in the actor's personal portfolio in your conscious mind.

SECTION II

Consumer Behavior and Sales

With our new understanding of the mechanisms of adaptation that are hardwired in every human being's DNA, we can now seek to understand its expression in exchange based societies of the modern world. These mechanisms, which were originally formed to allow prehistoric man to locate and utilize resources in nature for his sustenance and survival, must now be adapted to a new venue, our societies. While the Paradaptive Intelligence Network's mission has not changed, the nature of human environment has. Hunting and gathering still occurs, but now rather than seeking resources from nature, we now seek our resources, sustenance, and other vitals from individuals within our societies who specialize in the making or distributing of specific solutions. Roughly speaking, the "hunting" in the hunting and gathering activities occurs when we seek to trade our products, services, skills, or knowledge with others to obtain currency. This is reflected when seeking employment why we refer to it as job hunting. "Gathering" is when you seek to exchange your resources, your currency, for someone else's products, services, or knowledge. Or, some people just call it shopping.

This illuminates the yin and the yang of consumer behavior and sales, and why they are reciprocals. The difference is whether you are seeking to buy or sell, and why understanding one fully translates into understanding the other. And, in our societies, we play both roles innumerable times a day. It is this inability to separate the two, consumer behavior and sales, which drives the discussion of both topics simultaneously because one cannot occur without the other. And both these actions spring from the same source of mental machinery, the Paradaptive Intelligence Network. The regulatory action of the Paradaptive Intelligence Network controls all

89

transactions, whether you're the buyer or the seller. It is this same source that allows for the unification of disparate theories, wisdoms, rules, postulates, etc. to be combined into one coherent theory and starts the movement of organizing business activities into structured orderliness, removing it from the randomness and chaos once thought to be the defining character of business due to its subjugation to emotions. It is also the regulatory action of Paradaptive Intelligence Network controlling transactions and its foundational principles that makes it possible to remove business from the arts category study of style into a true science.

Perhaps it is best to think of the mind in this way: the purpose and function of the human mind is adaptation. The only master intellect serves is adaptation. And the mind has developed two general strategies for adaptation: 1) Innovation and 2) Relationships. In Innovation, the mind either alters one's behavior or the surroundings by examining the problem, designing a tool or implement, then evaluating not only its potential to solve the problem but the cost and risks of doing so, or changing our behavior to affect a desired outcome. Lacking the ability to change our behavior or our environment via Innovation, we have a second broad strategy, relationships. If we lack the skills, insight, knowledge, or resources to solve an adaptational problem, we form relationships to acquire that which we don't have ourselves in hopes of obtaining it from others. In sales, both of these general strategies are employed to solve adaptation problems.

10

FEAR AND INNOVATION ADOPTION

"If we worked on the assumption that what is accepted is really true, then there would be little hope for advance."
Wilbur Wright, pioneer of flight

In every sale, in every business transaction, *something* is sold to or by *someone*. So there are two elements to every sale, *something* and *someone*, an object and a relationship. The *something* is a product, service, or knowledge – a tool, an inanimate object for all intents and purposes. The relationship is the dynamic of emotions *between* the two parties. Both run concurrently. Of the two, the *something* is more important in one-time-only and low repetition of sales scenarios. The importance of the relationship grows with the frequency of repetitiveness of the sales or with the level of risk involved to the buyer. While the importance of the relationship may approach the importance of solving a problem, it will never surpass it. Buyers seek innovation to solve and nullify business pain points. Another way to state this is that buyers display innovation seeking behavior first and foremost. The process of innovation seeking follows a unique emotional pathway called an algorithm.

As we learned in Chapter 8, Emotions – The Language of Feedback, while only one Human Action Cycle can be pursued at any one time, it is possible to have two motives — one in the innovation pathway of a sale and another, separate motive for the relationship between the buyer and seller because these are two separate emotional algorithms. There is no hard and fast rule as to which pathway should be the focus at any one point. If you understand what is going on and how to identify and manage it, you, the salesman, will gain more latitude for creative adaption as your individual sales style and methodology evolve.

There are three types of sales markets: selling reduced uncertainty, commodities, and innovation. Uncertainty would have to do with insurance and financial products geared towards stability and reducing the impact of market swings or

FIGURE 10.1

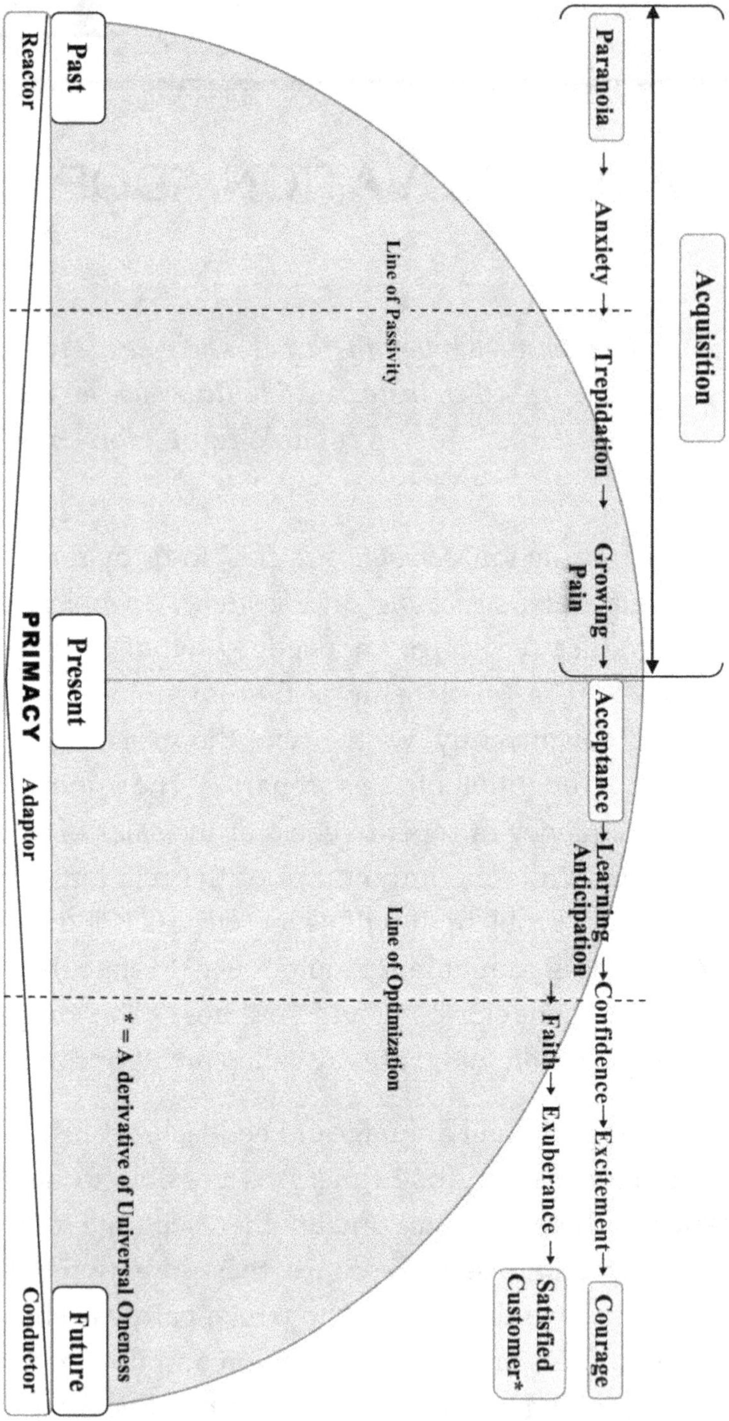

Acquisition Phase of the Innovation Emotional Tonal Algorithm

catastrophic events. Commodity sales are about selling goods and services that a business consumes in the course of their business on either a regular or irregular basis. Businesses accept the need to replenish these consumables. The third type of sales is innovation. This is where a change to the business' current operations or processes is being marketed in the form of a good, service, or knowledge. All three of these types of sales markets experience new products and services or changes in packaging to introduce to their evolving consumer bases. Change can be seen as a threat. This means the adoption process of innovation is governed by fear. Since fear is one of the basic corrective signals, we can now use the Paradaptive Intelligence Network to explain technology and innovation adoption and its relationship to fear.

But before we use the Paradaptive Intelligence Network to explain innovation adaption, let's review how the emotion state of fear governs innovation. Fear is generated by the reactor signaling a threat to the body or self. So, if fear is present, then that means that the reactor is vying for control of the body to some degree dependent upon the level of threat. So, to study fear, to study innovation adoption, one must study and understand how the two different "minds," the subconscious reactor and the conscious adaptor, vie for supremacy. As we'll see in this chapter, the more involved the reactor gets due to greater fear induction, the more irrational a prospect's behavior becomes, leaving less and less of the rational mind for the salesman to work with. However, just because there is irrationality does not mean there is not an opportunity for sales. To the contrary, once you learn the principles of Paradaptive Intelligence, it will teach you just exactly how to handle fear and its induced irrationality.

INNOVATION AND TOOL SEEKING

At this point, it is imperative to understand the difference between innovation and tool seeking. Innovation is an internal process whereby you create a new behavior or create an implement to solve a problem and nullify a pain point. This is working within your skill set and resources with a focus to the future. Tool seeking is when you are unable to innovate on your own and seek the new behavior or implement from someone else. If developing a specific tool economically was within your skill set, you'd have done it yourself. But, because your skill set or resources are not up to the challenge, you seek solutions, i.e. tools, from those with the resources, skills, and know-how. Because you're acquiring an innovation not of your design, it brings into question whether your skill set can even operate and utilize the innovation. This is the first evaluative action in looking at innovation and is past-based in its view. It looks to your past to determine the likelihood of successful innovation adoption based on an inventory of your current skills relative to the innovation and your resources. Once it is determined whether your skill set and resources are up to the challenge of utilizing an innovation, or will require assistance of some form has been answered, then the innovation goes through the same innovation/tool seeking evaluation as if you were developing your own tool.

What adds to the confusion is the word tool has a connotation as an implement of the hand, yet the word tool is often use to describe any alternative behavior that helps nullify a pain point. As an example, try this one "'You have one mouth and two ears, so a salesperson should listen twice as much as he speaks' is a great tool to use for those in the sales profession." Don't let this confuse you. Others may innovate, but if you acquire that innovation from them, you are acquiring a tool.

TECNNOLOGY DIFFUSION CURVE

Salespeople and marketers are a clever and observant lot as a whole. For many decades, marketers have used a model of the Technology Adaptation Lifecycle developed by Joe M. Bohlen, George M. Beal, and Everett M. Rogers at Iowa State University to help understand who and when technology is adopted in the marketplace. This model can be used to fit not only technology, but all innovation. In Figure 10.2, we see the standard Innovation Diffusion Curve and its five sections: Innovators, Early Adopters, Early Majority, Late Majority and Laggards. The Technology Adaptation Lifecycle model characterizes them as follows:

> Innovators (Venturesome) are the first to adopt. They are eager to try new ideas and are willing to take risks. They tend to be young and high in both social and economic status with many contacts outside their own local social group and community. They are also able to comprehend and apply complex technical data which is their main source of information in the decision making process. Firms driven by these types tend to be large and specialized.

> Early Adopters (Respectable) are relatively high in social status, well-respected by their peers, and usually high in opinion leadership. They tend be younger, more mobile, and more creative than later adopters. They tend to have few contacts outside their own social group or community. Firms driven by these types tend to be specialized. This group is also noted for having the highest contact with salespeople.

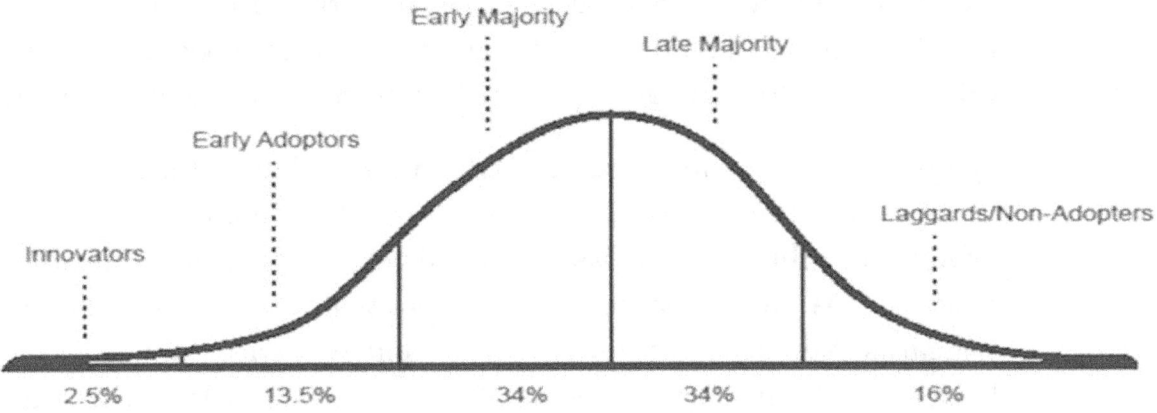

Figure 10.2

INNOVATION ADOPTION CURVE

INNOVATION ADOPTION LIFECYCLE

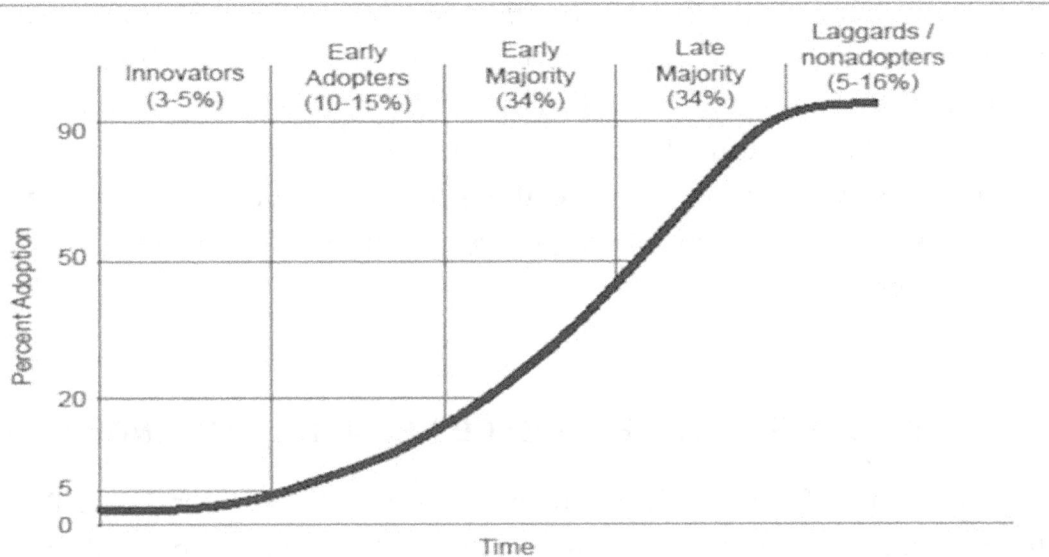

Early Majority (Deliberate) are those with above-average social status and will not consider a new idea until many early adopters have vetted the product. They tend to deliberate for some time before completely adopting a new idea. Firms driven by these types of individuals are average-sized with less specialization and have a lot of contact with mass media, salespeople, and early adopters.

Late Majority (Skeptical) tend to be below-average in social status and income. They are skeptical and cautious about new ideas, generally because their skills and knowledge are extremely outdated. They are less likely to follow opinion leaders and early adapters. Usually strong social pressure from their peers is needed before they will adopt new products. They tend to be older, clinging to past technology, which they adopted earlier when they were more likely to have been either an early adopter or early majority member. They make little use of mass media or salespeople and tend to be oriented more to other late adaptors than outside sources of information.

Laggards/Nonadopters (Traditional) tend to be low in the social status and income. They prefer current technology or old technology – the way they've always done things in the past. They are very suspicious of new ideas. They tend to be the smallest businesses with the least specialization. Laggards/Non-adopters tend to be "loners" with almost no opinion leadership. Their main source of information is other laggards and it often doesn't pay to court this group's business.

Despite being able to identify and apportion these segments, in its original design, there is nothing to tie this information in a useful manner to the salesperson's understanding of the marketplace. This is but one of many "black box" statistical analyses that we'll encounter in this book. This occurs when the causation or origin of the subject being studied is not known or understood, and therefore the only thing left for researchers is to measure the strength among associated variables and attributes. In this case, those variables are quantities and time relative to innovation development adoption.

PARADAPTIVE INTELLIGENCE NETWORK AND INNOVATION

If you examine Figure 10.3, you'll see the flow of Emotions Tonal Algorithm for Innovation. This graph perfectly exhibits all the emotions that prospects can experience in the course of a purchase and the order in which they will experience them. It is among the most important graphs a salesperson or sales manager will ever see in his or her professional career. It will allow salespeople and sales managers the ability to predict and quantify emotions in commerce. For the remainder of this chapter, we'll focus mainly on the past and present portion of this graph because it becomes the focal point of, and perfectly explains, innovation adoption.

If you reverse and mate the innovation diffusion graphs with Figure 10.2, pairing innovators with acceptance, early adopters with growing pains, early majority with trepidation, late majority with anxiety, and paranoia with laggard/non-adopters, you get perfect correlation and understanding of the underlying emotions driving innovation diffusion and thus market behavior (See Figure 10.3).

Emotions are the sole source driving innovation in humans. Emotions dictate to us whether to change our behavior to adapt to an environment or change our environment to adapt it to our behavior. So, in order to understand innovation diffusion, you must understand its underlying driver, emotions. The emotions displayed in Figure 10.2, the Innovation Diffusion Curve, represent the probability of various attitudinal states possible at first contact with a prospect, while the emotional tonal algorithm indicates the pathway that every prospect will follow on the way to making a sale. The emotions displayed in Figure 10.3 are in a specific order, and humans flow from one adjacent emotion to the next without skipping a step.

There are times and examples where it will appear a jump occurred over an emotional step(s) on the way to innovation adoption, but in reality, they just momentarily alighted upon an emotion, acknowledged, and satisfied it before quickly moving on to the next emotion in the progression.

Innovators

From Figure 10.3 we can glean several new insights into the workings of the salesman's environment. We learn that innovators live in the moment and are driven by the pain points of inefficiencies in their business. They accept change and innovation in their business operations as a way of countering the networking, experience, and wisdom advantage of rivals, thus focus on nullifying the psychic pain inflicted upon them due to business inefficiencies. They are unfettered by past experiences or phobias of other innovation adoptions; in fact, to them, innovation acquisition is just a normal life activity, and their skill and experience level is contemporary with current innovation technology. They are characterized by being youthful and high in social and economic status. They live in the present and accept innovation because they grew up in a silicon age where the quick pace of technological innovation was the background to their youth and formative years.

Additionally, they have not labored for years to acquire wealth or possession, so they are not vested in their accoutrements, figuring that they can replace any losses. If a salesperson approaches them, they will assume that you are vending older technology and products, which they are not interested in. They prefer and get their information from journals, magazines, and internet sources which are where all the state-of-the-art innovations are discussed and found. If they do sit down with you, it is only to acquire information to feed their adaptor's requirement for knowledge, which is not oriented to fixing a problem, i.e. pain point, but rather acquiring knowledge for knowledge's sake to compare against innovations in the same area. As a salesperson, you won't be sitting down with many, if any, of these clients. *They*

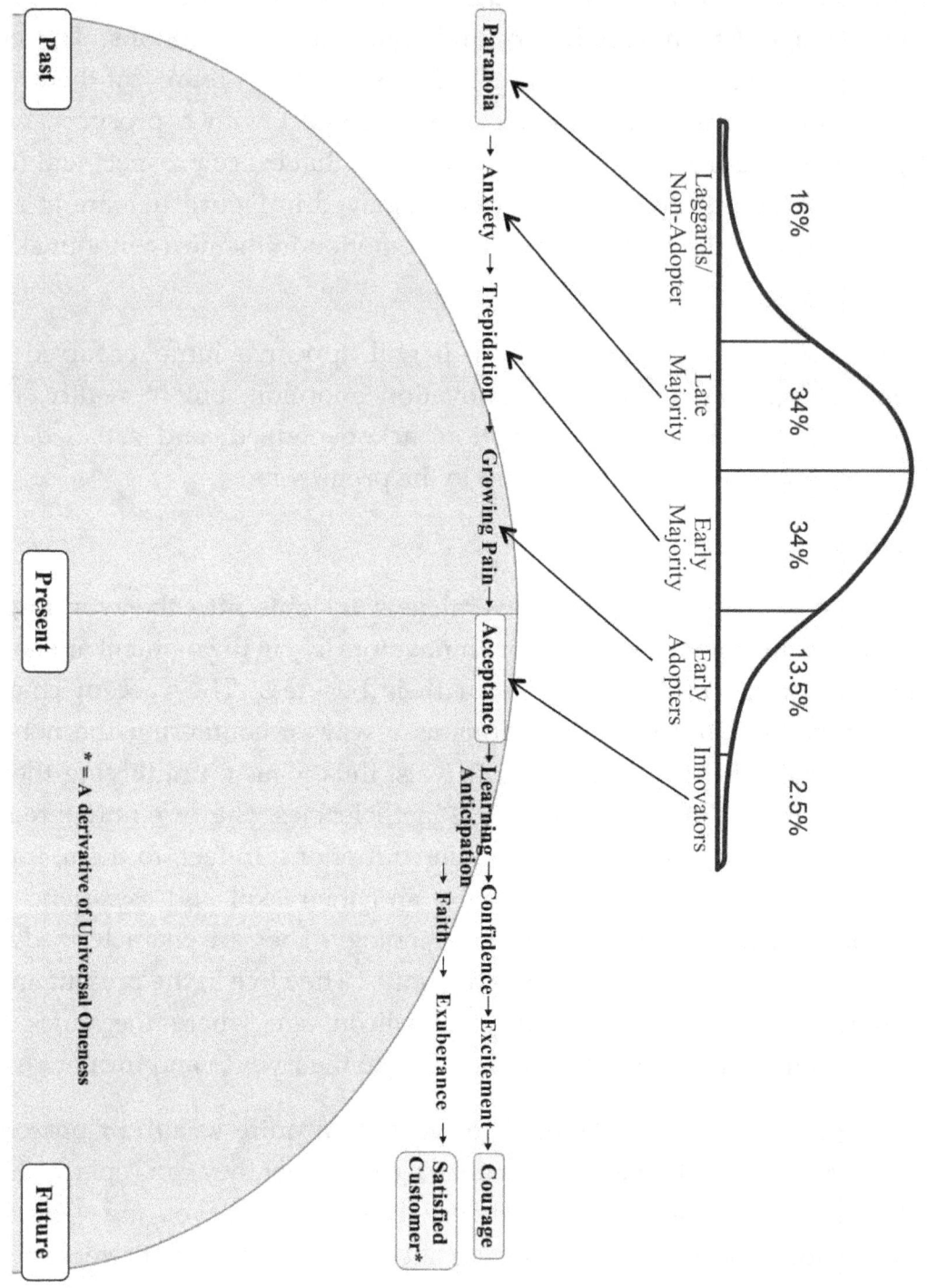

Figure 10.3

Innovation Emotional Tonal Algorithm Coupled with
Innovation Adoptive Curve

will contact *you* for an order — usually.

Acceptance is a very mild form of the basic emotion of joy. Having accepted the presence of a problem or issue gives people a positive direction in which to move and that was after all, what fear agitates towards, movement. The reactor is providing a reward, from the basic emotion joy, as a growth signal, for following its previous dictates to move away from the threat it perceived in the inefficiencies of their workplace and towards solutions and their pain nullification properties.

FEAR BASED PROSPECTS

As for others, early adopters, early majority, late majority, and laggards/non-adopters, the prevailing emotion is that of the corrective signal of fear. Innovation diffusion is a function of fear. The overall source of fear in the Innovation Curve is the perceived gap in the prospective clients' skills and ability to adopt and integrate innovation into their business and the added disruption it will cause to an already suboptimal performing business. The amount of fear is determined by just how close their current skill level is to the innovation technology and methodologies needed to fix the issue(s). Another way to state the gap in perception of skill and resources/innovation needed is how old and out-of-date their experience and skills are compared to current technology. Since their fear is rooted in past experience and skills applicable to technology that is no longer current, it is clear why the Innovation Diffusion Curve in Figure 10.2 describes the past portion of the emotional tonal algorithm for Innovation. The older and more outdated their skills and experience, the greater the level of fear. In this case, fear is agitating them to move away from innovation adoption because the disruption to their business and the energy needed to implement changes is proportional and commensurate to their lack of skills and experience needed for implementation. The greater the amount of fear that must be overcome, the greater amount of energy a salesperson will have to expend to convert that prospect into a sale.

Early Adopters

The first group of fear-driven adapters, early adapters, is governed by the complex emotion growing pains. This complex emotion is an acknowledgement that change is necessary and painful. Early adopters require the latest business innovations but seek to minimize the pain of disruption from innovation adoption by letting others, innovators, go first to work out any kinks of the product or service implementation process. They know business pain points must be addressed and want the latest innovations as soon as they hit the streets via salespeople. These firms tend to be specialized, which denotes expertise to a very narrow market. In order to maintain the image and expertise of a specialized, narrow market leader, proprietors must aggressively seek every advantage the market can offer. They tend to be younger because, again, they are closer and more comfortable with the rapid pace of innovation that paralleled their formative years. Specialized firms must rapidly evolve in their field to keep that specialization advantage, ergo, they have a relatively high tolerance for change, and their skill and experience level is just slightly less commensurate with current innovation technology and methodologies than that of innovators.

Your objective as a salesperson is to convince early adapters or those passing through this emotional phase that the innovation adoption process will pose minimal disruption by your participation and that you will lead them through it. It will be further helpful to demonstrate that the product or service has already been implemented by innovation leaders, so the implementation process is well understood, thus reducing business disruption from implementation.

Early Majority

The next group on the Innovation Adoption Curve is the early majority. This group's threat level and resulting fear is that of trepidation. Trepidation is characterized as a significant level of agitation, but the rational adaptor is still dominant, although with diminished capacity due to corrective signal agitation. These firms are characterized as average sized firms. This means that they have enjoyed enough success with their business strategy to grow to a notable size. Their focus is to do more of the same that has led to their continual growth. But it is a controlled growth that they seek, meaning stability is now sought throughout the firm so that the firm's limited resources can be targeted at selected growth opportunities. Growth is still important to these firms, but they just can't afford to grow everywhere, all the time — otherwise chaos would ensue. Adopting new innovations will upset the stability within the firm. By virtue of the stability recently introduced to the structure of the firm, there has been no movement and no change, therefore it acknowledges that the gap between the firm's decision makers' skills and the pace and scope of innovation has widened considerably, creating much angst about their ability to understand, use, and implement innovation. This is why this group has considerable contact with early adopters in making a decision about purchasing innovation. They want to get a very strong sense of how much disruption will be caused versus the benefits gained. This is why this group is noted for their long and deliberate due diligence in their purchase decision process. Sure, solving their pain points is important, but the implementation plan is even more important. And the best source for an implementation plan is the salesperson and his or her expertise. This is one of the strongest motivating reasons why early majority adopters have such heavy contact with salespeople.

Your objective as a salesperson is to convince early majority adopters or those passing through this emotional phase that the innovation adoption process will produce benefits to them in excess of the cost, resources, and disruption of innovation adoption. A salesperson needs to convince them that the inconvenience of implementation will create greater stability for them over the long haul, allowing them to extend their more-of-the-same business strategy.

Late Majority

The late majority's fear level is classified as anxiety. This means that fear is in greater control of the mind's apparatuses than rational thought pursuant to innovation. These tend to be older firms. Think of them as cash cows. They have a long business history of success and see innovation only as a means to keep the cash flowing with as little effort as possible. Growth isn't really a motivator for this segment; rather, maintaining cash flow is. Innovation is seen as a means of cash flow through extension of their current business model, not a change to that business model through new capabilities.

This group represents the widest possible gap that can be bridged between the rate and scope of current technology and the capabilities and comfort range of the decision makers. This is also the source of their anxiety. They have significant fear levels because their skill set toward innovation adoption is widely inadequate. Because their innovation adoption gap is so wide, their biggest concern is whether it is even feasible for them to pursue it. It is for this reason they have the greatest contact with peers who may have similar problems and have already pursued innovation adoption similar to what you're offering. Their biggest fear is that the disruption of innovation adoption could have a significant impact on the profit flow, which is their primary business mission, or even have a fatal effect on their business. This information is not obtainable from a salesman, which is why they seek input from peers who have already traversed a similar business path to theirs.

In addition, because the offering of the salesperson is so laced with fear due to the gap between their skills and resources, and that needed to partake of the salesperson's adaption plan, their agitation expression highly stimulates them to move away from the source of the fear, which is the salesperson. So, the only reasonable course of action is to pursue the innovation through surrogates, i.e. peers who have implemented this or similar products, who are less threatening but still possess extensive product knowledge.

Your objective as a salesperson is to convince late majority adopters that they can accomplish the innovation adoption process by showing them peer firms that have successfully done this, survived, and thrived. Further, by buying and implementing their innovation, the benefits will extend the period of cash flow, keeping the cash cow viable for years to come. Every salesperson, if courting this market segment, should have an older generation peer firm groomed and ready to act as a selling agent to showcase your product, if your product has satiated the previous markets of innovators, early adopters, and early majority.

Laggards/Non-Adaptors

This segment of the market's underlying emotion is paranoia. Paranoia is marked by irrational fear. It may also invoke the Fight, Flight, or Freeze. There is no opportunity for rational discussion regarding innovation with this segment of the market. It would be nice to assign a cause to this irrationality, but by definition there is no rational cause to irrationality. However, we do know it is based on some past bad experience, either directly or vicariously. Nor is this market segment of any use to the salesperson. There is no methodology to convert or argument that can be applied, to make the irrational rational, to make the incoherent coherent. The inhabitants of this segment, in all probability, couldn't explain to the salesperson the source of their irrational fear of innovation if they wanted.

The only value to the salesperson that this segment affords is that it is easily recognizable. Conspicuous will be the absence of any modern business tools considered normal for businesses of their type. A few questions will suffice to inform the salesperson that there is something decidedly off-kilter with this prospect. There is no hope for a sale at this type of business. The salesperson who doesn't understand this may see a prospect ripe for the sale, being in such need for innovation. Those that know better, however, will move on quickly to greener sales pastures elsewhere and apply their time to prospects where there is the actual potential of a sale.

AMBIVILANCE

There is a curious event that can happen – ambivalence. This occurs when two forces come into opposition, such as the reactor and adaptor, or two opposing HACs. In the case of adaptor and reactor opposition, the agitation of fear from the reactor is equally balanced against the adaptor's desire for adaptation. Two imperatives, save the body from harm and adapt, are perfectly balanced against each other. People often use the phrase "I'm of two minds on this topic..." Well, in fact they are. Their two minds are their reactor and their adaptor and their conflicting prime directives. Adaptation threatens stability, which is strongly desired in early majority adaptors, who have a "more of the same" business philosophy, versus the adaptor's desire for knowledge that brings flexibility for a greater range of adaptation to their market segment and growth. Knowing this as a salesperson, it will be easy to tip the scales in your direction by focusing on threat reduction while feeding the adaptor with encouragement that the world is changing and they need to adapt to stay viable and grow.

In HAC opposition, a single action could impact two or more HACs and bring them into opposition. Buyer's remorse is a prime example of this type of HAC opposition and will be discussed in Chapter 15. In HAC opposition a single action can bring a growth signal which is opposed by a corrective signal. Opposition occurs when growth signals oppose corrective signals. If a single action brought multiple growth signals, then the action would be further endorsed and pursued more heartily. The same goes for corrective signals. If a single action brought forth many corrective signals, then the HAC that brought forth the corrective signals would be paused and modified, or abandoned.

LINE OF PASSIVITY

Ambivalence also marks the Line of Passivity. It is at this point that the reactor is exerting equal control as the adaptor for control of the body. Up to this point, as emotions progressed from low intensity corrective signals towards high intensity signals, the adaptor, while impacted by intentional disruption from the reactor, was still in control. This disruption was passive, meaning that, in this particular case, fear was being dealt with in a controlled, non-reactive manner with reason, logic, and imagination, albeit in a compromised capacity, and the agitation expression to move away, while present, was not manifest. But beyond the tipping point of the Line of Passivity, progressing towards higher intensity corrective signals, the agitation expression to move away contained in a corrective signal, starts to assert primacy. But because the adaptor still has some control over the Paradaptive Intelligence Network, it tries to moderate or walk back the actions of the reactor (Figure 10.4).

The best understood example of this is passive/aggressive behavior of the corrective signal anger. The corrective signal anger is directing impulses to the body to fight back, so the reactor forces the person to utter an aggressive, challenging statement or behavior, which the adaptor tries to immediately moderate or walk-back with a softer or even conciliatory action or statement. If the defining corrective signal is fear, then the prospect will approach you for contact, then cancel and reschedule it frequently. This passive/flight action by a prospect is very confusing to a salesperson who has not read this book. They'll be wondering "are they really interested in my product or just jerking me around?" What is really happening is a conflict between the two brain processing centers, the reactor pushing away and the adaptor seeking to engage and adapt.

This is an indirect approach to action, which is a defining characteristic of emotions just beyond the Line of Passivity. In sales, this takes the form of prospects at the trepidation level of fear. They no longer want to deal directly with what has been generating fear, the presence of the salesman. Instead of working with salespeople, they prefer to examine the technology indirectly, through peers who've successfully implemented the technology. This is the manifestation of the agitation expression to move away from what is causing the threat – the salesperson. This indirect method of dealing with what is generating fear persists all the way through the escalating corrective signal with diminishing ability of the adaptor to moderate the manifestation of the core response driven by the basic emotion element of a corrective signal. This indirect action persists with direct action becoming more pervasive until the full corrective signal is achieved at the end of the continuum and full, direct action occurs. Put another way, the more intense the emotional corrective signal, the less the adaptor is able to modify the impulse to fight back (anger), escape (threat), isolation/loss (sadness), or move away/fight back from unwholesomeness (disgust).

PRACTICAL EFFECTS OF FEAR

Innovators, between 3-5% of the market, are not driven by salespeople. Laggards/nonadopters, between 5-16% won't be accepting an appointment to sit down with you unless you provide a commodity type product. So between 8 and 21% of the market will not even speak to most salespeople. This means that your market, as a salesperson, is comprised of early adaptors (10 - 15%), early majority (34%) and late majority (34%). These groups are pain point driven. At best, no more than 83% of the marketplace will be eligible for salesperson activities (excepting commodity product sales). And of that 83%, 34% will rely more on peers initially than the salesperson in moving through the sales process. So realistically, less than half, 49%, will be viable prospects which can be moved into the moment, accept that they have a problem (a pain point), and are inclined to solve it through a salesperson directed process.

It is impossible for a prospect to see anything of the present when their lens is the past. If the prospects have admitted to themselves the presence of a pain point(s) within their business, it means that past fears are no longer intruding and influencing their decision making as they look at their business in the moment. If

FIGURE 10.4

**Emotional Tonal Algorithm
For Innovation with Line of Passivity**

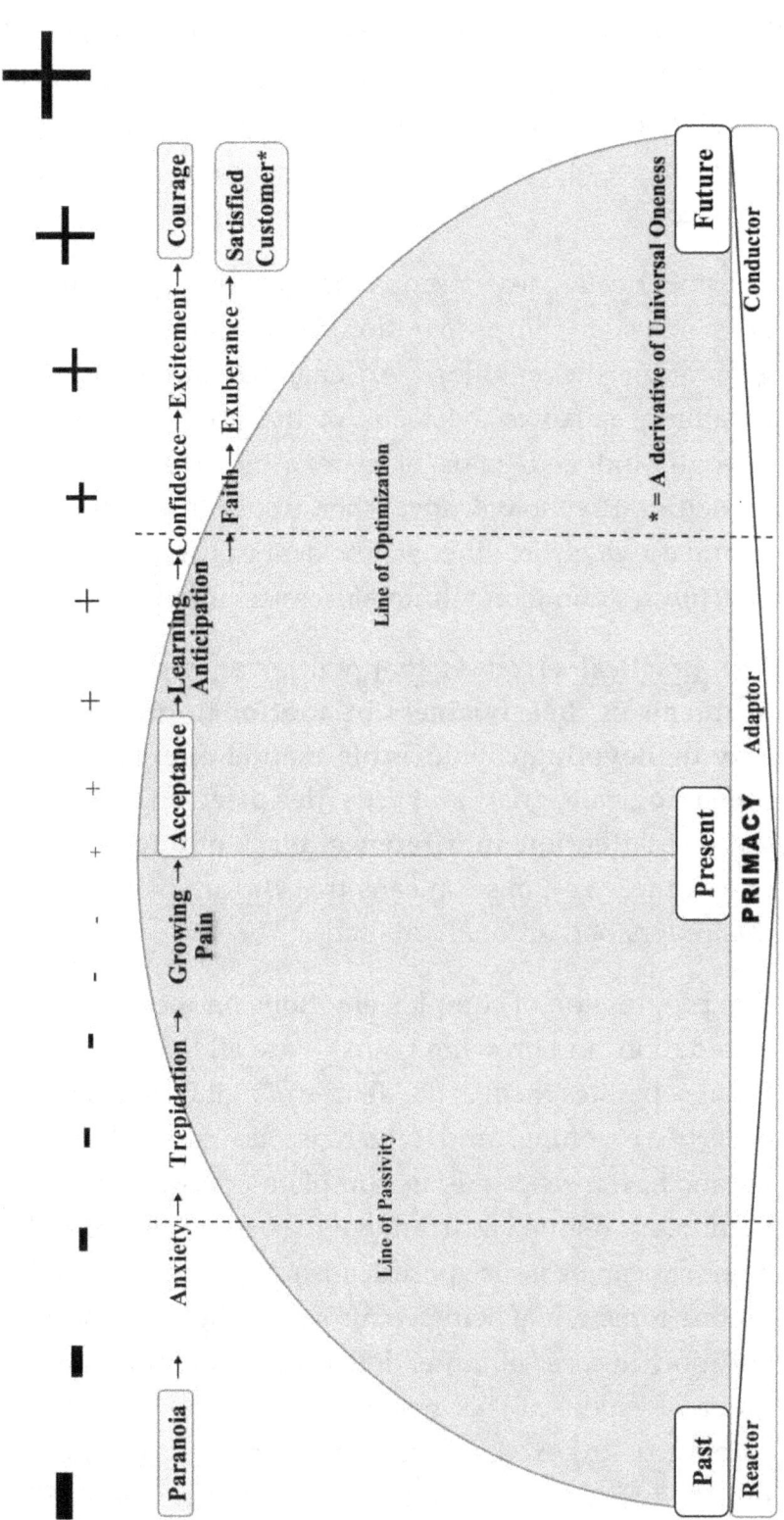

you've arrived at this point, you're at the entrance of the sales process. Technically speaking, acceptance is part of the pain nullification process. It is recognized as the emotional starting point of all sales cycles because, at this point, the prospects only know they have a pain point within their business, and it may not yet be well defined in their minds as to just what exactly their issues are. Remember, pain stems from an emotion feedback signal given from the reactor in the subconscious and will usually be ill defined or misunderstood by the vast majority of prospects. Fear, the main driver of business pain points, has several effects both psychologically and physically.

Physiologically, fear pumps hormones, chief among them adrenaline, into the body's systems in preparation for the perceived flight coming from whatever is generating the emotion. Adrenaline causes the heart to beat faster, changes breathing, narrows the focus of the mind, and fatigues a person quickly as the strength induced gains of adrenaline overwhelm the body's normal metabolic capacities. Psychologically, when under threat, the mind urges the person to leave, to move away from wherever he or she is at that moment. This creates a toxic swamp of activities going on within a prospect that the salesperson must wade through.

The practical effect is that while, as a salesperson, you're dealing with the problems of their business in a rational, problem solving mode, your prospects may be devoting considerable mental energy to override the psychological and physiological signals and activities directed by their reactors. This may present to you as inattention, indifference, a lack of understanding, or a lack of concern. Any one of these responses means that the adaptation plan you are presenting may be misunderstood or totally missed.

The progression of complex emotions on the fear side of sales — paranoia, anxiety, trepidation, and growing pains — are all tones, or shades of the basic emotion, fear. What separates them is the degree of agitation from the reactor versus the adaptor's orderly reasoning, and which is the controlling apparatus of the mind. With paranoia, the reactor is in complete control, and no rational thought is possible. Paranoia is defined as irrational fear; fear is in control of the apparatus of the mind. This fear can be issue specific, meaning someone could have a totally irrational fear on one topic while being composed, collected, and rational in all other respects. In addition, in cases of immediate threat, paranoia can also invoke the Fight, Flight, or Freeze Response. This response seems to be dictated by proximity as to which emotion is invoked – rage (fight) or panic (flight). Rage occurs when the threat proximity is imminent and escape is not possible. Flight occurs when the threat is eminent but there is a cushion of distance for escape. The Freeze response occurs at the interface between fight or flee. The brain rapidly cycles from fight to flee again and again, leading to a total lock up of the person because it is unclear which response, rage or panic, to invoke.

At the other end of the scale, growing pain represents the least intensity of fear. This is where only the smallest hint of fear is present and it can easily be managed and overridden by the rational adaptor. This is another reason why sales to the late majority take longer and require more energy — there is a basic communication deficit. Everything said between prospect and salesperson must be filtered through fear and its intentional interference of rational thought.

As advocated in this book, as a salesperson, you need to focus on the prospect's pain points in the most personal way to him or her. The vast majority of the time, the prospects are able to work within their tolerances and limits while discussing a pain issue to a greater or lesser degree. Occasionally, however, using this approach may evoke a response within the prospect that leads to an irrational or unexpected response. When you do, you need to stop your presentation and focus totally on the prospect as a human and not a potential income opportunity. An example of one response may be to stop your presentation and pray with the prospect for guidance. Or you can slam the brakes on your presentation, inject a couple of "whoas!" and ask the client what just happened: "We were going along just fine and then all of a sudden, you got uncomfortable. What was it that made you uncomfortable, or what was the straw that broke the camel's back?" The point is, your prospects are human and have fears and phobias; sometimes they can't help themselves. As a salesperson, you may often be in a better position to know what's going on in a business and are in a better position to guide your clients and prospects through these irrational moments.

MOORE'S LAW, EXPECTATIONS, AND FEAR

In 1965, Intel co-founder Gordon E. Moore predicted that computer circuitry capacity would double every year for the next ten years. Later, he modified that prediction to every two years. This prediction has held fast for over fifty years. As the capacity of the integrated circuits (IC) capacity doubled, its cost trajectory was the converse. So as chips became more capable, they became cheaper. This led to the integration of ICs into everything from spaceships to toasters. This progression set generational expectations towards technology, and thus determined comfort levels with the pace and scope of technology and all innovation. This exponential growth in silicon integrated circuitry is a useful tool in understanding the causational relations between expectations and fear, which is the main regulator of innovation adoption. This also makes it extremely important for the salespeople to understand as they approach prospects.

The saying in the' 80s, when VCRs were the latest high-tech innovation in the home, was "You need your grandchildren to program it." This phrase has been reshaped every decade for the technology *du jour*. In the 2010s, its current incarnation is, "You need your child to show you how to work your smart phone." This illustrates the relationship between youth and the acceptance of change. Moore's Law also explains why three decades ago, a person or firm a couple of years removed from their growth phase would still be considered an Innovator because the skills and experience were very close, or contemporary to the level of current technology. Today, being several years removed from the growth phase means that two or three generations of technology have occurred, and the gap between skills and experience of innovation adoption has the potential to widen at a much faster rate.

THREE PHASES OF INNOVATION ADOPTION

There are three general phases to a person's development: growth, stability, and decline. In the growth years, the formative years, a person is learning and in the process is exposed to technology. This is a world of constant stimulation from which an individual learns to manipulate artifacts in the world. This is usually a sheltered experience where there are parents and teachers to ensure that the ego does not put the person in dangerous or harmful situations. Learning and its subsequent failures have no dire consequences, thus the emotion of loss in any of its shades and blends are not attached to failure (with the exception of social failure). With limited experience, every situation is a growth opportunity, so the norm is growing and learning. The breadth of activities is fairly limited also at this time. Essentials — food, shelter, clothing, warmth, socialization, entertainment — are provided so that the focus can be on learning and acquiring essential skills and knowledge. Learning occupies the resources in the mind that generate, shuffle, and execute the Human Action Cycle. When one is in the learning mode, one cannot form or execute Human Action Cycles. As a person assumes more responsibility for his or her own necessities, he or she must devote less time to learning mode and more time and resources for Human Action Cycles that will provide the essentials.

During the second phase, the breadth of activities expands as individuals take on more and more of the duties of providing their own essentials. Because the breadth of essentials and their subsequent activities to obtain them widens, a person is said to have more and more responsibilities, which is a generality for a greater number of HACs targeted at essentials in various stages of action or suspension. With many more balls in the air, i.e. HACs, persons in this stage seek stability so they can pursue their HACs in a controlled fashion. When one of their HACs goes off course, they must devote time, resources, and mental energy getting it sorted out. When one HAC goes awry, it capitalizes the mind's mechanism to the exclusion of all else, excluding other necessities. The same goes for learning opportunities. Learning in the stability phase of life is limited. Necessity obtainment takes the majority of time. So learning must be metered so as to not impinge upon the obtainment of necessities. Failure from learning also carries greater consequences as the time to learn, fail, and sort out any fallout are time and resources that could have been devoted to necessities. There could also be fallout that negatively impacts one's ability to pursue HACs aimed at necessity satisfaction.

In the decline phase of life, biological deterioration erodes a person's ability to pursue HACs. With less and less capacity for HACs pursuit both physically and mentally, a person in this phase must choose which necessities must be jettisoned. Learning becomes a major liability because it further incapacitates the mechanisms of the mind, placing further strictures on the number of necessity HACs that can be pursued; thus, learning is avoided.

This is all important for salespeople to understand as they approach prospects. Because firms are comprised of and managed by humans, firms and their life cycles will mirror those who form the management which salespeople deal with. This is why we see in the Technology Diffusion Curve that innovators tend to be young. They are closer to or are phasing from the growth portion of their life to stability. This is why they are categorized as being in the present. Innovation adoption is part of their growth phase. They are acclimated to not only the pace of innovation, but also the monopolization on their mental faculties that finding and implementing innovation requires.

The further in time an individual moves away from his or her growth phase, the greater the disparity becomes between their accustomed pace of innovation and that which is occurring in the market place. An individual's accustomed pace of innovation is anchored to the rate of innovation as they left their growth stage. This is coupled to the increased need to supply their own necessities cuts into and diminishes their desire to seek out learning opportunities. This is why early adopters still tend to be younger, smaller, more specialized firms early in their lifecycle, but are removed from the pace of innovation they are comfortable with and have high numbers of necessities that must be considered. But they are not so removed from their growth phase that they have forgotten the value of innovation and still consider it to be part of their business cycle. They therefore seek out salespeople with their expertise and experience to acquire and implement innovation in the most expeditious manner possible. This proximity to their growth years is why they view innovation adoption as a growing pain, something that is necessary and beneficial but not necessarily liked, since they have acquired a taste for and expectation of stability and therefore look to manage the process expeditiously to minimize stability disruption pain.

Early majority adopters are even further removed from their growth phase and thus their expectations, i.e. comfort zones, of scope and pace of innovation are more outdated. They adopt technology out of higher levels of fear and move only when the fear of loss of competitive advantage outweighs the fear of disruption to stability. This is why a long, deliberate decision process to act is observed in this segment.

Late majority adopters have no comfort with innovation. They understand that they have problems that innovation can cure, but their expectations and experience of innovation anchored in their formative years no longer have any bearing on the marketplace of innovation, resulting in great anxiety. These tend to be older, larger firms populated by older individuals in management. Their primary consideration, fear, is whether or not adoption of innovation is even possible for them, since they recognize their skill set and the firm's composition has been constructed for stability, not innovation. This is why this segment of the Technology Diffusion Curve takes very few cues from salespeople initially and looks to other similar peer firms, or acquaintances, to assess the probability of a positive outcome versus catastrophic failure to their business when implementing new solutions to their problems. In short, their decision process is to determine the probability of continued existence versus collapse due to their dwindling capacity to juggle HACs, especially one that goes awry. A salesperson can't tell them this information, nor would they trust that information if it was offered due to the self-interest of the salesperson. Only those who have been through the process can, which is why they turn to peers to help make decisions.

Laggards/non-adopters never adopt innovation because they have no capacity for the new Human Action Cycles that innovation requires. These are people or firms that are already in decline and are already shedding necessities, such as recruiting new clientele. They exist totally for stability, the status quo, and servicing the clientele they already have in the manner they've always done so. Their overriding emotion is paranoia towards change, because they assume with certainty that any innovation adoption will lead to catastrophic results for themselves and their firms. Innovation equals death and must be avoided at all cost due to its disruption to stability and the certainty that it will go awry due to their diminished capacity for HACs with skill sets and expectations anchored in the very distant past. The sad and ironic fact is that the methodology or products to which they cling so dearly were at one time innovations themselves, and were not the refuge that they have now become, but were the vanguard of innovation in their day.

THE SHAPE OF THE MARKETPLACE

The Technology Diffusion Curve, which was intended to explain high-tech adoption, when coupled with the underlying emotions gives a much broader understanding to the marketplace for a salesperson or sales manager than originally intended. Its potential for understanding goes beyond technical innovation to become a model for all innovation. It gives shape to the marketplace and acts as a guide to the salesperson. It can align expectations with reality and guide the tone of the conversation between the salesperson and his prospects.

If the product you are vending is of an innovative nature, then you know the access to market will be highly dependent initially upon the marketing department's ability to gain publicity and technical interest in industry publications, both printed and internet. The salesperson's role will be limited initially to order taking. Knowing the shape of the market will also tell you when it is time to hit the road with your product and sales force, and what to look for in the early adopters segment.

We can apply a business' lifecycle to the Innovation Diffusion Curve and let it shape our understanding of the prospect's attitude towards the product you're selling. If the product is an incremental improvement on the old way of doing business, then we'll know two very important things: 1) there is already a broad penetration of this style of products in the marketplace, meaning we will encounter all phases of the Technology Diffusion Curve in the prospects we approach, 2) we'll know the distribution percentage in which we'll encounter them.

If the product you are vending already has an established market and low barriers to entry, then we can expect to see a constant filtration of prospects into the market. These new arrivals will tend to be younger, closer to their growth phase, and will seek out your product or eagerly await your visit. These new arrivals will constantly refresh and resupply your 'low hanging fruit' sales of innovators and early adopters segment but will only constitute 16% of your sales opportunities.

But because of their eagerness to adopt innovation and the fact that they are constantly filtering into the marketplace, they may be overrepresented in your actual sales because the other categories of adopters, while larger in number, take longer to procure, and thus fewer of them can be worked at any one-time due to the limitations of established business hours and practices and the fact that there are

Figure 10.5

Feed-Forward Feedback Cycle:

The Basics of the <u>H</u>uman <u>A</u>ction <u>C</u>ycle

and the Emotional Tonal Flow of Corrective Signal.

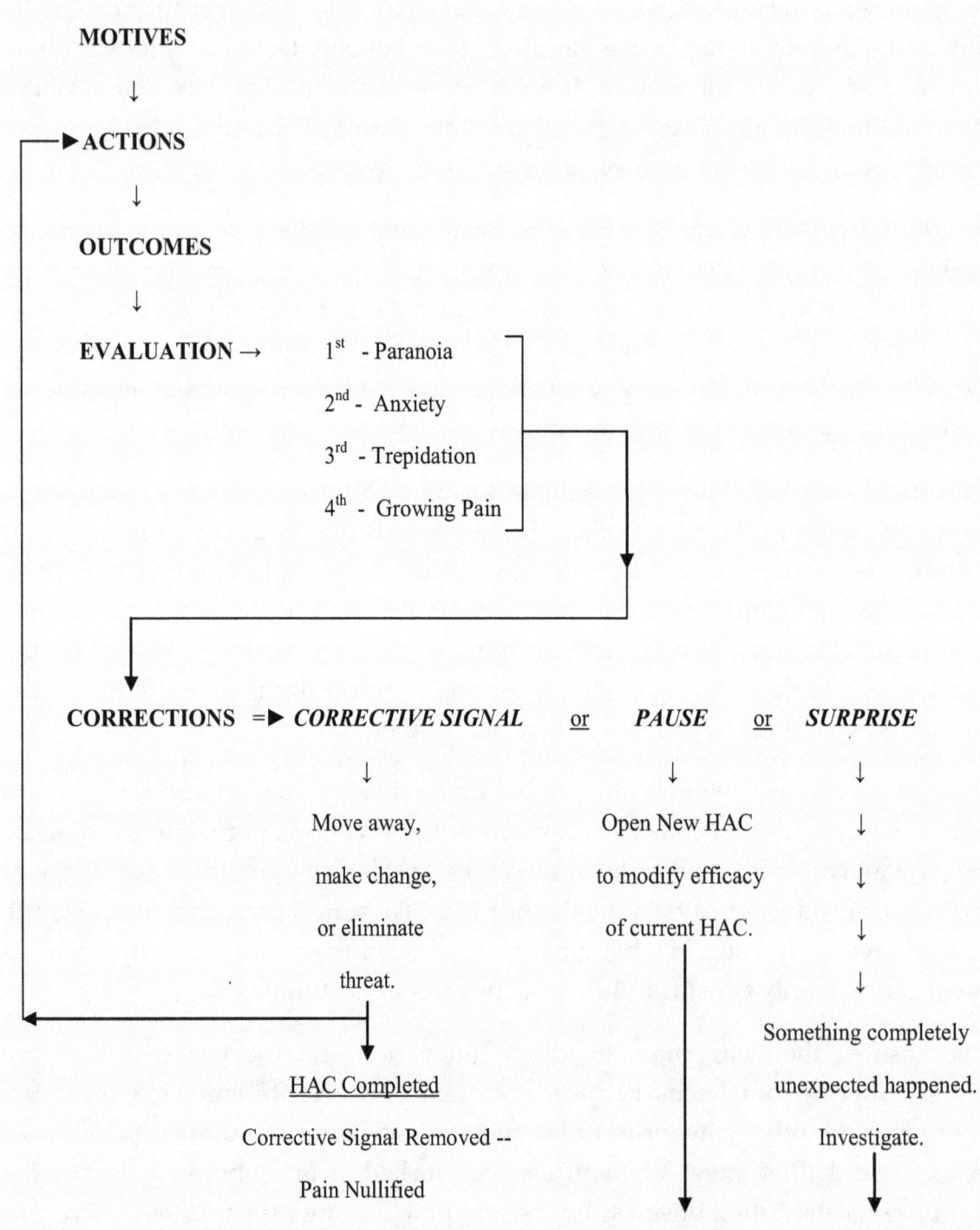

only forty-eight half-hours in a day. The tone of your opening conversation with the 'low hanging fruit' segment will not be focused so much on fear of innovation and disruption but on pain point nullification. The low hanging fruit are interested in overcoming competitive advantages of the bigger, more established firms in the market place. By removing their business inefficiencies with innovation, the firm can be more nimble and reactive to marketplace changes, which will allow them to shift resources to focus on creating competitive differences.

The early majority, 34% of your market opportunity, will take varying degrees of effort to consummate a sale because their measurements will be more precise, requiring extensive due diligence to ascertain whether the disruption to stability will confer any competitive advantage that can be driven to the bottom line. The initial conversation with these types of prospects will center on increased profitability, revenue generation, or decreased uncertainty. The first two speak to growth and competition, while the third speaks to their desire for stability.

The late majority, another 34% of the market, will understand that they need to adopt innovation. They've seen everyone else in the market already move to adopt it. Your initial conversation will start along the lines of brief explanation of the benefits — increased profitability, revenues, or decreased uncertainty — and then showing them case history or connecting them with peer firms that have already successfully adopted the innovation. Surprisingly, these firms require very little salesman attention initially because very little of what you say or do will be persuasive to the prospect. So why bother? The persuasion will come from the peer firms to which they speak. This segment of the market will either adopt your innovation or slip into the laggards/non-adopters based on their connections to their peers. The best strategy that you can use is to find one of these firms, diligently work them, getting them into contact with peer firms or in the early majority segment and leveraging them to become a spokesman in this segment. This gives the salesperson a clear strategy of what must be accomplished in this market segment in order to be successful.

The laggards/non-adopters, which constitute 16% of the market, pose another question altogether to the salesperson: "Are they worth the bother?" The odds say no. Is the business in decline? Are the principle decision makers holding out for retirement? If so, good! You've identified a non-adopter; now move on to a prospect who possesses a modicum of inclination towards innovation adoption and the probability of a sale is much higher.

TECHNOLOGY DIFFUSION CURVE REDUX

In this chapter, we talked repeatedly about the Technology Diffusion Curve. By coupling the foundational emotional drivers to this diffusion curve, we've seen that although it was originally meant to describe technology, it can now explain attitudes towards all innovation in the market place. This diffusion curve now can describe consumer response to all non-commodity products. Outside of commodity products like office supplies, barley to beer brewers, cleaning supplies, chemicals, et cetera, all salespeople are selling one form or another of innovation. This loosely means that you're trying to improve the way your customers do things. And yes, even commodities are subject to innovation.

The diffusion curve for technology is actually very arbitrary. It was derived from very basic statistical methodologies. A distribution of market adaption was projected against a timeline to develop a bell curve. That bell curve was cut in half, and further divisions were inserted using statistical standard deviations. This provides a basic structure for us to understand conceptually differing segments of the salesperson's or firm's marketplace. However, depending upon the age or newness of a market, there could be variations between differing markets' bell curves or the actual distribution of segments. All of which means that there is still plenty of room for human judgment when evaluating a particular market.

Regardless of the actual percentages of how your market varies, the constant is how those market segments think and react to innovation. The salesperson will never make a sale to the irrational laggards/non-adopters, and in the off chance a sale is made, the salesperson knows this market segment is just as likely to cancel the sale or give it back for reasons unexplainable. As for those in the late majority, early majority and early adaptors, they are driven by the emotions of anxiety, trepidation, and growing pain respectively. **The salesperson will still have to move the prospect through a HAC for one, two, or three of these consecutive emotions to acceptance by convincing the prospect they have the skills to successfully adopt your innovation, that their peers have done it, that the cost of internal stability upset is less than the value gained by the innovation, and that the internal upset will be minimized by an implementation plan developed and guided by the salesperson's experience** (See Figure 10.6). Moving your prospect through these emotional phases will bring the prospect into the moment, into the present, where he or she will receive a weak pulse of joy when he or she reaches acceptance of the fact that there are problems within his or her business that need a solution(s). This will open the door for a salesperson to present an innovation, commodity, or uncertainty product to the prospect.

RELATIONSHIP RESPONSE INVOKED BY FEAR

One of the interesting aspects of the self-preservation phase, the Acquisition Phase of the Innovation emotional algorithm, is that it evokes a relationship response in individuals. The best, simplest example of this is seen at the movies, or more accurately at a scary movie. During a frightening part of a movie, a young female can be seen instinctively clutching the arm of her date. This is just not a female response, but is universal to all humans. When in fear, we seek safety in numbers, we're moved instinctively to relationships for pain point nullification. Relationships will be the subject of Chapters 16 and 17.

This explains the perfect correlation between the observations of Bohlen, Beal, and Rogers when constructing the Innovation Adoption Curve Theory where all their described sectors, except for Innovators, will seek out and work with salespeople. Fear drives them to seek out relationships for pain nullification via relationships, whether it's peers, consultants, salespeople, or the amalgam of all three – a salesperson with a strong relationship with the prospect making them a peer acting in a consultive sales manner. Those who are irrational, those experiencing fear at its highest potential in the paranoia state, are not capable of rational behavior because 'rational' behavior is the sole domain of the adaptor. As described in this and earlier chapters, those experiencing paranoia are under regulation of the reactor, which has assumed full and complete control regarding this aspect of that individual's life. The term "rational" prior to this book was used in an imprecise manner that was more intuitive than definitive, the opposite of irrational. Without the understanding of the roles of the reactor and adaptor, the term 'rational' can't be fully understood. The reactor whose function is adaptation, must act with forethought and foreknowledge. So, irrational behavior then becomes to act without forethought or foreknowledge. But again, under this definition, our understanding of this distinction loses clarity because the reactor, acting "irrationally," is acting exactly in-line, as designed, executing its mission of protecting the body and self, which is rational because the reactor is an older, more archaic, system of the mind predating the adaptor, all of which indicates the evolutionary process in design. So it can be argued that irrational behavior is in fact rational behavior under the design criteria of the reactor.

Innovators are not under the influence of fear, but are working from the growth signal side, the positive agitation side, of the Vetting Phase of the Innovation emotional algorithm that internally drives individuals through impulses of joy to modify their behavior or environment. In this case, by seeking solutions through relationships via vendors and salespeople, they are attempting to modify their

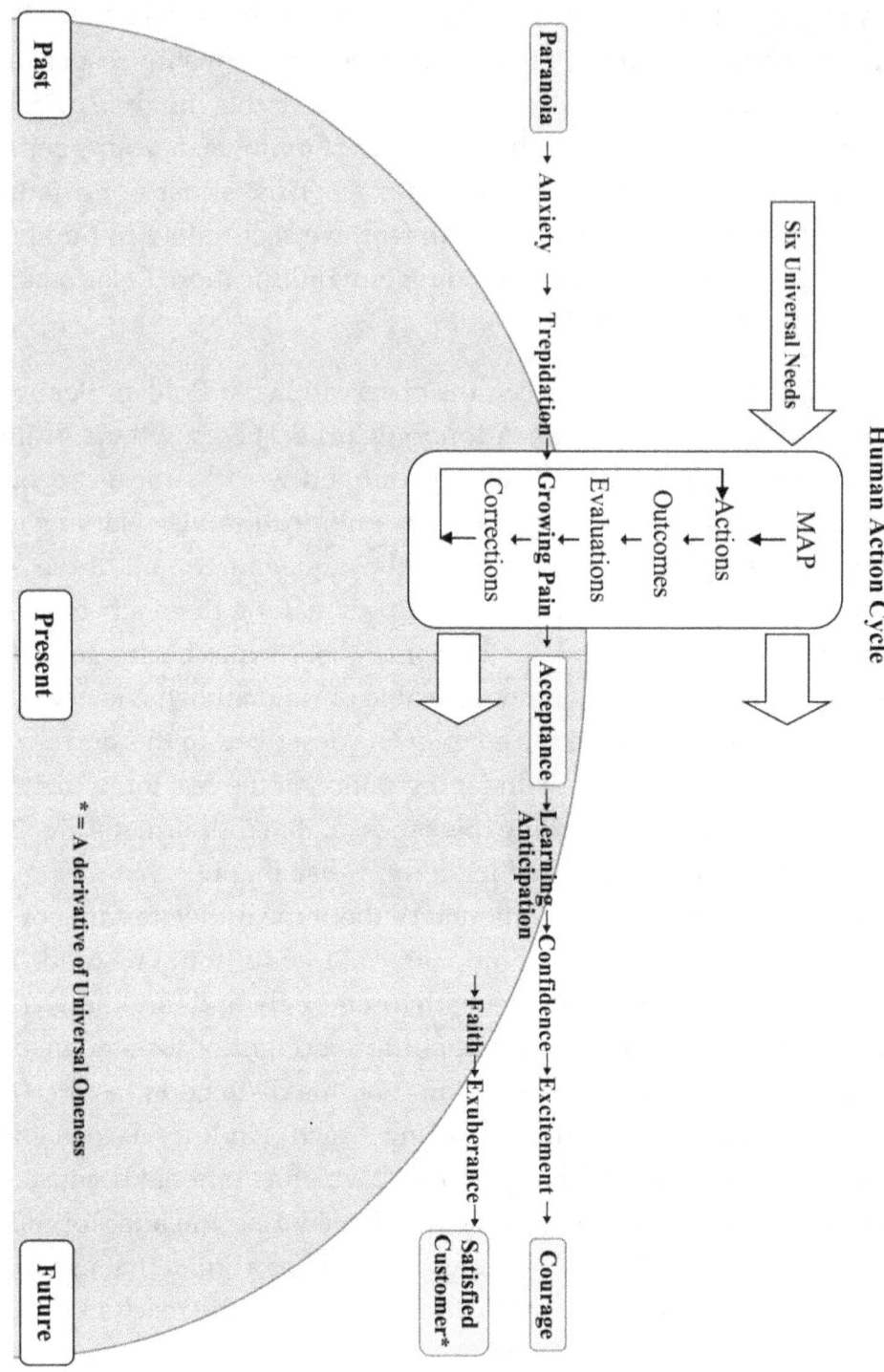

FIGURE 10.6

Human Action Cycle and
Feed-Forward Movement on Emotional Tonal Algorithm

environment through someone else's service or product. Bohlen, Beal, and Rogers observed a portion of the Paradaptive Intelligence system in operation but did not have the underlying structure or vocabulary of the Paradaptive Intelligence to describe what their analysis quantified.

11

CLOSING?! I DON'T NEED NO STINKING CLOSING!

59. THE LAW OF SALES

Second Corollary: Customers need to be asked to buy.
Third Corollary: Eighty percent of sales are closed after
the fifth call or after the fifth closing attempt.

of "The 100 Absolutely Unbreakable Laws of Business Success"
by Brian Tracy

Consumer behavior is the proxy of adaptation in exchange based societies. And closing is the most mystical of all events in sales. It is also the point of intercept between consumer behavior and sales. One of the highest praises that can be offered in sales is to say someone is "a real closer." Advertisements for sales positions often state they're looking for closers. Many salespeople harbor in their mind some image of a poised, self-confident salesperson offering a pen to the client, staring him down until the client takes the pen and signs the contract or the silver-tongued salesperson possessed of a flow of persuasion so smoothly delivered that the prospect simply is compelled to comply. That is some very strong sales kung fu. Incidentally, this is exactly why most business people hate dealing with salespeople at the conclusion of a sales cycle. They dislike having something 'done' to them. They fear that the salesperson will bring undue pressure or illegitimate persuasion to bear upon them at the conclusion of a sales evolution, for the purpose of meeting a sales quota, to their detriment. It also implies that closing is something you do to or perform on a prospect. This represents an egocentric view of closing for a salesperson. This construct connotes that the salesperson is working 'on' a prospect rather than 'with' them.

This is called offensive selling. It's offensive to your prospects. It treats the sales cycle like a conquest or campaign of dominance. It starts with management, whose mantra is "Sell! Sell! Sell!" setting the tone that the sales force is to go hither and take action on or against clients and prospects. Products are developed to help clients with problems. So just how does the original product design intent get twisted from "help" to "sell"? Regardless, this sets the stage for failure of the sales force by painting their bread and butter as victims rather than people in need. How you view your clients and prospects will determine how you view closing.

But is that how it is? And just what does it mean to "close"?

Just like in many other aspects of sales, these old concepts and images stem from sales mythology that are based on half-truths and misinterpreted observations. As delineated earlier, there are two approaches to sales. One is to find the client's pain points in the most personal way and show them a pain nullifying adaptation plan containing your product. The second is to educate and inform the customer's adaptor by giving a 'features and benefits' presentation on your product. In one methodology, you sell to the reactor, the other you sell to the adaptor. The former is a much scarier proposition for most traditionally trained salespeople. But why is that? Both have a place in the sales eagle's quiver. But the trick is to know when to use which, and that is a skill easily transferred to the journeyman sales professional when the parameters of use are understood.

The latter method, features and benefits, takes the traditional approach of educating the adaptor, feeding it with features and benefits to satisfy its main objective to learn in hopes that this will create the basis of a motive for a desirable outcome in a HAC that contains buying your product. The former approach, used by sales eagles, finds pain points caused by a corrective signal in the prospect and relieves them with an adaptation plan. Business in general, and its sub disciplines like sales, have been, until recently, a male dominated profession for centuries if not millennia. There are noted differences in the mental architecture of males and females in terms of emotional turbulence handling strategies. In many more cultures than not, males are supposed to be strong and stoic. Showing emotions, other than anger and aggression, are not signs of strength. So is it any wonder that these same characteristics have been built into business? There is a tradition, a perception, that emotions have no place in business, that business professionals are rational decision makers. Yet through our understanding of the emotions via the Paradaptive Intelligence model, we know that every action in business that interacts with the outside world will elicit an emotion. Therefore, it is impossible to separate emotions from business decisions, because emotions are foundational to how we solve adaptation problems. In Chapter 8 Emotions – The Language of Feedback, we learned that we have two very important emotion milestones on the emotional tonal algorithm chart that we need to manage for: acceptance and courage.

So why is the belief that business norms of the business professional are rational when we now know that emotions are integral to everything we do in business and sales?

It could be as simple as emotions were chaotic and messy for men. So, men simply created business standards that eliminated them. Couple this with the fact that much of what we know of business is derived from academia, whose impersonal observations failed to capture unmeasurable variables to them like emotions due to lack of useful psychological models.

As pointed out earlier, closings are also the most dreaded moment for your prospects if you're using a features and benefits sales approach. Up to this point in most features and benefits presentations, they've been in learning mode and probably weren't critically thinking about how to apply your product to their business. They were just having a good time gleaning new information for their adaptor. This probably is because you asked no questions that forced them to evaluate their emotions to formulate and update their emotional status towards your product as you demonstrated it, or got them to accept that they have problems in the most personal way. And even if you had, since there was no adaptation plan presented, they would not have been set emotionally to move forward. Up to now, they've had a positive, pleasurable emotional experience learning and connecting with you or advancing the relationship through their six universal needs.

While a positive emotional tone is great, it only signals to the prospect that they've done a good job learning, which in all likelihood was the motive to seeing your demo or presentation. Now comes the point in a traditional "closing" where the prospect decides to move forward with a "yes" or terminate the process with a "no." Saying no and terminating the gratification of basic needs for connection (due to the one-on-one communication and attention), esteem, and creativity, as well as the joy of exploration — which up to this point has been satisfying — will cause mental pain/discomfort to the prospect, which is why most prospects hate "traditional" closings.

Selling to the adaptor is safe and easy. Its mission is to learn. Salespeople interested in just purveying information satisfy the mission of the prospect's adaptor have reached their objective. So everyone is happy, right? The client learned something and the sales person made the client happy with education. Bad news, no sale was concluded for the sales person's time investment. Some may argue that a future sale may occur from this informational investment. However, in all probability, this information and education will serve as the basis for shopping around to your competitors. The reason for this is because the prospect in all likelihood has an ill-defined understanding of their actual pain point. Selling to the reactor is a scarier proposition for the classically trained. To sell to the reactor, a salesperson must instill either fear, anger, disgust, or loss in the prospect for it is only these emotions that generate pain points. Only the reactor detecting something in the environment that represents a threat to the body or self can create a pain point. And pain points are the source of all "closings."

ADAPTATION PLANS

We've discussed adaptation plans in passing in the past several chapters, but it behooves us to stop and take a deeper look at them. It is part of the salesperson's responsibility to describe just how the product will be incorporated into the prospect's business. It is, after all, a salesperson's expertise in implementing his products into their business that drives prospects to elect to work with salespeople. An adaptation plan could be described as a vision of how you're going to cooperate to resolve a prospective client's motive to nullify their pain points. An adaption plan has a beginning, middle, and end, and contains a product or service with an implementation plan. The basics of a salesman's adaptation plan looks like this:

> "You're going to cut me a check and buy my product."
> "The product will be shipped in X days and you'll receive it Tuesday."
> "At that time my people will install the product and train you."
> "You and I will implement and integrate it over the next two weeks."
> "It will solve problems X, Y, and Z by doing A, B, and C."
> "And you'll be happy because you'll no longer have to deal with X, Y, and Z."

The thing to remember is that you have the expertise about your product, how it is implemented/installed, how long it will take to train personnel on how to use it, how long it will take to implement, how long until the client becomes proficient and most importantly of all, how they'll feel about it at the conclusion. This properly sets expectations not only of actions to be taken, but also the problems it will resolve and how this will make the prospect feel. This has often been referred to as "assuming the sale," but in actuality, it is simply supplying the necessary scaffolding and framework the mind needs to get to the "courage" phase by eliminating unknowns, i.e. risk, and costs from their calculations in the excitement emotion phase.

As you can see, a pain-points-centric approach plus an adaptation plan is different than a features and benefits style presentation. The former is a call to action, the latter is just information. If you rely upon a features and benefits style presentation, you're counting on the prospect to create his own call to action. This is a lower percentage play for the salesperson because you're hanging your sale upon the prospect, who lacks your expertise in implementation, training, and specific outcomes, to put it together for you the way that you want it. Granted, there will be prospects that are capable of doing this on their own, but there will be a great many more that cannot. So to work efficiently, lay the adaptation plan out for them. You should be able to do this for them in less than thirty seconds.

COMMODITY AND PROCESS ADAPTATION PLANS

There are two types of adaption plans in sales: commodity and process. Each has different routes on the Innovation emotional tonal algorithm for fear. Commodity adaptation plans are described as essentials to a business; without them, they would go out of business. For examples, a doctor must have diagnostic tools and medicines for treatment; an air-conditioning repairman must have Freon (or whatever coolant gas is currently approved by the EPA) to recharge cooling systems; a beer manufacturer must have water, hops, barley, and yeast. Commodity adaptation plans are characterized by the "what."

Process adaptation plans are characterized by the "how." As the name implies, these plans are more about the way in which the commodity elements of a prospect's business are employed and utilized and other supporting structures. An adaptation plan for a beer brewer may be about new steam kettles, bottling line, bookkeeping, marketing or employee benefits packages; for a HVAC repairman it may be about how he stores regulated materials like Freon, stores and manages the vehicles records the Department of Transportation requires of company owned fleet vehicles, or the way invoices and charges are generated in the field. Products that are process adaptation plans will run the entire gauntlet of the fear basic emotions. A sales cycle may start with trepidation and culminate in a satisfied customer. In the corrective signal portion of the complex emotion of fear progression from anxiety to growing pain, as a salesperson, your objective is to remove threats or allay perceptions of threats related to your adaptation plan to move them to acceptance – more on that later. But the defining aspect between commodity and process sale applications is that commodity sales always start at the emotion acceptance, because these are business requirements which the prospect acknowledges they must have, bypassing the corrective signal side of the innovation algorithm.

FEATURES AND BENEFITS SALES ORIENTATION

Features and benefits, which salespeople have been misguidedly taught to lead with, is another example of sales practices lore not grounded in the circuitry of the Paradaptive Intelligence Network. Discussing features and benefits of a product without context of how that will directly nullify specific pain points in terms of the prospect's emotions is dangerous. By speaking of features and benefits without context puts the onus on the prospect or client to make the connections for you. By depending on the expertise and mindset of the prospect, the features and benefits sales approach is not in your best interest as a salesperson. Features and benefits must be presented in the context of how they will alleviate the psychic pain of fear or anger. But you will not be able to get to this point in a conversation or presentation until you address the prospect's underlying reasons for pain nullification.

Take pharmaceutical sales, for example, one of the most competitive, sophisticated sales fields. Salespeople are taught to lead with the features and attributes of their drugs. But is this really what a doctor wants to hear? The answer is "no." From the doctor's perspective, he has clients that need medicine treatments that perform a specific function. Many drugs perform the same function using different pathways. No drug is perfect; all have limitations due to their efficacy and side effects; therefore, no drug will perform uniformly across the board. What he wants to know is where your drug fits into his tool chest. By knowing when and in what situations your company's drug is best applicable, you reduce his fear of misapplication and undue harm to his patients and improve the quality of care he gives. Also, by leading with the strategy of implementation, which reduces his fear level of misapplication, you are able to discuss exactly how your product's attributes fulfill the implementation strategy in terms of how it is superior or solves medical problems for his patients. In this scenario, features and benefits is just passing information to satisfy the reactor's mission to learn in order to become more adaptable.

RIGHT UP YOUR ALLEY – THE VETTING PHASE

As you recall from Chapter 10 – Fear and Innovation Adoption, there is a continuum of emotions associated with fear, a negative emotion that agitates/pains the receiver to move away from the source generating the corrective signal. Prospects fear that their operations are costing them money, which threatens their survivability. The same goes for anger.

Anger in business usually takes the form of the complex emotions of frustration or some other complex emotion close by on the continuum of anger (See Figure 11.1).

A business man gets frustrated that some obstacle, some internal process like bookkeeping, machines not up to the job delaying production, or regulation compliance as just a few examples, is preventing them from performing their work in a timely fashion. Fear and anger create pain points for the person responsible for the business. Nullification of the pain that fear and anger generate in prospective clients are the main focus of salespeople in the Vetting Phase.

Prospects experience anger from either a boundary violation or from obstacles being put in their path as they attempt to achieve their motivations in business. This anger could be from a process that is inefficient, interruptive, or overly restrictive, or from supplies and materials that are defective or missing. Either way, it always comes down to control, or put more succinctly, the prospect's control over his business. Lack of control equals pain at the junctures where they have the least control of their business. This generally means relying on someone else for a vital product or service or outdated processes. The continuum of anger looks like this:

FIGURE 11.1

Continuum of Emotions for Corrective Signal Anger

Rage => Fury => Frustration => Annoyance

The more effective you are at demonstrating that your adaptation plan nullifies the prospect's pain points, the more positive he will feel about your proposition. The positive feelings the client will feel about your adaptation plan are actually five distinct emotional phases: acceptance, learning anticipation, confidence, excitement, and courage which culminates in the act of commitment. All of these emotions are positive emotion agitating the receiver to move towards/continue/repeat the process (See Figure11.2). This is the main portion of the pathway which all prospects, and thus salespeople, will have to traverse. The emotions from acceptance to courage, whether it is an innovation being acquired from someone else as a goods or services product, a commodity and retail product, or you're creating your own tool or service rather than obtaining it from someone else, is called innovation vetting. This is where closings actually occur when acquiring products from vendors. The most important concept to grasp is that closing is not a single event.

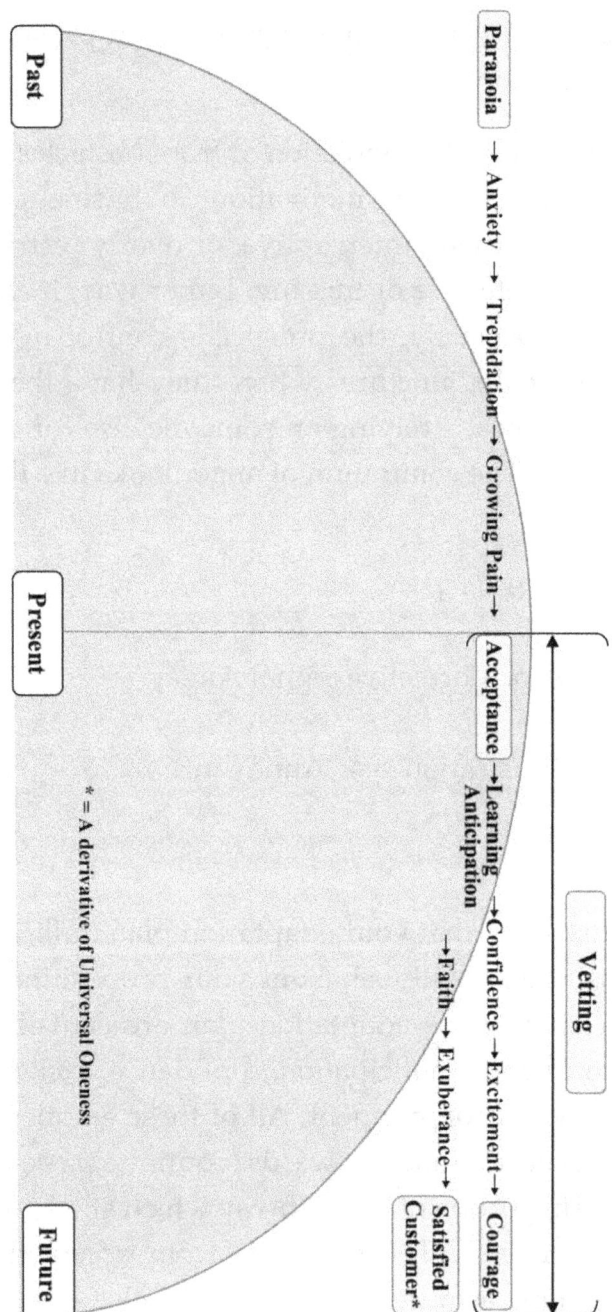

FIGURE 11.2

Vetting Phase of the
Innovation Emotional Tonal Algorithm

A closing occurs every time you resolve or demonstrate your adaptation plan's ability to nullify a prospect's pain point by satisfying one of the emotions of the Vetting Phase.

This is why it is your objective to find as many prospect pain points as possible and illustrate them in the most personal way possible to set up your adaptation plan as pain relief to their fear or anger. Every time you nullify a pain point, you advance to the next emotional tone in the Vetting phase. It does not occur at the conclusion when you ask for the sale. What happens at the conclusion when you ask for the sale is that the prospect evaluates the internal status of feelings towards your action plan, tallying the number of closings that occurred in the Vetting phase to see if they have arrived at courage. But if you wait until the end to ask this question, all the closings that you performed may get lumped into only one emotional tone adjustment. This is why question-based selling, which will be covered in Chapter 14, is so important. As you resolve a pain point, the prospect will be moved forward emotionally through your questions. Additionally, you run the risk that the customer will forget one or more of the closing/pain nullifications that your adaptation plans provides. Prospects may forget a major or minor point of pain nullification in a busy, long, or complicated adaptation plan presentation, but their emotional status never backslides as long as you are asking questions to keep tallying the emotional points you are scoring. In fact, the prospect may wrack his brain at the end of a presentation to recall all the reasons why he liked the adaptation plan so much. But the prospect is positive he strongly likes your plan. This is because you moved the client several emotional tones towards courage, even though the factual underpinnings for those feelings may have slipped his mind. But nothing lasts forever, and the emotion tone towards your adaptation plan will fade with time. The good news is that the emotion tone fades at a slower rate than the substantive, factual points of the pain nullification. Put simply, people are more likely to remember how they feel about something rather than the specifics of it.

One distinction of the Vetting phase is that it deals with projections. The prospect is trying to determine or project the efficacy of the adaptation plan that you are proposing. Because projections are not anchored in fact, but are "best guesses," little or minor issues take on the proportion of major road blocks. This is why it appears to salespeople that a client is "zinging them" with an objection. Point of fact is this is the client's first and probably only time mentally examining a pain point in detail and lacks the experience and depth of knowledge the salesperson has who's probably seen a multitude of implementations. The prospect just doesn't know any better and the salesperson is obliged to put the issue into perspective. This is called scaling the issue, putting it into scale of the larger proceedings. This is why the focus on pain nullification is so important. Comparison of a minor issue to the pain nullification of major business pain points is the true measure of what needs to occur, and you will constantly have to make that comparison for your prospects to get their emotional processes moving forward.

Acceptance

Up to this point, you have been dealing with a prospect's fear of innovation: now it is time to get them into the moment. At the emotional phase acceptance, the prospect must accept that he needs to find solutions to their business pain points. In order to do this, you need to "burn through" their ego filter, which may be preventing them from seeing their business as it really exists. Instead, the prospects may be seeing the idyllic business that is running properly and efficiently with only minor issues because their ego won't let them see the inefficiencies, waste, and missed revenue that could be reclaimed by your product or service. In order to "burn through" the ego, you must make their business' warts apparent to them in the most personal way possible. You may even need to be brutally honest in your critical, stark, professional assessment of their business. But in the end, they will thank you for making them see what was under their nose all the time. The essence of which is captured in the popular sentiment, "You have to be cruel to be kind."

Acceptance is the first emotion in the present. The prospect is looking at his or her business as it sits and exists in the moment, untainted by past experiences. As we noted earlier, customers will not even sit down to speak with you about pain point nullification unless they first recognize they have problems and can get beyond their fears of innovation adaption. Acceptance of this premise now makes it beneficial to examine your adaptation plan. After burning through their ego filter, prospects will form motivations and Human Action Cycles about what and why they need to adapt to in their present circumstances. There are two avenues by which acceptance occurs: via the reactor or via the adaptor. The prospect is responding to the psyche pain point generated in their reactor by a problem in their business that threatens their profitability. i.e. "Wow, I had no idea! I've got to fix this right now!" Or they respond to the adaptor's need to learn more to create potential solutions and flexibility in adaptation, i.e. "That's good information. I wonder if I've got that problem?" Both of these desires create motivation to move forward and begin the first step in the Human Action Cycle of creating a motive.

This leads to a choice to either fix the problem themselves or court several vendors, which exemplifies the difference between innovators and early adopters and the late majority adopters. Innovators and early adapters come to you with the "I've got problems that need to be fixed now" motivation. The later majority adapters are more likely to court many vendors and look at a broader spectrum of sales aspects than just focusing on the efficacy of pain nullification of your product or service because minimized business disruption is so important to them. So your goal is to move them to their next emotional phase, learning anticipation.

As advocated in this book, as a salesperson, you need to focus on the prospect's pain points in the most personal way to them to get them aligned on the reactor path of pain nullification so that the reactor's function of moving people towards pleasurable things, such as pain nullification, is working for you. Discussing pain points typical in their industry and exploring the prospect's particulars is one way to uncover specific pain points unique to that location. The vast majority of the time, the prospect is able to work within his or her tolerances and limits while discussing the pain point issues of their business. Occasionally, however, by using this approach, you may evoke a response within the prospect that leads to an irrational or unexpected response. Pain can make people irrational. When you do, you need to stop your presentation and focus totally on the prospect as a human in pain and not as a potential income opportunity.

Learning Anticipation

Learning anticipation is the second emotion that a salesperson must traverse in navigating the Vetting phase. Learning anticipation is characterized by the desire to learn if something new or a different approach will yield a positive result towards making a Human Action Cycle motive achievable. In this case, the HAC motive of the prospect is to make his or her pain point go away. It should be noted that pain point(s) may be a complex cluster of small and large interrelated problems, or a simple one-problem issue. There is no magic formula that says showing x-number of positive results will yield a change in the prospect's emotional state. But it is fair to say that you will have to demonstrate your ability to show positive direction toward pain nullification on at least one major issue in a problem before the prospect will be able to upgrade his or her emotional state from learning anticipation.

The English language doesn't really have a specific name for learning anticipation like we have for acceptance and the other emotions on the emotional tonal algorithm. Learning anticipation is about cataloguing known potential solutions. Some people might use the word "options" to describe this emotion, but this term does not totally reflect the key aspects of this emotion. The word "options" conveys a whole range of actions such as walking away from the pain point and ignoring it. While abandoning this motive may occur due to no suitable solution that could be ascertained, this will occur later in another emotional phase. The mind is geared to seek the widest possible array of solutions generated by experience, reasoning, logic, and imagination. This emotion is driven to find ways to possibly nullifying pain points or achieving the outcome of the motivation. Not all potential solutions are specific courses of action or reflect emotional content and drive to seek possible resolutions and remedies. If no course of action can be identified during the learning anticipation phase, then the HAC may very well abandon this particular objective of the motivation, or postpone further pursuit until a wider search can be made or wait for new developments in technology. If one or more possible solutions are generated, then those solutions are moved forward for pain nullification efficacy analysis in the next emotion in the algorithm. For these reasons, you should equate the emotion learning anticipation with solutions.

Confidence

The third emotion in the Vetting phase is characterized by the determination that a specific adaptation plan(s) can have enough of a positive effect to make the pain points go away and achieve the objectives of the motivation. Confidence is about projecting efficacy potential. The prospect will focus on whether enough of the positive outcomes learned about in this phase can be repeated, accumulated, or achieved to resolve the main issue(s). Another way to state this is the prospect will determine if the proposed adaptation plan is big enough or can be scaled up to a level to resolve the main pain point(s) of the motivation objective. This will be done in a comparative basis using, but not limited to, feasibility, practicality, efficiency, efficacy, and aesthetics. If the solution can nullify the pain points, then the prospect will become confident that your adaptation plan will work for him and upgrade his emotion to confidence.

In addition, in this phase the implementation plan will also be vetted for feasibility. Those solutions whose implementation is feasible and solution has efficacy will be moved forward to the next emotion on the algorithm as the emotion confidence is achieved. If an adaptation plan fails to produce any measure of projected pain nullification, then that particular adaptation plan will be eliminated from the pool of adaptation plans before moving on to the next emotion in the algorithm.

In the advent where multiple solutions are viable, the solutions will be ordered in terms of projected efficacy. The most efficacious solution will be the first to proceed to the next emotion of excitement. If the solution fails at either excitement or courage, then the HAC will return to confidence and grab the next ordered solution and advance that through excitement and courage, and so on. The HAC will continue this until a solution satisfies all the emotions of the Innovation emotional tonal algorithm or the HAC is paused for a HAC to modify some aspect of the original HAC, such as motive or goal, or is abandoned due to lack of a viable solution.

Excitement

The next, fourth, emotion that must be surmounted is excitement. Excitement is about projecting costs. This is where the prospect actually starts to visualize using your adaptation plan which corresponds with the emotion excitement. By visualizing the integration of your product into their world, they start to see questions about the actual integration and the costs in time and resources it will take to acquire and implement your adaptation plan. The main determination at this emotional phase is whether the cost of implementing your action plan outweighs the benefits and utility of those resources as they are already employed and whether those resources are available. Cost of the product versus resources available dictates the quantity that can be obtained. So, quantity is a function of excitement. Costs include time, resources (including money), disruption to business processes, and the like. If the benefits and utility win out, they will see themselves executing this adaptation plan and they will become excited that pain relief is within their resource reach.

In addition, the actual price of the product or service is measured against projected efficacy it will possess. This cost will be added to projected implementation costs and compared to the resources available to the individual. If the costs will exceed resources, that particular adaptation plan will be eliminated from the pool of adaptation plans. If the product is viewed as a commodity, then the learning anticipation and confidence emotions are quickly touched and passed to excitement, where cost from different providers is examined and is one of the main determinants of purchase.

It is at this point where salespeople generally try to redirect resources. One of the most common redirection methods is the "savings" ploy. If a prospect is currently using equipment and/or processes that are inefficient, the reduction in costs (resources) currently being expended can be transferred to offset the cost of implementing the sales person's adaptation plan, or released and returned to the prospect for other uses. This redirection sounds like this: "If you take your current resources that you are spending (or wasting) and buy my _____ (adaptation plan), you'll be saving X amount of dollars."

ROI, Return on Investment, style selling is another ploy aimed at this particular emotion phase. ROI selling is worthless, though, if you have not covered other previous emotional phases and the prospect isn't at the excitement phase. This is an example of one of dozens of previously promoted selling methodologies, made famous in the last several decades that appeared and became popular only to fade away. Because the emotional context was not understood, the application of Return On Investment selling would not always be effective. If clients are still in the learning anticipation or confidence emotion phase, they will not be willing to measure the projected costs against the projected benefits, which is the basis of the ROI selling system. This example should drive home the importance of topic matching to emotional stage in the Innovation phase of the emotional tonal algorithm.

Courage

Courage is the fifth and last emotion in the Vetting phase of the emotional tonal algorithm and implies an action is to be taken, the courage to do something. Courage is about projecting risk. Courage is also one of the most desirable emotional tones and gives the receiver a maximum dose of joy and positive agitation express, to encourage the self to take risks, which are needed in life to succeed. In the salesperson's universe, this is the prospect committing to an order by some physical action such as signing a contract, writing a purchase order, or writing a check. If they give you an objection pertaining to costs, by default, their emotional state is not at courage and they are still stuck at excitement and not yet ready to examine risk. At the courage emotional phase, they will have the courage to either tell you "yes" or deflect if they don't want to say "no."

The emotion excitement measures cost, which is different — it's about resources, while courage is about risk and evaluation of it. Risk is about what happens if it all goes wrong: What is the likelihood that it could all fall apart? What will be the fallout, the potential damage to their business aside from the lost resources needed to obtain and implement the proposed adaptation plan? Or, in the case of a commodity or common product, the risk of losing out on a better deal elsewhere. Economists call this opportunity cost. Quality of a product is a function of courage since higher quality reduces risk. Finally, if their assumptions were wrong, if their projection forgot to factor in some crucial element, or if the circumstances change shortly after a product is bought, how might the situation be salvaged, and at what cost? If the risks are acceptable or mitigated by guarantee, warranty, or return policy, courage is generated. Once courage is achieved, action is executed in the real world.

As described earlier, the Human Action Cycle combines all of the elements Paradaptive Intelligence Network to realize objectives and motives of the adaptor. Courage is a prime example of this architecture. In the process of Innovation, the reactor has had an opportunity to examine the solution selected to be implemented and has identified threats to the self associated with it. In addition, in the courage stage, the adaptor is actively seeking to identify any and all further risks which the reactor identifies and latches onto as threats. In order to overcome the reactor's purposeful disruption due to identified risks in the environment to the adaptor's orderly reasoning, a powerful internal incentive of joy associated with the emotion courage is necessary. This is why courage is one of nature's most desirable states and one of the most heavily rewarded. This also gives salespeople a direction in moving prospects at this stage. Internally, the mind is gearing up for internal rewards and the salesperson can complement this internal process by focusing on the rewards of the innovation or new tool to move the sales process forward.

Courage represents a shift from projecting results to obtaining real results. Up to this point, all of the evaluations of the adaptor have been performed on speculation. Once courage is achieved, all analysis is performed upon actual results. This is one of the salesperson's biggest challenges. While working with speculation in the confidence, excitement, and courage emotional stages, customers often lack perspective on functionality, costs, and risks. Without an estimate of likelihood of an occurrence of a possible negative event mated to a likely outcome, cost, or measure of failure, all the client's "objections" are equal. Without perspective, all potential obstacles, large and small, minor or significant become equal and become an impediment to the sale. It is the job of the salesperson to give the prospect perspective.

If several adaptation plans have made it to the courage phase, and risk is evaluated to be equal, then the individual will develop a mild form of anger – most likely frustration or something close to it on the continuum of anger, because selecting the proper course of action has now become a pain point. The pain point HAC currently in progress will be paused and the pain point of selection will become the subject of a new HAC that will more critically differentiate the adaptation plans of the first HAC that made it to the courage phase. If the HAC to critically differentiate the adaptation plans fails to produce the emotion courage, then another corrective signal of anger (frustration) is felt. The critical differential HAC will be paused and a third

HAC to more critically define selection criteria will ensue, and so on until a follow-on HAC produces the emotion courage. Once the emotion courage is reached in one of the subsequent HACs, this emotion will cascade back through the previous paused HACs, allowing each of the intervening HACs to reach courage until the original HAC examining adaptations plans is reached and a selection is made with risk having been refined by the follow-on HACs. If any of the follow-on HACs fails to produce the emotion courage, the individual will have accumulated numerous pain point corrective signals of frustration. Corrective signals agitate the individual to move away from the object causing the frustration, so they'll move on until a new development can break the logjam of equally rated solutions.

This avoid/move-away agitation may then force the individual to back off from trying to solve the problem and try the other major strategy of Paradaptive Intelligence – relationships. The individual will seek out expert advice from a trusted friend, a consultant or to form a committee. This is especially common when the original pain point HAC is a complex problem with many variables to consider which will produce a multitude of adaptation plan options after excitement. As a salesperson, you should be aware that business seeking innovation has most likely already experienced this progression more than once and learned that it is just simpler to go straight to the consultant or committee approach. This is the genesis of the "consultive selling" approach – more on that later.

A Quick Example

Let's put it all together and see how this works. Suppose you sell a computer product that has light accounting features and invoicing, a database of customers and transactions, and production scheduling for a service industry. You call upon a prospect that is currently handwriting invoices and has no database other than a filing cabinet that the prospect throws his duplicate copies into. His production and appointment scheduling is done on a Month-at-a-Glance desk planner. He acknowledges that he needs to join the computer age and organize many of the aspects of his business electronically and is interested in seeing what is available, which is why he's agreed to spend some time with you. Like most service industry business owners, he started off as a technician doing the actual service work before striking out on his own, so he's long on technical knowledge but knows little of business operating practices. You start your presentation by showing the prospect how his current system is causing him time and money to produce pain points and anchor his motivation to fix the problem. Because you've read this book and are using question-based selling, you get him to enunciate his acceptance and move his emotional state to learning anticipation. In his head, he's thinking, "*This guy knows where I hurt.*" You then list several directions in which he might move and the efficacy and history of problems associated with each ending with your adaptation. You ask the prospect if that about covers the possible solutions to which he replies it does as far as he can see. You've satisfied learning anticipation. "*Okay*," the prospect thinks, "*clearly this solution offers the biggest performance improvement. I need to examine this further.*" Next you show him how easy it is to invoice completed works. This pleases the prospect (internal shot of joy by satisfying confidence for one of the pain points). "*This gets me partway there by doing the invoicing. Maybe there's more.*" Next, you demonstrate how your product keeps and tracks the invoice information to create a database of his clients. Again, you get him to enunciate the benefits, moving him to confidence. At this point, he's thinking, "*That's two out of three — this just might do, even if it does nothing else. I can probably find something else to handle the scheduling if it doesn't.*" Now you demo the scheduler, which pulls information from the database so he doesn't have to do anything more than type the client's name, date, time, and work needed. The feature even prints a daily routing schedule and optimizes the route. He's wowed at this point. "*This thing will save me tons of time,*" he's thinking. His emotional state is excitement. He can see himself using the product.

He fires out one objection: "So how much is this going to cost me?" (Can you see now that cost isn't an objection, but the hardwired emotion of excitement that he's compelled by stronger and stronger doses of joy to fulfill?)

"Our price on this as I demonstrated," you reply, "is $175.00 per month, or $2,000.00 annual payment up front."

"Okay, I can handle that," he says, becoming visibly excited. "How soon can I have this up and running?" (Still assessing cost)

"We can have you up and running in five days once you get your computer and printer installed," you reply.

"So what happens if I don't like it, or something unexpected happens two weeks from now?" (He's satisfied excitement and now he's moved on to courage)

"Well, you do have the option to cancel the purchase in the first thirty days, and you'll get a refund for the year minus the first month's payment of $175.00."

"Sign me up then! Who do I make the check out to?" A satisfying answer to his minor "objection" of time frame, or the cost of the resource of time, moved him to courage.

It should be noted that all the emotions of the Vetting phase, acceptance, learning anticipation, confidence, and excitement, are growth signals and are tones of joy. With each emotional phase you move the prospect through the Vetting phase, the greater the intensity of the next emotion of joy the prospect feels. The process starts off with a mild joy payoff at acceptance and builds to complete, total, and full joy at satisfied customer. This is a good thing for the salesman because built in to these is an emotional element that compels the prospect to repeat positive experiences and move towards that which is giving him joy — you and your adaptation plan (see Figure 10.4). So, for the prospect, there is a built-in impetus and momentum to move to the next step in the sales cycle and repeat positive emotions. Some people have stated this as "Prospects want to be sold" or "Clients want to buy." Either way, it's another insight into the prospect's mind to help you phrase and position your adaptation plan. From a broader perspective, you have a prospect that is carrying some pain, and rather than dwell on these pain points, it's more comfortable and enjoyable for the prospect to pursue the pleasure and gratification of the positive emotions in the Vetting Phase, moving towards pain nullification. The game is rigged in the salesperson's favor once he or she understands the emotional constructs.

Now, that you've seen the whole emotion flow of Innovation in the Vetting phase, you'll understand that this is what most people call persuasion. **The art of persuasion is nothing more than the science of guiding a prospect through the five emotions of acceptance, learning anticipation, confidence, excitement, and courage.**

12

REFINING INNOVATION VETTING

"An ounce of prevention is worth a pound of cure"
Anonymous

With an understanding of the basic structure of the decision making process of adaptation in place, it's time now to refine this model

LINE OF OPTIMIZATION

Chapter 5 introduced the conductor as one of the three structures of the brain influencing human behavior with their biases and introduced the concept of primacy. Primacy indicates which of the brain's three processing centers structures, reactor, adaptor, or conductor has the primary share of control at any one point and to what degree control is being shared with any other of the brain's other processing centers. It is time to see how these processing centers interact and the influences they exert in the Innovation phase.

On the Joy side of the Innovation tonal algorithm there are only two brain processing centers that are sharing control, the adaptor and conductor. When not directing a human's adaptive actions, the adaptor is executing its bias of learning. Much of that learning comes in the form of feedback in the evaluation portion of the Human Action Cycle, while in other instances, the adaptor is specifically directing a human's activities specifically at learning. The conductor's bias is to optimize outcomes and the processes that produce those outcomes. In Figure 12.1 we introduce a new element of the Paradaptive Intelligence, the Line of Optimization. This line indicates the point at which primacy in control switches from the adaptor to the conductor. Both processing centers continue with their functions, but dominance in agendas switches at the Line of Optimization. This process can be best understood as a time-sharing arrangement to sort out which processing center, adaptor or conductor, is in control. In addition, this determines which processing center's agenda takes precedent in case of a conflict. The processing center of the Adaptor is designed to do the bulk of activity in all phases of human adaptation/behavior, but shares with other processing centers depending upon the external activities surrounding a person and whether they are good (joy), bad (corrective), or unexpected (surprise).

In this chapter, only the impact of the conductor upon the Vetting Phase of the Innovation algorithm will be examined. Figure 12.1 illustrates, primacy shifts halfway between the Present and the Future on the spectrum of Joy signals. Looking at how this line interacts with the Vetting Phase algorithms of emotional tones, it bisects the emotion confidence. How this manifest itself in behavior is that in the emotions acceptance and learning anticipation there is little regard to optimally defining the problem that is being accepted or the known solutions within memory are ordered which can bear on eliminating the pain point. Primarily these things just need to be identified, not optimized. However, at the emotion confidence, the solutions are evaluated and sorted based on their ability to relieve the pain point with a nod to which one is the best; best being comprised of which is the most efficacious, and secondarily, on first blush, as to which is the most efficient. The efficiency element is the influence of the conductor. As the Human Action Cycle continues towards the end of the Vetting phases, the next emotion, excitement, is evaluated with a much higher degree of the efficiency, optimization, with which the resource is going to be used. A greater degree of the evaluation in this emotion tone be will be conducted by the conductor to evaluate whether the expected nullification of pain point is worth the estimated expenditure of resources. While loss of resources may result in harm to the self in the future due to loss of capacity of resources, courage is an emotion that measures immediate risk of harm to the self. This is why the emotion courage is so much more sensitive to known risks than the emotions excitement is to lost resources. The conductor is heavily influencing the emotion tonal satisfaction of courage to optimize risk to the lowest possible value.

We can see how in the first half of the Vetting phase is concerned with just identifying problems and possible solutions and how at the halfway point, the emphasis shifts to higher and higher levels of optimization required for each emotion to be achieved.

FIGURE 12.1

Vetting Phase of the Innovation Emotional Tonal Algorithm
with Line Of Optimization

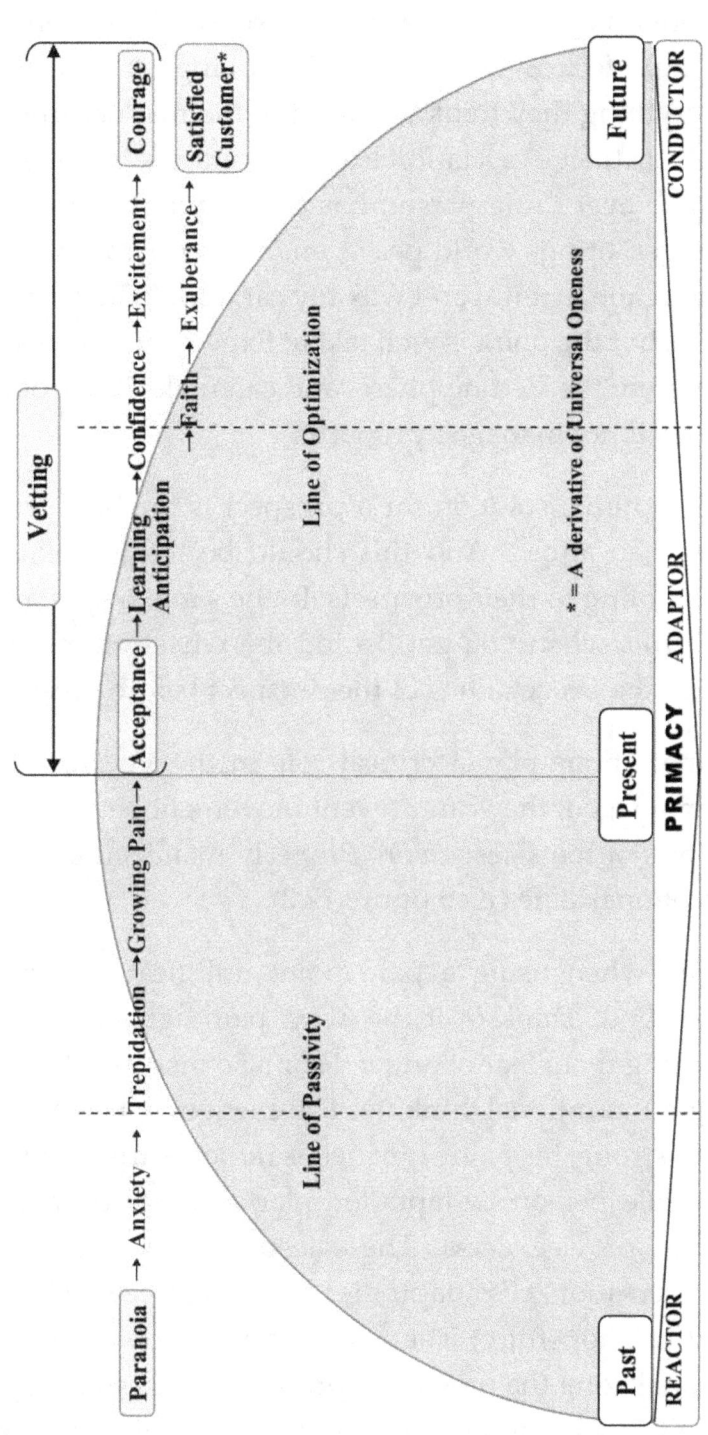

EXPECTATIONS

It's important to know how a prospect's mind will work if it's left on its own with no guidance from a salesperson. And left unattended, the prospect's mind will gum-up the works for the sales professional. Learning anticipation, confidence, and excitement are also the points of an interesting phenomenon – prospect expectations. There is no such thing as the perfect product; therefore, every salesperson's product is imperfect. Every prospect is looking for a perfect product that is free and does everything they think it should in the manner they believe it should be performed. This distinct expectation leads to some pretty interesting conversations like this one which every salesperson has at one point or another… "Sure your product cures hunger, brings world peace, and makes a damn good cup of coffee, but now you're telling me that it won't wax my car, too?" Granted, there is a modicum of hyperbole here, but the point is well taken. Expectations can lead to some serious disruption in covering the Vetting phase, and can make it impossible to move between emotional states if not managed properly.

The optimal solution for a prospect is the best product at the right time at a price they can afford. And this should be the template that all salespeople should be promoting to their prospects. In the same way that you check the mirrors, seat, and controls when you get behind the wheel of an automobile, you need to properly align the expectations of the prospect before presenting your adaptation plan.

Expectations play a critical role in the Vetting phase. If they are unrealistic and unmanaged, they can prevent movement between the emotion tones, thwarting the efforts of the salesperson. Properly managed expectations make it easier to change emotional states (See figure 12.2).

Even when using a pain point nullification approach, expectations need to be managed. Think of it this way: pain agitates people to move away from what is causing them fear or anger. Fear also disrupts thought processes and interferes with logic and rational thinking. The client may believe, irrationally, that because his fear is so strong, his pain point needs radical surgery and must be totally reworked, while the salesperson's adaptation plan calls for only minor adjustments in a couple of areas, or vice versa. The salesperson is not bringing any fear or anger to the conversation. His adaptor is free from threats, (like threats from his management "to SELL!", hopefully). The salesperson is probably the most rational thinker at the table in analyzing the prospect's problems. This should give you confidence to know that you're selling to people who are being influenced by fear or anger and its ensuing irrationality and that you may just have the most level head at the moment. It should also give you pause in dealing with prospects knowing that they may be just a little bit more than disadvantaged at the moment. And all this can be compounded by unmanaged expectations.

It is also notable to remember how unreasonable expectations are formed. Your prospect has formed a motive to stop the fear/anger pain, which has led to the formation of a HAC. That HAC contained an MAP based on the prospect's relevant experience to pursuing the HAC. Since this is a new experience for the prospect, and if he has done no market research of his own, then he will have no relevant experiences to draw upon. As you recall from an earlier chapter, imagination is the mind's tool to fill in adaptation plans and strategies when no relevant experience is present in his memory. So literally, the mind forces a creative solution to be made and put in place in order for the prospect to pursue an action plan. Without boundaries anchored in reality, the imagination will come up with unrealistic ideas, which then become expectations, such as a product that does everything he wants, in the way he thinks it should be done, requires no effort on his part, and is free. Unrealistic expectations are just an artifact of the mind's machinery forced upon your prospect by the mechanisms of adaptation. Simply asking prior to adaptation plan presentation if the prospect has done any research on the topic will tell you whether imagination or reality is driving the prospect's expectations.

Figure 12.2

MANAGING EXPECTATIONS

Unmanaged Expectations: <u>Imagination</u> based Human Action Cycle Plans

Acceptance   Learning anticipation   Confidence   Excitement   Courage

Managed Expectations: <u>Experience</u> based Human Action Cycle Plans

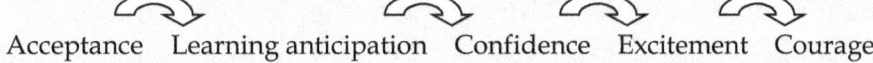

Acceptance   Learning anticipation   Confidence   Excitement   Courage

It all depends upon the action plan of the prospect. Is there an action plan for pain nullification or is the adaptor's prime directive – education – to learn an option for future use? Regardless, there are many ways and techniques for setting expectations. At the bottom of it all, you must get the customer to acknowledge that there is no perfect product, whether that's through amusing anecdotes, tales of your own imperfections, or those of your product's. But it must be made clear to the prospects, and what they need to acknowledge is, imperfections aside, your product is still the best adaptation plan at the right time that they can afford with the least risk.

Your response to ungrounded expectations will fall along one of these lines, "We tried that approach, but found it was too expensive...," "That would be nice, but currently, there is no technology that can actually do that...," or "We tried that and it didn't work very well for the following reasons..."

HUMAN ACTION CYCLE REVISITED

In Chapter 7, we learned about the Human Action Cycle. It's now time to tie that together with what we've learned about the Vetting phase. As you recall, the HAC is comprised of five steps: motives, actions, outcomes, evaluations, and corrections. In the sales cycle, the client's motives and action plan remain the same generally, but where the salesperson does his or her work is in the action, outcomes, evaluations, and corrections portions of the prospect's Human Action Cycle. The Human Action Cycle determines whether an emotion in the emotion tonal algorithm has been satisfied (joy) and moves the prospect on to the next emotion in the algorithm, or issues some corrective emotion to help the prospect adapt (Figure 10.6).

The primary function of the HAC in the Vetting phase is to project the various aspects of pain points and steps to resolve them. This system of projected analysis occurs for every growth signal emotion in the Innovation emotional tonal algorithm. During the evaluation phase of a HAC for acceptance it will project what the prospect accepts to be the problem (pain point); evaluation during the learning anticipation phase will project what are possible solutions and if enough have been accumulated; evaluations during the confidence emotion phase will project which solution will be the most efficacious and whether it will be efficacious enough to nullify the pain point; evaluations during the excitement emotion phase will project whether the resources necessary to execute the adaptation plan are available; and the evaluation phase during courage will project the risks involved with executing the adaptation plan.

As you discover a prospect's pain points and present your adaptation plan to nullify them, the client listens (action), observes how the adaptation plan will impact the pain points (outcome-projected), and evaluates how effective it would be on a

Figure 12.3

Feed-Forward Feedback Cycle:
The Basics of the <u>H</u>uman <u>A</u>ction <u>C</u>ycle
and the Emotional Tonal Flow of Growth Signal.

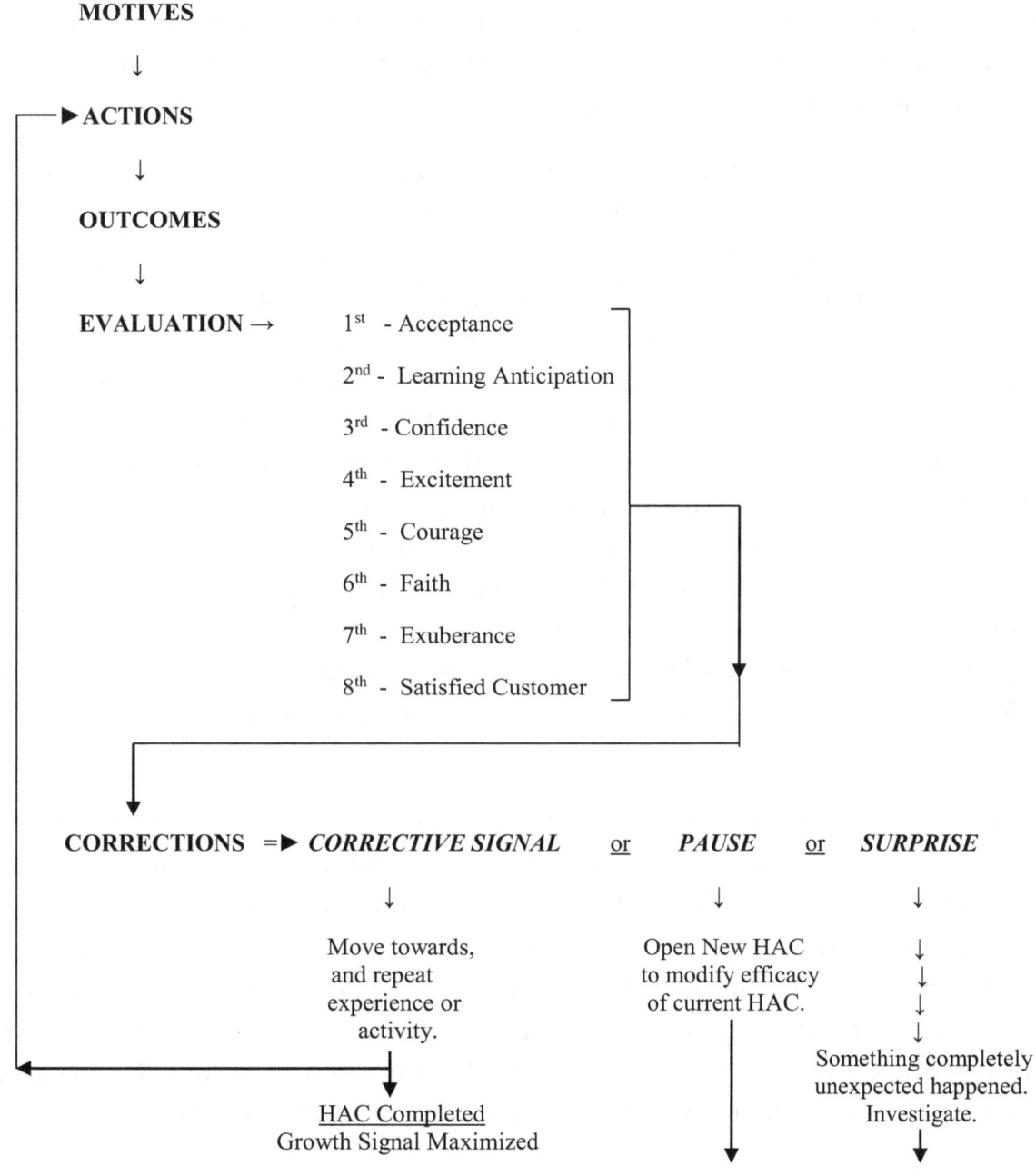

particular emotional phase (evaluations). When sufficient evaluations have accumulated, the prospect will go to the corrections phase of the HAC. If the projected analysis determines in the evaluations phase is sufficient, then a HAC correction is issued as a joy based emotion signaling the HAC to move to the next emotion in the Vetting phase. This is called a feedforward feedback cycle because it feeds forward in a specified sequence of emotions. The just completed, satisfied emotion positively agitates and directs the individual to continue upon the current HAC. A corrective signal in the corrections stage would agitate them to move away from the approach just tried and take another direction in order to achieve satisfaction of the emotion. Or it may, due to the corrective signal, abandon this HAC because it cannot fulfill the motivation.

There is a third action that can occur in the corrections phase, and that is to open a new HAC to modify some aspect of the adaptation plan to improve its efficacy (See Figure 12.3). This happens frequently at excitement as a prospect attempts to mitigate costs and other variables that may impact resources such as delivery dates and installation times. When a new HAC is opened to modify some aspect of the HAC currently in progress, the current HAC is suspended until the outcome of the increased efficacy HAC is completed. This works by pausing the present HAC to be modified while the modification HAC goes through to success or abandonment, cycling through all the same emotional tones (learning anticipation, confidence, excitement, courage, faith, exuberance, and satisfied customer) to create the modification to the suspended HAC. If the modifications produce the results desired, satisfied customer/universal oneness is achieved, concluding the modification HAC and the previously suspended HAC resume with the new modification, getting a new correction or growth signal and moving on in the emotional tonal phases.

All this may sound complicated, but it isn't (See Figure 10.6). If you remember that every decision, from what shoes to wear to whether to build a new nuclear plant, are all subject to the HAC and its five steps – motive, actions, outcome, evaluations, and corrections - and that the algorithm has eight joy emotional phases that it attempts to cycled through. Five in the Vetting phase – acceptance, learning anticipation, confidence, excitement, and courage, and three in the Application phase – faith, exuberance, and customer satisfaction (post-sale emotions are the subject of Chapter 14), then you'll understand a significant portion of the human adaptation process.

FIVE CLOSING IN EVERY SALE

So now that we understand that there are five emotional stages in every sale that must be satisfied before a sale occurs, it is now possible to really understand why and where the old fashioned and misunderstood concept of "closing" goes off the tracks. A prime example of this lack of understanding can be found in the quotation of author Brian Tracy that started Chapter 11 and shows how the typical sales person fights the Paradaptive Intelligence Network rather than working within its rules, principles, and boundaries. What is really occurring in the minds of prospects and consumers is emotional satisfaction. Emotional satisfaction and closing are synonymous. Since there are five emotions tones in the Vetting Phase, then there are five "closing" of emotional stages that must occur in a specific sequence, not just the signing of a contract at courage. And there are two styles in which to approach satisfying or "closing" those emotions.

TWO STYLES OF CLOSING

We looked in a previous chapter at the efficiency of salespeople. This picture can be further refined now as we look at the style of emotions satisfaction. A salesperson can create successful Vetting phase transverse by making the focus of their sales efforts to either the reactor or the adaptor of a prospect. As noted earlier, a sale occurs when a pain point is nullified. Pain points reside in the reactor functions of the brain. Eagles, the top sellers, focus their sales efforts on pain nullification.

They have found that this is the most direct, efficient route. The rest of the sales force typically sells to the adaptor with a features and benefits approach hoping that educating the adaptor will lead to a translation of pain nullification. This is an indirect route, with less control over how the prospect's brain will move from learning mode about your product to logic and application, provided that that is even a strong suit of the prospect. This is why top selling salespeople apply themselves directly to the reactor, which controls both the emotional generation of fear/anger pain and measures efficacy of pain relief of adaptation plans, rather than the adaptor, which looks to collect information, learn, and educate the self before coming up with its own adaptation plan that may or may not include your product.

Why does this matter? A quick example will illustrate the point. You have a molar in your jaw giving you serious pain. You go to the dentist who diagnoses the problem and says to you one of the two following statements, 1) "You need a root canal, and I can get that done for you Tuesday, but until then, here's some antibiotics and analgesics to control the pain," or 2) "Your nerve in tooth number 19 has become infected, which has spread to your jaw, causing the pain." The former is directed to the reactor (aimed at pain nullification), while the latter is directed to the adaptor aimed at educating. Given the pain that you're in, which of these two are you going to be most interested in? If you went with the adaptor statement, you'd be wrong but, for illustration's sake, let's consider it. In order to convert the indirect adaptor approach, you'd need to ask several questions. So what's the fix? When can we get it done? Is there anything you can do now to stop the pain? Is there anything else we can do in the meantime? All the while, the presumption is that you know enough to ask these questions and that the pain you're experiencing is letting you think clearly. Undoubtedly, all of us would, due to the pain, desperately glom onto the adaptation plan with the more direct reactor plan. The question is which type of salesperson do you want to be, the one offering an adaptation plan for pain nullification or the one offering education to the adaptor with features and benefits?

ACTION POINTS

There are four action points on the Innovation emotional tonal algorithm: paranoia, acceptance, courage, and customer satisfaction (Figure 8.5). These are notable because they mark not only a phase change in emotion but they also signal the commencement of a physical action.

Paranoia

This is the strongest emotion of fear in which the reactor is in complete charge with the sole mission of protecting the body and self. It may also trigger the Fight, Flight, or Freeze response. The emotional state of paranoia does not automatically incur a physical response. Physical response is a function of proximity. For example, someone may be paranoid about spiders and snakes. When you talk to them on the topic, they become irrational about the topic, but no physical response occurs. Whereas, if you shoved one of those in their face, they may swat it away (Fight) or simple run from the room shrieking (Flight). With older generations, not familiar with electronics or computers, they may have a similar reaction. Fight response occurs when a threat is imminent, when there's no room for escape. The reactor engages the emotion rage to protect the body by giving maximum effort for all-out mortal combat, even if that means short-term strength gains through hormone dumps like adrenaline that overtaxes the metabolic capacity of the body, leading to quick and catastrophic fatigue. The Flight response, panic, occurs when the threat is immediate, but there is room for escape. The same hormonal dump as fight occurs, but the singular focus is on escape and the reactor will run over or through anything in its way. There is no consideration for others when the reactor is in control. The Freeze response occurs when the threat's proximity is somewhere between or on the threshold of both fight and flight. The reactor rapidly cycles between rage and panic, unsure which one to invoke, which prevents the body from doing either fighting or fleeing causing the body to "freeze." In the salesperson's world the most likely of the responses they will encounter will be fight. This will take the form of being kicked out of somebody's office. Hopefully, the source of the fright was caused by someone else and not you leaving the door open for reconciliation later.

Acceptance

Acceptance signals the recognition of a pain point by the adaptor. Pain points are created by any corrective signal. This pain point is an expression of the negative agitation contained in the first level of the tri-valence signal in an emotional feedback signal. The adaptor can either ignore the pain point, rejecting the reactor's signaling of a threat, obstacle, boundary violation, loss, or something disgusting in the environment, and all with the potential to do harm to the body or self. The alternative is the adaptor can accept that pain point and create an action plan to deal with it. When the adaptor accepts the presence of a corrective signal, the reactor sends a growth signal, a small shot of joy, in the form of acceptance, as a positive emotional signal, that will encourage the adaptor to pursue actions and activities that will nullify the corrective signal. The adaptor will seek repetition of growth signals by taking further steps and actions to nullify the corrective signal.

A simpler way to look at this may be through a personal example. Let's say the reactor knows that your business is losing money on a product you're carrying. The reactor signals to the adaptor via a pain point of fear — a corrective signal. Essentially, the reactor is saying to the adaptor, "Hey, I've got a problem down here, and I need some help. I've identified something that is detrimental to the body, a product that is sucking up money that could be spent on me, the body. So I'm going to start bugging you to do something about it."

The adaptor's response is this, "Yeah, I got your message, and I agree. I need to do something about this product."

Reactor- "Great! Thanks for agreeing to do something about it. Here's a little shot of joy, which I know you like, as my way of saying thank you. This particular flavor of joy is called acceptance, and it's pretty watered down. It's just a taste of what I can do for you if you make this threat go away for me. If you keep working on the problem, I'll keep rewarding you with bigger and bigger shots of joy. Otherwise, I'll just keep bothering you, more and more, louder and louder, until you can't get anything done up there. And I'm going to do this until you get with the program."

Adaptor- "Alright, alright...enough. I said I'd start to figure something out." (A motive is born).

Reactor- "Good, 'cause I'm serious about this. And just so you don't forget about me, I'm just going to keep sending you little reminders, (corrective signals), to keep you on your toes. And I don't care how much that interrupts what you're doing. Just remember, you can make this stop anytime you want — all you have to do is figure out some adaptive behavior or action to fix this. And if it really gets bad, I just may take over and take care of it myself by hitting the fight button, or maybe I'll just hit the afterburners and run like hell."

Adaptor- "I get it! I get it! Look, I've put together an action plan on how to make your problem go away while you were threatening me. I talked to the conductor and it has agreed to work with me as long as I give it my best and that I don't hurt anybody. It's got a program for me to help me get this done. With all your constant yammering, interruptions, and threats, is it any wonder I was able to put a plan together? Now, if you'll just leave me alone, I'll get to work." (Behold, the birth of an action plan)

Reactor- "No promises."

Courage

The courage emotion phase at the end of the Vetting phase signifies the physical action of actual attempts to nullify the pain. Up to this point, all actions and activities had to do with finding and analyzing adaptation plans (solutions) to resolve pain points. This process is best described as projections as to how solutions will unfold upon implementation, and an attempt to understand how all the variables will react in the real world. The emotional phase of courage is when the act of projection ends and the implementation begins.

Knowledge is imperfect. There will always be unknowns when making predictions. Therefore, whenever an implementation plan is converted to action, there is always the risk that something was not accounted for in the calculations and projections. This creates unpredictable outcomes, which can be either good or bad. If it's bad, it can imperil the body, creating more threats that it resolved. This is a large emotional hurdle to overcome and why courage is one of the most desirable emotions within growth signals. A large reward is necessary emotionally to overcome risk (Figures 10.4 and 8.4).

Customer Satisfaction

This is considered an action point because it is at this point you cease to seek nullification to a pain point. The level of joy stimulus is so great that no further amplitude of this feeling can be achieved and all further inducements to continue on the path of pain nullification are removed. We are internally wired to stop when a problem is fixed; this is what customer satisfaction does. This is done to conserve energy. The mind is designed to conserve energy so, when a problem/pain point is nullified, it cuts off the supply of joy so we move on to other pain points and, thus, we are driven to constantly improve our survivability by not dwelling or working on pain points that no longer have potency. While this is a very good thing internally to an individual, it may not necessarily be the greatest of systems for the species or, for that matter, for the individual, either. However, moments, days, weeks, months, or even years after we have internally signaled to stop working a problem (pain point), we may become aware of a piece of information that totally changes our perspective of the customer satisfaction that was derived. Such as another product or service that solved a problem in a more efficient or effective way, or a vendor that sells the same product at a greatly reduced price. The customer satisfaction once enjoyed is now translated back into a pain point of having spent too much money or in having picked the wrong product.

CONFIDENCE IS A THREE-LEGGED STOOL

There is significant anecdotal evidence to indicate that during the confidence emotional stage, multiple points of support are needed to satisfy this emotion. There appears to be the requirement for triangulation of supporting points in order for satisfaction to occur. As of yet, there is no supporting research to explain this observed behavior and bears further inquiry. However, in the meanwhile, a good rule of thumb is to view the emotion confidence as a three-legged stool. It's incredibly difficult and quite perilous to attempt to sit on stool with only one leg. Sitting on a stool with two legs can be done, but it requires a tight grip on the stool top and the dependence on the long-term use of your legs to act as the third point of stabilization. It takes three legs to create a stable platform to bear the weight of a person safely. So, too, with sales. With one point of corroboration that the pain point will be solved, it will be very hard, but not impossible, to get the sales completed. And the chance of keeping that sale on the books without a cancellation goes up substantially. With two points of corroboration a sale has less difficulty of being completed but will require a lot of extra activity, constant attention, and support of the sales person to see this sale through and keep it on the books after the sale. The only safe way for a sales person to approach the emotion confidence is to create a triangulation of three or more points of corroboration that their adaptation plan will nullify the prospect's pain points.

EXCITED PROSPECTS

Occasionally, a salesperson is lucky enough to have prospects show up who have identified their pain points, done their homework, and sought you out because they are confident that your product has the potential to help them. Essentially, this prospect arrives at your doorstep already at the excitement emotional tone. They have examined the competition in price, and they are ready to move straight to courage by committing to the sale. However, for most salespeople there is always a competitor and these types of excited prospects, through their due diligence, are usually aware of your competition. What they are seeking is a more in-depth understanding of how your product works. Since they are seeking product knowledge, your best bet is to provide them with an action plan. While they were able to find your product's features and benefits on their own, what they lack is the implementation plan. But first, a few questions about their particular application are needed before an action plan to fine tune the total costs can be yielded. You can learn this by mixing in a goodly amount of SPAN questions (to be covered in Chapter 13). Usually, since they've already done their homework, they'll readily tell you about the pain points they're trying to nullify.

Excited prospects are more likely to see your product generically. They've done their research and identified several vendors whose product will nullify their pain points but as of yet are reserving decisions to any particular vendor until they've seen them all. In essence, they can't execute the excitement emotional phase until all the costs and benefits for each option can be weighed against each other. Now they are going from vendor to vendor, looking for nuances of difference and checking price and availability (both excitement attributes). They seem to be in control of the process, right? Wrong!

A top salesperson will take a proactive approach. A top seller will mix in a goodly amount of SPAN questions to not only pull information about their particular situation, but to also start tallying emotional tonal points towards courage, as well as use the 3F's to mitigate risk, specifically friendship and freedom of worry. There is no need to discount your product's price just yet due to competition.

But probably the most important thing to remember is that, although the excited prospect appears to be well informed, he or she doesn't know half of the picture. As a salesperson, you know more about the implementation and post-sales side of the transaction. By focusing the conversation on the post side of courage, it provides the scaffolding and framework to complete the customer's vision of choosing your product, which is really what they are missing as an excited prospect.

Let's take an example that is universal to everyone in the civilized world, buying a television. There is an endless parade of features, options, styles, technologies, and sizes. So, to sort through this, you create a matrix of product features, sizes, and prices of the big screen TVs that meet your specifications. Nothing for the salesman to do except show you the prices between the models that fit your matrix and the price, right? And that's what most salespeople do. Until the last salesperson you see. This salesperson read this book. He starts asking you questions and develops a strong rapport with you. He asks questions like: How many windows are in the room that you'll be putting the TV in? Where are they and where do they shine? What's behind the wall where you plan on mounting the TV? What type of TV feed will you be plugging into the unit? It turns out that many of the products in your matrix won't work well in the daylight levels, and in order to get an acceptable picture, you'd have to redo the curtains and blinds; this eliminates half of your product matrix. The size of TV you are buying requires more data content from the signal source that you currently aren't paying for. The wall behind the TV has a refrigerator and electric stove that generate a lot of electrical interference that certain manufacturers on your list are susceptible to, which will cause poor picture quality. All this information was not available to you in the sales brochures you perused to create your product features matrix, and as it turns out, that missing information made a whole lot of difference.

This implementation and post-sales expertise is the margin of difference in dealing with excited prospects, along with your understanding of the role of the 3F's and the six universal needs. Using questions will also uncover additional pain points the prospect had not considered, making the difference between you and your competitors.

NEGOTIATING VS. SELLING

In sales, there is a high probability that you'll run into the individual who wants to negotiate various aspects of the sale. Negotiation is a risk mitigation strategy. This happens at the emotion courage, where the risk analysis of your adaptation plan occurs. Many businesses and business people have a policy of never paying the sticker price and negotiating everything, thus decreasing risk to its lowest possible level. This falls under the HAC phase of corrections, where a pause is initiated on the HAC dealing with courage satisfaction of the presented adaptation plan to start another HAC to modify the current HAC's efficacy by reducing risk through price reduction or specific terms. The goal of negations is to reduce the overall commitment of resources and capital to the project and thus mitigate risk. It is important to recognize that negotiation is about risk reduction. Lowering the overall commitment in resources, intrusion, and capital to an adaptation plan lowers the risks if the adaptation plan fails for any reason. The prospect wouldn't have moved on from excitement and cost if he or she couldn't afford the initial offered price. As proof of the point, when you reach the magic number with a prospect, they say done and commit. If it wasn't truly about resources (excitement), they would then go into trying to expand the guarantee, warranty, or other risk mitigating actions.

Negotiations require a different set of skills of the salesperson, skills that have been covered well in other books and are not within the defined scope of this book. The good news is that it is easy to spot the difference between a principle negotiator, someone who has a policy or is committed to the principle of never paying the full price, and someone who is looking for risk mitigation.

The risk mitigator is committed to the sale. Risk mitigators see themselves using the product and are excited. You can simply ask them, "Do you see yourself using this product?" or "Are you excited about this adaptation plan?" to separate the risk mitigation camp from the principle negotiators. Principle negotiators will say "maybe" or "depends" as a psychological ploy for leverage and risk mitigators will say "yes."

Negotiation only occurs at the courage emotional phase. However, there are times when the budget of the buyer is set with no latitude for adjustment. But, upon closer examination, even this scenario is still risk mitigation. The buyer has achieved confidence and selected you as the preferred vendor; they've reached excitement because they view your price to be close enough that negotiations could bring it in line. And budgets are never fixed, they are guidelines. They are arbitrary surveys of resources without including the value they will receive for their resource allocation. Budget allocation occurs before value is known. Think of it this way: whether you're talking to the CEO, president of the firm, or some other decision maker down the line – their decision matrix is to evaluate the cost differential of your price over their budget versus their second choice. The value you're offering is already tempting; internally they are trying to explain to someone else why they're not getting what they really want, the best option for their business. Choosing the second best is riskier and risk is a form of a threat. The prospect's reactor will be actively signaling them to move away from the second best so they will be struggling to overcome this internal dissonance while justifying the choice of going with the second best option.

If someone starts to negotiate elements of a sale, it is a clear sign that a prospect has reached the courage emotional phase in the Vetting phase of the tonal algorithm. One of the evaluative processes in the excitement emotional phase is the prospect's attempt to discover or determine what negative byproducts will occur with the implementation of your adaptation plan. To accept your adaptation plan, the prospect will have to break or change old habits, methods, processes, procedure, and policies. This involves or requires the expenditure of energy on their part and the natural desire to get the most performance for the least amount of effort that is ingrained, DNA encoded, in everyone; it's called the economy of motion. Essentially, they're trying to determine if the overall package of pain nullification combined with the costs of change are acceptable. So by negotiating the terms of the sale, the prospect is trying to minimize the negative byproducts of resource consumption in coping with change, thereby mitigating the risk.

Understanding how their Paradaptive Intelligence is geared to work will put you in control in these situations. Knowing that it is risk that is driving the equation, you have a couple of options available to you. You can use implementation as the focal point to add value by minimizing business intrusion and disruption. You can talk about warranty and satisfaction guarantees or create a custom solution to lower the risk. Or you could add value to the deal as it sits. You could offer to add low cost (to you) accessories that have a large perceived value to the prospect. By adding value to the deal, you alter the value to resource cost ratio, thus lowering the risk. Or you can use all three options, implementation, warranty/guarantee, and value adding accessories to cover a bigger spread. Car dealers are famous for this – if someone can't pull the trigger on a deal, they'll throw in a set of floor mats, free oil changes for the first year, chrome hubcaps, a set of raised-letter tires, or give you a seven-day return policy plus they'll deliver it to you so you don't have to come back again. All low-cost offerings to the car dealer, but a big deal of risk mitigators to the buyer.

The courage process of risk mitigators includes negotiations, most typically to bring the adaptation plan within parameters they have not shared with you, whether it is cost, time, opportunity costs, or other resources, or a combination thereof. It is a process they expect to conclude positively, because they are mentally committed to implementing your adaptation plan; otherwise they would not be investing time in a negotiation. To them, negotiations are just part of the process, like writing a purchase order, or an internal proposal. In some instances, as with governments, this will become the basis of requests for proposal for bids.

And then there's the negotiator who does it for... well, other reasons. Typically, negotiations for these individuals fulfill some other psychological need other than business pain point nullification. It may be a misplaced sense of competition, a way of prolonging the personal attention the sales cycle garners, or a need to set them apart as special by negotiating a package specific to them. Here the understanding and use of the six universal needs will be extremely useful, because a negotiator is trying to use the sale in a misplaced effort to satisfy one of their six universal needs.

What is interesting is that when a negotiation becomes part of the sales cycle, the tables are reversed. You, the salesperson, enter the Vetting phase of the Innovation emotional tonal algorithm because you now have a pain point, a negotiation standing between you and the payoff desire of your HAC to make a sale. Now you are in a position where you are evaluating different proposed packages (learning anticipation) in an attempt to determine if the prospect will be reasonable and leave any margin price-wise for you, if it will be enough (confidence), and finally that the cost of not doing the deal versus doing it are satisfactory (excitement) that you'll be able to sell the negotiated terms to your manager (courage) and pull the trigger when the prospect reaches the same point emotionally.

COMMODITY SALES AND THE 3 F'S

Commodity adaptation plans have a unique sales path on the complex emotion fear tonal progression. They basically have no negative emotion involvement from innovation acquisition. The prospect already accepts the necessity of having your product. As commodity implies, the prospect likely sees little difference between your product and the competition's. While there may actually be substantive and technical differences between your products and the competition, from the perception of the prospect, they may all perform the same function and are therefore undifferentiated. This means that both learning anticipation and confidence are already satisfied. So, commodity consumers arrive at your door step with the emotional stages of acceptance, learning anticipation, and confidence already satisfied. All that remains are excitement and courage, or in other words, the price and risk of doing business with you. There are only three ways of obtaining these orders: lowest price, lowest risk and relationship (the subject of Chapter 15). This fact is captured in a phrase coined to help the reader remember - The 3 F's: friendship, freebies and freedom from worry.

Friendship

If your product or adaptation plan is undifferentiated from the competitions', the value of your companionship and <u>friendship</u> will make the difference between getting a portion or all of their business. A salesperson should focus on building a relationship beyond that of standard business. Your competitors will all build strong business relationships with your prospects. You need to move beyond that and determine ways of creating friendships with prospects and clients. This is the subject of Chapter 16. All things being equal, the business will go to the salesman that the client cares most about. Remember every client has the need for connection, among other needs. They want to feel connected with you if you'll let them. The best way to accomplish this, you'll recall, is to become known to them emotionally. By sharing your feelings first, you'll create a pathway of communications. By reaching out first, you will trigger their basic need for connection, esteem, creativity, and meaning as well as the adaptor's bias for cooperation that wants to reciprocate these emotional needs.

Freebies

Freebies are a way of expressing all the promotions and discounts that the salesperson can bring to bear as enticement for placing an order. Again, all things being equal, the salesperson with the best financial inducements will probably obtain the majority of the sales. Freebies also have an element of satisfying esteem needs from the six universal needs. Special deals make people feel special. There is evidence that strong relationships can impact the price; strong relationships allow those who enjoy them to charge more than the market low bidder, allowing for more profitable business.

Freedom from Worry

Freedom from worry is probably the largest and most flexible of the 3 F's for the salesperson. Companies and salespeople always promote their "service" as a way of separating themselves from the competition. This misses the point completely. Remember, your clients are driven by fear when relying on a third party — they are not concerned with service; they're totally consumed with relieving psychological pain caused by fear in securing a commodity product from a third party. Worry is a mild form a fear. Service only will appeal to them if it relieves their fear that your commodity adaptation plan — "buy from me" — will not add more issues, problems or concerns than the problem they are attempting to solve. Warranties, guarantees, and return policies help to address these fears. Price is not always the sole determinant of getting an order; terms of delivery can be just as significant, which is why terms of delivery are rolled up into this F. Clients want pain relief from fear, so you need to speak to them in terms of how these policies and offerings reduce their worry.

RETAIL SALES

Retail sales is similarly aligned with commodity sales. By self-presenting at a retail location, the consumer is showing that they are already at acceptance level emotionally, whether they're considering fast food or fashion clothing. By examining the price and features of the products on your shelves, they will move themselves from learning anticipation as they inventory your store to see if you have what they want, to confidence they're in the right place as they find things that apply to their issue, to excitement if the ticketed price is lower than their opportunity cost, and finally to courage as they pull it off the rack and take it to the register to purchase, secure that your return policy reduces risk to within limits.

The reason that retail sales is aligned with commodity products is that while they may be searching for unique items, specific to a vendor, consumers may also be seeking commodity products. Take clothes, for example. In some instances, the person is looking for a shirt that meets all their emotional stages in the Vetting phase that no one else has. Or they could be searching for a particular brand and item that most clothing stores sell, like Carhart or Levi.

There has been an interesting transformation in the emotions of retail since the end of World War II, primarily starting in the early fifties as industry shifted from war material production back to consumer goods. *Caveat emptor*, Latin for "buyer beware," has been the legal standard for several millennia and is rooted in common law from England, upon which our legal system is based. This legal principle is out of touch because it hails from a time when the consumer could actually see, feel, handle, and test the actual merchandise they intended to purchase prior to the act of purchase, where open markets were the norm. There was no packaging to be concerned with. All could be known about a product before money departed the consumer's hands.

After World War II, manufacturers had learned a thing or two about preparing materials for shipment during the war effort. With willing hands on the receiving end in the military to assemble products, the manufacturer could focus on packaging that emphasized efficiency, uniformity, and density rather than completed working products. In the post World War II era, the trend started of showing only an assembled floor or demo model of the product for the customer to examine. When the consumer went to make the purchase, he was given a boxed product pulled from the shelves which he took home, unpackaged, and completed any assembly required. They never actually tested or handled the product they actually bought, just a similar model. This became true for foods also, as prepackaged food no longer allowed consumers to directly handle the food they intended to buy, except for produce. In order to decrease the fear factor in buying goods in such a manner, warranties, guarantees, and return policies had to be adopted by manufacturers and honored by vendors to get the consuming public to buy products unseen.

Today, little is sold today that consumers can touch, feel, test, or operate except bulk goods, produce, and garments. This has an important bearing on all salespeople because it sets the cultural norm, raising the crossbar for all things being sold, including your product or service. Post-purchase expectations of products in terms of reversing the sale or exchanging the sale have risen in the consumer's mind as an expected right, reversing the *caveat emptor* standard of some three thousand years. This has only been reinforced by the advent of the internet. In order for consumers to purchase from a picture and description on a screen, they must feel that if it is not as pictured or described, they can get their money back. And if they don't, they now have the freedom and means to post or rate your service. This vendor rating practice, which started with eBay, has moved the internet to the forefront of consumer decision-making patterns. The Yellow Pages can no longer compete with the internet because of the lack of ratings, comments, histories, and critiques. They call this information "added value," but in reality, it is emotional content. Ratings are about feelings — the buyer is free to determine on his own what a four-and-a-half-star rating means in terms of risk (courage), or a one-and-a-half without criteria or agreed upon guidelines. Comments can tell a shopper about how obstacles were introduced or if a non-negotiable boundary was crossed; histories tell how trustworthy (a complex emotion of joy) a vendor is; critiques are a litany of corrective signal.

PROMOTIONS? – MAYBE

The marketing and sales profession has a term, promotions, that has a generalized meaning for any extra marketing or sales activity designed to create additional incentive for consumers to purchase the firm's products. But the term promotions, as currently used, lacks any precision, and is exactly what the Paradaptive Intelligence model dispels. It is important for salespeople to understand the correct usage of the word promotions and understand exactly how it fits within the Paradaptive Intelligence model.

Not all promotions are targeted at the same emotion satisfaction stage in the Vetting phase of the Innovation algorithm. Among other things, advertising can be targeted with a message to satisfy the emotion acceptance; it can be used to explain the product to people with latent or acknowledged pain points to satisfy learning anticipation. In addition, advertising can also be targeted to educate potential customers of your product's ability to solve specific pain points making it an exemplar in memory and will be brought forward to the adaptor in the learning anticipation emotional phase. Sampling, where product is given to prospects for the purpose of demonstrating its efficacy to solve problems, are targeted at the emotion confidence. Discounting, where prices are reduced, things are put on "sale" are aimed at the emotion excitement where cost resources are calculated against the pain point intensity. Promotions where value is added to a product, like giveaway contests of like or different products or experiences, whether it's a temporary price reduction, two for one, buy three get one free, or what-have-you, limited offers of warranty extensions, or free additional products or implements, limited time offer for free 20% extra product, etc., are targeted at the emotion of courage and are designed to reduce the risk in purchasing.

It is important for the salesperson to understand what each of these devices are designed to do so they are used at the proper time and in the right place in the sales cycle of the Vetting phase of the Innovation algorithm. The proper term for this genre of these sales devices should be more properly labeled consumer incentives, rather than be named promotions which has its own, very specific function, including an advertising element.

POINT OF VIEW & FIELD OF STUDY

At the beginning of this section, Section II, consumer behavior and sales were described as reciprocal aspects to the same event because one can't occur without the other and both processes are governed by the same Paradaptive Intelligence Network operating principles. This can be broken down further into two perspectives and how that relates to how we study business topics. One perspective is sales. An example of how the study of the same emotion changes with perspective is acceptance. In sales, marketing is the field of study that examines the emotions of learning anticipation, confidence, excitement, and courage from the sales perspective. On the other side, consumer behavior, the field of study of critical thinking is the study of the emotion of acceptance. In critical thinking, assumptions, presumptions, and foundations to perceptions are examined as support to the definition of a problem, issue, or in terms of Paradaptive Intelligence, pain points. Another example is finance. Finance is the field of study that examines the emotion of excitement from the business perspective. Financing studies the value of money in relation to time, opportunity costs, and the conversion of money to other forms of assets. The field of Economics is the study of learning anticipation, excitement, confidence, and courage from the consumer side. This concept is expressed in Figure 12.4.

FIGURE 12.4
Point of View & Field of Study

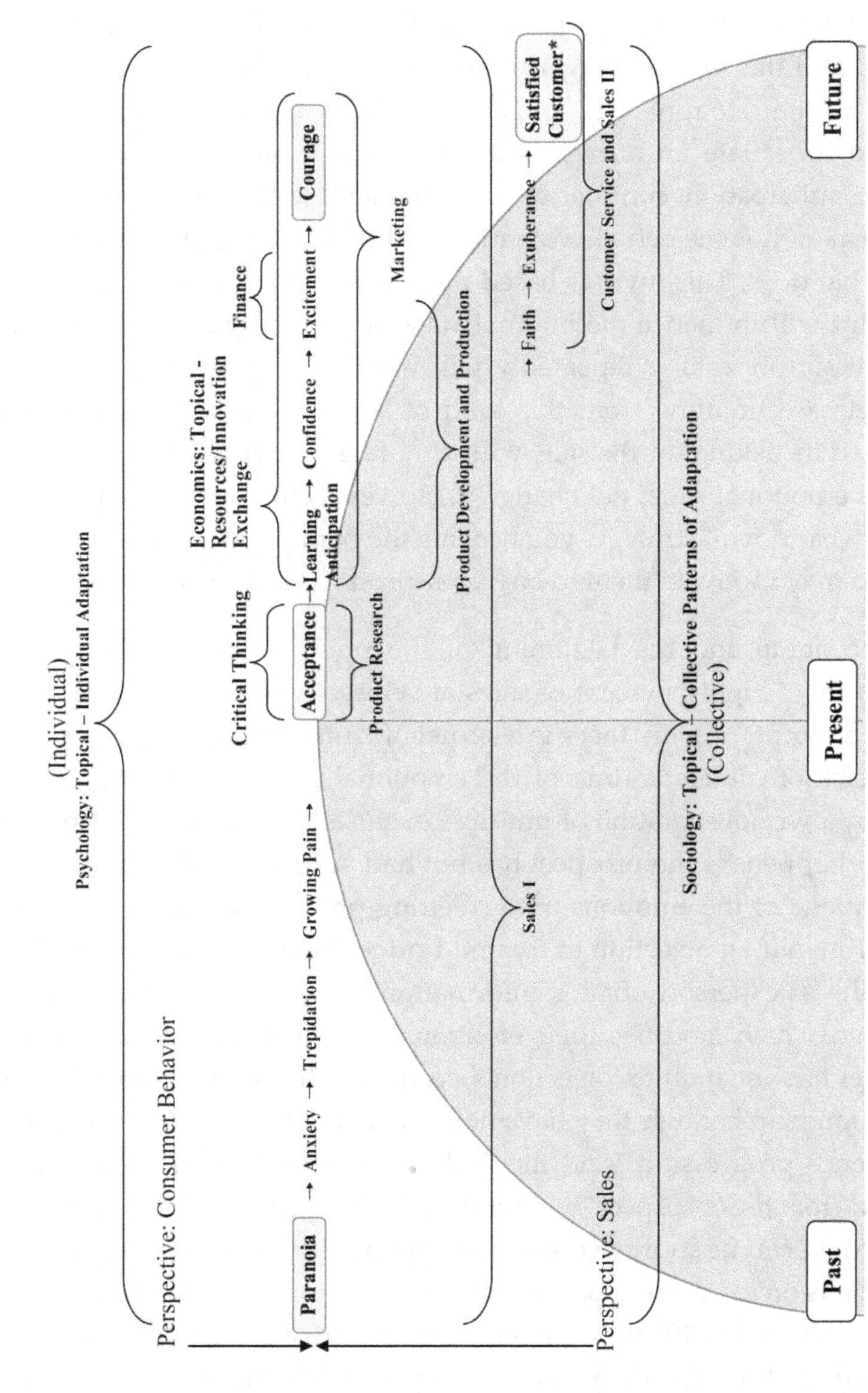

(Individual)
Psychology: Topical – Individual Adaptation

Perspective: Consumer Behavior

Paranoia → Anxiety → Trepidation → Growing Pain →

Critical Thinking

Acceptance →Learning → Confidence → Excitement → Courage

Economics: Topical - Resources/Innovation Exchange

Finance

Anticipation

Product Research

Marketing

Product Development and Production

→ Faith → Exuberance →

Satisfied Customer*

Customer Service and Sales II

Sales I

Sociology: Topical – Collective Patterns of Adaptation
(Collective)

Perspective: Sales

Past   Present   Future

MYTHS OF CLOSING AND OTHER NONSENSE

Multiple Closings Attempts

Sales lore holds that it takes X number of closing attempts of asking the prospect for the sale before a sale will be consummated. An example of this type of thinking was listed below the title of the last chapter. This puts the focus on the act of asking for the sale, as if this is what triggers a prospect to buy the product. While it is true that asking for the sale forces the prospect to clarify his internal emotional position in order to formulate an answer, the movement from one emotion level, whether learning anticipation, confidence, or excitement, to the next is not caused by asking the question, it is the actual evaluation of the material and its ability to nullify pain points that does. This myth is based upon the belief that the salesperson's action at this point will influence the internal state of the prospect relative to their product and that simply asking repeatedly will wear down the prospect. The internals of prospects are immune from this kind of 'wear' action. Remember the questions contained in 'asking for the sale' will stimulate the prospect to tally and *evaluate* his internal emotional state, not change it. However, by repeatedly pestering the client with a 'wear down' strategy, you become the pain point, which in only the best-case scenario may motivate them to buy your product, just to get rid of you.

Like the quote and the beginning of the previous chapter, some authors have claimed that "Eighty percent of sales are closed after the fifth call or after the fifth closing attempt." Again, there is a kernel of truth contained here, but because there was a lack of understanding of the emotional processes and the five emotions it requires, a wry observation of multiple events occurring was misinterpreted. What actually happens is the prospect has not had sufficient pain point nullification and is still at one of the emotions in the Vetting phase. They are not yet at courage, so they throw out an objection to try and bridge the gap to satisfy an emotion. At this point, the salesperson obtains information to the 'objection' and relays it to the customer, which modifies their emotional state further towards courage. But the customer has yet another 'objection' because he doesn't fully see himself using your adaptation plan because they have not satisfied the next emotion of the Paradaptive Intelligence progression. And the cycle repeats itself until all of the emotions are satisfied for the prospect to commit. This cycle of "objections" and further information can be shortened substantially or eliminated entirely if you focus your sales efforts on identifying pain points in the customer, and presenting your product in terms of pain nullification combined with a strong implementation plan to create a solid adaptation plan delivered in a way to satisfy the emotions of the Paradaptive Intelligence Network.

Multiple visits may be required to research and identify the pain points to be nullified, but this has nothing to do with closing. Instead, this has to do with pain point identification for nullification. Customers quite often know they have pain points but don't know exactly where they reside in their organization or operations. They just feel the symptoms. It may take you several visits to obtain information on exactly what the pain points are and how to fix them. Or, as occurs frequently in multiple-sign-off sales where different persons of interest have to approve or bless the sale in some manner, each person of interest could generate multiple visits to research their individual pain points begetting presentations of pain nullification.

It is interesting that the observation of five visits figures prominently in this "law of business." Is it coincidental that there are five emotional phases of the Vetting phase that must be accomplished before a sale can take place? Doubtful. It is more likely that most salespeople don't know what they're doing and the customer is directing them through the hurdles of the five emotional phases they must pass through.

Objections

Generally speaking, what have been mistakenly identified as objections which create callbacks and which also count as closing attempts are actually the prospect telling you what emotional phase you failed to move them through. In general, objections occur because insufficient pain points were nullified or the salesman is attempting to get the client to commit to a sale while the client is still emotionally somewhere else in the Vetting phase algorithm. Improper technique and understanding of what you're doing does not constitute a closing attempt. Under this terminology, asking for the sale is a closing rather than the nullification of a pain point, which is completely wrong. Objections are most often expressions of efficacy, cost, or risk. When the prospect offers up an "objection," he is asking you for rebuttal, because in most cases, he has no perspective and is relying on your expertise to inform him whether your product will nullify a specific pain point, or whether the cost in question is valid, overestimated, or inconsequential. If they weren't asking for rebuttal and reframing the cost or efficacy, why would they voice it to you? If it was a real, clearly defined cost, they would just include it in their internal evaluation of your adaptation plan, performed during the excitement emotion phase, without ever uttering it to you.

Remember, the game is rigged in the favor of the salesperson in that internally the prospect is seeking pleasure, and nullifying pain is pleasurable. They want pleasure and buying your product would bring joy to them. So an objection is not them trying to shoot you down, it is a plea for help to resolve a nullification issue from the confidence phase or the internal math of the excitement or courage phase so they can move to satisfy the emotion of courage which will give them a strong pulse of joy.

Getting the Prospect to Say Yes Three Times

There is an old sales truism that you need to get the prospect to say "yes" three times during a sales presentation in order to secure the sale. As with a lot of these sales lore sayings, there is a kernel of truth to it. As we just learned, there are five key emotional phases that must be negotiated: acceptance, learning anticipation, confidence, excitement, and courage. So, saying "yes," three times comes close to equaling the five closings of the emotional phases that must be achieved. In fact, an argument could be made that the three yeses referred to in the truism is describing saying "yes" to confidence, excitement, and courage. The presumption of this sales lore is the idea that saying "yes" equates to three pain nullifications. This may or may not have been true, making a prospect say "yes" about the beneficial aspects of your product. Agreeing that it's beneficial doesn't necessarily nullify the prospect's pain, but often enough, the three beneficial aspects just may be pain nullifiers to which the client said "yes." Just like a blind squirrel that occasionally finds a nut, someone using this method would occasionally stumble onto a situation where the "yeses" did correspond to pain nullification and the truism would be reinforced with a sale. This is like gambling; you only have to win one out of every X number of tries to think you're lucky. But, most likely, this is referring to the triangulation required in the confidence stage which requires three points of corroboration that the adaptation plan you are presenting will nullify all of the pain points. This truism, more than any other, underscores the need for a salesperson to understand how the mind works and what it seeks so that he or she isn't reduced to the luck of a blind squirrel.

AIDA

This acronym stands for Attention, Interest, Desire and Action. This acronym has been bandied about to describe the sales process by academics in business schools to the detriment of unsuspecting students for several generations now. This is another prime example of how having an improper understanding, vocabulary, and model of mind processes can lead to vague and useless tidbits that sound like they really would be helpful in the real world of sales. AIDA is a bit like describing changing the tire on a car in the following manner: Remove the spare, remove the tire, mount the new tire, and stow the old tire. While this captures the broad concept, it doesn't really tell you anything useful like stopping car on a flat, level surface out of the way of other traffic, or where the spare tire is. Nor does it tell you where to place the jack, how to operate it, or other nuggets like loosening the tire nuts before you jack up the car, and so on.

As this chapter clearly defined, the Human Action Cycle is the basic process of the mind. It cycles through five emotions that are satisfied in a specific order in a feed-forwards feedback-driven process through the emotional tonal algorithm. Each emotion has a specific requirement that must be met. This totally invalidates the AIDA concept. In the interest of recycling, the following is offered to give new meaning to the now defunct AIDA concept: Avoid Insipid and Defunct Acronyms.

13

PAIN POINTS AND
RIGHT TRACK/WRONG TRACK

"If you don't know where you're going, then you might not get there."
Yogi Berra

We discussed at length finding and using pain points of prospects to further the sale of pain nullifying adaptation plans, but it's time to take a closer look at the anatomy of pain points so that we can further understand and identify them. Let's review what we know so far. Pain points derive from the corrective signal portion of the six basic emotions. Fear is the leading corrective signal that salespeople deal with, followed closely by anger. As a corrective signal, fear tells the brain that something is threatening the body, urging it to remove the body from its present predicament. This could be competition, regulation, changes in economy, innovation, or other factors. The reactor, which is generating the corrective signal fear, is calling for a change in venue or behavior; this also means continued progress on the current path will lead to undesirable outcomes that will be detrimental to the body or self.

The second leading emotion driving pain points in business is anger. This is expressed more often as "frustration," a mild form of anger. A business owner knows that he has an inefficiency that creates an obstacle from him or his business to performing to its potential. The corrective signal anger is calling for the business owner to push back with aggression to change someone's behavior due to a boundary violation or remove an obstacle from the environment. We've also learned that the corrective signals, what we've been calling pain points, are comprised of three elements: agitation expression, basic emotion, and complex emotion.

Occasionally, a salesperson will run into a pain point driven by sadness (loss) or disgust (unwholesomeness). Because these are easy to identify and don't really conform to the main drivers of business, we will not delve into them. Besides, once you've mastered the techniques for understanding your emotion system and put it to work for you, you'll easily be able to understand the rare situations driven by sadness and disgust and how to handle them.

THREE TYPES OF PAIN POINTS

There are three types of pain points: Latent, Acknowledged, and Excitement. These three types of mental pain are driven by two factors in the business domain, acceptance and expectations. Acceptance is a measure of the prospect's attitude towards the pain point, and more importantly, what he or she accepts. Expectations occur when the prospect has entered a HAC with the desirable outcome (motive) of relieving the pain. The process of forming an action plan to achieve pain nullification will cause the prospect to form a set of expectations. These expectations will be based on memories and information that are applicable and available, or they will be newly fabricated by imagination because a plan is needed to move forward with pain nullification.

As we examine the three types of pain points, we'll use the common business activity of invoicing to illustrate their differences.

Latent

Latent pain points may not be immediately apparent to the prospect. The operative word here is "immediately." In our example of invoicing, this would be a prospect that is handwriting receipts on triplicate invoicing forms. This was state of the art when they entered business several decades ago. He has a nice, quiet, little business servicing the same customers he has had for the last twenty years. His business just putters along and he sees no real reason to change.

But when you probe a little deeper, you learn that he knows it takes a lot of time to hand write the invoices because he has to enter the customer information every time, even though they're the same customers over and over; he makes errors in calculation because the phone rings or he gets interrupted by employees when he's preparing the invoices. Oftentimes, they don't invoice for small, miscellaneous parts used in the service they provide because it's just too problematic to list and price all of it. Because they don't itemize on their invoices, inventory has to be manually surveyed regularly to keep necessary parts or materials on hand; when an error is made in the calculations, he absorbs the loss; additionally, employees spend additional time and labor to tally sales by hand for bookkeeping purposes. When that's done, the forms must be manually filed in a filing cabinet. When there is a question or dispute about a billing matter, the invoice must be searched for manually only to find that in many instances the invoice is misfiled or lost.

All of these would be considered pain points in any other business because they are spending labor hours over internal documentation, rather than spending those labor hours on producing revenue and profits. The client is actually aware of the deficits and knows full well what it's costing his business. But he chooses to continue to do business this way and ignore those costs. He may tell you this is because he just doesn't know a better way or that he just doesn't want to change things. Let's break those rationales down.

He doesn't know a better way because he hasn't looked. He hasn't looked because changes in this phase of the business have proven difficult in the past. The key word here is past. He is not living or operating his business in the present because he is letting past instances and fears cloud or prejudice his reasoning. But the most telling point of this whole scenario is that, and this is the common element to all latent pain prospects, rather than recognize his problems, he has chosen to accept and embrace those things that are giving him pain. By accepting and embracing these pain points, the prospect has tacitly acknowledged, or accepted (acceptance), the presence of a problem and the problems it spawns.

But one of the divine aspects of using the Paradaptive Intelligence in your sales activities is that, once you've identified which emotional phase the prospect is occupying on the fear scale, you know exactly how to speak to that prospect. In the scenario above, the prospect has accepted pain over pain nullification. Your communication direction to him should be something like this, "You know, you don't have to accept (the aforementioned issues). There are other ways to accomplish what you want to have happen and it may just make sense for you to explore them." This has a two-fold effect of indirectly relieving prospects of their present commitment to their course, and it appeals to their adaptors, which wants to learn; this is the source of curiosity in all humans.

Acknowledged

This is a prospect that knows and accepts the presence of a problem and is best summed up as a prospect who is saying, "There's got to be a better way." These prospects will be in the learning anticipation phase. Literally, they want to learn about the better ways. In our invoice writing scenario, this would be a prospect that has a computer system for creating invoices and receipts, but it may only dump to a customer database but doesn't tie into inventory, sales department totals, or other financial records. The prospect is familiar with the function of computerized invoicing, but it is badly outdated and greater distribution of data among other employees and departments is needed.

These prospects may not have formed a HAC for pain nullification. They may be stuck without the ability to form a HAC for several reasons. This occurs when the problem is ill-defined to them. They may not fully understand the origins of the pain point(s), so forming a HAC is out of the question. Or they perceive that these issues are emanating from a source in their business landscape not under their jurisdiction, control, or influence. They may feel that they lack expertise, such as with computers or accounting, to research and explore pain nullification scenarios. Since they have no background or particular expertise in this area, hence no grounding or experience based on reality, these prospects will use their imagination to create expectations as to what and how a new system would operate. This is where you hear phrases from prospects that sound like this, "I imagine it'll be easy for you to tie all this into…." or "I'm sure you'll be able to do X, Y, and Z, right?"

This is where your expertise as a salesperson comes in. As a salesperson with knowledge in the areas and functions your product touches, you can guide them through the process of evaluating the adaptation plan you are presenting. Knowing the specifications of your product will allow you to show them to which departments the new invoicing system could distribute invoice data. You'll be able to explain to them that all the different departments that want invoicing data all use different software and computer systems that may not be connected currently or play nicely with other systems in order to move them from their imagination-based expectations to more realistic goals, unless the entire company agrees to a single data system platform or a custom programmed system.

The point is to remember that acknowledged pain point prospects require knowledge and expertise. This knowledge and expertise you possess as a salesperson will allow you to not only highlight business pain points in the most personal way to the prospect, but also allow you to present and explain in your adaptation plan with the necessary details.

Excited

Excited prospects are obviously at the excitement phase. They have determined that there are potential solutions available in the marketplace that will nullify their pain points, and they are excited to make the problem(s) go away. They've evaluated which solution has the most pain nullification potential with the least amount of undesirable side effects and use of business resources (costs). These are prospects that contact you seeking your product. Initially, they may appear to be seeking a features and benefit presentation, but they have done their own research and traversed the confidence phase by themselves based on their findings, meaning their expectations are grounded in reality. In the invoice scenario, this is the customer who presents with an outdated invoicing system but has a laundry list of features available in the marketplace that he finds desirable and has selected your product.

However, just because their expectations are reality based doesn't mean the prospects have expertise in all the phases of the action plan. There may very well be issues surrounding their pain points that they may not have considered. As a sales professional, you must sniff out these gaps in their understanding to ensure the selection from your stable of the best products for their situation, budget, and business circumstances. In addition, you need to align their post-purchase expectation, otherwise their imaginations will be the source of critique as to whether they purchased wisely.

One of the biggest points a salesperson must understand about customers that contact a salesperson at the excited phase is that their information is usually incomplete. Aside from the aforementioned gap of acceptance, the prospect's excitement is probably not based on the full information. The prospect has probably obtained pricing information on your product only and may not be aware of the implementation costs. They've obtained excitement based on only half the adaptation plan – the product or service process. Their evaluation has not considered the cost of implementation. Before just blithely signing a contract with them, you need to make sure that they examine the true cost of a full adaptation plan. Having examined the three levels of business pain points, we can now create a matrix of how an excited prospect will present to a salesperson (Figure 13.1).

FIGURE 13.1

	Latent	Acknowledged	Excited
Accepts:	Pain	Problem	Problem
Expectations:	None	Imagination	Reality (?)

THREE BASIC GATEGORIES OF BUSINESS PAIN POINTS

In more specific terms, there are three main types of pain points encountered in business: increasing revenues, increasing profits, and decreasing uncertainty. All of these are control issues. Healthy businesses constantly work all three to improve the survivability of the company. But not only do these categories work at the macro level of the business, they also work at the micro level, down to the department and section level within a division. At the heart of every pain point is a process of the company. The human reasoning behind every process and business activity is what creates pain points. And as we have found out through Paradaptive Intelligence, every human activity that interacts with the outside world generates an emotion feedback signal. So, being able to understand the types of pain points that you're faced with as a salesperson will create another communication opportunity for you.

Increasing Revenues

Increasing revenues emphasizes the notion of increasing the overall volume of sales for the business entity. This focuses on the external contacts of the enterprise with other businesses or individuals. There are two ways to accomplish this: increasing the sales volume of existing customers or adding new customers. Of the two, expanding the volume of existing customers is the easier and less expensive route because the client's contacts have already been profiled for facial emotion recognition (Mirror Neuron System) and they "know you," producing better communications than with someone coming in off the street; their expectations have been aligned with the reality of your product; they know your product can help (learning anticipation); they know you can deliver enough of what they need to make a difference (confidence); and they are familiar with the costs of doing business with you (excitement), which is to make their pain point(s) go away. All of these are residual benefits from their last trip down the Vetting phase of the Innovation emotional tonal algorithm with you. So they have no fear of placing an order with you again (courage).

In fact, at this point, the dominant retained emotion for your clients is joy. They were successful in their last dealings with you, so their reactors are telling them to move closer to you and repeat the process for greater joy. This internal alignment towards you is your advantage against competitor intrusion on this client. By properly utilizing emotions guided by your knowledge of the Paradaptive Intelligence Network, you have hardened your clients towards competitors. Their adaptors, which drive them to learn and serves as their source of curiosity, will want to take a peek at competitors, but they will have to overcome the attachment of joy they have affiliated with you.

Increasing revenue by adding new customers is a much more expensive proposition. With new customers, you will have to expend greater time, resources, and energy to synchronize your Mirror Neuron System, align expectations, and to move them through the emotional phases of the Vetting phase. In addition, there will always be new prospects that you invest in that will never pan out, and thus represent a complete loss of your efforts.

Increasing Profit

Increasing profits focuses internally on the activities and process of the enterprise. There are only two elements to the operating expenses of a business: personnel and material. Increasing profits means focusing on the efficiency of each element. For personnel, the unit of measure of efficiency is productivity, or how much work each person can put out, and striving towards increasing that amount of work. The unit of measure for materials is consumption. This includes overhead expenses that consume money for upkeep, taxes, utilities, etc., as well as commodities and raw materials consumed in operations and production. The less money utilized to produce a product output increases profits. Productivity and consumption are both equal opportunity employers of pain points for prospects.

Uncertainty

Businesses do not operate in a vacuum. They operate in a complex environment that is constantly changing. These changes produce uncertainty for both small and large business as factors and forces beyond their control impact their operations. Examples of factors that create uncertainty include government regulation, competition, technological advancements, and the economy. Being able to mitigate these factors will reduce the fear level, hence the pain points of a business. The most efficient companies are the ones most able to weather changes produced in the uncontrolled areas surrounding your prospect's business. Intuitively, they understand money that is being spent on internal inefficiencies could and should be spent on increasing revenue and coping with business environmental changes and actions.

Insurance, a form of uncertainty mitigation, is one such form of the myriad of financial products companies can obtain to reduce their fear in uncertain times. Intelligence, or information, is another form of risk mitigation, which can range from political donations to industry publications that can keep a prospect abreast of pertinent changes.

PAIN INTENSITY

Up to this point, we've spoken of business-related pain as if all pain is perceived equally. This is indeed not true. Different companies may perceive the intensity of this business pain differently, even though the issues are identical. Just as every individual's ability to register and tolerate pain differs, the same can be said of businesses, which are comprised of humans with varying capacities for pain. So, collectively, a business' pain tolerance will be a weighted average of its employee's capacities. Intensity of business pain can be relative to other problems occurring within a business. Just like a person suffering a heart attack may not notice or complain to the arriving paramedics about a blister on his big toe, so too for businesses. If there are major internal problems to the company, the adaptation plan you're proposing to correct the blister may not be readily embraced because their focus is elsewhere. This is not to say that the divisional director, department head, section chief or manager that you may be dealing with doesn't feel the pain of the blister within their department. Also, this doesn't negate a company's willingness to deal with the smaller issue if the cost is relatively low and implementation requirements are minimal. Just don't be surprised that identical issues that your product and adaptation plan address do not elicit the same response from firm to firm.

As stated above, a business's pain intensity will be a weighted average of all the individuals within an organization. This is described as weighted because management, which controls and directs resources, will undoubtedly have a greater say on which problems and pain points hurt the most. However, line workers can have an important and crucial bearing on how business pain points are perceived within the organization. Business pain points can lead to employee discontentment, which will manifest itself as either decreased productivity, employee turnover, or both. So management may be forced to deal with a problem they consider to be insignificant because the burden of the byproducts of employee discontentment may be intolerably high. This is easy to remember if you keep in mind that all employees have Paradaptive Intelligence Network which will signal them to move away from anything that creates fear, disgust, sadness, and anger in their reactors, so ultimately any manager not attending to employees' environments will be held accountable to byproducts of the collective employees' reactors.

Doctors use a simple pain scale of 1-10 to rate a patient's perception of pain. Why not do the same with your prospects? Ask them to rate the importance of the pain points that you've identified and amplified in the most personal way. This will have two benefits to you: 1) it will either help illuminate to the customer the importance of exploring your adaptation plan, or 2) it will identify prospects that have low sale potential so that you can retract and concentrate on areas and prospects with greater potential.

It is recommended that you use a scale of 1 (least painful) to 6 (most painful). The six-point scale is recommended because it has no middle point on the scale, which forces the prospects to shade their responses towards really painful or not so painful so that the sales person can determine just how motivated they are to fix the problem, and the likelihood of a sale. It's also recommended that you keep such scale questioning to a minimum, using it only when you're unsure of the intensity of the clients' corrective signals.

PAINSCAPE

Now that we've examined the three types of pain points, the three basic categories of business pain points, and pain intensity, we can combine all these elements to form a map or a painscape of a prospect's perception of their business pain points. Figure 13.2 gives an example.

You can expand on this concept, which may need specificity for large complex sales with multiple sign-offs, or this may be overkill for a simple sale of a non-complex problem. But it is interesting to note that all sales eagles do this for every prospect, whether formally as above or quickly and simply in their heads. Doing so allows you to organize your sales presentation to best effect.

Figure 13.2

Company XYZ's Painscape

Increased Revenues		Increased Profits		Decreased Uncertainty
Existing	New	Personnel	Materials	Specific
Excited	Acknowledged	Latent	Acknowledged	Legislation on raw materials pending
I = 4	I = 2	I = 5	I = 6	I = 2

Intensity on scale of 1 – 6.

RIGHT TRACK/WRONG TRACK

Now that we have explored the notion of pain points created by fear and anger in prospects, we can now examine a segment of Peil's Emotional Feedback System model called the right track/wrong track. Humans have a unique ability among mammals, thanks to our enhanced cognitive and reasoning powers, to ignore feedback being provided by the Paradaptive Intelligence Network internally. It is this unique ability to ignore our internal signaling that contributes to our humanity. The interplay between the reactor and the adaptor also produces one of two responses: the right track or wrong track. In the feedback loop of the Paradaptive Intelligence, responses from the reactor are sent to the adaptor, which decides to act upon the input or ignore it, which in turn can either mollify the reactor or excite it to a higher level of urgency if the corrective signal is continually ignored.

Peil identifies two tracks that an individual will follow based on how he or she responds to the internal emotional signals presented by the reactor and its interplay with the conductor, which strives to make the individual the best that he or she can be. Built in to the model is the presumption that emotions exist for a reason. They are there to help individuals survive, grow, and succeed. To ignore them is to court peril. Yet, we have noted there are instances where ignoring emotional signals may be necessary. So there is no hard or fast rule as to which emotions to act upon and which to ignore. There are trends however, and these trends set individuals upon two distinct paths – right and wrong tracks. You receive emotional feedback to guide you long term to the right, proper, and healthy actions that will lead you to your greatest productivity and happiness. But, by continually ignoring what your reactor is signaling, you'll end up on the wrong track (Figure 13.4). In the long term, by generally following the emotional feedback from your reactor, you will end up on the right track (Figure 13.3). The Paradaptive Intelligence Network has been fine-tuned by countless generations to get you on and keep you on the right track to achieve whatever goals and motives you set.

The thought behind the right track/wrong track concept is that emotional signal action/non-action has consequences and has a cumulative effect upon individuals. And, as we have proven over and over in this book, businesses, which are comprised of humans, will affect the experience of the collective outcome of their constituent parts. An example of this is one bad decision can lead to another. We've all seen or experienced the scenario where a bad decision is made. Business people, like everyone else, have imperfect and incomplete knowledge. We are always making decisions with imperfect knowledge and we do the best we can. Sometimes we guess wrong despite our best efforts to produce a desirable outcome. Only hindsight can determine this outcome, and it will be signaled back to the individual as an emotion

Life On The Right Track*

When we can decode the messages of our feelings, the reactor helps us learn *the right stuff*. Just as pain and confusion characterizes the wrong track, the right track is marked by pleasure and purpose--- for nature not only pushes us away from ignorance, it pulls us toward our rightful destiny! Tremendous rewards are reaped when individuals discover the right track and support one another in staying upon it. With the emotional compass, people from all walks of life find new levels of purpose, creative motivation, tolerance, integrity, connection, honor, courage, and compassion. Group conflict, competition, and infighting gives way to camaraderie and win-win cooperation, creativity, synergy, loyalty, prosperity, and success.

Using multi-purpose emotional guidance is the actual "normal" state as defined by nature. Anything less than inner unity and outer cooperative community is less than we all deserve---and *we feel it in our gut that this is true*. For every painful wrong-track confused condition, there awaits a natural, meaningful, pleasurable right-track counterpart condition and destiny:

- These individual and group results are the natural predictable patterns of right track living. Right track living creates "winners", success stories, and self-actualized human beings. Just like the negative outcomes, the positive outcomes are not due to *genetic character qualities*; they are the *natural result of guided learning from the emotional sense*. These are the outcomes of learned *life strategies* that can be instilled under the right track conditions within virtually anyone. They are the hallmarks and rewards of *emotional intelligence---and they are every human's birthright*.

FIGURE 13.3

as to how you're performing relative to the desirable outcome you're pursuing through a HAC. But what can happen is the good choice (you thought) turns out to be a bad decision. Rather than back up and rethink your situation based on new information and your Paradaptive Intelligence feedback, you double down and proceed with an even riskier endeavor to make up for the losses of the first mistaken choice. Interestingly enough, this type of scenario can sometimes be driven by the Paradaptive Intelligence Network itself. Another type of instance of this is when you make a mistake and create another when you deny that a mistake was made.

Loss, one of the four basic corrective signals, signals you to seek replacement for what you lost. In the situation above, one bad decision (with the benefit of hindsight) can trigger one of the complex forms of loss that drives you to seek replacement of that which was lost, even if this means an even riskier move than what created the loss in the first place. It takes good judgment, which in turn is based upon experience salted away in memory by a properly functioning ego, to know when to ignore loss's impulses and when to cut your losses and run.

By constantly ignoring your reactor's emotional signaling, you set yourself up for bad decisions which lead to a tainted reservoir of experiences to draw upon when making future decisions. We all have seen or experienced these types of episodes or know of an individual that can never seem to do the right thing or get his or her life straightened out.

Another aspect of this is that a negative feedback cycle is initiated. When threats, obstacles, losses, and aversions are not dealt with, the reactor becomes more and more interruptive to force the adaptor to deal with the pain point. This means the quality and quantity of reasoning that go into an adaptation plan suffers, creating less and less effective solutions to which the reactor responds to even more forcefully.

Conversely, good decision making by predominately observing your Paradaptive Intelligence Network's internal signaling, gets you set upon the right track because your adaptation plan formulation is based upon a reservoir of proven strategies and experiences and the process is not interrupted by the reactor looking to enforce its primary bias.

Right track/wrong track can be a very selective process, though. Wrong track decisions in one phase of life does not mean a person will make wrong track decisions in all aspects of life. A quick example is the brilliant businessperson who is fabulous in the business arena, but a total wreck at home, or vice versa. These differences can be due to the reservoir of experiences for each distinctive area.

Life On The Wrong Track*

- Without understanding the teacher, humans *unconsciously* allow the disruptions of the reactor to affect their mind in ways that leave bad attitudes, and unsuccessful beliefs and strategies---*emotional baggage*---which brings further pain. Learning occurs, but it is mostly conditioned instead of conscious, and instinctive reactions become disempowering habits. In short, without the *evaluative* guidance of the Reactor, we can learn the *wrong stuff!*

- When we spend too much time on the wrong track tremendous detriments befall us, our families, our social and professional groups, and ultimately, our world. Without the internal compass mind and body are not united in thought and action and good people easily fall into universally predictable patterns of *inner conflict*, which underlie *all forms of outer conflict*.

- These patterns have profound impact on all aspects of life---resulting in outcomes from simple miscommunication, lack of energy and enthusiasm, and failure to learn from experience, to job loss, divorce, compulsions and addictions, ill health, and even violent criminal behavior. Such people are often called "losers" and these things are considered "normal" in a "world gone mad", but they are in fact, *biologically deficit states,* wherein humans are operating on half power, animal level, emotional guidance! Some such states are:

- These outcomes are not the result of genetic character flaws, they are facilitated by *predictable* and *preventable emotional dynamics* that can effect all human beings under the right (wrong track) circumstances. Emotion is an equal opportunity self-regulator, highly effective in doing its job---even if it is forced to operate against the mind of its owner! But these outcomes are *painful distortions* of nature's intentions. With the emotional compass, they are preventable and correctable. Even genetic predispositions for certain maladies (*) can be managed, minimized, or avoided entirely.

FIGURE 13.4

However, those who continually ignore their Paradaptive Intelligence Network emotions in one phase are far more prone to ignore them in other phases and become total wrecks in all phases of life.

Now that we understand how this works at the individual level, let's look at how this applies to business. The best example to illustrate this is Walmart. It started out as a small company, just like every other corporate giant at one point in time. But rather than accepting its pain points, it focused on solving its internal pain, concentrating on product handling and distribution efficiency to produce employee productivity gains.

The reverse of this is the small mom-and-pop store that isn't interested in changing anything they're doing because they tried to change something in the past once, and it took so much effort that it's not interested in going there again. That one experience has taught the owners the gain was not equal to the effort needed to implement it, so in their limited reservoir of memories, all change is bad. Salespeople often refer to this colloquially as "You can't fix stupid." Although it may appear intelligence is to blame for this type of business acumen, it is in fact rooted in a maladapted Paradaptive Intelligence Network where a business allowed one bad decision to begat more bad decisions, like not pursuing innovations.

We have learned techniques and progressions to understand and address a maladapted Paradaptive Intelligence. The question for each salesperson to answer is whether it is worth the time and energy to address this type of customer in order to put their Paradaptive Intelligence back on the right track or move on to a higher potential prospect. The old saying of "misery loves company" is true. People on the wrong track are miserable. They do not know how to relate to people on the right track because they don't share a common reservoir of good decisions that shape their outlooks. Small business owners will tend to seek out other like-minded business owners, so turning one wrong track business around could lead to many in a ripple effect.

It is impossible to give concrete rules for which specific emotional feedback emotions to ignore, and which ones to accept. There are exceptions to both, and choosing which route to take is based totally on the context which generated the emotion as a feedback signal. Two quick examples may help illustrate what is meant by the situational context. Recall the example in Chapter 7 where a co-worker is hurt and needs immediate medical attention. You drive like a demon to the hospital to save a life, exceeding speed limits and road conditions. Your reactor is giving you stern fear signals, literally screaming at you to slow down and move away from the course of action you are pursuing. But you ignore it because you know someone's life hangs in the balance.

In another example, you hit it off upon meeting a new person and he befriends you rather quickly. In the course of your conversation, he offers to buy you a drink, lunch, dinner, whatever, and you accept. At the conclusion of the meal or drink, the bill is presented, and your new friend pats himself down frantically only to sheepishly conclude that his wallet has been lost, stolen, or left at home. You feel bad for him, so you pay for the meal and then he hits you up for cab fare home. You offer to drive him or her home, but he won't hear of it and confirms he's good for it to pay you back. As part of the payback, he'll let you in on a little deal he's working on, but you'll need to front some money to the deal. Your HAC motive was to enjoy this person's company, which you've done, and your mind is directing growth signals to move closer to this person and continue the pleasurable experience. Even though your reactor is telling you to get closer, to get more involved with this individual, you come to your senses and realize you just met this person, and you don't really know who he is and walk away when the assistance you offered is declined with a grander request. This is good, because this is a typical grifter's ploy, in which a conman ropes in a mark for a bigger ploy. By ignoring your reactor's emotional feedback of joy, you've just saved yourself a lot of anguish.

SALESPEOPLE AS PAIN POINTS

Sales is a numbers game. A salesperson will have to find X number of prospects who will yield even a smaller amount of Y prospects whose profile will fit into your product's pain nullification envelope, which will then lead to a smaller subset of Z — closed sales. This means in order to become successful, you must collect a certain amount of "no"s. The immediate reaction for most salespeople is for their reactors to send a signal to their adaptors in some form of anger because they will interpret the 'no' as impediments or obstacles to their paycheck or quota.

Upon receiving your flash of anger, the prospects will also have a corrective emotional response, telling them to move away from you. This could be fear because your anger becomes a threat to them. Their corrective emotional display could be loss because they may have come to enjoy your company as a person, but they can't do business with you so the relationship must now end. It could be anger towards you because they sense you are blaming them for not doing your bidding and that violates an internal immovable boundary of respect. Or, it could be a form of disgust because they perceive your behavior as unwholesome just because they were unwilling or unable at this time to do your bidding by purchasing your product. By flashing your internal corrective signal to the prospect, you will reinforce to them a negative attitude towards dealing with salespeople, which will make it infinitely more difficult for you or other salespeople to approach them in the future, thus making salespeople pain points in their business environment. Break this cycle. Respond with joy.

The problem begins with your attitude and view towards prospects. If you see them as a means to a paycheck, then you will always respond to a 'no' with a corrective signal internally because your reactor will be telling you that you are off course in obtaining your paycheck and you need immediate corrective action. If your objective is a paycheck, then you will be disappointed, frustrated, and angry most of the time you're working. Instead, you need to reshape your HAC motivation to pain nullification in prospects. If you are focused on making people's pain go away, then you will never be disappointed except when, a) there was insufficient pain for your product and adaptation plan to nullify, creating joy over their well-being, or b) the prospect is wrong tracked, preferring pain, and in that case, you're giving them exactly what they wanted.

Instead, set yourself up for a corrective signal by positioning yourself for something positive from the basic emotion joy category. Thank the prospect for saying "no." Thank them for turning you loose. Let them know you appreciate them respecting your time and not wasting it with maybes or comebacks. Thank them for their honesty. 'No' is a statement of fact. Accept the facts and move on. Besides, as salespeople, we know the business environment is constantly changing, so a statement of fact today may very well change as prospects' circumstances evolve. By being positive and responding with joy, you will break the cycle of conditioning that salespeople are pain points for your prospects, and you leave the door open for future contact when their circumstances change, which they surely will.

Take ownership of your prospects. Treat them as part of your flock or network like you would with one of your clients. By taking ownership of them as a prospect, you will not be so willing to flash a corrective signal at them because they will have value to you regardless of their yes or no status because you will have added knowledge about a prospect to your repertoire and created an association that may be useful with other prospects. At the end of the day, they are still your prospect. Not every seed in the garden blooms at the same time. By taking a long-term approach of ownership of a prospect, you allow them and yourself time for development. Remember, at the very least, a prospect's adaptor drives him to learn because learning helps him adapt and survive. Even if they say 'no,' you've planted a seed in their adaptor. By flashing a corrective signal at them, you kill the seed. Nurture is what is called for, especially if you saw pain points in their present which they chose to live with now, but perhaps not in their future.

And the best fertilizer that you can use to grow your prospects is to utilize the six universal needs of the reactor. Everybody, including your prospects that have said no, needs their reactors tended to. If your competitor hasn't read this book, chances are he is not feeding his client's reactor's needs. Remember the 3F's? All things being equal, the business will flow to the salesperson liked best with the strongest personal connection. So feed the 'no' prospects their requirements of the six universal need:, freedom, power, connection, esteem, creativity, and meaning, and watch them come around.

PAIN POINT MYTHS AND OTHER HOOEY

Value Propositions

One of the current, trendy buzzwords to throw around in sales these days is "value proposition." Salespeople are supposed to state their value proposition to prospects clearly upfront, and this is supposed to establish the credentials of the salesperson's product and their value. There appears to be a whole industry of experts who will help you craft your value proposition. But the whole notion of a value proposition is bogus on the face of it, a euphemism invented and perpetrated by those who have no understanding of the actual workings of the Paradaptive Intelligence. Value is intrinsically internal to the individual. It measures desirable outcomes relative to others. A declaration of a salesperson's value cannot, and never will, replace an individual's internal schedule of relative value. It's preposterous to tell someone what they value.

More importantly, a value proposition, which is usually a flowery statement of abstract banalities, is an indirect way of attempting to state which pain points a product or service will resolve. It often leaves the prospect trying to interpret how exactly to relate what was just offered in a value proposition into something that will directly benefit him. Rather than waste time and confuse a prospect with a value proposition, why not just tell them what you do, "We make X, Y, and Z painless and profitable."

The concept of value propositions occurred because intuitively, subconsciously (that pesky reactor), people understood that pain nullification was the aim of all commerce but lacked the structure, vocabulary, and understanding of the Paradaptive Intelligence in the business domain to explain what they felt. Value propositions are a vague, fuzzy, egocentric way of telling a prospect what you will do for them and should be banished from the salesperson's repertoire and replaced by direct, factual statements regarding pain nullification of the prospect's circumstances.

Consultive Selling

Consultive selling is another one of those buzzword euphemisms floating around the sales industry at present. When you ask sales managers just what exactly consultive selling is or to define it, you get just as many different answers, but they generally include the notion to "act more like a consultant than a salesperson." This kind of fuzzy thinking leaves most sales professionals hanging in the lurch.

Consultants have explicit and detailed knowledge about specific industries and the particular problems owners and managers in that industry face. In other words, they are experts on pain points in a particular industry. Further, consultants also have and offer adaptation plans for those pain points. This is identical to the process of selling described and recommended in this book. So, consultive selling is a pain nullification centric approach to your prospects with adaptation plans to remedy the pain points you illuminate.

"Consultive selling" occurs when perfect alignment of the salesperson's motive occurs with the prospect's. The prospect's motive is to relieve psychic pain. The salesperson's motive must be to relieve the prospect's psychic pain. It cannot occur if the salesperson's motive is to "sell" or "make a sale." The salesperson can change his motive; the prospect can't. This may seem like a minor point, but in reality, it is a huge factor in the feedback that the Human Action Cycle produces while trying to achieve a motive through the Innovation algorithm. Producing feedback in the form of emotions for "making a sale" motive can be vastly different than that of making the prospect's pain point go away. This is what top sales people do; they change their motive which gets them working cooperatively with prospects.

Risk Tolerance

You constantly hear about risk, in business and economics, even in this book. But can anyone tell you exactly what risk is or what it measures? The answer is no, because until you understand the mechanisms of the mind and speak in terms of those mechanisms, you're just whistling in the dark. Risk implies peril. Peril, as students of Paradaptive Intelligence now know, is a form of fear. The fear stems from the reactor when it senses a threat to the well-being of the body or self. It relays this finding to the conscious mind in tri-layered signals including impulses to move away from the source, a basic emotion tone in the corrective category fear and a specific complex emotion. This signal agitates the individual to physically remove himself from the threat, which may be an impossible task if the threat is caused by an abstract rather than a physical threat, such as imperiling your money in a venture with a high probability of failure.

So, risk is also a measure of possible loss, which, if it happens, has the potential to threaten the well-being of the body. And as we learned earlier, it has the potential to begat even more bad decisions. Think of the gambler that always doubles down no matter how much he loses.

Peril is interpreted by the brain as fear because, basically, the mind equates money as an intermediary to food, shelter, warmth, and other bodily necessities needed for survival. As the threat enlarges, the reactor's agitation signals increase. This increasing agitation disrupts concentration, focus, reasoning, logic, and all other higher functions of the mind, creating a psychic pain until its demands to flee are met.

So, risk tolerance would be a measure of pain tolerance. It measures how much higher brain functions can be retained relative to the intentional disruption from the reactor demanding response to a threat. But this is a faulty measure. Even a small amount of peril increases the disruption of higher order functions of the brain. Just because the adaptor has not totally yielded to the reactor does not mean that it is functioning properly. The more peril, the more poorly higher order brain functions of the adaptor will operate to the point where reasoning, logic, etc., are no longer possible.

An article recently appeared in a major news/politics/business publication espousing that fear is a good thing. Fear injects adrenaline into our system, which sharpens our senses, quickens our reactions, and increases our strength. Their message was, essentially, "Who wouldn't want to walk around feeling like Superman?" Aside from the fact that this state carries a high penalty in metabolic exhaustion that is corrosive to the body, over time, repeated exposure to high levels of fear hormones causes detrimental health consequences. The author of this article lacked awareness and understanding of the emotional content which drives fear, even at low levels. Little did the author realize the mind's higher order functions are purposefully and intentionally being interrupted and degraded by the impulse to flee by the reactor so as to break the adaptor's grip on the mind putting the reactor in charge. So, when someone tells you they have a high-risk tolerance, that may be true, but they are also brain impaired to some degree. I wouldn't let them make any decisions for you concerning your health, wealth, or family when they're exercising their risk tolerance.

It pays to keep this in mind as a salesman because, as you work with prospects, you'll see that they may not always get everything you are trying to show them in a pain nullification strategy. Be patient, for they may just be a little brain impaired at the moment if there's risk and peril involved in your adaptation plan or in their present circumstances.

14

SPAN

"In life, it is not the answers that are important. It is the questions you choose to ask."
Anonymous

So far we've explored the Human Action Cycle as the foundational element of the Paradaptive Intelligence Network that produces emotions as a feedback signal. We next explored how emotions are constructed in the adaptor forming trivalent signals containing the binary agitation expression, one of six basic emotions, and complex emotions of tones or blends that interact with the adaptor and conductor in controlling emotions and thus human behavior. In Chapters 11 & 12, we established the flow of complex emotions from one complex emotion to the next in the universal progression, feed-forward continuum of emotions that all humans go through in making decisions that is called the Vetting phase. In this chapter, we will establish the necessity and vital role that questions play in emotions and sales.

There are several well-known sales methodologies, referred to by different acronyms, that are about question-based selling. Many have well written books displaying meticulous statistical research on the efficacy of different types of questions used in the sales process. These tomes take partial or incomplete understandings of the subject matter and spin them into methodologies that yield nominally more productive results. But, beware. As in politics, wags will take a limited set of facts and spin them into a unique perspective to set in motion their desired outcome within the recipient, which smacks of manipulation. This spin is meant to misdirect and obscure.

While these books can help salespeople improve their results when used properly, what is missing from them is one word: why?

Statistical analysis, while a fantastic tool, is a backward-looking technique. It can only explain the strength of relationship (or lack thereof) between variables as they existed in the past. Statistical analysis of this nature relies on the premise that past behavior will predict future actions. While this can be helpful, it isn't always accurate and produces a spread of anticipated results. In sales, this is like talking to a mirror looking over your shoulder at your prospects and clients. Because these statistical analyses based sales questioning methodologies lack the proper vocabulary or understanding of what their statistics are trying to describe, they will never be able to help the salesman understand what is it questions are doing internally to prospects, making them nothing more than mimics to the types of questions outlined as productive. Wouldn't it just be easier if you understood the mechanisms of the emotional machinery that your prospects are using to make their decisions? SPAN is a methodology that will help you do just that.

As a word, SPAN connotes a bridge between two points or a gap. And it is no coincidence that is exactly what the SPAN methodology does, bridging the gaps between the emotional tones discussed in Chapter 12. But, SPAN actually serves as an acronym to four types of questions: Scenario, Pain points, Adaptation plan, and eNunciation that will guide you to a more directed method of question-based selling.

QUESTIONS

We all know what questions are and what they can do for us. Or do we? In the Paradaptive Intelligence Network, questions are the links that bridge and move us from one complex emotional state to the next. And the best part is you already know how to do this! We have all done this or seen a child upset at skinning his knee that comes to a parent or adult to tend to the wound. The upset child will fuss and whimper while a Band-Aid is applied to the knee, and the adult finishes with the ubiquitous question, "Does that make it all better?" To which the child will sheepishly replies "yes" and stop his/her fussing. Great homily, right? But, what has that got to do with sales?

Answer: Again, more than you can guess.

Questions work from and are driven by the adaptor. In previous chapters, we learned that the main mission of adaptor is to learn. Questions seek information for the purposes of learning. The more we learn, the more flexibility and potential solutions we have for adapting to new circumstances. Better adaptability translates into higher success and survivability. The conductor demands more than just survivability of us and drives us to be the best we can be, influencing the adaptor to seek the best information. We want to know more about our environment and the

186

people that populate it. In sales, we need to know what our clients do, the problems they are encountering, and what they feel about it. Through the Human Action Cycle, we formulate questions to help focus adaptive solutions and potential solutions for our adaptation plans. As a salesperson, you are agents of adaptation in the form of the products and services. Salespeople, also as agent of companies, have to create new adaptation potential solutions for the problems your prospects and customers are experiencing.

Answers, however, come from and are driven by an entirely different process. In previous chapters, we learned that the reactor's main mission is self-preservation, to protect the body. We learned that it has six universal needs that help it succeed in this mission when interacting with other people. Third on the hierarchy of universal needs is connection. Humans are social animals because nature has settled on and wired our brains for self-actualization of ourselves and our identified tribe as a survival strategy. This wiring coupled with the adaptor's bias for cooperation compels us to answer questions when posed to us. The cooperative survival strategy can't work unless humans are driven to connect to others, and questions are the highest form of connection.

But to understand exactly what questions do emotionally, let's break it down a little bit further. Asking a question confers no emotion except to the asker. Hearing a question posed to you does not create emotion either, nor does mentally processing the question and formulating an answer. However, enunciating the response does create an emotion. Remember, in the HAC, only actions that interact with the world create emotional feedback signals. Thinking and listening do not interact with the world. Speaking, on the other hand, does. If you lie, you'll feel bad (a corrective signal) or if you answer truthfully, you'll feel good about cooperating (a growth signal).

In addition, the act of enunciation forces the Paradaptive Intelligence Network to determine the inner emotional state in preparation of the feedback signal it is about to send to the adaptor for execution. If you just presented an adaptation plan to the customer by demonstrating your product and its fixes to a problem, thus decreasing their pain induced by his or her fear or anger, then your prospect will move on in the emotion tonal algorithm. It is the act of enunciation that helps change emotions. Going back to the boy with the skinned knee homily, asking if it is all better forces the child's Paradaptive Intelligence Network to evaluate his feelings, and answering will move him to a new emotional tone, one where the threat of pain is greatly diminished.

Expanding this to the business sales cycle, you'll realize that it is not enough to simply demonstrate or show prospects a solution to a business fear-based (or other basic emotion) pain. While their adaptors may be thinking that your adaptation plan fixes their pain points, only an action that interacts with the world will get their reactors in sync with their adaptors. You must get them to enunciate whether your solution is of value to them. In this way, you can actually manage your prospects' emotions.

SPAN

SPAN stands for the four stages of the sales cycle in which question based selling occurs. SPAN is an acronym for **S**cenario, **P**ain points, **A**daptation plan and e**N**unciation. Memorizing this will help you stay focused on the types of questions you need to ask in order for your product or service to be purchased.

S – Scenarios

Scenario questions are designed to illicit general information about the prospect's company, department, and responsibilities. This is important to know because you will need to shape a plan of not only what pain points exist within the business, but also to learn whether you are speaking to a laggard, late majority, early majority, early adopter, innovator, or excited prospect. The purpose is twofold; first, to give you context upon which to formulate an action plan that will allow you to nullify the prospect's pain points with a well-crafted adaptation plan, and second, to create opportunities for synchronization of the Mirror Neuron System. These are some of the type of questions you might ask:

> Tell me about what your firm does?
> What is your role and what are your responsibilities?
> How long has your firm been in business?
> Are there other divisions or departments that you interact with or report to?
> Who will be involved in making decisions when it comes to new technologies and processes?
> Who will also need to have buy-in to any innovation introduced into your department?
> What was it about me or the product/services I offer that interested you?
> How do you think I might be able to help you?
> What systems or technology are you using now?
> How long have you been using the equipment/process in place?
> Is your business growing, at a standstill, or in decline?
> How do you feel about bringing innovation into your firm at this time?

Do you consider your firm to be innovative, adopting technology as soon as it's widely available, or does your firm like to see it tested and tried by the industry before moving, or only when it's absolutely necessary to keep the company's revenue flowing?

P –Pain Points

Most business people are trained or develop the practice of speaking about their businesses in terms of goals, objectives, and problems as issues. This is because it has been frowned upon, considered unprofessional, to discuss the emotions behind why they're doing what they're doing. It is safer to frame dialogue in terms of actions and activities. While this is useful information, it is an indirect approach to identifying what is motivating the prospect. And it is at this juncture that SPAN sales radically depart from other question-based selling techniques. The goal of these questions is to illicit what emotions are motivating the prospects' participation. Are they interested in expanding their adaptability by gaining knowledge of products that pertain to their business (feeding their adaptor), or are they trying to nullify pain points?

If they are just interested in information, there is no potential for immediate sale, and the salesperson should provide them with a brochure or web address and cultivate a relationship with them before moving on. It is the salesperson's choice to develop a relationship — become known — to the prospect's Mirror Neuron System, in the event that this account may become active in the future, but at this point, there is no guarantee that this investment will pay off for the salesperson. It is important to note the difference between a prospect that is being motivated by emotions with the purpose of gathering information on solutions to address their problems, or if they're just trying to increase their knowledge base for future contingencies.

If they are motivated by emotion, it will either be joy or one of the basic corrective signals: fear, anger, disgust, or sadness. The salesperson's job is to identify which of these is the motivating emotion. For example, let's say you're a pool salesman, and your firm installed a pool for a client that has moved and desires a pool at his new home. His joy of swimming and a backyard aquatic lifestyle are certainly a driving emotion — he wants to repeat that joy. But, he has a budget, time frame, space limitations, and fears that any one of these will derail the project or go over budget, threatening other aspects of his financial health and well-being. So then the mission is to discover which elements of pool ownership created the most joy and replicate and repeat those while presenting an adaptation plan based upon the project's constraints.

The above example exemplifies whether or not joy is involved as a motivator, but there will always be one of the basic corrective signals involved. Generally, business pursue pain nullification, pleasure is the pursuit of individuals. Almost always the culprit will be fear or anger in a business environment. Fear and anger create mental pain. These pains agitate the prospect to take action to move away from the pain, and if that isn't possible because that would mean leaving their job, then their alternative is to remove the pain point. Anytime there are inefficiencies or disruption of regular work processes, this puts the prospect into fear mode. The unknown and its unpredictability creates fear because resources could be threatened and put at risk for unknown payoffs. This is why it is essential for the salesperson to identify the source(s) of a prospect's fear or anger, or his pain points. Questions that will help a salesperson get to the root of pain points look like this:

> What is it that keeps you awake at night when you think about your business?
>
> When you're driving to work in the morning, what is it about your day you look forward to? What do you dread?
>
> What are the three biggest headaches you face on a daily (weekly, monthly, annual) basis?
>
> In what ways do X, Y, and Z (pain points) make you vulnerable?
>
> Who does it make you vulnerable to? Competition? Management?
>
> If there were three things you could change about this issue, what would they be? Why?
>
> Do these inefficiencies impact or ripple throughout your firm?
>
> How do they impact other departments?
>
> How does it make you look to other departments?
>
> How do the people in your company react to these inefficiencies? Frustration (Anger)? Avoidance (Fear)?
>
> What gives you the greatest grief (Sadness) in your job?
>
> In what areas are you the hardest on yourself (Disgust) in managing your firm?
>
> How do you feel when your customers or employees do X (a known inefficiency or friction point)?
>
> How do you handle this scenario (a known inefficiency or friction point)?
>
> What part of your work and responsibilities do you feel you have the least control over?
>
> What makes you the most frustrated about your work?
>
> What obstacles prevent you from creating more profits/efficiencies/volume/etc?
>
> What do you find yourself getting angry about at work?
>
> Is there something within your work flow that annoys you?

What do these annoyances/obstacles make you do? Do you stop what you're doing and attend to them or ignore them?

How much time to you spend working around these obstacles/annoyances/frustrations?

Do these obstacles disrupt your thoughts, business process, or work flow?

How much money do these accumulated disruptions cost you?

Salespeople have been classically trained to "qualify" a lead or prospect. This traditionally has been described as determining whether the person you're dealing with has the authority and freedom to purchase your product and determine if your products meet their needs. As learned earlier, there really are no needs, except the six universal needs of the reactor of individuals that populate a firm. What they have are pain points that need nullification. Asking the above type of question will give you a more exact sense of qualification of the prospect. The most important vetting you can do is to determine their motivation. If there are no pain points, then the prospect is not motivated to purchase your product or service and is just adding to the information wealth for future contingencies.

Often there are multiple scenarios where a prospect is experiencing pain points and the salesperson's product(s) addresses and mitigates multiple pain points. Pain point questions can also determine where the prospect falls into the emotional tonal algorithm as being either at the acceptance stage or learning anticipation.

A – Adaptation Plan

Having uncovered the prospective customer's underlying pain points, you can now look to start formulating an adaptation plan. Your adaptation plan will consist of specific products and services picked from your inventory and an implementation plan specific to the prospective client. Having created an adaptation plan, you now need an action plan on how you're going to present this information to the prospective client. Your Motive to help the prospect by nullifying their pain points combined with your Action Plan make a MAP of your actions at that account. But your adaptation plan is just a projection, your best guess. The prospect is the ultimate authority on how, where, and when to implement or receive new goods and services, so you'll need to fine-tune the implementation with the prospect, which is going to require more questions.

You'll want to ask adaptation plan questions of the prospect for two reasons. Firstly, there may be additional implementation costs that you'll need to know about before you quote a price. For example, do they need after-hours delivery, installation, or training? How about weekend service? Will equipment or personnel be available to off-load, or will you or they have to schedule these at additional costs? Secondly, by incorporating these types of questions, you stimulate the prospect to come up with answers (esteem) which satisfy the six universal needs of the reactor, or to come up with creative solutions (creativity) or work collaboratively (connection) to work out these details. This also has the benefit of "assuming the sale." This gets the prospect thinking in terms of when, not if, they are going to make the purchase, guiding them in the excitement phase to conclude that the costs are less than the benefits. Working on the when also takes advantage of the prospect's adaptor's bias for cooperation. The prospect already has a built-in bias to cooperate with you.

There are two styles in which you can accomplish the use of adaptation plan questions, set piece or on-the-fly. In a static, set piece format, you can do your presentation or product demonstration, and then ask a series of the following questions as a transition to obtaining commitment. In an on-the-fly format presentation, you can work these questions into the format to create a dynamic presentation.

Either way, examples of questions of this nature would be:

> My experience has shown me this type of implementation works well. Does that work for you?
>
> How could we improve it?
>
> Do you prefer the first of the month, the last, or does it matter?
>
> Do you see any problems with this?
>
> Who else would need to be involved with this aspect of implementation?
>
> Based on what factors will we grade the implementation?
>
> Who from within your firm will be responsible for ongoing training and management of this system once we complete the implementation?
>
> We can start implementation X days after your commitment. Will that give you enough time to prepare for the product?
>
> What steps do you need to accomplish internally before we can begin implementation?
>
> What kind of assistance from me do you need before we begin implementation?

N – eNunciation

Studies have shown, and your own experience will tell you, that you are far more likely to remember exactly what you've said than what someone else has said. The mechanics of formulating speech to answer questions engages more parts of the brain, and this higher level mental activity creates greater instances for the mechanisms of memory versus static listening, no matter how active the mind is engaged on the topic. By using this simple fact, the salesperson can generate greater penetration and retention of the salient, positive pain point nullifying aspects of your presentation. As a salesperson, with your product knowledge and experience, it's easy to calculate specific benefits of your product for the prospect and most salespeople make the mistake of doing just that. The salesman would be far better served to lead prospects through the process of calculating the benefits themselves and have them enunciate it. In this way, you make it difficult for the prospect, who has been participating in your presentation up until now via Scenario, Pain Point or Adaptation Plan questions, to resist further participation. Also by doing so, you enable the prospect to calculate and supply the projected savings and benefits, which makes it very, very difficult for the prospect to conclude the process by saying 'no' to the sales. With this methodology, you are not selling to obtain a "yes" but are positioning the prospect so that it is impossible for him to say 'no' because he is the one who calculated the benefits.

Examples of this type of questions are:

> Does this product do everything that you need it to do?
> Is there anything that it doesn't do that you need it to?
> Is there anything that it needs to do that I didn't address?
> If it is deficient, is there a way to work around it within your organization?
> How much time would this save you?
> What would you do with the X amount of hours a week this would save you?
> How much would doing Y increase your revenues?
> What would the amount of new revenues generated be?
> Roughly, what would you calculate the percentage of revenue increase to be?
> How much would doing Y increase your productivity?
> How much will you save on material cost? Decrease labor cost?
> Will this product decrease your uncertainty about ...?
> Will you sleep easier knowing that you won't lose your company over Z?

STRATEGY

The prevailing wisdom and lore of sales is that your objective in a presentation to a client or prospect is to describe the features and benefits of your product to them.

This could not be more utterly wrong or false.

While there is some efficacy in this approach, it relies upon the fortunate coincidence of some feature or benefit randomly striking an interest in the prospect before they become bored and quit listening. Percentage wise, you will make random connections. When it doesn't, you'll just be another salesperson who wasted their time. The second half of this process also relies on the prospect forming a Human Action Cycle to obtain your product. As discussed in Chapter 4, we learned that one of the main objectives of the adaptor is learning, which it is always performing in coordination with the ego. By taking a features and benefits approach, you are educating the client's adaptor and hoping that information will become a motivation – desirable outcome – to initiate a Human Action Cycle to obtain your product This is a haphazard, uncontrolled approach that produces nominal results, yet is considered effective.

The purpose of SPAN questions is to find the pain points produced by corrective signals that the business is experiencing. It is far more productive to discover and work with what fears are driving them in their business. It's a waste of time to pursue non-problems or minor issues if they are producing little to no fear or anger, hence little to no pain, when there are much bigger problems at hand that are producing intense emotions. Intense pain points are what must be removed and satisfying the complex emotions of the Vetting phase in order to move your prospects through the emotion courage will generate a sale.

Most male salespeople will shy away from strong emotion. Until you've read this book, you probably won't know what's coming at you. Females, for structural reasons, are typically prepared to handle these emotional turbulences much better than men. This is because men are geared to lead with problem solving while women are geared to lead with cooperation. Intense emotions are not problems, and thus are difficult to deal with for the basic male mental architecture without practice and a good understanding of emotions. Men are more interested in finding out what caused the intense emotional outpouring and fixing it at the root. Women, on the other hand are geared for cooperation, hence their first impulse is to empathize or sympathize rather than look for a course of corrective action. But as was pointed out earlier in this book, training, as an adaptive behavior modification, can change these basic impulses.

This discussion of mental archetypes is important because what comes next may sound antithetical, as a salesperson, you need to zero in on the pain points and illuminate them in the most personal way as possible. The point is not to be cruel, but to make the prospect aware of what the real problem is and the seriousness of it. If you're talking to a business owner, you need to be discussing the pain points in terms of lost revenue or profits, why the business is not moving forward, the competition is moving ahead of them, or the toys that they want to own but can't afford. With business or corporate managers, the conversation is generally the same, but with the emphasis on their status within the business, and not the toys of their personal life.

The more intense an emotion you can evoke, the better your adaptation strategy will appear. One of the elements of corrective signal pain is that it will move the person experiencing it away from the source of the pain. The more painfully you present it, the more motivated the prospects will be to move away from it. By offering them an adaptation plan, you take advantage of their desire to <u>move away</u> from the pain and <u>move towards</u> an adaptation in your product that takes away their pain points. When done properly, prospects may even cry if their emotions on the subject are intense enough.

Therapists do this with their patients. They pick at festering psychological issues to expose them and get them out in the open so they can be confronted, dealt with, and resolved. So, too, with salespeople. Whether the issues are business based or personal, the approach must be the same because they both are dealing with the same root cause - fear, anger, or some other corrective signal. It may not be too farfetched, if you are a good salesperson, to think of yourself as a business therapist because you are essentially doing the same thing, helping people overcome painful issues. Just think to yourself, how effective would a therapist be if he or she were too afraid to ask questions that may upset the patient?

For example, let's say you sell some form of product that has accounting software features. You could go the educational approach and discuss the features and benefits of your product that will keep track of financial registers, segregate taxable revenue from non, generate daily accounting reports, etc., or you could just go straight to the pain point and ask the prospect how much money and time he or she is losing by accounting by hand, and what he or she would like to be doing with that money and extra time.

EFFECTIVENESS vs EFFICIENCY

All humans have emotions (excepting those with psychopathy personality disorders which mute emotion intensities) and thus a basic understanding of the workings of the mind. Salespeople, as a breed, have a better sense about these things, and gravitate to this profession. Thus, most salespeople that have been in the profession for a period of time have demonstrated a level of effectiveness that allows them to hold their jobs and produce an income. But sales leaders, those that stand heads and shoulders above everyone else, often referred to as "eagles", work differently — they work *efficiently*.

By this, we do not necessarily mean they find the most economical route to drive between points as they go about their daily business. Using the methodology discussed in the previous section on strategy, they quickly rip into the clients' pain points, offer them adaptation plans, write the contracts, collect the checks and then leave. They do not waste time dithering or talking about items found in the office because they are animated and allow themselves to be known (Chapter 9) while executing SPAN questions. In doing so, they align the customer's expectations because they know the adaptation plan they have presented is going to fix specific illuminated pain points. Clients see the salesperson as knowledgeable and respect him because he knew exactly where and how to filet back the pain points to expose them to the salve of their adaptation plan in minimal time.

Top sales performers use questions as a way of demonstrating and establishing their expert credentials by asking about problems they know to exist. They do not waste time by asking if the prospect is experiencing a known problem; they ask questions to determine how bad it is, how painful it is. By carefully choosing questions designed to demonstrate that they know the prospect is experiencing known problems, pain points their product is designed to address, they change their perception in the prospect's eyes from someone who's fishing for information to someone who knows the answers. All the questions in the previous section of this chapter are good as a template, but should be modified to your particular circumstances to probe for pain points you know exist in your industry or sales niche that your product is designed to address. In this way your questions will accomplish two things, 1) You'll determine just how intense the pain points are in the business, which will help you formulate an adaptation plan, and 2) you'll establish your bona fides as an expert on the situation by assuming a problem's existence rather than guessing. If it doesn't exist, the prospect will tell you straight up and you can move on to another client who does have known pain points.

Because this sales cycle approach cuts straight to the pain of the matter, gets a contract and check, and gets the salesman out the door. He is able to see more customers and close more deals. That is why sales eagles are able to produce higher volumes. Their sales cycle is devoid of wasted time with the customer and themselves. These eagles can accomplish all this because they are not afraid to make the clients feel and recognize the pain their business is causing them. If you are not doing this, then you are wasting time, energy, and motion to satisfy your personal needs to be "nice" to the detriment of your personal finances, your clients' time, and possibly your employer's well-being. It may be necessary for you to review the six basic needs to find out which of your reactor's needs is intruding into your business activities and redirecting them to outlets in your personal life.

COMPOUND QUESTIONS

Now that you have the basics in place for a SPAN question-based approach to sales, it is time now to increase your efficacy. So far, we have looked at **S**cenario, **P**ain points, **A**daptation plan, and e**N**unciation questions. Yet, even those can be improved upon. In Figure 8.1, you'll see that all of nature's most desirous feeling tones are mostly the sublime forms of the six universal needs. Combining these needs with SPAN questions can improve their efficacy.

The six universal needs are the needs for: freedom, power, connection, esteem, creativity, and meaning. As you recall, these are hierarchal in organization and have to be satisfied in sequential order. In reality, as a salesperson, you will be only dealing with the last four — connection, esteem, creativity, and meaning — because you should, as a matter of basic proficiency, be dealing only with a decision maker at a business. By definition, decision makers have already satisfied the first two needs by virtue of title and authority, and you've checked to see that they are free of contractual engagements that would prohibit them from purchasing your product. In the business environment, if the person you're dealing with cannot enter into a contract or write a check or purchase order, then he or she does not have power.

This leaves connection, esteem, creativity, and meaning as useful tools for the sales professional.

Connection

Connection allows you to connect and relate your adaptation plan to other business or opinion leaders who might be using your product or similar processes. Or you can use the converse argument that because they used your products or similar processes, they became business or opinion leaders because they've embraced products like yours. Connection also fosters and facilitates cooperation. So, don't be afraid to ask for information that might help tailor your product demonstration to the specifics of the prospect's business, such as the name of the person who might be most impacted by these features or that function.

A quick example of the importance of connection is the history of communications technology. Harnessing the use of radio waves for broadcasting was followed shortly by ham radio, CB (Citizens Band) radios, and finally its modern-day incarnation of the cell phone. Connection and its conduit, language, have certainly been a powerful force in shaping our world.

Here are examples of questions that emphasize connection:

Do you find communication with your customers (employees, suppliers, etc.)

a challenge?

Has miscommunication cost you profits?

Did you know that company X uses this same process/product?

Have you seen anyone else in your community using this product?

Would it surprise you to know that this product is used by thousands of people in this area?

How often do miscommunications or incorrect information cause disruption to your business?

Did you know that the leading companies in your industry have switched to this product?

Esteem

Esteem is an expression of worthiness relative to others. The conductor urges and guides you to make the most of the knowledge you acquire. This all ties in closely with honor. Honor derives from adhering to the rules and strictures of society while maximizing your knowledge and talents. We don't honor serial killers of thieves, nor do we honor people who live by society's rules but don't push themselves to full potential. Those that do push to their full potential usually become the leaders of their peers, groups, neighborhoods, communities, and societies, and we honor them for their leadership. In sales, these would be the first to adopt innovation in their peer groups, whether that is innovators, early adopters, or early or late majority.

Esteem can be used to create and foster feelings of confidence and honor. You can feather-in encouragement in your dialogue with prospects by assessing their applicable talents and expressing that their skills for the product adoption process shows you think highly of them, which is a form or respect, another type of honor.

There's no doubt that honor plays a strong role in every society. Some honor the family name, while others erect monuments to those who maximized leadership potential for their societies, or to honor those that have "given it all" in battle. People leave money for scholarships or build buildings in their names at universities; doctors have hospitals, wings, departments, or chairs named in their honor. Creating a sense of worthiness in your prospects will bring them the confidence needed to make innovative purchases or try new suppliers.

Examples of esteem questions include:

You're not worried about being able to implement this product, are you?

Do you know you're among the first to purchase this product?

How's it feel to be a market leader?

If other clients have questions, would you mind if they call you?

This'll be a piece of cake for you, wouldn't you agree?

You'll do just fine, don't you think?

You're going to worry your competition when this is done, aren't you?

Creativity

Creativity is by far one of the salesperson's greatest allies. As we've learned, prospects expect the salesperson to guide them through the innovation adoption process. But even though you're their guide, there will always be particulars about the prospect's business that you won't know. One of the greatest mistakes a salesperson can make is to assume that they will have all the answers. You know the sequence and variations to make the adoption process work after the sale, but only the client will know which specifics of the adoption plan will work for them, so ask them. Make that part of the demonstration or presentation. Not only will it make it interactive and keep prospects involved, but they will also receive emotional fulfillment by creating solutions for innovation adoption in the adaptation plan.

Creativity has the ability to manifest emotional fulfillment in many needs categories. By expressing creativity towards the implementation of the product, they will feel connection through the banter and exchange of ideas in brainstorming sessions. By having the answers to problems, they will feel great esteem aside from the joy of creating a positive outcome.

> Examples of question cultivate creativity include:
>
> What do you think we should do about X?
>
> What's the best way to accomplish Y?
>
> How would you propose to do Z?
>
> Is it possible to do X and Y?
>
> How can we accomplish Z given your time frame?
>
> How can we work around this concern?
>
> Is there another angle that we can take regarding X?

Meaning

Meaning is also a source of compound questions. This is the desire to make sense of it all, to understand life's connections. While life's answers may not necessarily be found in the adoption of innovation at work, the resulting reduction in chaos and control that it brings can add to the sense of connection to and orderliness of their prospect's business, thus giving their world the appearance of meaning.

Examples of questions that create meaning include:

What are you going to do with all the time/money/ resources that you'll save when this project is complete?

So how are you going to re-organize your business after this?

How much room will this clear on your plate?

How do you think this will impact employee morale by reducing the workload?

This should give you one less thing to worry about, right?

How will it feel to be back in charge of your business again?

PHRASING FRAMING

Along with the questions discussed in this chapter, there is one other point concerning dialogue with prospects that must be brought to attention. Almost all products have some sort of metric to convey their efficacy. When discussing these metrics, it is crucial to always frame your phrasing is a positive manner. For example, there are two ways to state probability, 1) 50% chance of success or, 2) 50% chance of failure. As a salesperson, you must always state the chances for success or improvement. Never discuss failure or chances of negative outcome with your product. That's what satisfaction guarantees are for. Failure is a threat. Discussing the failure rate of your product links your product or service as a threat to the prospect's business. Once the prospect's reactor identifies a threat, it will actively signal a person to move away from the threat. Remember, people have no control over their reactor, they can only ignore it when possible. Once a reactor identifies a threat in the environment, it will never stop signaling to move away from it. Don't let that threat be you, or your product or service.

In fact, the only time it is permissible and advisable to discuss failure and threats is during the acceptance emotional phase. As a salesperson, you must selectively choose to discuss those threats to a prospect's business to which your product or service remedies. To discuss threats or failure beyond the acceptance emotional phase may brand the whole topic as a threat to the prospect's business, forcing them to move away from the whole concept. It is okay to remind them of a threat identified earlier, especially when describing how your adaptation plan will nullify the pain of that particular threat.

Even in a scenario where the prospect states the reciprocal of a metric you just quoted them, "…you mean that 31% of the time you're unable to fix problem Y…" resist your cooperation bias's tendency to confirm what he just said; instead rephrase back to your stated metric, "…that's right, 69% of the time we can solve problem Y…"

CONCLUSION

The underlying principle of SPAN is to gather necessary information about your prospect before developing and presenting an adaptation plan. Often, a salesperson is contacted by a prospect seeking information about their products. The salesperson dutifully makes an appointment, shows up, and is obliged to start discussing the features and benefits of his product. If you are doing this now without having asked scenario and pain point questions, STOP! If you were planning on doing this, DON'T! An unfocused adaptation plan is one of the quicker ways to kill any deal. We discussed earlier the concept of efficiency in top performing salespeople. SPAN selling is the key to their efficiency. Also discussed earlier in the section on the Vetting phase was the excitement emotional tone. Excess features presented in a features and benefits style of action plan is not only indirect, inefficient, but a waste of time unless that feature can directly go to mitigating a prospect's pain point. Additionally, in the excitement phase, excess and non-applicable pain mitigating features become a burden, not a benefit. Extra, unused features become a liability, forming the precept in the mind of prospects that they are paying for a whole lot more than they should to get a bunch of features that they don't want or need. These extra features make it difficult for the prospect to get excited about your product. And lastly, if you're not talking about the prospects' pain points, then you've probably lost their interest and are boring them. If this happens, it's doubly hard to get their attention again, even if you do stumble upon one of their pain points because they have quit listening and are probably preoccupied with figuring out ways to conclude the meeting. This notion of not over-selling is captured in the old sales saw of "Quit selling while you're ahead."

SPAN is a flexible system. It may not always be prudent to start with Scenario questions and work your way through to eNunciation questions. Indeed, many salespeople specializing in a specific industry often know scenario questions and answers so well that it may be best to jump right to the pain point or action plan questions as you see fit. Either way, be flexible and take your cues from the prospect by looking for tell-tale clues that will tell you their emotion status. Let your knowledge of the six universal needs guide you to create questions that not only let you identify prospect pain points and create specific adaptation plans, but also create questions that will satisfy their internal six universal needs.

SALES CONVENTIONS AND OTHER HALF-MEASURES

Question Based Selling

Question, interrogatory, based selling has been a staple of sales techniques from time immemorial. It is capable of producing reasonable results when done properly as it currently is practiced, but not optimum. The reason why optimum results will elude those currently using this sales convention is because the goal of the questions is unclear, with no intermediary goals or established pathway leading to a sale. While certain industries and companies have developed progressions of questions that led to high probabilities of sales, they really didn't know what they were accomplishing. That's because, until you've read this book, you really don't know what you're doing in sales. The practitioners of question based selling have been missing vital information, the other half of what questions do internally to move prospects along the path of their adaptational machinery. Take Neil Rackham's 1988 book Spin Selling, arguably the finest book of its type. Yet, using its methodology, one can never reach the full measure of sales potential they have within them. Its well-constructed observations backed by statistical analysis can only measure the strength between observed variables but is incapable of establishing a cause and effect relationship. Question formation strategies alone are only capable of inference and conjecture resulting in a sophisticated "mimic me" approach to sales. Its approach is to teach you the parameters of question formation, not the parameters of how consumers' and prospects' minds actually make decisions. Conjecture is fine if you've got a narrow market segment whose prospects always present in the same way to a salesperson. What happens when some outlier crops up in your sales day? How do you handle new situations that don't fall within neatly constructed question patterns? How about when you change products, divisions…companies? By not knowing what is happing inside prospects' minds, but only a strategy to formulate questions, you will be half prepared to reach your full sales potential.

Question-based sales strategies serve two purposes. First, it serves as a template for new sales hires. Second, a company, when training a new hire, can quickly teach them questions they are to mimic, reducing training expenses by producing a clone army of salespeople. This gives the new hire a reasonable chance of being productive quickly, while lessening the cost of training new hires to the company. But if there is one thing that is widely agreed upon in the sales community, it is that change is constantly occurring. The neatly dovetailed questions learned in training lose potency over time as technology, government regulation, competitors, and consumer demand change the mix in the field for salespeople.

As stated at the beginning of this book, the intent here is to inform the sales professional. Cloned sales people are a different market completely and will find more suitable books on the market to address their limited designs.

15

AFTER THE SALE SALES

"Care and diligence bring luck."
Thomas Fuller

"Work would be terribly boring if one did not play the game all out, passionately."
Simone de Beauvoir

U p to this point, we've talked about sales as if a sale is completed by the act of a prospect committing to a business relationship with you by signing a contract, writing you a check, or generating a purchase order. This, in fact, would be misleading. Getting a signed contract or purchase order only represents *half* of the sales process; the second half starts at this point, and any failure in the second half can and will negate all your sales activities that occurred in the Vetting phase. There are still three emotional tones in the Application phase where implementation occurs that must be negotiated in order for the sales to stay on the books, faith, exuberance, and satisfied customer (See Figure 15.1).

And up to this point, the sales process has involved mostly words projecting the use, benefits, and costs of an adaptation plan. But after the contract or purchase order, goods or services start to show up, be performed, or both. The prospect, who has now graduated from prospect to client, has formed an image of himself using the product or service and it is imperative that what is delivered matches the client's mental projection. The word "closely" is used because the client is biased positively towards your product and service. He sees himself using the product, and this generated a good deal of excitement prior to producing the emotion courage. He is not going to nitpick your product or service because he is inclined to believe that it will work to his satisfaction or he would never have obtained the courage to commit to the purchase. Throughout this book, the notion of an adaptation plan, which is a

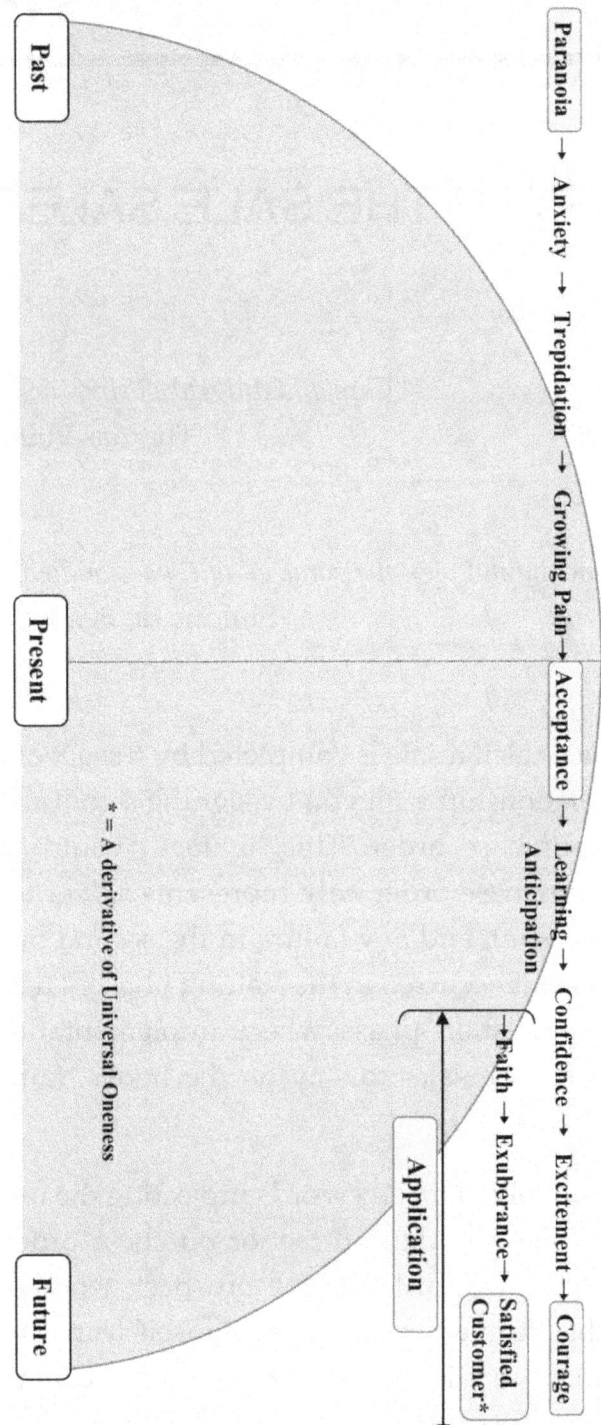

FIGURE 15.1

Application Phase of the
Innovation/Tool Seeking Emotional Tonal Algorithm

combination of implementation plan plus the product or service, has been repeated abundantly. The reason for this is about to become very apparent. In Figure 15.1 we see the Application phase is comprised of the three aforementioned emotions of faith, exuberance, and satisfaction/satisfied customer. All the emotions of the Application phase are based on the adaptation plan. Faith is the evaluation of the implementation plan – actual versus projected. Exuberance is the evaluation of the product/service – actual versus projected. Customer satisfaction is a composite value of the optimization achieved in both the emotions of faith and exuberance.

COMPANY'S HOME STRETCH

Up to this point, the salesperson has been laboring relatively alone while pursuing the sale, thus controlling most of the aspects of the sales activity. But once the product or service is applied to the client the salesperson usually welcomes the addition of other players from his or her company to the sales process. And unless you're selling a service that you can perform alone without any outside aid, such as consulting, the remaining emotional phases of Figure 15.1 can't be successfully traversed without the addition and intervention of a new element, the company – the people and its products that you represent. Those in your company not actively involved in current sales, are in the next. Even those in indirect support positions effect costs which impact the price, which will play a role in the next client's excitement emotion phase. So, up to now, their presence has been a background influence. But with the signing of an order, their activities take center stage and will have a bearing on the post-sale emotions of every sale.

The three emotional phases that must be traversed in the second half of the sale, faith, exuberance, and satisfied customer, represent the client moving from a state of predicting the outcome of your adaptation plan to complete knowledge as to the exact fitness of that adaptation plan. These three emotional phases are much easier to traverse than those of the Vetting phase because of the inherit acceptance and commitment of a positive outcome rather than the skepticism common to the Vetting phase. This positive outcome bias is the product of the HAC evaluation phase which is biased to interpreting outcomes in the rosiest, yet realistic manner and the ego's confirmatory bias to only let in information that confirms objectives.

However, this advantage of bias towards success can be offset by the complications that are added to the sales process as more people from the seller's side get involved. With each person that gets added to the process of delivering the purchased product or service, the potential for miscommunication and deviation from adaptation plan increases exponentially. This process is also accelerated, too, by the necessary involvement from the client's side by people that weren't involved in the sales process. This means that a whole lot of people with unmanaged expectations have just joined the process. We'll come back to that in a bit...but first, let's look at the emotions of the home stretch.

FAITH

Faith starts at the moment the prospect becomes a client by committing to the sale financially and by deed. Faith is about tallying the projected costs of implementation against actual cost. As soon as the client has committed, his expectations are on the clock. However, faith exemplifies the positive bias towards your product or service and its successful conclusion as the basis of his or her expectations. In achieving the emotion excitement in the Vetting phase, the clients recognized and evaluated the projected cost in resources of accepting the adaptation plan of the salesperson. Now at the start of the implementation, they start to see those outgoing costs of time, effort, and resources as changes start to occur to make way for the new. They have no way of knowing if their calculations will hold true to reality, yet they persist, believing that the benefits to be delivered upon or near the completion of implementation will outweigh the outgoing cost at this phase. The emotion faith is characterized by the outgoing expenditures of resources with no significant levels of benefits yet discernible. This is why faith is one of nature's most desirous emotions (Figure 8.1). This high and powerful level of joy agitation is necessary to overcome the negative agitation of other HACs that may be impacted as outgoing resources accumulate with no joy based agitation from the expected benefits to offset them.

This is also why there is value in keeping the client's attitude positive and doing a little cheerleading during this time, especially since a salesperson is more experienced in the implementation process than the client. Remember that other client HACs are being impacted negatively with corrective signals all the while during implementation. Use that knowledge to keep the client upbeat, especially in the face of all the changes which is a threat to stability. In the faith phase, more than any other, clients will be more dependent upon your knowledge and experience with your product as well as your attitude to set the tone of theirs.

Failures at the emotion faith may occur because the alterations or changes to the client's current business practices or procedures that are needed to implement the new adaptation plan can't be accomplished. This can happen due to a) miscalculation upon the client's part, or b) necessary questions and vetting of resource expenditure to implement the adaptation plan were incomplete. This is why your best insurance as a salesman for this phase is to have a solid implementation plan expressed in the adaptation plan.

Failure to move beyond the emotion faith may also occur due to too wide of a variance from the implementation plan. Deviation from the implementation plan means extra resources not planned for had to be expended. These additional expenditures can take two forms: extra or excess costs not foreseen or creation of new problems and issues in the firm not anticipated by your product or service which incurs unforeseen cost in time, labor, money, and resources to resolve.

In summation, the emotion faith is about comparing the actual costs of implementation to the estimated projects which set expectations. Whether the sale is complex or simple, its implementation plan — the emotion faith — plays a critical role. Even in the simplest scenario of a commodity purchase at retail, say a famous brand of vacuum cleaner, faith plays a critical part. In this scenario, you buy a vacuum at your local retailer and they give you a big box, with a shiny picture of the product on the outside. You take it home, open the box, and extract a disassembled vacuum cleaner. But in this setting, the hardware is not included to complete the assembly. You never get to assemble the product to see if it cleans as well as it was advertised. Or maybe the instruction manual is not included. You're more likely to get a corrective signal of anger because someone has put an obstacle in your way because you know you're either going to have to take it back and get a refund or exchange, or contact the manufacturer for the missing parts. This is a real deviation from the implementation plan which was probably set in place by the shiny picture on the box informing you that this is what lay inside, waiting for you. Or the converse could happen — the vacuum cleaner is easy to assemble because everything was in the box with good instructions. Either way your Paradaptive Intelligence Network will be tallying the actual costs. Whether it's a complex computer solutions or simple commodity products, if the implementation costs stray too far from the projected, the customer will cease the implementation, cancel the deal, or attempt to renegotiate in light of the actual expenses incurred. None of which are good for the salesperson.

Buyer's Remorse

Faith is the point at which a phenomenon occurs called "buyer's remorse." This is when the buyer experiences a corrective signal emotion due to the transaction. They've written you a check in the courage phase and lost the use or security of that money. Every client has or had a HAC that was driving them to put money aside or work within the business' cash flow. Their pre-determined margin of security, the difference between cash flow and operating cost, is the function of a HAC for security. This is evident by the fact that the prospect had the money to make the purchase of your product. With the loss of security by having spent money on a HAC to fix a pain point(s) in other business areas, the prospect is now receiving a corrective signal on his performance of the HAC to save money or live within certain cash flow parameters. His Paradaptive Intelligence Network is telling him that his security is threatened, and he will be driven to seek their money back. Every time you or a prospect loses or departs with some portion of your accumulated estate, the basic emotion of loss or threat is triggered. Everyone experiences it to one degree or another. If the emotion triggered is threat, then they will have the urge to flee. If the emotion triggered is loss, they'll seek to replace what was lost. An example of this emotion gone awry is a hoarder, whose emotion signal of loss is so strong and overpowering that he or she can't bear to depart with anything. In business, hoarders are called clients with "buyer's remorse." It's easy to tell which case you're dealing with – if they ask for their money back, they're seeking replacement and you can deduce they are being driven by the corrective signal of loss. If they just want to cancel the sale, they are trying to flee the deal and are being driven by fear. Knowing what the dimensions are will help you ask the right questions to get to the bottom of their desire to cancel the sale and create and action plan to get the sale back on track.

This might also be the case of two competing HACs, one to save money or have security in one's cash flow versus the one to nullify pain. In the end, the client can't have both HACs succeed at the same juncture in time. One of them will take a hit, either security through savings or nullifying pain points/fixing problems.

But how did this occur? Corrective signals generated by pain points are designed to disrupt the adaptor's processes, including the evaluation of risk. So why didn't the buyer's remorse issue become known sooner? If you recall at the beginning of the book, the Paradaptive Intelligence model states that all human actions generate emotions. We used the thought experiment of formulating the perfect crime in your head, which generated no emotion. It was only upon implementation, when and action is taken, that emotion is generated. This is a prime example of the rule. The client was projecting, just thinking of, the cost and benefits of your adaptation plan. No action was taken, no money departed hands. And as you recall in an earlier graph, Figure 8.5, courage was listed as an action point. Due to the design of the Paradaptive Intelligence Network, no emotions can be generated until an action occurs, so there was no way for the HAC focused on security to make its presence known until an action was taken, i.e. courage obtainment in a pain nullification HAC.

Your best strategy is to be proactive, knowing that in every client there are HACs whose focus will be impacted by the action point of courage to your sale, so get them out into the open. Before accepting the client's contract or order, unless it is a repetitive type sale, have a little speech or homily prepared to the effect that all though there will be some unknowns and doubts, you'll both work through them and in the end their business will be much better off.

Some salespeople accomplish this by pausing before formally accepting a signed client order and asking "Are you sure you want to do this?" This is a great technique for quelling buyer's remorse. By doing it immediately after the prospect has taken the action of signing the order, their HAC for security has been fully impacted and you'll get an immediate whiff of whether there's to be any buyer's remorse. By doing this immediately after signing but before formally accepting the order, you'll also take advantage of other HACs the client undoubtedly has. For instance, almost all prospects have goals to be trustworthy, consistent, decisive, aggressive, etc. By querying the client upon signing, you invoke those other goals, those other HACs, to counteract against the awakening of the security HAC. Let these HACs to be trustworthy, decisive, consistent, etc., go to work for you. These additional HACs will create an internal dispute among the client's HACs (as discussed in ambivalence) between security and the goals of being trustworthy, consistent, aggressive, and decisive, and will, in all likelihood, keep the prospect from doing something they'll regret, like cancelling the order. After all, the pain point that originally brought the salesperson and prospect together will only reassert itself later. Now, if the prospect cancelled the order due to the security HAC, his HACs for trustworthiness, decisiveness, aggressiveness, or consistency will work against the salesperson because they will send corrective signals to the adaptor if they come back and ask for the order again after cancelling it. This is what the complex emotion embarrassment signals, which is a blend of the basic emotions disgust (with themselves) and fear. The salesperson then becomes the source of a corrective signal, which will agitate the prospect to move away from you due to embarrassment. Quite often, the prospect will then go and buy from a competitor with an inferior product or at a higher price to save themselves of the corrective signal of embarrassment of being inconsistent, indecisive, or untrustworthy. Those salespeople who have not read this book will be at a loss to explain this type of behavior and occurrence. As a salesperson, do yourself a favor and be proactive about buyer's remorse.

Your communication strategy at this phase is to communicate to the client that he has work to do before the benefits can be realized, but it will be worth it. He will shortly be able to regain that lost money in the benefits that your product confers. It's also important to share with the customer that he has lost nothing. What he's done is exchanged or transformed one form of his estate (money) into another form (your product or service) with your adaptation plan. Not only has he lost nothing, what he gained will relieve him of fear's pain, allowing him to be more productive or profitable. So he lost nothing and gained considerably, adding value to his operations. Don't make the mistake of redirecting the conversation back to a features and benefits of your product as a way of re-securing the sale. That doesn't respond to the basic emotion of loss or fear due to impact on other HACs that is driving the buyer's remorse.

EXUBERANCE

This emotional phase of exuberance starts the moment one of any of the anticipated benefits occurs. Exuberance is about tallying actual pain nullification against projected pain nullification. Pain nullification efficacy will also be validated at this stage, which was the whole point of the HAC. It is at this point that pain nullification actually occurs, validating the client's vision. More typically than not, this phase is marked by many small validations rather one single stroke of pain nullification. Because the pain nullification can happen in incremental steps due to incremental installation steps in the faith stage, it can creep right past a client, which is why you need to ask questions like, "Just like you planned, right?", "That's got to make you happy, right?", or "How's it feel not to have to worry about X, Y, or Z?" In this way, the client will be moved to constantly update their internal status.

Exuberance is also marked by increased positive agitation from the reactor. It will be intensifying the notification to the adaptor to move towards you and your product, to repeat the pleasure that they are now starting to receive at making the pain go away. So at this point the more moments of validation you can introduce into the client's circumstances, the more motivated he or she will be to increase the rate or tempo of implementation.

This emotional stage is also marked by accounting. Failure at this stage can occur due to failure to nullify the pain points to the degree projected. As the points of pain nullification and validation accrue, the client will be internally tallying them against the projected efficacy. Each client will be different, and there is no set rule that can be applied to all situations because you're dealing with client internal value scales. But since you know now that this internal tallying is taking place, why not, as a communication strategy, ask questions of the client like "What will this project have to look like for you to consider it a success?" or "How will you determine that this implementation was a success?" You might even sneak this kind of question into the faith phase as a way of keeping the client motivated and focused on the end goal.

Failure at this stage can occur when the client's internal tallying finds that the pain nullification varied too far below the projected. This can happen one of two ways. Either the pain nullification efficacy was overestimated, or the pain points were greater in scope or quantity than anticipated. It is not uncommon for both types of errors to occur because there is absolutely no way anyone can predict or determine the future when evaluating an adaptation plan. This is why it's vital to have a communication strategy at work in this phase to find out what the client is measuring. If your questions yield a pattern of the accounting process that looks like it will not end favorably for your product, you will have some forewarning and may be able to salvage the situation. Perhaps the client is ascribing properties of your product into the equation that are not related or do not exist to the adaptation plan or undervaluing the certain properties. If your product or service fails your client's internal accounting process, the net result will be his or her realization that he or she just traded one set of pain points for another and expended resources in doing so.

SATISFIED CUSTOMER

The satisfied customer emotional phase is marked by the comparison of the two previous emotions, faith and exuberance, to each other. Satisfaction is based on positive tallying of both implementation (faith) and pain nullification efficacy (exuberance) together. Failure to achieve either emotion will result in failure of satisfaction which has the strongest joy delivery of any growth signal. One thing that is unique in Application phase is that neither faith nor exuberance has to be fully satisfied before going on to the next emotion. These emotions are implementing in the real world, which may be different from the projected world of the Vetting phase. For example, it may take longer or cost more resources to implement an adaptation plan yet, once installed, exuberance occurs because the projected pain nullification occurs. In their accounting phase of each of faith and exuberance, both are compared to actual performance to projected performance. Deviations from projected in both, if present, are accrued and be scored negatively. The greater the deviation from the projections, the fewer the points of validation will occur leading to fewer moments of the growth signals of faith or exuberance. The objective of the whole process is to nullify pain points. It is for this reason that pain nullification exuberance growth signals will figure more prominently and be given more weight in the client's mind than the implementation growth signals of faith. If expectations were met, no deviations were accrued and a positive balance was scored for meeting expectations. If costs were less or the product or service performed better than expected, greater positive results were accrued. The reactor tallies this score giving more weight to the pain nullification score and produces a total. The take away point is small deviations from the proposed implementation plan will be outweighed by the product or service's ability to nullify pain.

If that total is negative, the customer will not achieve customer satisfaction. If the score is positive, then expectations were met or exceeded, then the reactor sends a much higher agitation signal indicating a higher degree of satisfaction as a growth signal. So customer satisfaction begins at the moment the client's internal accounting process tips from neutral to favorable towards your product. If the pain nullification concludes satisfactorily and the resources needed to obtain and implement it were less than the costs, the customer will feel a higher agitation of satisfaction. This initial moment of satisfaction does not necessarily come at the conclusion of implementation. It may come at any point in the implementation process. But what may also occur is that implementation may uncover or create more pain nullification on other issues not initially projected and may continue to accrue as well as the joy of satisfaction already accrued. An example of this may be that staff and crew morale may go way up that was never projected as a benefit, creating a better, more flexible work atmosphere leading to more productivity.

But satisfaction is a fleeting substance. Because the business circumstances surrounding and leading to the initial pain points are constantly shifting due to industry, consumers, economies, markets, innovation, legislation, and as your client's business grows or contracts, the few moments of joy will slowly yield to change. While the actual satisfaction of your adaptation plan may fade as the above circumstances have impact, the memory of the joy will not. That memory will be deposited in the client's memory by his or her ego. This memory will harden your client to competitive pressure. When new pain points start to rise, the memory of the joy of satisfaction you brought to him or her will be one of the first things the client will draw upon as he or she searches the memory for applicable experiences and exemplars to form a new HAC for the pain points of the future.

But don't become complacent just because your customer is currently satisfied. Initially, your product may perform well, meeting and exceeding all expectations. But a technical glitch can occur that requires follow up from other facets of the company. If those services create more pain points, the once satisfied client can start to develop pain points with other facets within their business.

Satisfied customers are eager to share their stories of joy. Telling others about their pleasurable experience is another way for them to extend and increase their pleasure by creating meaning and satisfying their six universal needs. Also, their conductors, which drive them to be the best they can be for themselves and others in their society, will push them to share their experience so that others may share in the benefits.

FIGURE 15.2

Application Phase of the Innovation Emotional Tonal Algorithm
with Line of Optimization

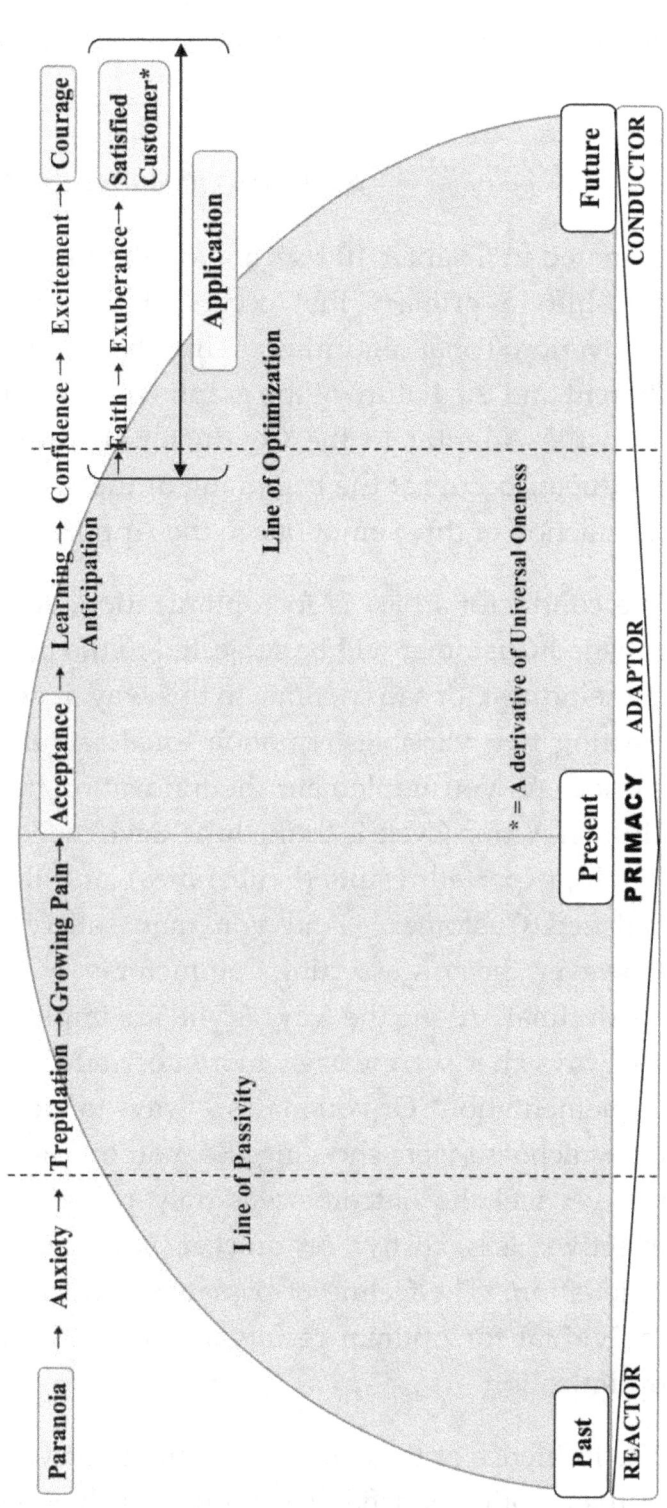

This is the source of referrals, a salesman's best friend.

In summation, we can now see that while the act of committing to the sale starts with courage, the sale consummation does not occur until the accounting process of customer satisfaction occurs, making the sales after the sales portion, the Application phase, even more important than the Vetting phase.

APPLICATION PHASE OPTIMIZATION

As noted in Chapter 10's section on the Line of Passivity, so, too, must we address the shift in primacy that occurs at the onset of the Application Phase of the Innovation Tonal algorithm. This shift occurs at the halfway point between the Present and the Future of the graph where the primacy/time sharing majority shifts from the Adaptor to the Conductor (Figure 15.2). This shift in primacy to the conductor occurs at the beginning of the Application Phase, prior to the attempted satisfaction of three emotions in the Application Phase.

The conductor's bias is for optimization, so the emotions faith, exuberance, and Satisfied Customer will be subjected to the internal urges/steering for optimization in their quest for satisfaction. In this way, it creates a range of evaluative feelings by creating two variables: emotion tonal satisfaction and efficacy. Here's how this works. As you implement the innovation/tool derived in the Vetting phase, the Human Action Cycle is trying to achieve each emotion as envisioned in resource cost (Faith), expected results (Exuberance), and the summary of those two elements in Satisfied Customer. And you may satisfy these emotion exactly as expected. However, the now asserting Conductor is forcing examination of whether the results are optimal. Along the way, as you are implementing the Innovation plan, you may see ways that were easier, more cost effective, or faster ways to accomplish the implementation. Or you may see ways to increase the efficacy of the desired results for which you were shooting. So, you may achieve the exact results they were look for, yet feel the outcome was only passable due to discovery of a better, more effective, less costly, or quicker way during the application of the selected innovation. The feeling of passable results is the bias of the conductor driving an individual for optimal results and that there is still work to be done to achieve optimization.

The influence of the conductor is progressively greater and dominant, culminating in the emotion Satisfied Customer which is heavily influenced by the Conductor's bias. This is why customer satisfaction is so difficult to achieve. Not only must you delivery the innovation/tool on time, on budget and have it produce the promised results, but along the way then customer must believe that there was no other better way to achieve the results. This may be impossible if the customer preferred a different innovation/tool solution in the Vetting Phase but was limited in resources, forcing them to select a solution within their means, but not optimal. This is where the concept of good versus great comes in. A good result satisfies all three emotions of the Implementation phase but is not optimal to the conductor's bias, where a great result not only satisfies these emotions, but also meets the conductor's bias for optimization.

This creates another avenue of questioning about a customer's choice and the framing of the results. If the customer is selecting a solution limited by resources, then the implementation plan must be framed as a good result. If the salesperson knows that the solution option selected is the most optimal, it can be framed as great. While there may be other, different solutions from competitors, the salesperson must be aware of how their solutions compare in optimization of both implementation and results. When a customer has a complex problem seeking to satisfy many different pain points, different vendor's solution will have different points of efficacy on each of the specified pain points. So, a customer will rationally seek the highest average of satisfaction across the pain point spectrum. While not all of the solution elements within the product you may be vending are optimal compared to the individual points of competitors' products, your solution can still be the optimal solution due to the highest average of satisfaction and achieve Satisfied Customer. Even if indications are you will deliver a good result if the customer was limited by resources and thus selection of solutions, this leaves an opportunity for upgrading in the future and that a good solution is a gateway, or stepping stone, solution to later achieving an optimal, great solution.

And like everything else human, differing DNA combination will set differing levels of optimization sought in general. This leads to the notion of laziness. While we are all driven biologically to seek the greatest results for the least amount of effort to differing degrees, as a species, there is a spectrum of individuals who will be driven by the conductor's bias for optimization. So laziness can be expressed as a combination of someone driven to conserve resources (Chapter 12, Line of Optimization section) plus a low drive for optimization from the conductor's bias.

COMMUNICATION

As noted earlier, the second half of the sales cycle is accomplished in conjunction with your company. As a salesperson, you may not have direct control over the new players introduced. So the role of the salesperson turns from solitary actor to that of manager and orchestrator. The most important skill that you bring to this new role as manager and coordinator is communication. This includes both written and verbal communication. Now, as a student of the Paradaptive Intelligence, you know that your communications with everyone within your organization will generate an emotion within them. As a salesperson and the lead on the sale, the order you write along with special instructions, notations, and other pertinent information becomes the motive of a HAC for every person involved in the adaptation plan's fulfillment. The more information you provide the better your company's supporting players' motives and action plans for the fulfillment will conform to what you promised the client. Because you now know that you will be creating emotions within people in every portion of the company that come in contact with your clients' orders, you will need to manage that communication process.

The relationship emotional tonal scales will be different than that we've used for the sales cycle but the problem solving/adaptation algorithm is universal (see Figure 10.4) which was based on fear/pain nullification. The emotional tonal algorithms used for employee management are not the subject of this book, and any discussion of those emotions would be better served in a book centered on that topic of management. But even though the tonal algorithms will be varied for the different players you come into contact with inside your company, the skills, tactics, and techniques are all the same when you identify the proper emotional tonal algorithms.

It is important for you to control and manage the emotions you invoke in others in your company as a salesman. By keeping your communications style to one that produces positive communications, you will help your orders be processed and implemented by the company. If you yield to the temptation to air a grievance or use anger to correct some action within the company concerning your order processing, no matter how well deserved, you will create a negative emotion in others towards you and possibly your order. And these others, who are supposed to be helping you to implement your orders, may not be able to separate their negative feelings for you from your clients' orders. Negative emotions will be telling your support team to move away from you, hence to move away from your orders also. So your clients, innocent third parties in any internal fracas, will receive the brunt of any negative emotional blowback, which can result in a backslide of the hard work you've done to move the client towards satisfaction.

Most sales cancellations occur in the faith or exuberance emotional phases because management of companies don't know what emotions occur in this phase of the sales cycle. Management typically recognizes that, with a commitment at the courage emotional phase, a change takes place. They recognize that there is a distinction between order getting and order fulfillment. Generally, after the sale, when a company obtains an order, that order is sent to a different set of individuals, teams, or departments to complete the sale, which in their mind is delivering the product. Nothing could be further from the truth. As was demonstrated in Figure 8.5, the sales process is a flow of precise emotions in a specific order. If the salesperson departs the process at the point of a sale, courage, he has left the job half done, and the sale is in grave jeopardy. The salesperson, if he is now using Paradaptive Intelligence based sales techniques, sold the product to nullify specific pains. If he is not there for the adaption plan implementation phase or has not given specific, detailed information to the order fulfillers, then the customer will have been abandoned in mid-sales cycle. The chances are very likely this sale may be cancelled. Salespeople have always called this the "follow through" or "follow-up." In reality it is finishing the sales cycle for specific pain nullification covering the faith and exuberance emotional phases of the emotional tonal algorithm of the sales cycle. It's delivering on the promise made during the growing pains emotional phase to guide the implementation of the innovation. By abandoning the clients in the Application phase, you just justified and recreated the fear you alleviated in growing pains portion of the Acquisition phase as well as failing to fulfill the adaptation plan you presented.

CONCLUSION

A sale is like a bet. The customer has put his money on the table and bet that he will get the results he projected. If the results occur, you (the salesperson) get to keep the money. If the projected results do not occur, the client will seek to regain their money from you. Or failing that, they will seek to take what they deem the equivalent from your hide by broadcasting aspersions about your character or that of your company's to anyone who will listen. And with the internet, a lot of people are listening these days. And like all bets, there are odds involved. If you stay in the sales loop and manage the Application phase processes, then your odds of keeping the money are extremely good. But if you quit after the emotion courage, then the odds will greatly shift against you. If you have any desire to work with a client in the future when their circumstances change again, then you would be well served to be a central player in the Application phase process. It is the only path that leads to a satisfied customer. The outcome of the application of your product or service will lead to whether your relationship with that particular client is upgraded or downgraded in their eyes. And this has particular bearing not only on you the salesperson, but also with how they view your company.

MYTHS AND OTHER SALES LORE

In sales management, there is an axiom that says internally you need to sell to your coworkers just like you sell your clients. As with other myths, not fully understanding the mechanisms of the brain and emotions has led to an axiom that misses the true nature of what is transpiring. Salesmen are very good at intuitively managing the emotion algorithm of clients. They've been doing it for as long as there have been salesmen. They also use those skills to manage the emotions of others, including internal company resources. Because they are using the same emotional sales management skills for a different purpose, it *feels* like they're being sold. But they are not.

Internal company staff are not being motivated by fear or anger (we hope). Your client's orders are not pain points to them (or they shouldn't be). They are not attempting to make decisions regarding the potential solutions available for pain nullification or assess their efficacy. Because salespeople apply their emotional management skills on others, these types of tactics get mislabeled as selling. Only individuals who are trying to nullify pain points through a second party's adaptation plan that involves the exchange of consideration and are being sold.

16

RELATIONSHIPS – FEAR AND LOATHING, TO MENTION JUST A FEW

"With friends like this, who needs enemies?"
Anonymous

As discussed at the beginning of Chapter 10, there are two components to every sale, something and someone. This chapter will focus on the someone, the relational aspect between buyer and seller. In selling, the salesperson is trying to create an action in the buyer, so it is the buyer's emotional state that is the center of interest. If the tables were reversed and this was a case of a reluctant seller, everything would still apply, only in reverse.

Frederick F. Reichheld, in his book, *The Loyalty Effect*, states:

> "Loyalty is dead, the experts proclaim, and the statistics seem to bear them out. On average, U.S. corporations now lose half their customers in five years, half their employees in four, and half their investors in less than one. We seem to face a future in which the only business relationships will be opportunistic transactions between virtual strangers."

This paints a pretty gruesome picture of business. The growth of the internet and e-commerce seems to bear this prediction out. But is that how it is?

It may well be the case in the executive suites where the customer only shows up as a statistic, one of many among the types and volume of sales that are neatly divided into continents, country, states, districts, territories or industries. It's easy to believe loyalty is dead when you don't have to look a customer in the eye. It is this aloofness that leads to the statistics decried by Mr. Reichheld, and quite frankly, is responsible for the poor performance and lackluster sales of modern businesses directed by the executive level. What this book exposes and lays bare is universal for all. The hardwiring described is present in every human and active in every transaction of

221

commerce, regardless of geography or culture. It is the lack of understanding of consumer behavior and what facilitates buying decisions that leads to business policies and behaviors that are antithetical to their stated goal of increasing sales.

Janet Robinson states, "Repeat business or behavior can be bribed. LOYALTY has to be earned." She's right - mostly. If all you are using to advance the sale of your products or services are price, distribution, and promotion, then you are leaving money on the table by ignoring the necessary and required human element of the relationship between buyer and seller. Fortunately, for the readers of this book, this chapter will bring a new understanding of how to manage the relationships between the buyer and seller.

TWO SEPARATE EMOTIONAL PATHS FOR ALL SALES

Somewhere near the beginning of time, when the first two salesmen met on some nameless road, the argument commenced as to what was more important to consummating a sale, the relationship between buyer and seller or the product. Until now, until this book, there was a presumption that product and relationship were all mixed up into one big tangled fur ball that we just haven't been able to unravel yet. The truth of the matter is, when linked to the actual mechanisms of the mind, there are several separate emotional pathways that occur concurrently on every sale, whether it's person to person or a faceless transaction on the internet. The product, the *something*, whether tool, innovation, service, or behavioral change, invokes its own emotional pathway, as discussed in previous chapters. The *someone* that is the relationship between buyer and seller may involve up to three other relationship emotional tonal algorithm pathways concurrently, the intra-personal relationship between the buyer and seller, the relationship of the buyer to the seller's tribe (his company) and the buyer's relationship to the tribe that may have produced a specific product (the brand).

Man is a social creature and his brain's construction and mechanisms of adaptation are organized around furthering this predisposition. So there are two elements to which the Paradaptive Intelligence Network must accommodate, intrapersonal relationships between individuals and relationships between an individual and tribe which is a collection of organized people. Relationships are important from a survivability standpoint. As we've learned in earlier chapters, the flow of communication and credibility of information in the Acquisition process is very much a function of the relationship between salesperson and prospect. Individuals, prospects, with poor, hindered, or under-developed adaptation skills or capabilities in a particular area can acquire better adaptation plans through relationships. That's why prospects seek out salespeople or their companies — to acquire their adaptation plans. But in addition to this individual element between salespeople and prospects, people are designed to have relationships with collectives of organized peoples.

The basic unit of collectivism is tribalism. All collective groups of people are tribal in nature to the Paradaptive Intelligence Network. In man's development, all societies originated from humble tribal beginnings whether it was Hittites, Sumerians, Visigoths, Celts, Saxons, Vikings, American Indians, Incas, etc. Belonging to a tribe confers certain benefits. The collective community offers protection through the greater strength of numbers and the ability to collectively nurture and feed the young, sick, injured, or old. So the Paradaptive Intelligence System is built to accommodate this need to evaluate and relate to a collection of people in order to obtain benefits.

SEVEN TYPES OF RELATIONSHIPS

There are seven basic types of Relationships:

1. Intimate
2. Companionship
3. Professional
4. Institutional
5. Competition
6. Rival
7. Conflict

All these relationships are very similar in the Joy portion of the emotional tonal algorithm, but differ significantly in the corrective signal portion. While all relationships can evoke any corrective signal, the list below is focused on the predominance of what occurs in the normal course of the described relationships. The rationale is based upon which corrective signal that predominantly would prevent an individual from entering into that type of relationship again once a known danger of its type is registered in a memory as an exemplar.

Intimate

Intimate relationships are companionship relationships with the opposite sex with the inclusion of one or more of mating/childrearing strategies encoded in human DNA. Lovers leave — therefore the corrective signal portion of both is based on the basic emotion of loss. There are two varieties of intimate relationships:

- Lust is the mating strategy based on physical attraction and visual signaling.
- Pair Bonding is a child rearing strategy based on communication.

Companionship

Companionship – our friendships are based on joy that these relationships bring us via the fulfillment of the six universal needs. Friends can betray us so the corrective signal portion of this tonal algorithm is betrayal, which is a boundary violation and invokes the basic emotion anger.

Professional

Professional relationships occur in tribal settings. An individual has elected to join a group of people, a tribe, to further a motivation. Tribes have structure, and thus leadership, therefore the relationships of this type are either that of equals or subservience/authority. Professional relationships come in two varieties.

- Vertical Professional relationships are based on power. Employees have the power to fire their supervisors through collective poor work performance and supervisors have the power to remove individuals for the same reason. This is threat based and invokes fear.

- Horizontal Professional relationships with co-workers and clients have no power over each other and are based on mutual assistance. Lack of assistance creates obstacles and invokes the basic emotion of anger. The worst that can be done in a horizontal relationship is to say bad things about you creating impediments and obstacles for you in your job, trade, profession or industry, or in the relationship with your supervisor. These are obstacles and boundary violations that create anger.

Institutional

Institutional organizations can violate processes and rights and invokes the basic emotion of disgust with unfair actions. Examples of institutions could be governments, clubs, churches, organizations, brands, clubs, tribes, etc. For example, a person may not be interested in joining a club because the last one they were in made unfounded claims about the individual's dues payments and then revoked his membership without so much as allowing him to provide proof to refute the claims. Or, a brand that advertised like crazy telling the consumer their product was the greatest, only for the consumer to find that it did not live up to those promises, is a boundary violation. Anything associated with that brand would be considered suspect in the future.

Competition

This is a reactor-driven relationship in obtaining scarce resources with multiple persons within your identified tribe.

Rival

This is a reactor-driven relationship in obtaining scarce resources with a singular person within your tribe and usually someone very close in the level of your skills or attributes upon which you are competing.

Conflict

This is a reactor driven relationship in obtaining scarce resources with someone from without your identified tribe.

For the purposes of sales and this book, we'll focus only on horizontal client/salesperson relationships and institutional relationships because of their connection with the institution of brands and organizations. In this way, we can explain why customers and prospects might like you but not your product, company, or brand, or vice versa.

HORIZONTAL PROFFESIONAL RELATIONSHIPS

The relationship between a salesperson and a prospect is essentially focused upon the prospect evaluating the information being conveyed about the adaptation plan, and determining the chances of doing future business together (See Figure 16.1). The greater the level of the relationship, the greater likelihood that the information being offered by the sales person will be accepted unchallenged.

This is made possible by the human action cycle that can pause and swap out different motives in a micro-second, giving you the sense that it is all one, seamless activity. The Innovation and Relationship HACs swap seamlessly between furthering the motives of "I want to help this person by selling them my product," and "I want to develop a relationship with this person (or not)." Because salespeople usually execute their profession eyeball to eyeball with prospects, which stimulates empathetic signals to their Paradaptive Intelligence Network via their Mirror Neuron System, which in turn influences the cooperation bias of the adaptor and altruism bias to do their best for others, courtesy of the conductor, they are more susceptible to the influence of relationships. These influences are hard to escape

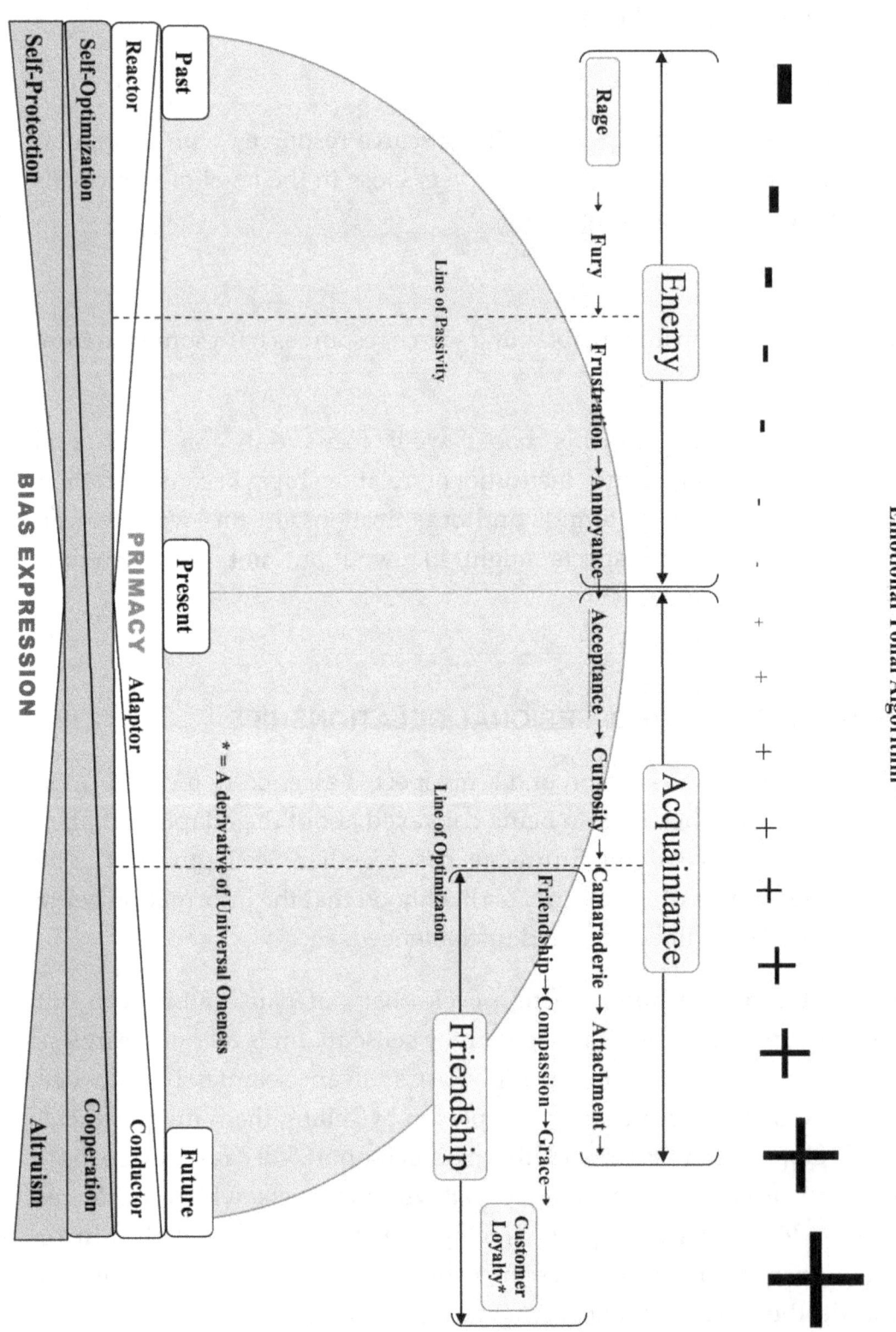

FIGURE 16.1

Horizontal Professional Relationship
Emotional Tonal Algorithm™

given our hardwiring as social creatures. These relationships exist and will influence all transactions between salespeople and their clients and prospects. This also leads back to the themes of a previous section, and why management makes decisions towards its clients and selling that are often antithetical to the goals of selling, forgetting the face-to-face nature of sales where the rubber (a firm's product) meets the road (the client's wallet).

Though the Innovation algorithm and horizontal relationships are separate, these paths influence each other through the ego. Remember, it is the ego that allows information into and out of memory and the adaptor, so it can pull information from each of the separate emotional pathways to help the conscious mind, the adaptor, nullify pain by finding the right tool/innovation. However, this is not necessarily a two-way street flowing in equal directions. Innovation is problem solving. In business, if the tool doesn't solve the problem, i.e., doesn't nullify the pain, it will be abandoned regardless of the underlying relationship. The presence of a negative agitation expression from the client's competition (threat) or obstacles (anger) is too persistent and pernicious to overcome the goodwill of a relationship

But these two pathways can complement each other at differing times. If the adaption plan is good and nullifies pain, then the relationship with its deliverer can be enhanced. But this won't occur until the conclusion of the innovation seeking emotional tonal algorithm, and *only if* the individual/company reaches the satisfied customer emotional stage. However, the relationship emotional tonal pathway can influence the innovation seeking emotional pathway in two ways, 1) by setting expectations, and 2) by increasing the credibility of the adaptation plan.

Setting expectations is straightforward. Doing business in the past with a salesperson led to pain nullification. The expectation is that doing business with you now will also lead to pain nullification and joy. So the perception of the client will be that you can help, already putting you effortlessly at the learning anticipation emotional tone or further, such as greater confidence, in the innovation seeking emotional tonal algorithm based solely on the history of your relationship. For any salesman this is a huge advantage over the competition. In addition, because of your history, clients will be more willing to take the assertions of your adaptation plan with less fact and back checking. This increased credibility is also a tremendous advantage over competition, but it will only come if your relationship is in the friendship phase of the relationship emotional tonal algorithm or greater.

Sometimes it's easier to understand how things work by looking at the converse. You'll often hear clients and prospects speak ill of other businesses and competitors. This is often expressed as some variation on the theme of "He sold me a hunk of junk," or "Their products are pieces of excrement." This sentiment indicates that the person or company purchased a product from the described person but was never able to get to beyond the faith or exuberance, and thus did not reach the satisfied customer emotional tone of Application phase. Because the promised or calculated pain nullification never occurred or the implementation cost exceeded what was described in the adaptation plan, the individual attaches blame to the *someone*. This blame is ascribed to the source of the information from which their calculations were based, the salesperson. It won't be attached directly to the company for whom the salesperson worked, but indirectly for hiring a scoundrel like that salesperson. In the Innovation emotional tonal algorithm, at any phase when the innovation is determined to be unable to nullify the pain point, the tool/innovation is abandoned. And based upon the situation of the abandonment, the salesperson's position on the Relationship emotional tonal algorithm will be evaluated and updated.

THREE PHASES OF THE
RELATIONSHIP EMOTIONAL TONAL ALGORITHM

In Figure 16.1, the horizontal relationship emotional tonal algorithm is broken into its three phases: Enemy, Acquaintance, and Friendship. Each of the phases represents distinct portions in the relationship between salesperson and your clients and prospects. And as with the Innovation emotional tonal algorithm, this pathway shows a continuous flow of emotions from the highest intensity emotions to lowest for both positive and negative that are associated with business relationships. You may encounter clients and prospects at any phase of emotion on the negative side of the continuum. If there is no past boundary violation or you did not create an impediment to the individual's goals prior to meeting them, then your relation automatically starts at acceptance. And like all other emotional tonal algorithms, one cannot skip or bypass an emotional tone, but rather move through one tone at a time sequentially. But unlike the Innovation emotional tonal algorithm, the relationship emotional tonal algorithm exhibits no action points. This is because this emotional tonal algorithm does not represent a seeking/searching behavior. It merely reflects the strength of a relationship by increased intensity of emotion, both joy and corrective signal.

For example, if you look at Figure 8.3, you'll see several emotional phases associated with the basic emotion of anger. At this point, you should start to see that the names, labels, and terms we use for emotion tones serve as indicators of emotional intensity, and are relative to each other. One label, name, or term signaling the strength or variance in an emotional pathway is relative and is only understood relative to labels for other intensities of the tones of emotions within the emotional pathway. So depending on the situation, more intermediary emotional tones of those labeled may apply, but this does not detract from the overall usefulness of the diagram or understanding of the pathway in regard to the negative emotions of the Relationship emotional tonal algorithm.

ENEMY

The Enemy portion of the relationship emotional tonal algorithm represents the past oriented phase of a relationship. If a client or prospect's emotional state, also called attitude, is in the negative, then you've done something or are being related to someone who was injurious to this person. The client's reactor is signaling him or her to move away from you. As a salesperson, your job is to help people by nullifying their pain points. In all likelihood, these clients feel that you or the exemplar they relate to you wasted their time, money, or other resources by violating the cooperation bias of the adaptor in past dealings.

Interestingly enough, the Enemy phase gives us a good understanding of the importance of the relationship relative to the adaption plan. Even if someone doesn't like you, pain point nullification takes precedence, but only if your product is unique and is not interchangeable, replaceable, or substitutable. People will still do business with you despite increasing negative, corrective signals towards you on the relationship algorithm. In fact, it is considered a sign of business acumen to be able to do business with one's enemy when required. However, this can only go so far. This concept needs to be refined just a bit. People will do business with you, even if they don't like you, i.e. have negative emotions towards you, up to the point where the adaptor remains in control. The tipping point, the Line of Passivity, is going to be somewhere between frustration and fury (anger), depending on the person's ability to override the agitation expression coming from the reactor. After frustration, provided there are no exceptions, the mind will become more irrational than rational, thus the ability to override the agitation expression will become more difficult before becoming overpowering. Once beyond fury, the likelihood of doing business will diminish due to the increasing irrational state of the buyer. At this point on the Enemy phase of the continuum, you begin to see passive/aggressive behavior. Incidentally, the term passive/aggressive is another misnomer that has crept into the American lexicon. Before Peil's work and this book, there was no foundational theory to ground the observed behavior of aggressive behavior followed by passive behavior designed to mollify any turbulence the aggressive behavior initiated between the parties. Aggressiveness is the dominant behavior of fury. Passivity is the subordinate emotion. Therefore, the term would be more accurately described as aggressive/passive behavior. There is *almost* no opportunity for business dealings or relationships at the rage emotional tone due to the total irrationality of their behavior and dominance of the reactor's mission to preserve the body and self. If your product is so unique and necessary to a buyer that without it he or she will face extinction, pain point nullification may take precedence over his rage, but it's improbable. At this point, it depends on what is the biggest pain point – you or the issue they're trying to resolve. The prospect's reactor is actively, overridingly telling them to move away from both you and the issue, so you have no reliable way of predicting a sale at this emotional tone in a relationship.

The practical effect of this is that the client's ability to deal with minor inconveniences and irregularities in your business deals will diminish as you move further up the corrective signal intensity side because the client will be devoting more and more mental effort into overriding corrective signals from the reactor, and will have less and less capacity of the adaptor to deal with nonconforming issues. This is why the actual breaking point is case specific. A regular, non-problematic transaction can be "stomached" by someone with a more intense corrective signal than someone dealing with a bunch of exceptions from someone that annoys them. The rule of thumb is that the less a client or prospect that dislikes the salesperson has to think about the deal, the more likely the deal will go through. This is important to salespeople because, from time to time, something outside your control will go wrong in a transaction. All is not lost as long as you know that if there is some novel aspect to your product, you're still in the game as long as you put together a seamless, thoroughly vetted adaptation plan that requires no action other than for the buyer to hold his nose and do the deal. The take away point here is just because they don't like you, your company, or your brands, doesn't mean that there's not a sale to be had.

Rage

This is the most intense form of the emotion anger. It is measured by the total irrationality towards the object of dislike and the overpowering desire to strike out at it, to push back. At this point, all negative corrective signals in their most intensive form are indistinguishable from each other due to the utter incoherence and irrationality towards a person, place, or thing.

Fury

This emotional tone represents a shift in balance between rationality to irrationality. The prospect will start to show aggression towards you in aggressive/passive form. Just as discussed earlier in the book in the acquisition corrective signal phase, the prospect will be showing indirect active corrective signals, in this case aggression from anger, and then try and walk it back as the adaptor exerts what little control it has left to moderate the aggressiveness with conciliatory remarks. When it comes to potential sales, this tone is the limit, for clients who need to do business with you but have negative emotions towards some aspect you represent, but there must be significant separation between you and the alternative, though. The client's need will be measured by the cost of alternative products or services. There will be displays of animus towards you that will occur randomly just because the client won't be able to control themselves all the time, and this aggression will certainly surface around any irregularity in process or slightest deviation from their expectations.

Frustration

This emotional tone represents a feeling of anger towards you by a buyer who is willing to do business with you as long as there is moderate separation between you and the alternative. While the buyer is mostly rational, your presence is still causing significant disruption to the adaptor's processes. There will be no direct display of animus to the salesperson unless a modest irregularity to the proceedings occurs.

Annoyance

This emotional tone represents a feeling of anger towards you by the buyer who is willing to do business with you if there is only a minor separation between you and the alternative. The buyer is rational with only a slight disruption to the adaptor's processes caused by your presence, which they tolerate. Tolerance is the act and the feeling we experience when suppressing the agitation expression contained in a corrective signal, like annoyance. There will be no display of animus unless a significant irregularity to the proceedings occurs, at which time you can expect to see slight, if any, animus displayed.

ENEMY PHASE
- MOVEMENT BETWEEN EMOTIONAL STATES

The Enemy phase of a horizontal professional relationship emotional tonal algorithm is characterized by empowerment and anger. When someone has been injured by someone else, either by a boundary violation or creating an obstacle to some goal or motive, then the other person has power over them. The need for power is one of the six universal needs and is foundational to relationships. Empowerment is the installation and confers power to that person to make and be responsible for change. The removal of the ability to create change is called disempowerment. If someone has the ability to create boundary violations or impediments for you, they have power over you. Good business relationship cannot develop or exist in the *active* presence of a boundary violation or obstacle to one of the two parties, so the removal of the source of violation or impediment is foundational to any hope of developing a positive relationship. This is different from what was discussed in the previous section which was discussing injurious actions. This is not only significant to client relationships, it is also essential in employee/employer relationships in sales. If your employees work in a climate of fear or obstacles, then you as an employer will never experience their creativity or loyalty.

There are companies that do not permit fraternization between their employees and outside salespeople. This in no way negates the business relationship and the need to manage it. Prospects are hardwired to have relationships, especially ones where pain points are discussed and judgments lead to commitments. In short, if the emotional tonal algorithm of Innovation is activated by engaging a salesperson, that means that there is a *someone* involved, and therefore the relationship emotional tonal algorithm pathway is automatically invoked.

APOLOGY RULES AND MECHANISMS

Apologies are the way that one moves between any corrective signal algorithm in relationships stepping down clients and prospects from higher intensity corrective signals to the present. This applies equally to fear, anger, loss, and disgust.

The way in which a salesperson improves his or her relationship in the enemy phase is to first stop the injurious or boundary violating/impeding action. This is first accomplished by owning your responsibility for causing the negative emotions to the person. This can be as simple as an apology. This lets the buyer know that you know you caused or contributed to the situation. This will satisfy annoyance and move the individual to acceptance if their beginning emotional state was annoyance. This will also prevent any further intensification of the buyer's negative emotions. The rest is well known, even biblical in nature. Secondly, you must remove any future potential for the problem actions to resurface and demonstrate this to the injured parties if their relationship emotion starts at frustration. An apology that includes the phrase "and this will never happen again, and here's how we're going to prevent that…" will cover both the frustration and annoyance emotional phase which are both passive emotions, being to the right of the Line of Passivity (Figure 16.1). Commitments to not repeating the behavior removes any future potential threat. Thirdly, you must make whole any damage you incurred to the satisfaction of those injured to remove any history and memory of pain from the past if their starting emotional state is fury. By making reparations, it removes or nullifies your actions as an exemplar from memory of injurious behavior.

Making reparations is an active response. This is required and easy to identify because if the person you've injured is aggressive/passive, this is an active response to your actions clearly indicating that they are to the left of the Line of Passivity and are experiencing the emotion fury or greater. Active actions, aggressive/passive behavior, by the client or prospect require active responses by you, hence reparations. In sales, this could be an adjustment in price, discount on the next order, include at no cost some valued accessory or service, or any number of other options in this vein available to a salesperson. This may also involve letting the person who was affected release his or her anger, scorn, venom, etc. upon you. This is called venting. The client's or prospect's active, aggressive/passive response may also take the form of complaints to a third party. Just remember, when the client's or prospect's action moves from passive/internal to aggressive/external actions, your apology strategy must contain an active element as well.

And the last rule of apologies is contrary to all traditions most have been taught about the matter. Most people have been taught to lead with an apology and this is supposed to set things right. This is completely and utterly wrong. It can't and won't satisfy the emotions of the offended client or prospect unless their emotion is the lowest form of a particular corrective signal. As demonstrated throughout this book, you must deal with the client or prospect at the emotion stage they are experiencing and de-escalate their emotions into the present. As just learned, if the client or prospect is at fury and you're starting out with an apology which is aimed at satisfying annoyance, you're not addressing their emotional stage. Always start with the emotion stage they are experiencing and work backwards towards the present and acceptance. The quick rule of thumb is to lead with the most intense emotion stage they are experiencing in forming apologies and work other necessary elements into the apology in order as you move down the corrective signal emotional algorithm.

Often, people feel that saying you're sorry should be all that is necessary to resolve a threatening situation, which is the case if someone is annoyed with you or other lowest corrective signal tone in a relationship. But if the threat or anger runs deeper, saying you're sorry just won't cut it, psychologically speaking. The conscious mind, the adaptor, which is receiving the apology, has no control over how the reactor will respond to a threat. So, in order to repair the situation, some careful questioning to determine where their reactor is with the threat or anger you're creating will be necessary to determine your apology strategy. One of the difficulties in choosing the level of apology is determining what the agitation level is if it is passive. Both annoyance and frustration are to the right of the Line of Passivity, which means both of the emotion levels will not be aggressively presented; both are being internalized. So how do you tell at what level their anger is trending at? The answer is easy if you remember that the function of the Mirror Neuron System's function is to outwardly display internal emotion states. Unless the offended is expending prodigious amounts of concentration suppressing the expressions of the Mirror Neuron System, you will be able to access their internal state by the level of their agitation. Their Paradaptive Intelligence system is giving them agitation to move away; this translates into directives of action, movement. Someone experiencing frustration will be antsy, fidgety, whereas someone experiencing annoyance will be more sedate.

While the enemy phase of the relationship tonal algorithm is rearward in its gaze, looking into the past as to what you've done to cause pain (psychic, i.e. pain point), it also presumes that you will also continue to cause pain in the future. This is why it is so vital to acknowledge your responsibility and the steps you've taken not to do the same in the future. If you do this properly, you will have removed any past (fury), future (frustration), and present (annoyance) potential for causing pain to the buyer, thus removing a threat, obstacle, or boundary violation.

Making whole any disruption or damage due, whether direct or indirect, is an entirely different action compared to verbal apologies or assurances. This is business, and it may not be worth your while as the cost of making reparations may outweigh the future gains of their business. It just depends upon you and what you think the impact will be upon your reputation in your industry. But keep in mind that negative information floating around in the industry about you will not create positive emotions and will make it harder for you to gain the loyalty of future customers by starting you off in the Enemy phase of the relationship emotional tonal algorithm for having demonstrated your potential to cause injury to others, an unwholesome activity, thus setting the expectation in new prospects that you will do the same to them. Reparation doesn't have to mean paying them out of pocket. The injured party can be given special dispensation in future deals, i.e. discounts, to work towards reparations. After all, it's better to get a smaller profit margin than no profit margin at all.

17

RELATIONSHIPS AND CUSTOMER LOYALTY

An ounce of loyalty is worth a pound of cleverness.
- Elbert Hubbard

Whose bread I eat, his song I sing.
- German Saying

Having explored the corrective signal phase of the professional horizontal relationship, which is described as the self-preservation portion of the relationship algorithm, this chapter will focus on the self-development and self-actualization portions of relationships called the Acquaintance and Friendship phases, respectively. The Friendship phase's programming serves the biological function of engaging an individual in behavior that can be beneficial to survival and procreation. This is linked to curiosity, which in turn is linked to the adaptor's primary mission to learn. This is an important aspect of the human psyche to the salesperson. As an example, let's look at the converse of engagement-disengagement. Boredom, disengagement, is the lack of engagement in activities that do not provide self-development. The business equivalent of this complex emotional blend, stagnation, is that of loss plus either anger or fear, depending on the level of stimulation with which the reactor wants to prod the adaptor to get it moving in a different direction. So, knowing that a business that has reached a plateau will drive business owners and managers with corrective signals of boredom, which the business owners feel as stagnation, will drive them to seek and engage in relationships that will help them develop their business. This makes the friendship phase a powerful ally to the salesperson. This is the source of all social networking whether it is via digital social or personal networks. Maybe, you don't have the answer, but in your travels and working with other businesses you might have come into contact with someone who has a solution that may be right for your particular problem. This is why if you, as a salesperson, when calling on a prospect's place of business with "Sell, Sell, SELL!" on your mind rather than the proper mission of being there to help, you're not working within nature's structure and functionality of the Paradaptive Intelligence Network. Remember, there are two basic strategies that we've been equipped with, 1) create and modify tools (modifying our environment) and 2) modify our behavior, which includes creating relationships to gain resources, knowledge, and adaptation plans from others. This is the source of the phrase "consultive selling." By being a purveyor of not only your specific adaptation plan, but also acting as an agent of connection to others with their own adaptation plans, you've added value to your relationship with any prospect you encounter.

The self-actualization phase, the Friendship Phase, is about evaluative emotions that drive us to be the best we can be, or achieve the best possible of outcomes of our actions. They drive us to evaluate what worked and didn't, and how we can improve. In relationships, this is about helping others so others will help us reciprocally. By helping others we've identified as having resources, talent, skills, or behaviors that are beneficial, we strengthen our self-selected society, which in turn strengthen our chances of not only surviving, but succeeding to the greatest extent of our talents by motivating others via the cooperation bias of the adaptor to reciprocate with theirs.

ACQUAINTANCE AND FRIENDSHIP PHASES

Just like the Innovation emotional tonal algorithm, the Relationship emotional tonal algorithm is a joy-based algorithm of emotional tones. (Figure 17.1) Your buyers will be rewarded and compelled to seek deeper relationships with you; they're hardwired for it, and it is universal. So, the game is rigged in your favor. This flow of joy-based, approach/repeat signaling is broken into two phases, Acquaintance and Friendship. What separates the two is respect and loyalty. Respect is acknowledgement. It is applied to tribal members as well as nontribal. It is applied in greater degrees towards others as one progresses through the Acquaintance phase until maximum acknowledgement is attained upon obtaining the emotion attachment. Loyalty, emotionally speaking, is a modification to the emotion attachment of varying intensities that allows for the nullification of imperfections in others. The Acquaintance phase is marked by its complete lack of it, whereas the Friendship phase is defined by attachment of loyalty at varying intensities at every emotional tone in this phase of the emotional tonal algorithm.

FIGURE 17.1

Horizontal Professional Relationship
Emotional Tonal Algorithm with Line of Optimization™

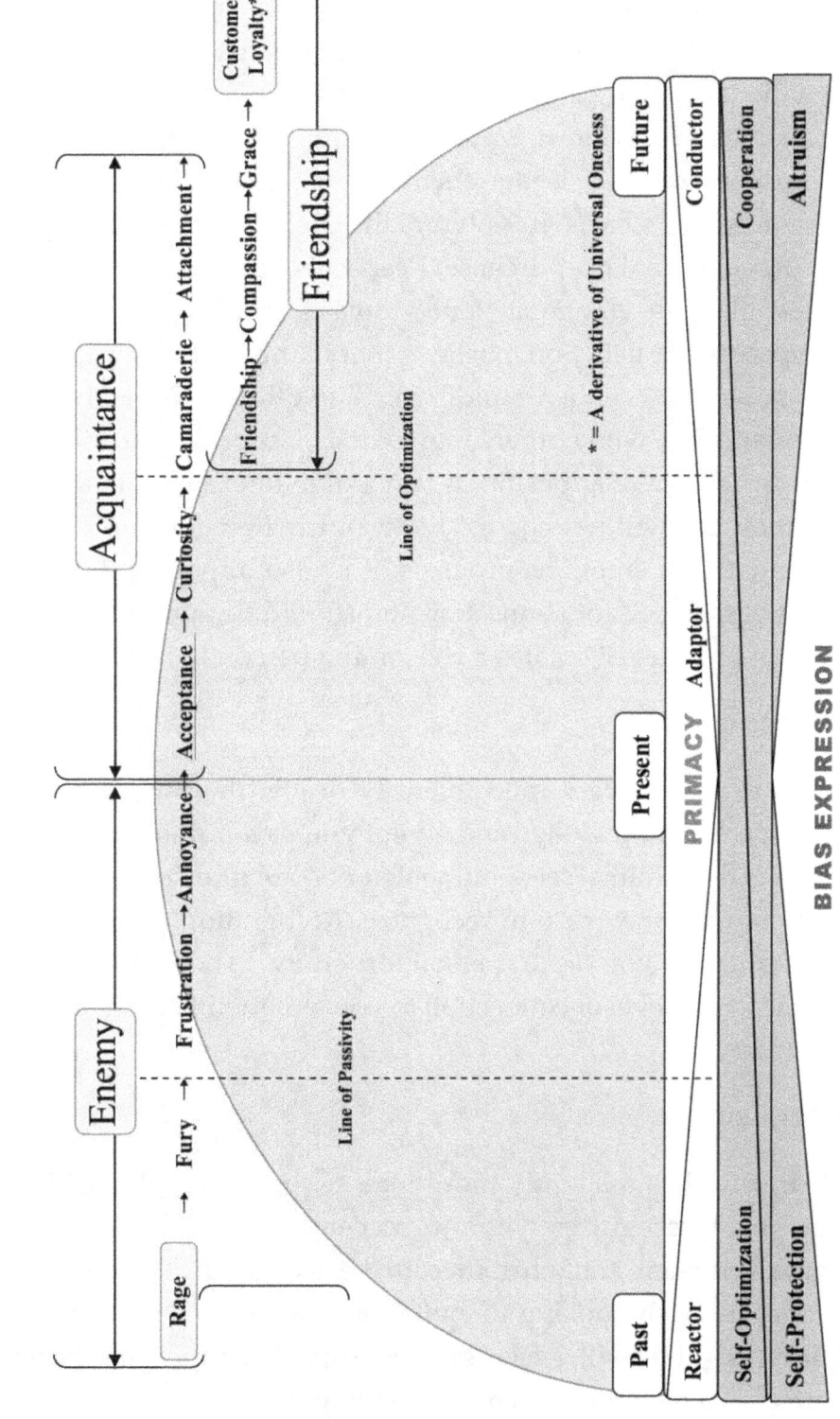

ACQUAINTANCE PHASE

The Acquaintance phase is marked by the application of respect and exploration. In business, this is not about learning about the product, but rather about the personal aspects of the salesperson, prospect, company, or brand. The strength of the business relationship will be determined by the prospect or client's emotional tone, not the salesperson's. While this process is going on in both the prospect and the salesperson simultaneously, it is the client/prospect's feelings that will set the tone of the relationship because it is always the prospect/client that must commit to an action, courage, to make a purchase. Respect is applied in increasing intensities with each movement in emotional tones toward attachment where the maximum level of respect is applied. Some believe that all human beings are due respect and quickly grant acceptance then rapidly move to other emotional tones such as curiosity and camaraderie, while others may be much more cautious or jaded in attaching more respect to the relationship. It is possible to exaggerate application of respect, but it cannot and will not change the way the Relationship emotional algorithm and its foundational emotions progress. It is also important to note that respect is a huge part of the need for connection and should be applied to clients and prospects upon contact because it creates a welcoming persona.

Acceptance

This is a very, very mild intensity of joy, the minimum threshold. At this point, prospects acknowledge and accept you as a human and potential business partner. This is the minimal recognition that you are due, the token respect they would afford any human they care to recognize. Recognition is the key to acceptance; they are recognizing you as a person or entity. They are also acknowledging a low satisfaction level of connection to you as a member of their society, clan, business, or industry.

Curiosity

Curiosity has a slightly more intense, positive value of joy. This emotion from a prospect recognizes you as someone of different, special, unique qualities, achievements, and attributes to be explored. This works towards the need of connection. By looking to explore more about another person, you will find more instances that will create greater respect for their character or achievements and attaches a high level of connection to you.

Camaraderie

Camaraderie contains a low to moderate level of joy in its agitation expression. In this emotional phase, esteem is the need most satisfied since a buyer is finding commonalities between themselves and you that they find worthy. There is also the recognition of you as a fellow traveler whose journey on the road of life is commiserate with theirs in some respect(s). The strength of the relationship is based on shared histories, experiences, philosophies, attitudes, and activities found through exploration and it attaches a low level of esteem as a worthy companion. By finding commonalities in others and assessing their importance to the world, we are able to measure our worth indirectly and develop our esteem.

Attachment

Attachment contains a moderate amount of joy in the complex emotion. The other individual's experiences, attributes, and achievements foster the strongest levels of esteem to you. The prospect feels enough common ground that they should continue life's journey in your company, creating esteem and a sense of worthiness in you. In addition, this emotion fosters and provokes a sense or desire for self-development between you and your companion.

FRIENDSHIP PHASE

In the Friendship phase of the Relationship the emotional tonal algorithm is driven by the strength of creativity and the two-way exchange of assistance creating meaning in both lives. Humor also arises from this source of spontaneity, spontaneity being synonymous with creativity. Creativity is living fully in the moment, which defines the Friendship phase, whereas the Acquaintance phase was about exploring background and past experiences or attributes formed in the past. If the creativity or spontaneity is not to our liking, we might think the person is "goofy, strange, or weird," stifling any further development of the relationship. The unique aspect of meaning is a search for understanding and a measure of positive impact upon others. So, while the Acquaintance phase was about exploration for commonality and worthiness, this phase is about "being yourself" and providing mutual assistance. This phase also marks the exchange of favors and gifts.

Friendship

Friendship contains a significant amount of joy expressed in the complex emotion. Psychologically, this emotion expresses closeness not available to every person; this closeness separates this individual from most people you know. You seek out this person's company due to the level of joy each time this relationship is renewed. This emotion is based on the ability to provide connection, esteem, and now creativity for the first time. Creativity comes from feeling comfortable enough for spontaneity. Humor is often the source of creativity. If this creativity is received well, the prospect will develop a low-level sense of creativity with you.

This also marks the point in which you allow someone within some personal boundaries that you would not normally let people violate. This aspect attaches a modest portion of loyalty to the person invited within your boundaries. Any imperfections noted are deemed to be minor and non-threatening. You'll look first to this group, as well as the rest of the individuals or entities in this phase in hierarchical order to seek help to fix problems and resolve business pain points.

Compassion

Compassion has a moderately high level of joy. This primarily comes from greater understanding of the dimensions of your friend. This greater understanding allows you to understand what makes your business friends tick and the emotions they are experiencing, thus making it easier and safer to see their point of view and circumstances. This empathy makes them more predictable to you, thus allowing you to lower boundaries that enable them to penetrate more closely to your unguarded business self. The highest level of creativity occurs at this level because of the ability to work conjointly on complex problems without fear of betrayal. Any imperfections in people in this circle are accepted.

Grace

Grace, in this sense means being favored, even among business friends and associates. Think club, clique, posse, gang, or group. This emotion provides high levels of joy. This is your inner circle of closest business allies. This emotion is driven by the need for meaning, which seeks understanding. Meaning comes from the ability to positively impact someone else's life by providing mutual comfort, assistance, and advice, which this emotion level provides a low level. This group of friends provides significant amounts of connection, esteem, creativity, and meaning to you and you to them. There is a significant amount of loyalty attached to this group, and all known imperfections are dismissed.

Loyal Customer

This is the full expression of positive joy of the complex emotions that can be expressed to another human in a business setting. This person provides maximum amounts of joy as well as satisfying connection, esteem, creativity, and meaning to you, which is reciprocated. Imperfections known and unknown are irrelevant. The loyal customer is a derivative of self-actualization or what others may call "universal oneness." But these latter terms are more aptly applied to personal relationships. Business relationships have a different context, hence the loyal customer label.

BIAS INTERACTION

Relationships are the domain where human bias comes to full fruition. Graphs 16.1, and 17.1 demonstrate important interactions of the biases present in all relationships that occur between the subsystems of the Paradaptive Intelligence Network discussed in earlier chapters. The four main biases of relationships are self-optimization and altruism of the conductor, cooperation of the adaptor, and self-protection of the reactor.

By looking at Graph 17.1, it can graphically demonstrate that self-optimization and self-protection closely parallel each other. In the sales environment, this is seen often when prospects are receiving a corrective signal from either you or some aspect of your product or service; they tend to vocalize statements such as "it better be a heck of a deal if they expect me to do business with them." This bias is the foundation of the circuitry for the risk and reward behavior that grounds much of the science of economics. As risk decreases, risk being synonymous with the corrective signal fear, the less the reward is needed from external rewards such as money, which are replaced with internal rewards of joy as relationships progress along the relationship algorithm in play in any given scenario. The self-optimization bias represents the reward element and the self-protection bias represents the risk element of the risk/reward behavior mechanism, giving deeper understanding of why people react the way they do in exchanging their resources for other's innovations, services, or knowledge.

The conductor's self-optimization bias also interacts with the adaptor's cooperation bias at the same time in an inverse ratio. The more a person in the relationship produces corrective signals in others, the less likely that person while be driven to cooperate with the source of pain (corrective signal) and more likely to focus on their interest. This also explains why salespeople see the attitude of "What's in it for me?" in relationships that are in the Acquaintance phase of the relationship of a relationship algorithm. There is a high prevalence of self-optimization in the lower stages of the Acquaintance phase of relationships that diminishes as the adaptor's cooperation bias becomes more dominate in the Friendship phase. This explains why we are more interested in helping our closest friends with little regard for our receiving any benefit from our interactions with those on the highest end of relationship algorithms. This is also the source of the misunderstanding within the sales profession of those who believe relationships are the most important part of sales. As discussed in earlier chapters, pain point resolution is always the driving force in human actions; relationships play a part in how that pain point resolution is achieved.

And finally, we can now examine the interaction between cooperation and altruism which becomes much clearer. As relationships develop in the Friendship phase of a relationship algorithm, the conductor's bias of altruism interacts with the cooperation bias of the adaptor that shifts an individual's adaptational focus to cooperating in achieving the motivations and goals of those who produce the strongest growth signals (joy) in them. This is the social glue that holds human societies together and makes man a pack animal.

LINE OF OPTIMIZATION

The bias of the conductor manifests itself differently in relationships than is does in the Innovation algorithm. The conductor is still driven to maximize relationships as in the Innovation algorithm (Figure 17.1), but this manifestation takes a different approach. This still occurs half way between the Present and Future on the graph where the adaptor and conductor are in equilibrium. However, in relationships this is marked by giving of one's time or possession to others freely.

The strength of relationship as measured by the emotions of the algorithm that have been satisfied determines the degree to which one will give of themselves. So someone who has satisfied the emotions friendship will give of themselves, but not to the same degree as someone who has satisfied the emotion grace, but certainly more than what might or might not be given to someone at the curiosity point of the algorithm. The emotions to the left of the Line of Optimization (Figure 17.4) are under the predominant control of the adaptor, so giving of oneself to someone occupying these emotions only happens if it does not interfere with the adaptor's mission to evaluate the person in the Universal Needs emotions of Connection, acceptance and curiosity, and is of little value or cost to the giver.

It must be noted that the Line of Optimization passes thru and predominates the emotions of the need Esteem. By giving of oneself at the emotions in esteem, helps a person establish themselves in the social order by identifying who they are comparable to (camaraderie) and by having that estimation of comparability and compatibility affirmed by the emotion of attachment. So the Acquaintance phase is bisected by the Line of Optimization and all the emotions of the Friendship phase occur under the predominance of the conductor. This introduces the notion of sacrifice. To sacrifice is to give something of importance, value, or needed by an individual freely to another for their benefit and betterment over that of the giver. This leads to another interesting phenomenon that occurs in the emotions of Meaning, grace and satisfied customer. The emotion grace is the point where people are willing to throw themselves on hand grenade to protect others before themselves.

So, what are the practical effects of the Line of Optimization to the salesperson? Gift giving and favors (given without expectation of reciprocation) create powerful internal signaling within others to further relationships. Do not underestimate the power of breaking bread with your clients, whether it is breakfast, lunch, diner, or dropping by with homemade cookies. Favors are especially potent devices for developing relationships. If your client needs the favor of product now with delayed billing, after hours service, or thousands of other exceptions, don't miss the chance to move your relationship forward through these means. Favors and gifts while still solving their pain points in an optimal manner are what hardens your clients from competitor predation.

FULL COMPREHENSION
OF THE SIX UNIVERSAL EMOTIONS OF SALES

Now that both the Innovation Algorithm and a relationship algorithm (Professional Horizontal and Institutional) have been dissected, a deeper, fuller meaning of universal needs can now be examined. A need is defined as an internal, DNA encoded, imperative to engage in a particular type of behavior for which internal reward stimulus is provided. As this pertains to sales, this means engaging in Innovation behavior to solve business sales problems with external entities from your company, thus necessitating the activation of relationship algorithms dependent upon the type of entity you are engaging. These algorithms are the device of fulfillment for universal needs.

Looking at Figure 17.2 , we can now see how the Innovation algorithm satisfies the universal need of Freedom in the Vetting Phase and how Power is satisfied by the accomplishment of the emotions of Implementation phase. The Vetting phase clearly delineates how decisions are made which is by definition freedom in choosing one's direction or path in life. The Implementation phase delineates Power as one implements change to their world. Power can now be early seen as the ability to make changes. It also explains why Freedom and Power come before the other

Scott Syverson

FIGURE 17.2

Freedom & Power Satisfaction
Six Universal Needs
Emotional Tonal Algorithm for Innovation

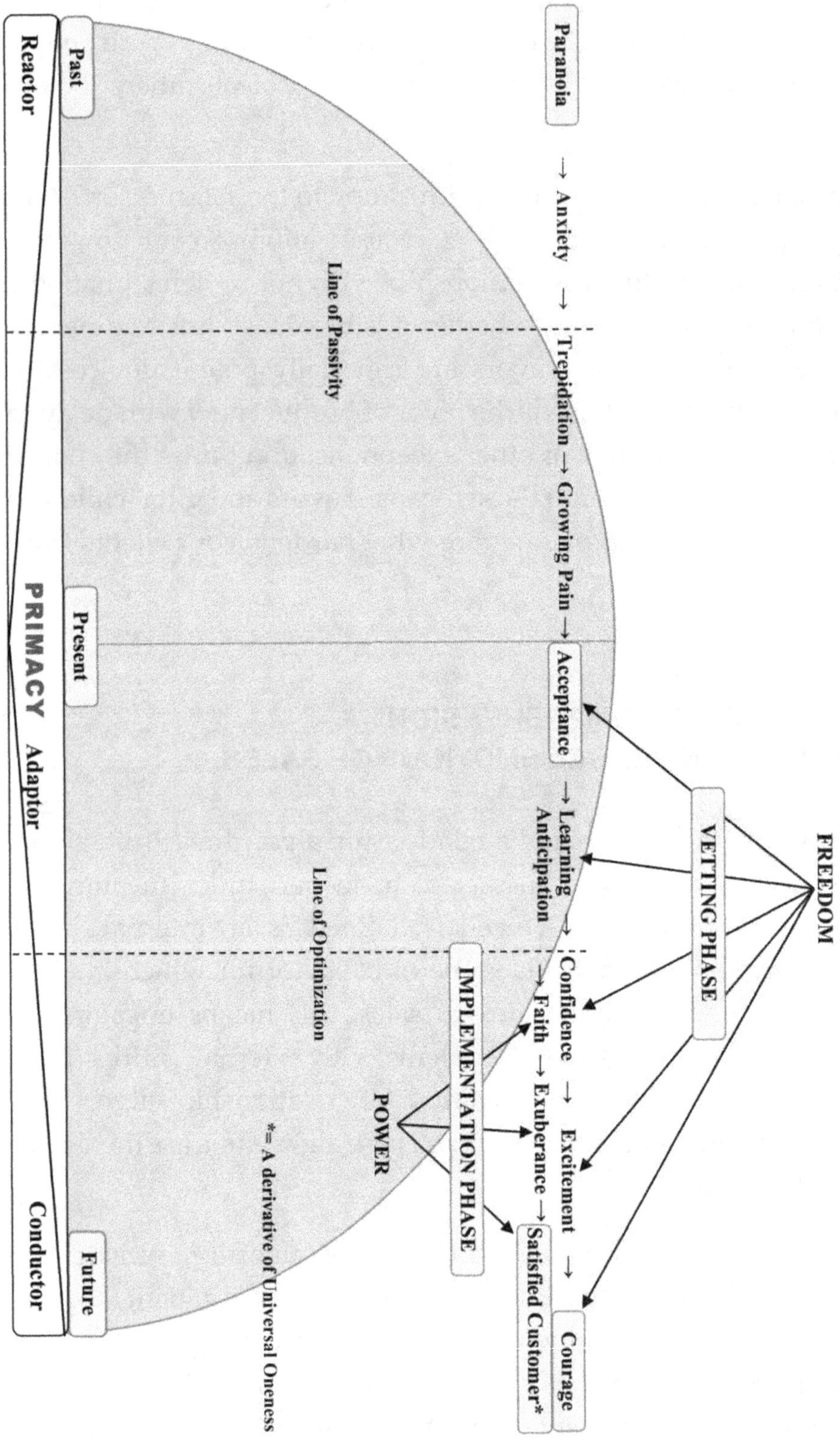

Paranoia → Anxiety → Trepidation → Growing Pain → Acceptance → Learning → Anticipation → Confidence → Faith → Excitement → Exuberance → Satisfied Customer* → Courage

VETTING PHASE

FREEDOM

IMPLEMENTATION PHASE

POWER

Line of Passivity

Line of Optimization

* = A derivative of Universal Oneness

Reactor — Past

PRIMACY   Adaptor

Present

Future   Conductor

244

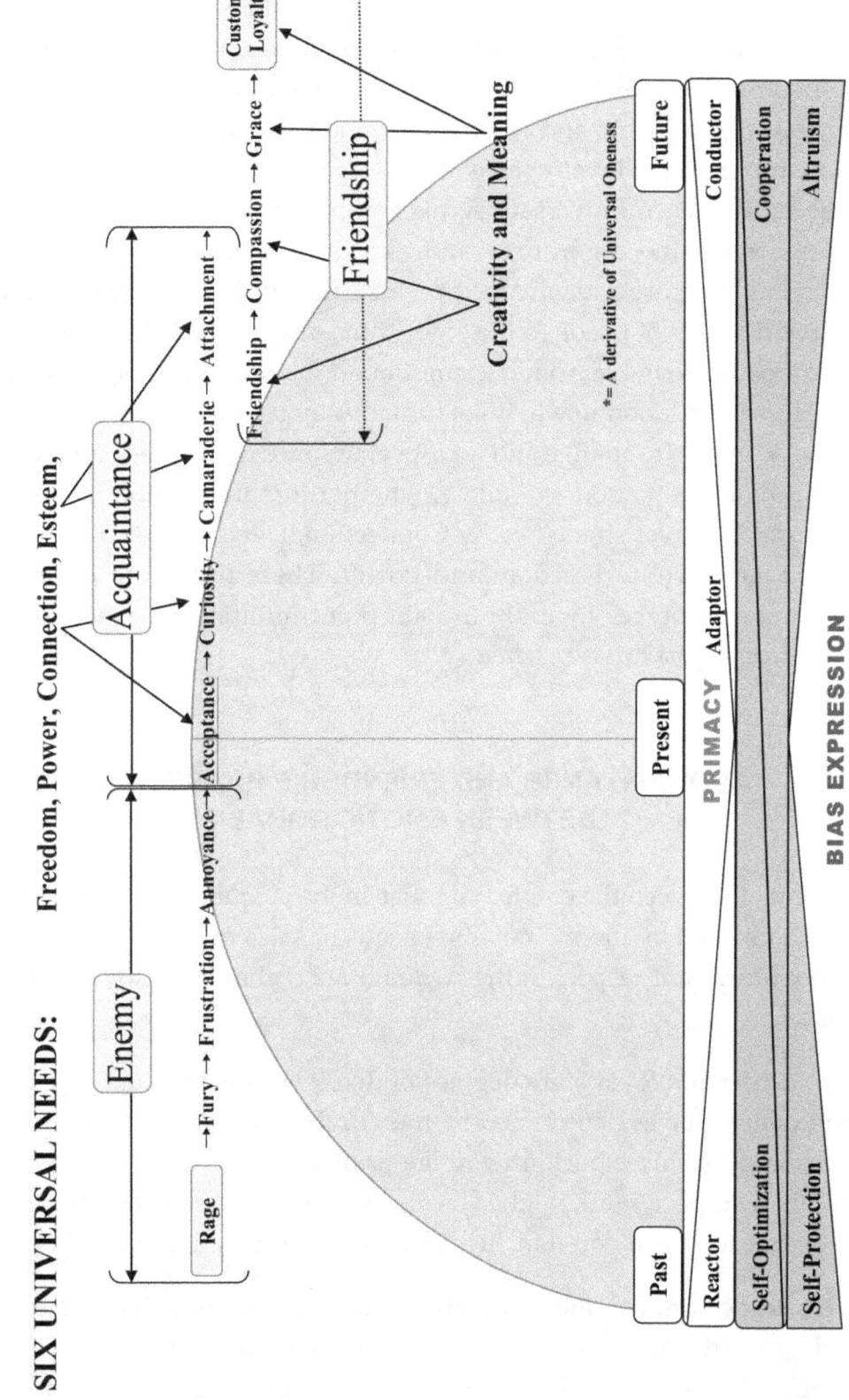

FIGURE 17.3

Six Universal Needs & Professional Horizontal Relationship
Emotional Tonal Algorithm™

universal needs because Freedom and Power are personal to an individual and are the most utilized in securing survival.

In relationships (Figure 17.3), it can now be demonstrated how the universal needs of Connection are satisfied by the emotions acceptance and curiosity, Esteem is satisfied by the emotions camaraderie and attachment, Creativity is satisfied by the emotions of friendship and compassion, and Meaning is satisfied by the emotions of grace and customer loyalty (an equivalent form of universal oneness). It can now be observed that each universal need is comprised of more than one emotion. It also explains why the algorithms and thus the over-arching universal needs are hierarchal in nature and why the process stops when an emotion cannot be fulfilled. The relationship of needs to the algorithms also explains the motive force, why we are compelled to move from one emotion to the next, in an algorithm. This structure also gives foundation to why the Human Action Cycle is compelled to give internal feedback signals to change and adapt behavior to achieve as many of emotions in an algorithm as a situation will allow, whether it is Innovation or Relationships. This structure also gives shape to why Connection, Esteem, Creativity, and Meaning are a secondary level to Freedom and Power. These needs are most associated with developing resources to apply to pain point nullification when an impasse in the Innovation algorithm is reached.

ACQUAINTANCE AND FRIENDSHIP PHASES – MOVEMENT BETWEEN EMOTIOTIONAL STATES

Movement between the emotional tones in the Acquaintance and Friendship phases is accomplished by the six universal needs of sales in the reactor (Figure 3.1) and by the application of respect in the Acquaintance phase and loyalty in the Friendship phase.

Both respect and loyalty are degrees of deference given to another individual based upon their value as determined by the number of emotions they satisfy within you on the relationship algorithm you are applying to them. Lower levels of deference are called respect, while higher levels of deference are called loyalty. Deference is the degree to which you'll include another in your activities or thoughts.

As a salesperson, you interact with decision makers who have already satisfied the needs for freedom and power. The movement in the acquaintance phase is accomplished more predominately by the needs for connection and esteem, while movement in the friendship phase is predominately accomplished by creativity and meaning. As noted earlier, salespeople qualify who they speak to in an organization by seeking out the decision makers. Decision makers already satisfy the baser levels of the six universal needs by having both the freedom and power (Figure 17.2) to make changes in the work place.

In Figure 17.3, we can see that there is a weak followed by a strong emotion for each of the four universal needs of connection, esteem, creativity, and meaning. The architecture for this process is as simple as it is powerful. The weak emotion in relationship is directed at others when achieved and extended it to them. The strong emotion occurs when it is reciprocated. Weak is an internal state directed to external; strong is when external signals are received to confirm that same state in others at which it is directed. This explains why we make such powerful connections and why a salesperson can affect several levels of emotions towards and individual to foster better relationships without it being perceived as artificial and thus a negative. Our brain is structured so that the differential between our status on a relationship algorithm may be different from our client's or prospect's without consequence, in fact, it is a natural occurrence that brains are constructed to equalize if possible. The strong emotional ties, as we perceive them, occur when someone is projecting a weak emotion from one the last four of the six universal emotions towards us that we have not yet achieved ourselves towards them. When that emotion in the relationship algorithm does occur, we receive the internal joy signal of not only satisfying the weak emotion, but it is immediately followed by the strong emotion signal as we are now able to process the reciprocating signaling from the other individual. So internally, we receive two shots of escalating joy in rapid succession. This can all be boiled down to something very simple -- in building relationships, somebody has got to go first. We are rewarded internally for going first to build relationships with the small dose of joy for extending ourselves when we satisfy the weak emotion in a universal need. The Mirror Neuron system is vital in this process; it is the source of feedback that controls our Human Action Cycle. When our actions, guided by the feedback and adjustment cycle of the HAC, allow us to let someone else to achieve that same emotion towards us we receive another shot of joy for fostering it in others. In the end, it is all the same amount of internal joy that gets dispensed, the difference is in the timing based upon who in the relationship goes first in extending emotions. Knowing this, as a salesperson, it is always to your best advantage to be the person going first. Extend yourself and conduct your affairs so that your clients receive that double dose of joy when weak and strong emotions are simultaneously fulfilled. This is the essence of defensive selling.

While some people may claim it is artificial and possibly manipulative to approach a relationship with goals and measured milestones, *Sales Psychology 101* advocates that part of good client/sales relationship management is knowing exactly where you stand with your customers and what you can expect from them. Knowing the emotional phases, their sequence specific emotions, and the driving forces to satisfy them allows the salesperson to create language that can make clients and prospects more comfortable. This will allow for maximum transfer of information between both buyer and seller that the relationship will allow, which is beneficial to both parties.

INSTITUTIONAL RELATIONSHIPS

Institutional relationships are an outgrowth of tribalism. As noted earlier, all human civilizations started as tribes, whose core is familial interrelations. So the emotional progression of joy for institutional relationships reflects a connection to a familial group. This is accomplished by swapping out friendship for kinship in the joy emotional progression of emotional tones. In all other respects, the joy tonal algorithm is the same as a horizontal professional relationship. (Figure 17.4)

If you think about it, when you belong to a political party, church, organization, club, etc., the further you progress your relationship and involvement, the more kinship, or sense of connectedness of a familial nature occurs as the relationship moves into the Friendship phase of the tonal algorithm. It's also just practical, too. You can have a friendship with another human that can interact with you directly, but you can't with an organization. There's no facial expressions to exchange or decipher, no humor or witticism that can be exchanged, etc., with an organization. But an aggregate of personalities, intentions, and actions, can be compiled which becomes a composite human capable of a relationship with a person. On the other hand, on the corrective signal side, there are two possible progressions and are completely different from the Innovation emotional algorithm, and one is of a type not yet explored. Institutions can violate rights, rules, and processes which are the threads that stitch together a voluntary collection of people. The rules, rights, and processes create boundaries. Boundary violations produce anger. However, engagement in activities that is unwholesome trigger disgust. Dishonesty and lying are unwholesome and trigger a response of the basic emotion disgust. While only an individual can lie, an organization can act upon a lie. Just like only an individual can break a rule, it takes two members or more of an organization colluding to break a rule or lie. Disgust is the more likely corrective signal to be triggered because breaking rules is a form of dishonesty. The four quarters of the disgust, starting with weakest intensity, are dislike, repugnance, revulsion, and hate. Think of these four segments in the sentiments in which they're often expressed: dislike – "I don't like

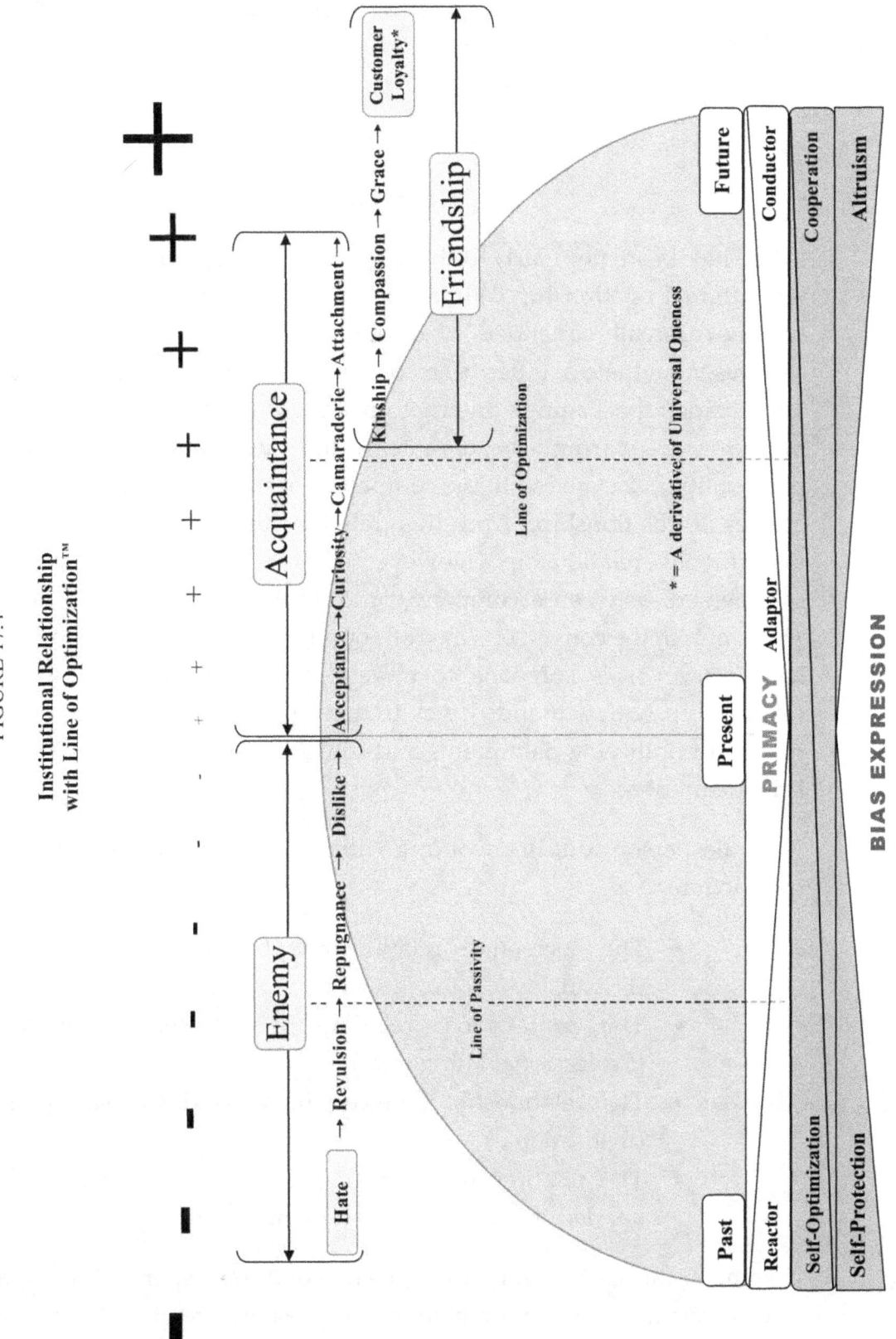

FIGURE 17.4

**Institutional Relationship
with Line of Optimization™**

you," repugnance – "I can't stand you," revulsion – "You make me sick," and finally hate – "I hate you." The Line of Passivity for this progression is between repugnance and revulsion. In all other respects, this progression of corrective signals works just like the other corrective signals previously explored.

BRAND MANAGEMENT

What has been popularly dubbed "brand management" is in fact just another institutional relationship. While this part of the Paradaptive Intelligence Network was never really intended to develop relationships with inanimate objects or services, nonetheless, it has been co-opted by modern product managers. Images in advertising, packaging, internet postings, and logos, as well as product performance, warranties, guarantees, and customer support create a composite personality associated with the companies of the products or services provided and creates a relationship. And this relationship is no different than any other institutional relationship. However, this is a third-party relationship to a salesperson, between a company/product that they are vending to the prospect. Think of it in the converse: we've all found products that we like, but sometimes the local purveyor is someone that we're less than charmed with, but still, our relationship with a brand drives us to seek them out because the product has a history of nullifying pain points and some level of loyalty has been attached in the Friendship phase.

So a salesperson could be working with up to four relationships algorithms in one transaction:

- The personal relationship between buyer and salesperson. (Friendship)
- The professional relationship between buyer and salesperson. (Professional Horizontal)
- The relationship between buyer and the salesperson's company. (Institutional)
- The relationship between buyer and the brand of product being vended by the salesperson. (Institutional)

In some instances, the brand might be that of the salesperson's company, making the salesperson a direct vendor, company representative of that product, and therefore he would only be dealing with two relationships. There are many examples of how to look at these relationships and how they can impact sales. You could have a personal relationship with buyer at the emotion level of compassion, for example.

You tell your buyer about a special you're having on Brand X. The buyer has tried Brand X and didn't have a good experience. While he may listen patiently, because you're friends, he is not likely to buy based on his relationship with Brand X. However, if you're friendship is at the emotion level of grace or better and you asked him to do a favor for you because you're under some pressure to move some product, he might buy a little from you and figure out a way to dump it or move it later. He might do this because in the Friendship phase of relationships, it's about mutual benefit and it is a completely different HAC to help a friend than it is to buy a product with which you've had previous bad experiences. Or you might be new to the client, but the client has a long history with your company. You offer him a brand with which he has no experience – his relationship with the brand is at acceptance - and it sounds like a good deal. So he buys, knowing that if the product doesn't work out his relationship with your firm will offer him some sort of make good or return gesture.

Brand managers create this relationship with the brand as a fail-safe against bad local distributors so that local consumers will seek and demand the product in a "pull" marketing strategy in case the local vendor is ineffective in creating a "push" strategy in the market place due to weak relationships. Again, this is reassuring to salespeople because there are up to four ways to affect the communications between buyer and seller in a positive way to increase the chances of a sale. Product managers managing brands often have specific goals in mind, such as wanting customers to think certain things when they think of their brand. This may be quality, value, innovators, or other brand descriptors. With our understanding of Paradaptive Intelligence, we can now see how these different descriptors are related to the innovation vetting cycle, which will be useful in achieving confidence in a product, or excitement if they are positioning it for the emotion excitement, and so on. But, remember, these descriptor messages will either be muted or positively influenced by the relationships involved.

But is this the right goal? It is most definitely not. Brand managers are managing a relationship (See Figure 17.2). Trying to put theses descriptors such as value, quality, innovation, etc., is like trying to describe an intimate relationship as "innovative," or a companionship relationship as "quality." Instead, it would be more accurate, and certainly more beneficial, to manage brands to the institutional relationship emotional tonal algorithm. As a salesperson and the go-between between company and consumer, they often see the brand management programs employed in the advertising and images projected by companies at the field level. This can be disconcerting, because the salesperson may know that the image projected cannot be accomplished by him or his firm, creating a pain point for the sales staff because he has no say in the relationship between consumer and the product managers.

AFFECTATION OF EMOTIONS IN SALES RELATIONSHIPS

There are sale people who affect emotions they don't actually have towards a prospect or client. This can be either bad or good, depending on two provisos. One, the salesperson has to be a successful enough actor to carry it off or the insincerity will create a corrective signal in the prospect. Secondly, the salesperson's image must be attractive to the prospect in some way. The reason for affecting emotions that you are not experiencing relies on the cooperation bias in human adaptor. Emotions of business relationships tend to be synchronous. Both parties tend to move mutually up or down together through relationship emotional tones via visual signaling of the Mirror Neuron System. If you are acting towards a client or prospect like you have achieved, say, attachment, this puts subtle pressure upon the mind of the prospect to act in a reciprocal way via the bias for cooperation. Thus, the salesperson a can use this false communication bridge to convey product information. But there are limits of what can be done with emotion affectation in relationships.

To affect an emotion is to act or put on airs through your actions and facial expressions to be picked up by the prospect's Mirror Neuron System and reactor seeking to satisfy its six basic needs. Let's say you, as a salesperson, have just met this potential client once for a very short time and are at the emotional level of acceptance in this relationship. Upon meeting them the second time you say, "Hey, how's it going with my compadre?" or "How's it going with my little buddy?". These two simple questions convey many emotional tones. First, by asking a question, opening communication, you're acknowledging their presence which signals acceptance. Starting the greeting by saying "How's it going…" you're demonstrating the curiosity. By using the word "my" you're expressing attachment. You're demonstrating ownership, which signals connection, and by using the word "buddy" or "compadre," you're signaling camaraderie. So in one simple sentence, you've conveyed the first four emotions in the emotional tonal algorithm for business relationships. "How's my man?" signals the first three emotions. "How's the rat race? Are we winning?" gets the first four. If you're introducing someone you're at attachment with to another person, you might say by way of introduction of the prospect, "Carol, I'd like you to meet my friend…" and with a gentle hand to the prospect's back communicates even more. Now, you're expressing friendship by stating the emotion and trust by touching. By placing your hand on the back, you're reinforcing friendship, because touching of this nature does not generally occur until the mutually beneficial stage of the Friendship phase where trust is a foundational element. You're also signaling mutual beneficial behavior by introducing him to your circle of relationships. Touching another's core demonstrates an intimacy, i.e. trust, established in the Friendship Phase; touching another's limbs signifies a lesser relationship emotion such as attachment, because it takes no trust to touch these parts of the body. Touching a limb is a possessive act denoting the emotion of attachment.

Shaking hands, is a ritualized greeting in the Western world which must be learned. It is not our natural instinct to grab or make contact physically at acceptance or curiosity. Touching in relationships generally occurs around attachment and camaraderie but may be culturally advanced or retarded by customs. When we look at the six universal needs, connection refers to the mental connection, not the physical. Esteem for a person must be derived before someone would be desirous of physically touching someone else, usually their limbs. Esteem, one of the six basic needs comprised of attachment and camaraderie, is where the motivation to touch occurs. To touch is to attach. In attachment, the person develops a sense of claim upon another person and the need to touch that possession is an extension of that claim. This is why you see fist bumps, high fives, and other touch rituals that signify esteem needs have been met.

Another ritualized affectation is manners. Manners are a form of acknowledgement extended to others for the purpose of striking a tone of congeniality, which is another form relationship signaling. A hand shake in western cultures signals acknowledgement and then manners affect a higher level of relationship, generally by accommodation and giving, usually seen at the entrance of the Friendship phase.

There does appear to be rules to affecting emotions. One cannot generally affect more than three emotional tones beyond what they are experiencing. To do so will set up a corrective signal to the other party. The person receiving the affected emotions will be thinking something to the effect of *Whoa, not so fast. Where does he/she get off thinking he/she can do that to me.* Or, *Wait a minute, I've got to rethink this because I'm certainly not on the same page as this person,* if you go beyond three. Affectation only seems to work in the acquaintance phase, beyond which affectation creates a threat in others as someone who is presumptuous. It only works in the acquaintance phase because not enough information has been collected by the client or prospect about the salesperson to make them predictable, which is a necessary precursor to trust, which in turn is the underpinning of the Friendship phase.

The second proviso requires that you be attractive to the party receiving affected emotions, whether it be charismatic, humorous, or physical attractiveness. This is relying on the first component of the trivalent structure of all emotions. This element directs an individual to approach/move towards a person or move away. Being charismatic, humorous, or physically attractive generates growth signals of joy to approach. The other's reactor's cooperation bias can only work when someone is being directed to move towards you.

Some salespeople will see affectation as manipulation. Others will see it as good salesmanship. The application of this mechanism will depend on the persons involved, the situation, and motives. The purpose of this book is to illuminate the mechanism and principles of operation and not to enter into philosophic debates. This is a tool, and like most tools, they all have their proper uses.

E-COMMERCE

The trend today is for companies to skip the middlemen and purvey their products directly to the end user when possible. The internet, as a direct medium, has spurred much of this trend. There is the presumption that doing business on the internet is emotion free and therefore doesn't require a relationship. This presumption could not be more wrong.

Just because two humans are not interacting in an internet sale does not mean that a relationship does not exist on the buyer's part. Remember, they are buying something from someone. The relationship circuitry is hardwired and automatically engages anytime there is a transaction. Since our forefathers first traded seashells for obsidian knives, food for animal hides, et cetera, the activities have always involved another human being, thus engaging our social mental machinery to guide us in the transactions. Faceless transactions started with the first coin-operated vending machine, or one could even say with the advent of post systems and catalogue sales, but one can't deny its recent perfection in the internet, which has moved the loci of business and commerce into our homes. The proof of this continuation of relationships has been hiding in plain sight on our screens. When a buyer finds a website that can sell them what they want, they are at the emotional level of acceptance. They accept the site as a legitimate seller of the tool, product, or innovation to nullify their pain points.

Take feedback. Buyers love to rate vendors. It's on auction sites, it's on every savvy online merchant's site. There are whole sites devoted to rating internet purveyors. In fact, a whole industry has developed for rating purveyors. When a bad transaction occurs, the buyer's scorn is motivated by their conductor to do right by others and warn them off of bad sellers. So why would buyers who had a good experience be compelled to rate a vendor? Clearly, they got online, made a purchase, and got exactly what they expected. End of story. So why rate them when expectations are met? The reason is the positive experience of fulfilling their expectations may move them to the curiosity emotional stage of the relationship by creating an internal reward of joy. Most certainly, exceeding their expectations will move them to the curiosity emotional stage. They are curious to learn what they can do for the vendor because they are hardwired to try and develop a relationship. So they help by rating them positively. A second successful transaction may move them to camaraderie. This is when the buyer puts them on their FAVORITES tab. They have found a fellow traveler that knows just what they want because of their like-minded focus. Another successful transaction may move them to attachment. This is when they put them on their social media pages as their favorite store or vendor showing ownership, which is attachment, and so on down the line.

Good internet purveyors have been haphazardly attempting to use this hardwired aspect of relationship building. For example, after a transaction with a first-time buyer, a purveyor may notice the first-time buyer's status and send the buyer an invitation to join his buyer's club. This channels the buyer's curiosity into examining the benefits of developing a deeper relationship. Or the buyer may send a customer survey of his or her experience. Action on these two examples, survey and buyer's club, rest solely with whether that particular customer's emotional state was increased from acceptance by the transactional experience.

Smart internet purveyors also try and learn about the likes and dislikes of purchasers, the ostensive purpose is so they can provide advertisements that they like while getting more targeted bang for their advertising dollars. But what this is trying to connect with is the emotion of camaraderie by saying "Look, we're alike — we know just how you feel by giving you the product information you want." Of course, this doesn't work if the buyer is still at acceptance or curiosity. This need for a relationship is evidenced by specialty chat rooms at vendor websites for like-minded customers to enhance the sense of camaraderie.

Smart e-commerce purveyors can study and use the relationship tonal algorithms to learn how to convert random search engine pairings with purchasers into strong relationships by following the specific emotional path of the Acquaintance and Friendship phases. And, if they blow a transaction, their customer service staff can certainly benefit from knowing and understanding the Enemy phase in handling disgruntled customers using their knowledge of corrective signals.

RECOMMENDATIONS

Studies have shown that a typical satisfied customer tells three people of their experience while bad experiences are communicated to ten people. Why the disparity? Using our understanding of the Paradaptive Intelligence Network, we can now shed some light and understanding on the subject. Consumers and prospects are internally wired to seek satisfaction by solving and removing pain points. We learned in earlier chapters there is an internal system of greater and greater joy that is delivered as reward for advancing through the emotions of acceptance to satisfied customer. The folk-saying "the satisfaction of a job well done" captures and recognizes the pleasure the Paradaptive Intelligence Network delivers for pain point nullification. The key word here is <u>internal.</u> The internal reward system is not designed, other than expression through the Mirror Neuron System upon your countenance, to spread your pleasure. This is why clients are not normally moved to spread the word unless requested. This also explains why the stance of satisfied customers is "If asked, I would recommend your product." This willingness, when asked, to favorably rate your product or service to others is also based upon the assumption that the transaction left the buyer at a level greater than acceptance. Again, this is seen in savvy internet purveyors who ask for ratings after the conclusion of a transaction. Those not moved by the transaction beyond the emotional state of curiosity or better won't bother to rate the purveyor. Those that do rate are likely to give a positive rating because the completed transaction just gave them an impulse of joy as they moved positively upward on the Relationship emotional tonal algorithm. Rating a purveyor after receiving an impulse of joy will make raters overstate the quality of purveyor and artificially increase his ratings due to the adaptation hardwiring of the human brain.

Negative experiences, on the other hand, are driven by a completely different mechanism in the Paradaptive Intelligence Network. The need to share with others unsatisfactory experiences and outcomes is driven by the conductor. The conductor's bias is to do right by others, and preventing them from experiencing the same unsatisfying experience you just had is a step in that direction of optimizing that relationship. Giving of your experience (negative) to others so they do not fall in the same trap is a favor, "Listen, I am doing you a favor, don't do business with Company XYZ." Doing right by others is an external function; others, by definition are external to your internal environment. This is why they are driven to externalize the unsatisfying outcome and spread the word vociferously.

CONCLUSION

We started this section, Section II, with a synopsis of the path in which memory and adaptation derived from optimizing survival and mating success. As you recall, prior to our adaptation system, the Paradaptive Intelligence Network, an animal, like a lizard, would wander about randomly contacting food, mates, and predators. A haphazard way of conducting life, but it works – minimally. The Paradaptive Intelligence Network strives to put us in the anticipated position to contact and obtain that which is desirable and needed for our survival while avoiding what is detrimental. This also goes for salespeople. You can wander about and make random sales and survive – possibly. But your Paradaptive Intelligence Network is designed to put you in likely, anticipated positions of success. Where you've made one sale once before, you're more likely to make a sale in the same spot in the future. The Relationship emotional tonal algorithm portion of the Paradaptive Intelligence Network is there to help you become repeatedly successful by building bonds between humans for mutual support and success. Understanding how this mutual support and success is built upon the satisfaction of the six universal needs of the reactor will make you and your salesforce something to be reckoned with whether you're a sales rep, a brick and mortar retailer, or internet purveyor. The choice before you is what type of sales animal do you want to be? A sales lizard wandering from sale to sale or a sales eagle that can zero in on a sale from a mile away, swoop in for the sale and is off for the next sale in an instant, all with the invitation to come again, soon. Managing your business relationships with the principles outlined in this book will allow your sales career to soar to unparalleled heights.

MYTHS AND OTHER TWADDLE

Loyalty Is Earned

As we've learned in this chapter, the buyer/seller relationship is built on progressively fulfilling emotional stages by satisfying the six universal needs of the reactor. However, somewhere down the line, this notion that "loyalty is earned" crept into the popular consciousness. When asked, "Just how do you 'earn' someone's loyalty?" the answer invariably begins with, "By doing X, Y, or Z." But if you examine just exactly what is described in X, Y, or Z, you'll find that it generally describes fulfilling emotional stages via satisfying the six universal needs. So what does the dictionary have to say? Several dictionaries commonly describe earn as "to labor for, receive as merit, or to gain as profit." None of that really applies to how loyalty is developed. Development is really the key. Development of loyalty is based on the fulfillment of the reactor's six universal needs, with emphasis on the needs satisfaction for creativity and meaning.

Repeat Business Is Not Loyalty

Many salespeople confuse repeat business with loyalty. Repeat business can be bought, i.e. bribed. Lowest price is an example of a bribe. Someone looking to spend the least amount of money may consistently buy your product until someone else comes in with a lower price. Loyalty involves the fulfillment of emotional stages.

All that is necessary for a transaction to occur is the emotional state of acceptance in the presence of opportunity, opportunity being synonymous with convenience. So, convenience and the most minimal positive emotional state are all the ingredients necessary for a buyer/seller relationship. Sounds like the very grim description of random acts of commerce between strangers that started this chapter. This is fine if you do not expect or desire to do business with the same party more than once. But customer loyalty is a key factor to a salesman and a company's success, as we'll learn in the next section, which means you'll need to put emphasis on satisfying the six universal needs of the reactor and managing the emotional stages of the Relationship emotional tonal algorithm.

How to Win Friends & Influence People

Dale Carnegie's 1936 book *"How to Win Friends & Influence People"* is considered one of the seminal books for practitioners of sales, and produced good results for those that read it. This book is of the "mimic me" variety because it told sales what to do, but was unable to explain why, where, when, or what it was predicated upon. Now with our understanding of the Paradaptive Intelligence model, we can see that much of what Carnegie had observed was about the Relationship algorithm and how it worked. He did pretty good job but could only take it so far without a deeper understanding of the Paradaptive Intelligence Network's mechanisms, functions, and operating rules. For example, he identified calling someone by name "the sweetest sounds to a person's ears", which we now know was the emotion acceptance in a relationship algorithm at work. He demonstrated the need to focus on problems and issues, not people's choices delineating the Innovation from the relationship algorithms involved. This is focusing on pain points. Blame for a problem is focusing on a relationship algorithm, and blame always is reductive, thus destructive to whatever type of relationship that is in play. Influencing people under Carnegie's precepts we now know to be the Vetting phase of the Innovation emotional algorithm. And the list can go on and on. But the overall problem for this approach is that if you ran into a situation not covered in his book you had no information to formulate actions. And this is always the crux for "mimic me" books.

Now, with Sales Psychology 101, a much deeper understanding of what Mr. Carnegie was trying to convey can be gained as a supplement to execution of the rules and operating principles described therein.

SECTION III

OTHER APPLICATIONS OF THE
PARADAPTIVE INTELLIGENCE NETWORK

Once the underlying structure of the mind and biological function are understood and the operating principles of the subcomponents are appreciated, they can be used in other areas of the sales arena. Primarily, knowing how the mind works will allow you to better manage those working in the sales field and to recognize and avoid manipulation. This section will focus on these tertiary benefits of understanding the Paradaptive Intelligence Network with the presumption that if one knows how a system works, you will be better prepared and able to manage it for the results desired. The following pages look at applying our newfound understanding of Paradaptive Intelligence to sales management.

18

ILLEGITIMATE PURSUASION AND MANIPULATION

"They say honesty is the best policy. By process of elimination, that means dishonesty is the second best policy."
George Carlin

This book has advocated knowing and being prepared for all the emotional phases every client must go through in order to make a purchasing decision. Knowing how the Paradaptive Intelligence Network dictates what prospects are thinking allows you to anticipate the type and level of communications necessary to guide their purchasing behavior. This is not to be confused with manipulating your prospects, which is an entirely different matter.

It is believed that people can control others by manipulating their emotions. This is not possible, at least not without the permission of the subject. As we know, emotions are feedback derived from the outside world about how that individual's actions are performing relative to achieving the aims/motivation of a Human Action Cycle. You can *influence* this internal process in others by providing false feedback via actions and facial expressions. But again, it is important to remember that individuals are not bound to the emotional feedback you provide their reactors, false or otherwise. For the most part, they have the ability to reject and ignore any emotional signal they receive from the reactor up to the Line of Passivity. However, having said this, we cannot ignore the fact that by providing false feedback, someone with devious designs can create emotions in others that are not truly related to their actions. This can range from telling someone a "white lie" to make him or her feel good (falsely derived joy, most likely exuberance) to creating an unnecessary corrective signal like fear by making them worry about something that isn't really evident or has an extremely low probability of occurrence. This unduly and falsely influences someone's emotions and occurs by taking advantage of one of the primary architectural features of the human mind by pitting the reactor's primary bias against the primary biases of the reactor or conductor.

COOPERATION BIAS

At the beginning of this book, we distinguished the three levels of the emotional mind: reactor, adaptor, and conductor. As you recall, we share the common function of all three with all mammals. All mammals have adaptor functionality, but being able to make simple tools and limited active learning resides with just a handful. For the most part, a fully developed adaptor is the providence of humans, and the conductor's functionality is shared with all mammals, albeit in a very limited way. It is important to understand that cooperation is a function of the adaptor. It has been said that man is a social creature, which is just an indirect way of acknowledging the built-in element of cooperation in all of us. Let's look at how that comes about, what purpose it serves, and why it's important to the professional salesperson.

From birth to our early teens, the reactor is the primary brain function in control. The adaptor and conductor are still in development until about twelve years of age where the adaptor becomes dominant, with the conductor still developing. Adulthood occurs when the conductor becomes fully developed and functional, usually in the late teens to early twenties. The reactor's function is to protect the body and connect the brain to the body. The reactor is learning to coordinate the limbs and form communicate with speech, as well as other physical activities necessary to move and service the physical requirements of the body. In order to protect the body, the primary mode of operation is *competition*. In order to ensure survival, the brain is programmed to compete and, if necessary, take what it needs from others. This is manifest in children's penchant for competition in sports and games. We've all seen T-ball games where children hit the ball and run anywhere they want, pick up the ball and just throw wherever. And we've all seen toddlers grab food from siblings or playmates without thought or consideration. That's just the actions of a reactor unchecked by the still developing adaptor or conductor, ensuring the pleasure and survival of body. Another example is children over-reacting to perceived threats, impediments, unwholesomeness, and losses.

Around twelve years of age and through adulthood, the adaptor develops to become dominant, controlling the functions of the brain. In order to learn for maximum adaptability, its primary focus shifts to surrounding individuals, and the dominant mode is *cooperation*, which is itself a form of adaptation – adapting to those around you. In order to absorb the maximum knowledge (like social norms, rules, behavior and culture – and even style) to increase our survivability by living in a group, tribe, or societal setting, we are programmed for cooperation to both give information to others and receive it. It is cooperation that is at the core of all human societies.

Man is not a solitary creature. He lives in groups, allowing different skills and talents to benefit the group as a whole. This wouldn't be possible if we were not heavily programmed for cooperation. Here are a few quick examples of how this is manifested in the teen years: cliques, gangs, clubs, squads, and groups that seem to sprout in junior and senior high. Team sports become more proficient, not just because of increased physical dexterity and development, but because of an inclination to be part of a team and perform cooperatively as a group. Another example is girls going to the bathroom in groups for mutual support and protection.

Adulthood begins when the conductor adds a controlling element to the adaptor, influencing the cooperating element into being the best that the individual can be for himself and others. The dominate mode of operation in the conductor is a balance of self-actualization and altruism called *self-optimization*. This serves the function of ensuring the survival of the individual by optimizing his or her skills and performances which not only enhances his or her survivability, but also the well-being of others within their identified society thus increasing the survivability of the tribe or society he or she lives in. Self-optimization is unique to each individual and is one of the defining attributes of the individual's personality. Sometimes it's easier to illustrate this by its absence. The 1954 classic book *Lord of the Flies* by William Golding describes the descent into savagery by youths whose conductors had not yet developed to influence their behavior, giving a realistic, albeit fictional, description of life without the conductor.

If you have any doubts of this functionality, the importance, and strength of cooperation in the human genetic code, let's bring it full circle for you. In Chapter 9, we learned about the Mirror Neuron System and its function of displaying and deciphering human expression. Why would nature expend so much energy and put so much importance on facial expressions if emotions are *internal* signals? Why display them *externally* as an expression?

The reason is because facial expressions facilitate cooperation.

If you know how you're feeling emotionally and you are signaling others around you how you're feeling by your expression and body language, then those around you will know how to address you and at what level to communicate with you to assist you in either corrections (disgust, anger, fear, or loss) or repetition (joy). Visual and physical expressions of emotions are a way of asking for others to help you in the spirit of cooperation. If you think of the people who you've come in contact with throughout your life, those that you've taken an instant liking to or have liked the best, such as your friends, all share one characteristic: they read your emotions and went with your flow. They found out how you were doing or where your thoughts were at and made that the topic. With you, they made and exercised total emotional cooperation by co-opting yours. By doing this, they created a very positive emotional state in you that made you want to reciprocate and adopt their emotional states. All good salespeople innately do this. This is also why the myth of discussing something in a prospect's office has had positive, albeit accidental, success. By taking a moment to identify and adopt the emotional state of the prospect, you create an opportunity for positive communications. Dale Carnegie's books and training take advantage of these aspects of the Paradaptive Intelligence Network without understanding what they are actually doing or the overall framework within which what they advocate works. This comes dangerously close to manipulation by giving feedback signals solely to effect someone's emotions. You're internally geared for this sort of emotional cooperation; you just need the assurance that it is right to do so and that emotions are not only expressly allowed, but required for optimum sales and profits. If you do what is natural, adopt your prospect's emotional state and make it yours, rather than focus on your internal agenda of making the sale, you'll find your ability to identify their pain points and offer adaptation plans will be greatly improved.

And this is just another reason why you should animate. If you don't, you frustrate the natural programming of cooperation built in to all humans.

THE POWER OF QUESTIONS

Now that we understand the built-in bias towards cooperation, we can understand the power of questions. As a salesperson, one of your primary tools in getting a prospect to help identify their pain points is questions. Questions are direct appeals for cooperation, begging for response. In its simplest form, a question is a request for information. It signals interest in the knowledge or opinions of the person being queried. It is a compliment because it assumes the person being asked the question has the power to help the person asking. Asking non-rhetorical questions subjugates the asker, shifting power to the person being asked, saying "you have something I want."

All these subliminal messages empower the person being asked. In Chapter 3, we learned of the six universal needs. Questions are the only form of communication that engages all six needs. A question:

1. Acknowledges the *freedom* of the person being asked to respond or not
2. *Empowers* the person being asked to make things happen by helping or not
3. Creates a *connection* between two people via information
4. Grants the recipient a measure of *esteem* by shifting the power to them
5. Provides the recipient an opportunity for *creativity* in responding
6. Gives the recipient *meaning* by allowing them to help another

So if you can balance using the power of questions and animating your response to the answers, you'll be well on your way to having optimized, positive communications. It is only when you shut down one or the other that troubles begin.

CONDUCTOR BIAS AND MANIPULATION

As learned earlier, the conductor evaluates your actions in the outside world for acceptability with respect to the best effort/outcome for you and the best for others. Those who wish to manipulate the emotional system take advantage of this subsystem. They will try and convince you that your actions are unacceptable by developing arguments that skew your actions as not being favorable to others. The most common of these types of arguments is the "you're not being fair" argument. The concept of fairness is based on the arguer's strategy to play upon your conductor's bias by defining fair in such a way that your actions should benefit the arguer more than they benefit you. People will also try to subvert the conductor by creating premises of acceptability and fairness by such tactics as "You believe that it's only (fair, just, right, natural…) that X should happen, agreed?" By phrasing the statement as a question a person creates a very powerful manipulation because it layers the adaptor's cooperation bias on top of the conductor's bias by attempting to redefine the terms of acceptability. Don't be fooled by these types of strategies and manipulations. Your best approach is to understand there are two ploys here, one to the adaptor and one to the conductor. Start by deconstructing this manipulation. "I'd like to agree with you, but X doesn't always take into consideration of …" is an indirect approach or you could go with the direct approach "I disagree that X should happen…" and then go on to rebut the premise of the conductor manipulation. Refuting the premise of the speaker's conductor manipulation is best accomplished by a statement as to what you think is fair, how all individuals who are party to the suggested actions of the speaker should be treated. This will now put subtle pressure on the manipulator's adaptor to cooperate.

FALSE FEEDBACK

Now that you know the internal structure of the human Paradaptive Intelligence Network and how it operates, it's time to look at intentional misinformation, known colloquially as manipulation. Because of the strong bias towards cooperation everyone is wired with, they are programmed to believe what you express, both verbally and emotionally. The difference between lying and manipulation is the inclusion of false emotional feedback in manipulation. You can falsely tell someone something is red when it's blue, and this may only cause the individual to feel anger towards you because you gave false information to him or her, and by doing so, you become an obstacle to what he or she is trying to accomplish. But when you tell them you're feeling blue and act like it when you're not, you're supplying false emotional signaling to their Paradaptive Intelligence Network. This is done as an attempt to direct in others the emotional feedback their reactors will produce to their adaptors.

As we know, the target will receive and most likely react to their internal signaling for correction and change their behavior and actions. For example, you may try and "guilt" or "shame' someone into doing something by portraying to them that their actions have hurt you in some way or by accusing them (falsely) that their actions do not measure up to the conductor's prime directive. Intuitively, but indirectly, people take advantage of the conductor's drives for people to do the best for themselves and others. So having hurt someone (falsely), you come into internal conflict with your adaptor's primary directive, which produces a negative emotion, agitating you to change your ways. You might hear something like "You're killing me here," "That's not fair," or "You're being _____(stubborn, deceitful, impossible, righteous, unfeeling, etc.)." The conductor's bias is where we get our sense of fairness to others; it's another way of creating opportunities to do the best possible to others. Similar ploys may be directed at the adaptor's bias of cooperation where you might hear something along the lines of "Come on, work with me here." There are dozens of examples of the various types of manipulations that work against the prime directives of the adaptor and conductor, and most readers are familiar with them, so an extensive examination of manipulations is contrary to the aims of this book. Sufficient to say, being aware of the mechanisms in play will give salespeople adequate knowledge to identify manipulations directed against them, say, by prospects arguing to reduce the price by attacking or manipulating you. Your best option when you hear a complaint/manipulation in one of these situations is to ask the person how, exactly, you hurt them or are not cooperating. Get specifics. The sham will fall apart sooner, rather than later.

Because of your built-in bias for cooperation, there is really no defense against manipulations other than experience. Once manipulated, experience will guide you to seek more information before accepting someone else's emotional displays and signaling. This is called being skeptical. Once a manipulation is exposed, it triggers a powerful emotional response of betrayal. Betrayal is a deep sense of loss. The loss is that of trust, and trust is a euphemism for cooperation. It may also trigger disgust because the manipulation may also be evaluated by the reactor to be unwholesome. Either way, the emotions of betrayal and disgust signal that a basic covenant of your Paradaptive Intelligence Network has been violated, which will eventually initiate anger as a boundary violation.

Illegitimate persuasion occurs when someone tries to pit their corrective signal against another party's adaptor or conductor's bias, or both. They may feel angry over some boundary violation and use guilt, a form of shame signaling disgust with one's self for making an error, to make you feel it was your fault. However, there may have been no legitimate boundary violation in the first part of what they consider an obstacle, such as the price of your product or some other term of the sale, that is in fact a legitimate requirement on your part. They may illegitimately tell you that you scare them, making you the threatening party, in hopes that you will modify your cost or terms to be less threatening. They may claim you are unwholesome, such as taking advantage of people in their times of need, in hopes that you will again modify some aspect of your adaptation plan for their benefit. Or, lastly, they may claim a loss, such as the loss of friendship over the terms of a deal "a friend wouldn't do this to friends..." And just as easily, these ploys can be used on prospects and clients.

Using manipulation as a sales tool is a very bad idea, even just once. Eventually you will be discovered, and your credibility will be irrevocably damaged, not only with the recipient of the manipulation, but with everyone within earshot of it. And in a world of social networking, search engines, and the internet, there isn't anywhere you can go on the planet that is out of earshot. Some people say using deceit is guile, which has a positive connotation. However, it is clearly just another form of deceit, which is a violation of the adaptor's prime directive of cooperation and just plain bad business — it has no place in the salesperson's quiver.

CON MEN

Con men, or grifters, have been around as long as man's had emotions. It is important to discuss them and what they do, because many prospects confuse salespeople for confidence men, and sometimes with good reason.

Con man is short for "confidence man." Their modus operandi is to gain the confidence of a mark and use that against him fraudulently for financial gain. But how do they do it? They have a very high-level feeling for, albeit intuitive and unstructured, the Paradaptive Intelligence Network and its directives. They use this knowledge to manipulate a mark into voluntarily giving the grifter his money, taking it by deception rather than force. Con men have the image of gentleman thieves who do not resort to coercion or force to obtain other peoples' money. They are perceived as takers, which is true, but how they weave their web of deceit is by giving. To gain a mark's confidence or trust, they use the Paradaptive Intelligence Network's adaptor's cooperation bias and Friendship relation algorithm. They devise "tales" about themselves that they know the mark will find appealing and connects with their Companion algorithm in the acquaintance phase (Acceptance, Curiosity, Camaraderie, and Attachment). Then they share intimate details (fabricated) about themselves, thus signaling they trust the mark (Friendship phase), who reciprocates and then shares intimate details with them, which the grifter uses to further manipulate the mark. Next, the grifter offers to help a mark, shifting to the Friendship phase of the algorithm with a get-rich-quick scheme that turns out to be a sham. A grifter uses false information to escalate the relationship in the Companion relationship algorithm so that the information of the particulars of the scheme will be taken with little or no skepticism.

Con men succeed because they manage and manipulate the mark's Paradaptive Intelligence Network and the emotions it produces. Salespeople just manage them. An ethical salesperson truly believes their product or service will help a client. It is this distinction that is lost on many people, leading to confusion between the two. That, and there are still some industries that use the same manipulative techniques as con men do in their sales efforts— mainly car sales.

Big cons were widespread in the early twentieth century. Gangs of specialized con men would enter a region, set up one of the three types of big cons, fleece as many people as possible, and then move on to another area. Because communications were limited early in the last century, it was difficult for people and law enforcement to check the credentials and identities of people. But better communications have vastly curtailed this criminal activity to the point where it no longer enjoys or employs the number of practitioners it once did.

The following are the steps in a "Big Con":

> "Putting the mark" – Locating and investigating a well-to-do victim.
> "Playing the con" – Gaining the victim's confidence.
> "Roping the mark" – Steering him to the inside man.

"Telling him the tale" – Permitting the inside man to show him how the mark can make a large amount of money dishonestly.

"Giving him the convincer" – Allowing the mark to make a substantial "tester" profit.

"Giving him the breakdown" – Determining precisely how much he will invest.

"Putting him on the send" – Sending him home for the money.

"Taking off the touch" – Playing him against the "Big Store" and fleecing him.

"Blowing him off" – Getting him out of the way as quietly as possible.

"Putting him in the fix" – Forestalling action by the law by creating legal peril if he squeals.

By the way, the 1973 Academy Award winner movie for Best Picture, The Sting, was based on the steps listed above, and if you go back and watch the movie, it breaks the movie up and labels each of the above movements.

So let's put this into a Paradaptive Intelligence perspective…con men purposely manipulate the relationship emotion tonal algorithm so that a mark is more likely to believe what the grifter tells him, counting on loyalty to silence any disquieting and discordant signals the mark's reactor might receive in "playing the con." Next, the grifter steers the mark to the inside man – "roping the mark"- which satisfies learning anticipation. The con man has something that can fix the mark's pain point. The mark's pain point is assumed because everybody has the pain point of not having enough money (acceptance). "Telling him the tale" satisfies learning anticipation by explaining how, for just a relatively small amount of money, the mark can obtain riches that are outside his current ability to earn and how he can do it. Additionally, "telling him the tale" also works towards the mark's conductor's bias to do his best towards others, because he will be sharing a small amount of the windfall with his newfound buddy, thus helping him out by providing the buddy's only missing ingredient, money. "Giving him the convincer" satisfies confidence by proving the low risk, surefire nature of the venture, making it easy for the con man to give the breakdown of how much money they need to make it work ("giving him the breakdown"), which satisfies excitement, and put the mark on the send for money ("putting him on the send"). Once the mark gets the money, he quickly hands it over to the con man, courage having long been satisfied. Now the mark is running on faith, convinced that his decision was sound and that he will reap riches. This false reality is removed in "taking off the touch," exposing the true risk in the venture as the whole deal goes south. There will be no emotion past faith, and the HAC is abandoned because it can no longer fulfill the motive of making money. Instead, to forestall any violent or negative blowback from the mark, the con calls for the introduction of a new corrective signal, fear. This comes in the form of a threat, such as being arrested for being party to some illegal or immoral aspect of the venture. This sets the mark's Paradaptive Intelligence System's emotions at either anxiety or paranoia, giving him massive signals from his reactor to move away, to flee, and quickly! Con men use the mark's own Paradaptive Intelligence Network to get the mark to remove himself.

By now, you've already found that this book's material has been proven valid every time it's applied correctly. The truths of the theory put forth here are self-evident in your own life. But for those few who are still not quite convinced, the above example is just another confirmation from a different quadrant from science, business, or your life. Con men are masters of manipulating the human psyche. Many clever criminals have spent countless hours studying man and his weaknesses to exploit. While con men and grifters may not have understood the Paradaptive Intelligence Network to the degree of precision that readers of this book will, they clearly had identified the pathway that was required to con people out of their money, thus confirming beyond all doubt the veracity of the emotional pathways and mechanisms described in this book.

With the steps of "the big con" in mind, let's look at car sales.

Step 1 is accomplished by advertising. Car lots and dealerships use high energy ads to arouse prospects into visiting. Because the marks are self-selecting or "volunteers," the salesmen really don't have to research their marks other than media research to place ads and tested formats of their ads to get the type mark they need. Step 2 happens at the lot. When a mark appears on the lot, he is quickly greeted by a friendly salesperson, "playing the con," that's going to help him get the car he wants. By doing so, he presents himself as the mark's agent when, in fact, he gets paid by the dealership, and therefore is, and always will be, *their* agent. Think of it this way: have you ever been greeted on a car lot by a salesperson that says, "Look, I'll help you to the best of my ability, but I work for the dealership and at the end of the day, I have to protect their interests"? Fat chance. You'll also see salespeople saying things like, "I can get you a really good deal today on this car," "We're having a special sale today," "I think we can get an extra X dollars off this car for you today," "We can deal on this car — I'm in tight with the manager," or hundreds of variations of this theme. The goal is to make the mark feel that he is special or that it's a special day, all to gain his confidence in his new found "friend's" help. Next, they get to the convincer, Step 5. They put the mark behind the wheel of a car for a test drive, the ostensive purpose so that he can get the feel of it or determine if it has any unwanted problems or characteristics. In fact, its main objective is to get him fired up (his reactor's pleasure seeker) and focused on getting a new car, creating a sense of desire to obtain new car pleasure in the mark. Now they go to the Step 4, "telling the tale." They start talking money, and as it just so happens, this car is on special, has a promotional rebate, etc., so the mark can save a large amount of money. Now the salesperson must steer the mark to the inside man (Step 3), the finance manager, who'll work magic. But first they need to "give you the breakdown," a.k.a. Step 6, in order to determine how much the mark can put on the car as a down payment. After that is determined, Step 7, putting him on the send, is next. The mark fills out credit applications, which the inside man pursues with his banking partners to get the mark the "best deal." Here's where Step 8, taking off the touch, takes place. The big store is a concept within the grifters' society where they get marks to play against a rigged process. It started off by actually opening stores, not to sell product, which they did only for cover, but to get marks involved in shell games, Three Card Montes, rigged card games, or a host of other small cons. So the mark sits, and sits, and sits… Now, as salespeople, you're used to selling things on credit or financing, and the process we're used to bears no resemblance to what occurs at a car lot or dealership. The purpose of making the mark sit serves two purposes. One, they actually do need to exchange paper with finance institutes but, secondly, they need the mark to stew. Remember, he's put his finances in the hands of people who won't let him see what's happening. He's always kept at arm's length in this process. That is because their goal is to maximize their profits, not minimize his payments, which they do by kickbacks and side deals with financial institutes for the volume of deals steered to them. Remember, this is a rigged process. By making the mark wait, they know it will create a sense of peril (to the proposed deal) in him. By it not happening right away, they want him to feel thankful when it does, because he's been imagining all that could go wrong to squirrel the deal while he's been stewing. Chances are the deal was approved within minutes after the paperwork was submitted, but they needed him to wait and worry in order to get him to the proper mind frame to sign the contracts the minute they present it. As soon as he signs, they hand him the car key, and the car is waiting for him, ready to go out front. This is the blow off, Step 9, which entails getting him out of the way as soon as possible. The buyer is so stressed from fear, waiting, and worrying, that he wants to escape the confines of the dealership without knowing why. The worry of the deal going south has been accumulating in the brain of the buyer. Worry is a mild form of threat. So the accumulated corrective signal to flee is expressed in signing the contract, grabbing the keys and getting out the door to his newly purchased vehicle. Step 10 takes place in the next day or two when the mark gets a call from the salesperson, who congratulates him on the exceptionally hard bargain the mark drove. This indirectly puts pressure on the mark, making him believe if he tried it all over again today, he'd not do nearly as well, that the mark caught the dealership in a moment of weakness. It puts him "in a fix" in that if he gets buyer's remorse, he'll never get as good a deal as he just did.

All the elements of the Big Con are there, just slightly reordered and updated for the times. One of the primary differences is that con men usually involved their marks in something illegal or immoral. Selling cars is a legal activity allowing a slight restructuring of the con steps. The effects are still the same, a manipulative process designed to part a prospect from his money in the most advantageous way for the dealership.

How many other salespeople have the luxury of getting prospects to step into an environment in which they control all the variables and a team helping to manipulate a prospect? The answer: none. People who go through this process know or sense at some level that they've been manipulated. And for many individuals, this is their only contact with "salespeople." This is why salespeople, in general, have a bad image and reputation, because one relatively small segment of the sales domain practices manipulative tactics.

Since this format is an industry "best practice" for car sales, we all end up eventually having contact with some form of this big con. All the pieces of the con are there, just reordered slightly to suit their needs to control your emotional feedback and take advantage of modern processes like advertising. Your only defense is to find car purveyors who don't subscribe to this methodology and support them. But if you find yourself in the grips of a manipulative process, your best defense is to recognize what it is they want to manipulate and then react in an unpredicted manner. Chew out the sales manager, loudly, in front of the other customers in the manipulative pipeline. Don't worry, he can take it—he knows that he controls the process. The real damage you do is when you upset their carefully choreographed manipulation of other marks' emotions in the pipeline and spook them into bolting. Be unpredictable—a loose cannon on the decks of their dealer "ship." Bust up their play, inject your reality upon them, and become their pain point.

19

SALES MANAGEMENT

"Life is a succession of lessons enforced by immediate reward, or oftener,
by immediate chastisement."
Ernest Dimnet

"Doubtless the world is quite right in a million ways; but you have to be kicked about
a little to convince you of the fact."
Robert Louis Stevenson

To date, the emotional process that occurs between prospect and salesperson has been covered. But that is only half of the equation. When a salesperson walks into a prospect's location, he carries with him the training, policies, and attitude that his firm's policies and practices engender. It would be remiss to not look at the emotional equation of the salesperson at work when they are not with customers and prospects because they are so instrumental to the performance of a salesperson.

Salespeople are a unique breed in the business world. As external agents of the company, they spend a goodly amount, if not the majority, of their time in "Indian country," using the colloquialism from our nation's founding. Because they are unobserved by management and fellow company employees, they occupy a shadowy world between a company and its clients. Because part of the role of a salesperson is to be an advocate for the client or prospect within the firm, they often seem to be at odds with the firm. But this is a vital role. The sales force and its salespeople are the only real link to the outside world. The marketing department's function is to coordinate the company's activities through third party media like print, TV, and radio for differing markets. Sure, the marketing department may do marketing research to provide management with homogenized, filtered, and statistically ordered views of the world, but this isn't a true two-way connection to the real world (as a reformed marketing researcher, product developer and marketing manager, I can attest to this). In fact, the primary function is to obtain information for management without management getting its hands dirty from the clientele. And the information provided is only as good as the question asked (the subject of an upcoming title).

This shadowy world evokes images of the salesperson as one who is free and unbound, which leads to both high levels of trust and mistrust at the same time by management. Because of the unusual half-in, half-out netherworld that salespeople occupy, management is presented with a difficult proposition. Although uninformed management will try to distill this process down to metrics that are a quantum of cold calls made, follow-up calls, presentations, delivered proposals, etc., the essence of the sales process can't accurately be judged by these metrics. Management's willingness to take this approach is based on the lack of understanding of the emotions and rules that all people, salespeople and otherwise, operate under and is forced to make evaluations based on broad statistical averages. This hides the true measure of effectiveness of their sales training, marketing strategy, sales support, and sales force effectiveness because the unique nature of the work cycle of sales where every situation, due to the differing attributes of each prospect or client makes uniform measurement of performance impossible. Signed contracts measure only the culmination of the emotion courage. Due to this varied nature of attributes, there can be no uniform direct measure of work output of a salesperson other than to measure the client's uniform emotional states of the Innovation emotional algorithm universal in all clients and prospects. A delivered sales presentation does not measure learning anticipation, nor does charting follow-up calls measure confidence towards your product by the prospect, etc. However, the best tool for sales management professionals to ensure a compliant sales force is the one that resides in all salespeople, their Paradaptive Emotional Network. By engaging and harnessing this tool properly, the sales manager's role will change dramatically for the better. Those that buck and frustrate this internal mechanism will enjoy results of a different stripe - minimal compliance, high turnover, slow growth, and less than enchanting sales volumes.

There are many strategic and tactical decisions regarding distribution channel management that are better suited to other books. The emphasis of this book is to increase the efficacy of the sales force where the rubber meets the road, when salesperson meets client or prospect, no matter what the tactical or strategic path. By applying the techniques advocated here, you may find that a malfunctioning or underperforming distribution channel may not be due to tactical or strategic mistakes, but rather to correctable sales force management issues.

FOUR PRIMARY SALES MANAGEMENT FUNCTIONS

There are variables in the sales environment that management can't influence, such as the economy, legislation, innovation and the impact it has on overall customer demand, and competitive activity. However, there are four main management functions that shape the sales force and thus control its performance to a large degree. They are supervision, selection of personnel, sales training, and motivation of the sales force. All four of these areas can be enhanced by understanding and utilizing different aspects of the Paradaptive Intelligence Network to support management's efforts to achieve the company's goals.

Supervision

Companies have a right and obligation to direct the work of those who they employ. So in companies that choose to field an in-house sales force, there are several things to keep in mind when formulating a management strategy. In supervision, there are three objectives that must be met: accuracy, clarity, and conflict avoidance. Accuracy refers to telling your sales employees to do the right activities at the right time, not only so they perform and work by the appropriate policies and procedures, but also so that they understand their role. Your work directives become the motives of your employees. An example of poor clarity is the sales manager that orders his employees to "Sell, Sell, SELL!" Sales are the by-product of helping prospects with problems, i.e. pain points, with your products and services. Clarity refers to succinctly telling, in an understandable and unambiguous way that minimizes confusion, what it is they are to do. This refers to the desired outcome of the motive. Where sales managers go wrong here is micro management. They tell employees how to perform every aspect of the task thinking this is clarity. What is actually occurring is the employees Paradaptive Intelligence Network is overloaded to the point of dysfunction with an overly complicated motive, which it considers the entire litany of micromanaged activity directions to be, and whose by-product is the disengagement of their adaptive mental machinery, since there is no latitude for problem solving and adaptation. Lastly, conflict avoidance refers to giving work directives that are not in competition or in contravention of other work directives, so that desired outcomes do not conflict with one another. An example of this is giving two number one priorities to an employee in the same time frame. There can only be one priority. The word priority denotes attention above all else. Giving an employee another task in the middle of a priority can have the same effect.

In sales management, knowing exactly where to direct your sales forces activities is a matter of supporting the strategic aims of the firm's management. Accuracy of directives is a function of the adaptors of management as they attempt to devise new strategies to cope with and adopt to the ever-changing business climate and meet their goals. Work directives, if accepted by your sales professionals, will become the motives of a Human Action Cycle. Therefore, your salespeople *will* develop emotions about the directives given them. One could simply assume that a salesperson's own Paradaptive Intelligence Network will help them keep on track to obtain their directives, in which case, one wouldn't need to do anything. And while this would be right, an opportunity is missed with that stance. No matter the clarity with which you tell an employee what needs to be done, at some point there will be miscommunications because there is a difference between directives and the motives they become. Desired outcomes not communicated become imagination-based action plans. This is because your words, written or spoken, will be interpreted by the employee's vocabulary and its definition of words, not yours. They may understand what you said differently because the words, expression, inflection, or tone you used have a slightly different meaning to them; after all, no synchronization is perfect. Or, their attention may have wandered or was interrupted while reading or listening to your instructions. This is a fact of business life. So rather than wait for the inevitable, be proactive to get and keep things on track. Ask your employees how they feel about how they are doing regarding the directive once they have had an opportunity to implement it and generated internal feedback. Their Paradaptive Intelligence Networks will act as the perfect diagnostic tool for you because they will tell you which of the six main types of emotions they are experiencing, which will point you in the right direction to fix any problems or get out of their way.

Asking employees how they feel about things is a radical departure for many managers. This is because deciphering these signals prior to this book was a messy and fearful endeavor, with little usable information obtained. Because asking about their feelings had so much downside with little gain, the norm became not to talk about emotions in the workplace. As a manager, you learn far more about your organization's operations by asking about feelings and following up with clarifying questions. The typical approach under the old paradigm was to ask for a progress report. Some employees might take that as a challenge that you don't think they can do it, or that you don't trust them. Others, perceiving that they may not have met your expectations, may skew or shade their answers to what they think you wanted to hear or even outright fabricate a response. Asking about their feelings has a totally different approach. It focuses on their opinion, on *them*, and not the work. Everybody loves to talk about themselves — it's part of the hardwiring for cooperation. It's an indirect, softer way of obtaining better information about their performance. Expressing feelings is hardwired in humans for cooperation, which is why we have facial expressions depicting our internal emotional status. It is this built-in cooperation mechanism that leads to the company rumor mill which can have destructive and corrosive results on a company's well-being. Being proactive and asking about your sales staff's feelings will positively channel this natural and required activity into information you can use as a manager.

Knowing and understanding your employees' emotions is extremely beneficial. It allows you to understand when you're over- or under-controlling your staff. You hire salespeople for their flexibility and adaptability; the optimum level of this occurs when your sales people are meeting all six of their universal needs. Every salesperson is different and each operates differently. Work directives, which are necessary to systemize operations, are by definition one size fits all. Yet, there always are a myriad of ways to incorporate a work directive if coached properly. Otherwise, sales staff may become frustrated because a directive could curtail one or more of their six universal needs. And remember, the universal needs are hierarchical, so a directive that impacts a need low in the hierarchy could have a large impact on the employee's performance. Negative emotions, by design, will interrupt employees' thought processes, preventing them from efficiently doing their jobs. This is leaving money on the table for a sales manager. A sales staffer that is preoccupied with an internal corrective signal just won't be as productive as you need him or her to be, which will impact your position in the company. This can also be said for the salesperson in the field that comes upon a prospect that is feeling Loss due to a family member's demise; the prospect won't hear a thing that you have to say about business, products, and adaptation plans until you deal with his or her emotions. So if it works for your sales force in the field, don't you think it should be part of your process as a supervisor? At a minimum, you should be leading by example. At the best, your sales force will respond more favorably to you because they believe you care, you've removed obstacles that increase productivity, and you're being proactive, making changes and fixing their pain points sooner rather than later.

All this communication relies upon two different elements, trust and respect. Respect comes from you hearing their concerns *and responding to them vis-a-vis cooperation*. This is part of the cooperation hardwired circuitry of the human emotion system. In the 80's, one of the hot, new waves of management practices was to sit and listen to employees' emotions. This practice fell upon the dung heap of management fads that failed to understand the basic human structure of the emotions system. Managers would dutifully hold sessions, which soon became known as "bitch" sessions because they listened but didn't respond. Listening is not cooperating. Cooperating is sharing information. This means telling employees why you can't do everything they want. They may not know or understand the limitations and constraints placed upon you by your superiors, or their superiors, or how you arrived at your decisions. Sharing that information is responding, cooperating. If there is no limitation, be flexible enough to change something, to remove the obstacle that's causing consternation.

The second element to succeed is having trust. They must first trust that you will not use their expression of feelings against them or belittle them. This is easy to do if you remember that every emotion they feel is valid. Your feelings about their feelings are irrelevant. Your goal is to remove any negative feelings/corrective signal that are disrupting their mental focus so they can operate at their optimal level, precisely as they would with a prospect living in the past that is having difficulty moving into the present so they may accept the adaptation plan being offered. This is done by either removing or altering some element causing the impediment or offering information that allows them to change their perception of the problem, which is short for modifying the HAC that is being impacted.

Conflict in work directives is clearly a topic involving the Paradaptive Intelligence Networks of your sales team. The telltale response in your staff to look for is anger. Recall that anger occurs when an immutable boundary has been violated or an obstacle has been placed in their path to a desirable outcome. Conflicting work directives satisfy both definitions. By giving conflicting work directives, you've given them an impossible task. This is unfair, and being unfair is an issue of respect and cooperation. Everyone requires respect — that is part of the cooperation hardwire set and the minimum threshold for a positive business relationship — and your conflicting directives have caused you to violate the cooperation boundary of the adaptor. The other way that conflicting work directives can be interpreted is that they create confusion, which requires effort and time to sort out. Wasting time and effort on nonproductive activities is an obstacle to achieving their goals and making money. When you see anger in your employees, seek clarification as to which of the two violations, impediment or boundary violation, is the source and rectify it.

Selection of Personnel

When looking to hire employees, several steps are involved, such as identifying the need to hire, developing selection criteria, collecting candidates, reviewing candidate documentation, interviewing, and induction. At this point in the process, managers are trying to identify aptitude for their type of sales, whether it's retail selling to the final consumer, or industrial selling to resellers, business users, or institutions. For institutional selling firms, their selection process is further refined for the types of sales jobs they expect their people to perform, trade, missionary, technical, or new business selling, all of which carry further aptitude requirement refinements upon the sales manager.

But what does "aptitude" mean in hiring situations?

Generally, it refers to the personal characteristics an applicant brings to the job, such as intelligence, analytical ability, communications capabilities, honesty, work ethic, etc. But now that we know that the sales process is directed and controlled by a prospect's or client's emotional machinery, and mastering this machinery has the greatest impact on a salesperson's success, you need to add another criteria to the selection process and make it among the top elements, if not the top characteristic you hire for, Paradaptive Intelligence (PI).

PI hunting in salespeople is comprised of two aspects: communications and problems solving, but not in the normal context of the old paradigm. By communications, we mean a candidate's ability to speak to others' emotions, which includes identifying them and responding to them effectively. By problem solving, we aren't referring to their ability to complete puzzles quickly, but to create pain nullification strategies and present them in an effective Paradaptive Intelligence compatible manner.

Having learned how high PI is a predictor of sales success, you can now formulate a hiring strategy around identifying this characteristic. But first, it's important to look at the old paradigm of hiring to see the former pitfalls and how they have led sales managers astray. In the old paradigm, typically, a sales manager would select for the highly favorably characteristic of "experience." The belief there was that experience at some other company was an indicator of potential success at their firm. But what does "experience" get you? You do get some indication that they are reasonably capable and comfortable working by themselves in the field, unguided by supervision and have adequate communications skills. But that seems to be a relatively low standard of qualification. You want the best — after all, your income and livelihood depends on this individual's performance. Getting an indication of the applicant's abilities in unguided work, communications, and work ethic can be ascertained from résumés, job history, and an interview. But typically, there is no screening for PI. This can be accomplished prior to the interview with a written test or during the interview with standardized questions that allow you to evaluate candidates relative to each other. Your aim in testing the candidate is to create scenarios both typical and atypical to the type of sales he would be expected to perform. Give the applicant typical and non-typical customer responses and then ask him to identify which emotions are involved and what his response to it is. If you need assistance in this type of screening, you can contact the SPAN Consulting Group, LLP via the internet or phone listed at the end of this book for a consultation to formulate questions specific to your hiring needs.

Another pitfall of screening for experience is failing to understand what "experience" really means. All sales companies, up until the advent of this book, trained their salespeople with the classic features and benefits approach. The first thing that a new salesperson finds out is that features and benefits have absolutely nothing to do with how the customer looks at problems. Through communication, perseverance, and luck, a new salesperson will find customers who educate the salesperson to their perspective on how they see their product. This is typically a salesperson's first brush with pain point selling. Experience in a salesperson is the process of abandoning features and benefits selling for pain point selling, albeit their understanding of pain points is limited only to what his or her customers educate them to.

The process of seasoning a typical salesperson is highly industry specific. This means a salesperson that was a top performer at one company may be a dud at another company. The pain points learned by random contact with prospects pertain only to that industry. This is a highly inefficient process because most customers and prospects are unable to articulate their fears and anger or even understand them or their relevance, let alone communicate them to a salesperson. A salesperson without Paradaptive Intelligence sales training or who does not have a high level of innate PI, has a low probability of translating prospect fear and anger into useful information, thus the emotional content of selling from one industry typically gets lost. This is why "industry experience" is highly sought, because it has some emotional portability. Some portability is still a crapshoot because the salesperson's understanding of pain point selling was based on someone else's product, not the ones an applicant will be selling. Unless it's a commodity product, the new salesperson will start again at a features and benefit sales model, based most likely on your sales training of features and benefits, and start the "seasoning" process all over again. The reason for this is a journeyman salesperson may stick in one industry long enough to stumble upon "hot points" (pain points) of that industry and short cut his or her sales approach in a modified pain point selling approach, but may not really know or understand what he or she is actually doing. He or she just knows that focusing on certain points of a prospect produces a higher probability of a sale and does it by rote. So hiring a journeyman salesperson with industry experience may just lead to hiring a salesperson with a limited bag of tricks that may not translate to your company's marketing profile. This is why PI testing is so important. If a salesperson possesses good abilities in reading peoples' emotions and dealing with them, they you will have a much higher probability of increasing your income based on their performance, once you've trained them in Paradaptive Intelligence selling in conjunction with your product's pain nullifying capabilities.

The best of the top performers, though, operate intuitively on Paradaptive Intelligence selling techniques. PI sellers have skills that are easily transferable from one company to the next, from one product line to another. They know what to look for, pain, and how to extract that type of information from clients and prospects. Because their initial focus is not on application of features, they are able to co-opt the prospect's emotional algorithm, opening better communications to probe for points of pain. Their adaptation plans are adapted for the specific emotional set discovered in the prospect, directed at pain nullification and the proper emotional station in the Vetting phase where the prospect is residing, and followed by relevant questions designed to identify and allow changes to the prospect's emotional state through enunciation.

It has been said that the best hiring strategy is to identify the skill set of your best performers and hire that archetype.

This is a fallacy wrapped in a misunderstanding surrounded by misguided intentions.

Until you've read this book, you've had no idea what that skill set actually is, how to identify it, and therefore how to select for it. Secondly, intuitive salespeople with high PI are exceedingly rare. That's why they say, "They broke the mold after they made 'em'." And, lastly, this approach ignores the hidden gems in your sales force that can be polished into top performer status with the right training. The priority should be to look for individuals with high and equal levels of PI and analytical skills because both skill sets are necessary for successful salespeople. When those characteristics are not available in the hiring pool, select for strong analytical skills first. Strong analytical skills types have a strong affinity for PI sales training because it is a process they can identify with.

And, finally, the last pitfall in hiring a top performer from another company stems from the emotion acceptance. Every product is designed to address specific issues or problems. This specific design criteria upon which the hire candidate's experience is founded is an affectation of what problems and issues the product designer considers important and accepted by their targeted prospective clients. When you hire someone from a competitor or allied field, they will bring with them the accepted problems and issues from their previous employment, which may have considerable overlap with the design philosophy of your product or nothing at all. This exposes the extremely large variability of the hire prospect's skills portfolio. While a hire candidate's idea is of accepted problems and issues in an industry is dependent upon what products they've been exposed to in their career, their skills and understanding of the Paradaptive Intelligence Network is a much more stable indicator of what they can do. No matter what the accepted issues and problems a product is designed to fix, a salesperson with high PI can shift their foundational sales strategy to any industry. And what they accept as foundational may not necessarily be the same accepted issues of the design parameters of your product. The point is this, bet on their Paradaptive Intelligence Network skills, and not their industry experience, which unless you have specific tests for, is nothing more than a crapshoot.

If you need assistance in identifying and selecting for these traits, the SPAN Consulting Group can assistance you in setting up a screening process for this type of criteria recruitment.

Sales Training

Renouncing features and benefits training and changing your paradigm to SPAN selling is among the largest, most impactful change you can make to your organization. Maintaining a direct sales force is one of the most expensive, yet most potent marketing tools a firm can possess. There have been many books written on sales force management, with dozens and dozens of anecdotes of how industry leaders like Proctor and Gamble, IBM, and Microsoft dominated their industries due to their sales force. As discussed previously, accuracy in directing your sales force activities is vital. Directing them to perform unproductive and wasteful activities is taking a chance with your career and the firm's resources. Features and benefits selling fit this type of activity. Features and benefits selling is indirect and requires the prospect to make the connection between the benefit and the nullification of their pain point to create their own adaptation strategy. Because psychic pain disrupts the higher mental process such as reasoning, thought, and logic, training a sales force in features and benefits training is setting them up for failure because you're betting on impaired prospects being able to put logic and reasoning together regarding your product. This also assumes that reasoning and logic were in their inventory in their first place. Still, prospects do and are able to make these connections, create their own adaptive strategy, including your product, and sales occur. People in general, and prospects specifically, generally are able to handle some level of disruption from their Paradaptive Intelligence Network and perform higher order thinking, but not everyone, and not always — it is dependent upon the intensity of the corrective signal. But the bigger question is have you positioned your sales force for optimum sales performance with this type of training and direction?

The more prudent and productive approach would be to have your sales force address the Paradaptive Intelligence Network of prospects directly by doing the thinking for them and then couching that thinking in emotional terms that their prospects are feeling. In order to do this, you need to implement training in the processes of the Paradaptive Intelligence Network presented in this book. Salespeople should not leave your training program until they can recite - backwards and forwards, inside and out — the attributes of the Paradaptive Intelligence Network. Additionally, to make that sort of redirection in training successful, it also requires a reversal in most companies' training philosophies. In order for the Paradaptive Intelligence Network training to be successful, sales force trainees need to understand the emotions of their prospects, which means they must also understand their prospects' business processes and industry. The typical management thinking is that their only obligation to a sales force trainee is to explain the features and benefits of their product. The rest is the responsibility of the salesperson to figure out once he hits the field. Or they hire "industry experience," which we now know is a marginal indicator of success. Either way, this is a haphazard approach to something that directly influences your paycheck and career as a sales manager.

Instead, this book advocates that companies put the most emphasis on industry training, followed by, to a lesser degree, company processes that would have bearing on the products' implementation and operations, followed by the normal level of product operation, features, and benefits that they would normally give a trainee (See Figure 19.1). The reason behind this is straightforward and logical. The expertise in the industry and process will normally already exist within the company; after all, someone had to research the industry and company processes to understand the problems of the target market and design a product or service to fix them. Secondly, this will shorten the time necessary for a new trainee to be fully productive by removing any confusion created by unfamiliar context and parameters encountered at the clients' sites, undermining the sales process with indecision, tangents, and uncertainty of the product's application. Remember, your salespeople are selling an adaptation plan which is a product or service coupled with an implementation plan. If they don't know the industry or the firm's business processes, how can they present an effective or acceptable implementation process? Lastly, by being conversant in the prospect's industry, they will be able to zero in on pain points quicker, build trust with the prospects by honoring the cooperation bias with their empathy and understanding in exchanges of the prospects' plight, and be less distracted by non-relevant information presented by the prospect. A shorter sales cycle means greater volume potential for the firm or the need for fewer salaried salespeople, both of which add to a firm's bottom line.

By incorporating the philosophy towards new sales hires presented here, you provide your new salespeople the proper, stable foundation upon which the features and benefits of your product can be anchored. By taking this approach, you create a sales staff that comes out of training straight into a consultive style of selling without any aging or "experience" gathering required. By doing so, even sales by new sales

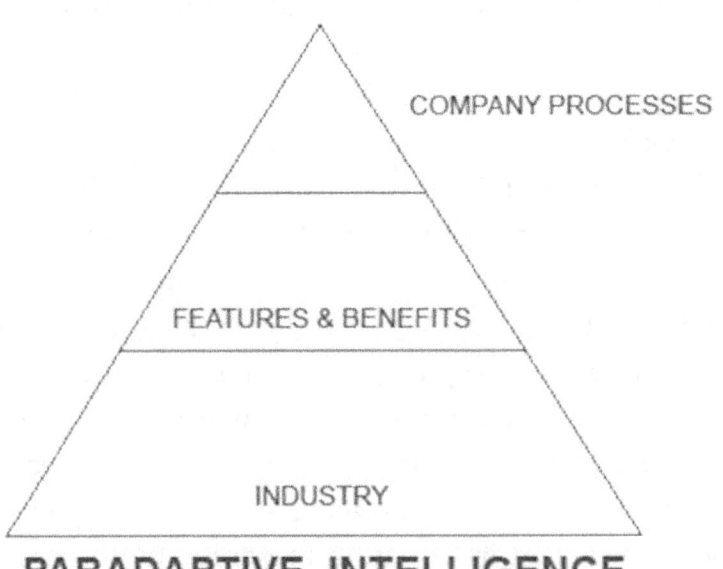

staff will generate strong emotional attachment by your customers to your salespeople, hence your company, which hardens them from competitive pressure. Besides, your sales staff is destined, to one degree or another, to abandon features and benefits selling as they stumble forward and find pain point selling instances on their own. Doesn't it make sense, and don't you owe it to them, to change your training regimen to build upon necessary business process and industry knowledge, which is where they'll end up anyhow, if they survive most companies' misdirected training efforts?

Motivation

All people, salespeople included, are internally motivated by their conductors to perfect themselves, their skills, and their abilities to maximize their survival. However, in sales, additional incentives are required. This is because the salespeople work outside the immediate control of supervision normally. To ensure that the salesperson works towards the company's goals and does not pursue other agendas, companies offer incentives as a means of exercising control from a distance. For example, salespeople are a gregarious, outgoing lot that enjoy talking to people. This gives them pleasure, which their Paradaptive Intelligence Network directs them to repeat. While conversation may give pleasure to the salesman (fulfilling the need for connection), it does not support the company's needs of selling products, so sales incentives are provided so that the salesperson can self-modulate his activity and make choices between the pleasure of conversation and the pleasure of earning money.

Every sales company must decide to what degree they want to control their sales force. This control is measured by two factors - the choice to pay salary or performance incentives, or both, and in what proportion. Salaries are offered by companies desiring high levels of control. This control comes at a cost, though, to the company. Performing non-sales related activities takes time away from the pursuit of sales. This reduces the possible universe of sales for each salesperson by utilizing business hours to execute company directed activities. To offset the lost sales of the salesperson due to the unproductive activities, companies must provide salaries for the lost income from commission and bonuses. For example, many sales companies spend significant amounts on internet sales management tools that require their salespeople to use their valuable working (or personal) time to enter in how many phone calls, cold calls, letters, research surveys, proposals, signed contracts, etc. they perform each day. These are unproductive in that they do not directly support the sales activities between a salesperson and a prospect; rather, their entire function is to give management the illusion that they are managing the sales process. It is illusionary because outside, and even inside, salespeople to a high degree, are autonomous. They will make their own decisions about what and how they will go about their work. That is, after all, what they were hired for, their adaptability and decision-making skills in an unsupervised setting.

Another motivation factor is performance incentives. Incentives are forms of compensation or other desired commodities offered in exchange for work performance, usually measured in completed sales. Incentives work via the basic emotion of joy, which agitates and directs individuals to approach and repeat experiences. In an exchange based society, money, as a medium, buys pleasure, joy, security...survival. People, long before science confirmed it, recognized that better long-term results could be achieved in controlling other people's activities by dangling a carrot...joy, rather than the stick (fear/ threat). Incentives provide a constant, positive, ever present tool that works directly with every human's Paradaptive Intelligence Network to guide behavior.

Another form of motivation of little or no cost to the sales manager is praise. Each salesperson has motives to be successful in many different ways. They create motives and action plans which they run through a HAC to achieve those results. When you recognize those efforts with praise, you are providing the positive external confirmation of achieving that motive. While the act of selling is usually motivated and rewarded by financial remuneration, there are far more motivations of your sales staff that only praise can provide positive confirmation of success and provide them with an internal shot of joy of satisfaction.

A quick example is flattery. You want to present to the world in a specific way (motive) by having a professional appearance. You accept that you don't currently have a suit that presents you in the specific fashion you want (acceptance). You go to a chosen suit purveyor to purchase a suit to the specification of that motive (action plan). Arriving at the suit purveyor, you see he has many suits that can fulfill motivation. You try several suits until you finally settle on the one you want and purchase it (learning anticipation, confidence, excitement, and courage). After the tailoring is done you pick up the suit and wear it the next day with a carefully selected shirt and tie feeling like you're presenting a professional appearance to the world in the way you anticipated (faith). You look in the mirror and see the type of business professional that was your objective and you hope others will see the same thing as you. At work people notice the new suit and genuinely compliment you on the look. These external confirmations from others on your motive achievement gives you more shots of joy, exuberance, reinforcing the internal satisfaction you achieved via the Innovation emotional algorithm up to this point. Since the suit was within your budget and getting tailored right was accomplished, plus external compliments have added exuberance, satisfaction is tallied as both faith and exuberance were positive. This external recognition reinforces the positive agitation expression of self-actualization/satisfaction to approach/repeat the experience. This is why flattery makes you feel good. Also, praising their non-vocalized motives will raise their opinion of your observational powers and situation awareness, creating or reinforcing their perception of you as an observant and aware leader. This will open the door for mentoring opportunities by fulfilling the six basic needs of connection and esteem by working for and being associated with an excellent leader.

As a sales management professional, when you realize that everyone of your sales staff has a multitude of motives in regards to their professionalism, like being on time, being organized, being accurate, informed on your products attributes, improve their volume, and on and on…you will realize you have the ability to highly motivate your staff without money. Sales are usually rewarded with remuneration and therefore do not require praise. It's already received external reward reinforcement in the form of commission. Praise of something, some effort, which has already been receiving external reward is a waste of the sales manager's effort and time because it is redundant and adds nothing to the salesperson's internal Paradaptive Intelligence system to repeat the experience. However, what you can complement the salesperson on is the growth of their sales or landing of new or different types of accounts that they haven't brought in before, the quality of their paperwork, consistency, and other attributes for which they will never receive a commission or sales incentive. The only caveat is that you must observe the salesperson carefully to determine what motives they are trying to achieve before rewarding it with an external reward of a compliment and praise. To compliment someone on something that they have no motive to achieve will only serve to change their opinion on your perspicacity.

Sales Pitch Blasts

In one of the most egregious examples of misdirected sales training, certain drug companies used to train their salespeople to recite features and benefits script about a product without interruption in a one-way blast of data. The trick, as far as they were concerned, was to make this blast seem conversational. As a training aid, they were supposed to light a match and finish the script before the match burned to the fingers. First off, when you are speaking, your reactor is focused on translating thoughts into action in its role as the connector between mind and body. When speaking, you are less likely to observe the body language and expression of the person you are addressing. If by some chance you did observe them, you undoubtedly would have observed them becoming irritated with you for violating the cooperation bias. You were speaking at them, not with them, which is not cooperating. Even though this features and benefits script blast was directed at a sophisticated audience with high capacity to translate the technical data, the clinicians are often unable to focus because they are distracted. And what were they distracted by? By now, you should know the answer. Most doctors have their own practices, which makes them small businessmen. They have concerns about product quality, meeting payroll, supplies, equipment, personnel issues, and the like, as well as industry issues, not to mention quality patient care. Pain points in their business processes and industry disrupt their focus. This will happen no matter how sophisticated the audience because nature has designed it that way. But enough doctors are able to compartmentalize (subdue reactor agitation expressions from corrective signals in their business) their emotional distractions long enough to allow their adaptors to acquire new information, which the adaptor craves for expanded adaptation capabilities. Still this approach left half the process undone unless they included an adaptation plan. What the clinicians really want to know is when and where to apply this product. The primary concern of a doctor is providing the best care for his or her patients. Every product has a different pathway, and thus different target markets, including drugs. The adaptation plan is what should be led with, the features and benefits providing the logic and reasoning behind that plan. The clinician is going to figure out on his own how to apply it or even if he will prescribe a drug for his own reasons. So why not beat them to the punch and give him a ready-made solution? At least this way, at a minimum, you can influence his decisions, if not direct him as he emotionally moves through the Vetting phase.

Cold Calling

This match-duration blast approach is typical of sales companies that don't understand the emotions of cold calling. Cold calling is a necessary element of sales. But what most salespeople don't understand, until now, is that their intrusion *will* cause an emotion within the prospect. In most cases, the intrusion is unwanted, yielding a corrective signal negative emotion by the prospect. But by playing to their adaptors with brief statements of the type of education and pain nullification you offer, with a promise you're leaving in the next thirty seconds, will allow you to nullify the pain point your intrusion generates. Your only goal is to ascertain whether there is follow-up potential. Find out, leave, and call to book an appointment at a later date at their convenience. Your goal is not to squat and force a sale. Sometimes that will happen organically, because the prospect has a burning pain point that needs immediate salve and has the time to speak with you, but that is rare. Your best bet in cold calling is to start by acknowledging that you are interrupting, and emphasize the fact that you are leaving, which will generate a positive emotional response of relief upon which you can further build with that quick offer of education and pain nullification if they're interested. By casting offers at both the reactor (pain nullification), and adaptor (education) you've broadened the opportunity of success for the prospect to say, "Yeah, I'd like to hear more. Why don't you call me to set something up?" Additionally, by stating your intent to leave in the next thirty seconds, you relieve the prospect of ignoring you while they try and think up reasons why they can't talk to you right now or ways to get you to leave. You've already solved one of their problems or nullified that particular pain point, namely that of your interruption. Now they can hear your offer of further pain nullification or education without further distraction.

THE QUOTA GAUNTLET AND INCENTIVES

Quota

The most misunderstood and abused element within the sales profession is the use of quotas as a motivation tool. A quota is a formal, stated expectation of performance that contains a threat. If there was no threat contained, it would be called a guideline. It says, "We expect you to do this…or else!" If you do not achieve the number set, you have failed to meet expectations. Failure to achieve the expectations of someone who has power over you activates a powerful corrective signal in the Paradaptive Intelligence Network, fear. Power is the ability to bring change, bring unwanted change — harm — to someone. And as we have learned, fear agitates and directs a person under its influence to leave the threatening situation as well as intentionally disrupts logic, reasoning, and thought until the individual responds to the threat. And every salesperson works under this threat for a significant period of time if a quota system is in place. This threat is especially potent if salespeople witness other sales staff removed for non-achievement of quotas. Whether the quota is monthly, quarterly, or yearly, a salesperson will be working the majority of the period with his or her performance below the quota because it takes time to accumulate sales before reaching the quota threshold. It may be argued that many salespeople are confident that they can reach their quota numbers and give it no thought, and thus do not spend the majority of their time working in a fear state. There is some validity to the argument, but its supposition is the salesperson's confidence is based on the presumption that he or she will have the full working period to achieve the quota. This assumption never factors in illness, injury, disease, family emergencies, or a multitude of other events such as environment disruption, business disruption, etc. that occur in life.

Threatening employees will get short-term results, but it has a long-term corrosive effect that is hard wired into every human's Paradaptive Intelligence Network. Sales managers are generally good, decent people, and would never go home and beat their child or spouse for good measure, just to introduce fear into their relationship. Nor do they threaten their customers. Yet, due to tradition and lack of the understanding of the hardwiring of the human brain, they will flog the very people their livelihoods depend on with the unveiled threat contained in a quota, thus setting many of their salespeople up for failure and most for under-performance. Your salespeople will not understand what their brains are doing to them, unless they read this book. This threat manifests itself in many ways. A salesperson under a threat may constantly have thoughts such as "I hate this job," "This job sucks," or "I've gotta get a new job." If you question them closely, they may not be able to tell you exactly what it is about the job they hate or why they need to get a new job. Very often, they like a great many aspects of their job. This is the silent and pernicious action of a quota and its threat element acting upon their psyches. As they are perpetually bombarded by their Paradaptive Intelligence Networks responding to a threat, they will eventually adopt this negative attitude, which will eventually lead them to seek employment elsewhere. Good salespeople will have this type of change in attitude for no apparent reason, causing a sales manager to scratch his head, wondering what happened.

Salespeople have many motives about work: they desire to be liked by their co-workers, have a good relationship with their boss, to help people, to meet people, to make money. Thanks to the simple architecture of the HAC, a salesperson, or any employee for that matter, can have many motives about work and servicing multiple HACs about work at any given time. But if just one of those motives turns into a viable threat, like quotas, it can override the positive feedback of joy from all the other HACs cycles. Remember the reactor's mission is to protect the body and it will not tolerate a threat, despite whatever other joy might be associated with it. So, even a good salesperson can't override the negative emotions a quota generates forever and will eventually succumb. These vague, unspecified feelings of unease accumulate and grow with time as the reactor ramps up the intensity, pushing harder and harder to force a response to the threat. Sometimes, salespeople can correct their attitude by investigating the threat and removing it, by negotiations with management, or recasting it as a challenge. But most times, it's irreversible because they have no idea where it's coming from. Once the negativity takes hold, it becomes the lens through which every action of the company is viewed, creating a snowball effect that culminates in "burn out." "Burn out" is the accumulated effects of threats and obstacles in the work environment.

Another variation of this is the lack of earnings. If a salesperson can't make enough money due to the quota, or his inability to create sales due to poor training, support, or supervision, his survival is threatened. Again, the salesperson's brain is bombarded with corrective signals to leave. Firms experiencing high turnover in their sales force most assuredly are creating high threat environments that their salespeople can't ignore or override.

The most important thing to remember is if a company creates a negative emotion rich environment by threats to their sales force, it is automatically forcing its employees to flee. And the first to flee will be your top performers. Top performers are the most mobile. They have skills and talents that other firms covet and thus have the least tolerance to threat environments. Those in your sales force with lesser talents are less mobile, and have fewer options or alternatives; therefore, they are more likely to try and ride out the storm or persevere in threatening environments. This has the effect of dumbing-down your sales force to the least competent denominator. Firms in this type of downward spiral set a negative feedback cycle (wrong track) that is tough to break. Top sales performers exit, leaving less competent salespeople, who management threatens even more with additional quotas or other threatening actions to get more out of the reduced capacity sales force. These increased threats create more agitation from the sales staff's reactors, thus interfering with the rational thought processes and making them perform to an even lesser degree than they are otherwise capable of, which results in an even more threatening posture from management, ad infinitum. Firms on this path see:

- Reduced yields per salesperson.
- Higher turnover.
- Increased training costs.
- Decline or no gain in market share because no customer loyalty can be attached to the sales force.
- Higher incentive dollar expenditures to maintain sales.
- Shorter average longevity in their sales force.
- Low motivation and morale levels in their sales force.

Incentives

An incentive is a promise of reward for performance. It contains no threat, only the promise of reward. Thus, any failure to collect an incentive does not agitate and direct a person to remove himself or herself from the scene. Instead, failure to collect pleasure can activate the basic emotions disgust, anger, or loss depending on the context of the Human Action Cycle in play in the salesperson. If the salesperson saw the reward within reach and then blew it with a bad decision or some variable within his control, he will become disgusted with himself. The basic emotion disgust agitates the person to remove the unwholesomeness or, in other words, not to blow it again by repeating that unwholesome mistake. If the variable that prevented him from achieving the incentive was not in his control, he may experience either the basic emotion anger or loss. If the person sees that the variable that caused him to lose the reward was created by someone else, he will experience anger because they see that other person's actions as intentionally putting an obstacle in front of him. This will move him to push back with aggression to remove the obstacle. In addition, that interference violates the adaptor's cooperation bias as well as the conductor's bias to do your best for others, which will also trigger anger. If the variable that caused the failure was in the environment and not controlled by anyone, it will trigger loss, which agitates the salesperson to seek replacement. Or, in other words, to try again. Often, this is expressed in the concept of luck, as in "it was just bad luck."

The Gauntlet

Most often a sales organization will combine these two different systems, which guarantees muddled results. Generally, it works like this: a quota is set, with incentives only available after the quota has been achieved. It is a unique twist on the "carrot or the stick" analogy but, in this case, they get both. The carrot is tied to the stick, which threatens them until they come into possession of the carrot. Mostly, they just get the stick. This also goes by another name, the Gauntlet. Of the two, incentive (joy) and quota (threat), the brain is hardwired to ignore the incentive, and the reactor focuses solely on the threat contained in the quota because its job is to preserve the body by avoiding threats. Studies have shown that the vast majority (75%) of salespeople are quota driven (pain nullification), with the remainder being money driven (joy). The numbers vary, but usually the ratio is around 3:1. This makes perfect sense in light of the Paradaptive Intelligence Network's priority on threats. By using a quota system, you set your sales force up to work towards pain nullification — the quota threat — and not sales maximization (joy) by a margin of 3:1. Another way to look at this is only one quarter of your sales force is focused on maximizing sales. The rest just want to make the pain go away and stop when that is accomplished. Again, the greater question is have you positioned your sales force for success or failure by pain/threat driven motivation, and how much good is your incentive system doing? Are you fighting nature's hardwiring in your salespeople, or are you working within its parameters to maximize the firm's sales? There is a better way.

But before we can discuss a better way, there needs to be some foundational underpinnings put in place. From the discipline of economics, we need to learn and adopt the Law of Diminishing Marginal Returns. This law states that with an expenditure of X amount of effort, you will capture Y amount of the market. It further states that for each unit of capture, you will have to expend increasingly larger amount of effort. In sales, this means that low-hanging-fruit sales can be picked up easily, but after that, each sale will become increasingly more difficult and time consuming than the previous sale because the prospects are more skeptical, have more technical issues, are more remote or further away, have more internal issues and players to deal with, etc. This means that one sale may take an hour of the salesman's time, the next two, the next four, and so on. This is not a linear progression. The effort scale to produce sales is exponential in the cost to the salesperson. This is a law, meaning it is universal and every human is subject to its parameters, and no matter how much one wants to wish it away because it does not fit well with one's perspective, opinion, or business traditions, it will be in operation.

Salespeople are extremely observant and they understand the increasing difficulty of getting the next sale as the easy sales are exhausted. They live the Law of Diminishing Marginal Returns. They will make choices as to how much of their lives they are willing to sacrifice beyond the expected 40 hours per week to obtain more sales. And this decision will vary from quota period to quota period. A salesperson may need to pay hospital bills or want a big screen TV, boat, or other motivations and thus be willing to expend more resources and work longer, taking time away from family and life outside work.

This is a temporary choice and not a lifestyle decision.

The second biggest abuse of the quota system, other than using quota as a motivational tool, is quota creep. Managers expect that if you did X amount last year, then that should be the minimum you do next year before getting into incentive money. This type of expectation is in contradiction of the Law of Diminishing Marginal Returns. It forces salespeople to make a decision of lifestyle, your life becomes the family or it becomes the company. Quota creep becomes a threat in the hardwiring of the reactor's mechanisms to the salesman's lifestyle and sets up the salesman for failure by pushing him further and further from his chosen priorities and lifestyle until it forces him to leave due to burn out. If quota increases are not tied to some business/economic metric then you are guilty of quota creep and are punishing sales excellence. This arbitrary increase will make your salespeople become angry with you, the sales manager and the company, because their Paradaptive Intelligence Network will be forcing corrective signal into their brain telling them you are putting obstacles in their path. This is why a sales manager is fought by the sales staff every time he announces new quotas. The sales staff literally can't help themselves — you're fighting Mother Nature — their hardwiring, and operating against the parameters of the universal Paradaptive Intelligence Network. A price or content change in your product is the only time a quota change is acceptable. The effort to obtain sales remains constant due to the Law of Diminishing

Marginal Returns and unless there is some significant change in some variable that makes it easier to sell your company's products or services, there is no basis in logic or reasoning to believe that if a salesman did X amount in sales this year, next year he should do X + 1, outside any learning curve.

The best model for incentive development has been available in marketing and sales management textbooks for decades. It is stated as:

Can a salesperson:

(Make any changes to produce results towards the incentive?) +

(Make enough changes to reach the incentive?) +

(Do they desire the rewards?)

HEY! Hold on just a minute here!

Isn't that exactly the same thing that happens to prospects in the Vetting phase!? Isn't this learning anticipation → confidence → excitement just stated differently?

Some bright person stumbled upon a portion of the universal Paradaptive Intelligence emotional tonal algorithm for Innovation but didn't have the background and scientific foundation to understand what was discovered.

This sales incentive model is instructive in other ways. First and foremost, it recognizes that salespeople choose whether or not to participate in an incentive program and to what degree. And since it is established that a choice or decision is being made, we can directly apply what we know about the process in the Vetting phase to sort this out. First, we know that learning anticipation is about exploring new and different approaches to pain point issues (quotas, incentive participation, etc.). So the salesperson will examine what he can do differently that may yield higher sales. Then he will determine before putting in any effort if it will be enough to bring about a reward/incentive (joy) in the confidence stage. No one wants to waste time and effort if there is no payoff. And lastly, he will ask himself if what is actually being offered in the cost/benefit analysis of the excitement stage is worth the effort. There are two components in the excitement stage, direct and indirect. The direct element is the amount of incentive being offered. The salesperson will evaluate if the remuneration is commiserate for his expected efforts. If it's not, he'll pass on participating in the incentive plan. The indirect element is any unintentional consequences of participating in the incentive plan. This means quota creep and its punishment of sales excellence. If quota creep is practiced by his company and its punishment of their sales excellence is severe enough, he'll pass on participating, and thus nullify any motivation you expected the incentive would bring. Remember, the excitement emotion is about weighing benefits against resource costs. And despite any protestation you as a sales manager might be forming in your mind at this moment, you have absolutely no control over the salesperson in the excitement stage. The evaluation will be performed by each salesperson value system, not yours. So, while it's convenient for you to forget the threat that quota creep creates in your sales staff, it is biologically impossible for them to ignore.

There is also another aspect about this model of incentive construction that is also highly instructive. It demonstrates why mentoring is the only style of management that will achieve permanent results with sales staff. Just like a salesperson with a prospect, the sales manager can insert himself into this internal salesperson process and perform a little "consultive selling" to influence the salesperson's thoughts of incentive pursuit. With a mentoring approach, the sales manager can work with individual sales staff in the learning anticipation stage to show them new ways and approaches to create new sales beyond what they are already doing. In the confidence stage, you, the sales manager, can encourage your salespeople by sharing your confidence in them that they will be successful with the new approaches, thus giving and increasing their confidence that making changes will lead to incentive payoff. Mentoring, working one-on-one with individual salespeople, works upon the cooperation bias and allows the sales manager to plug directly into the salesperson's psyche without interference or reservation. The same information shared in a group setting becomes a work directive and is handled differently by the Paradaptive Intelligence Network, thus lacking the same efficacy. It is impossible to effectively mentor someone while threatening them; the reactor will just shut it down due to threat presence and initiate a desire to distance themselves from the sales manager.

There is an embarrassingly large portion of sale managers that ignore these laws of nature, science, and the universal mechanism of man's psyche and insist that quotas are the only way they can control a sales force. While you can threaten a sales force into temporary performance gains, you will induce unnecessary and unwanted turnover that will hurt your firm in the long run. The best performing sales forces have the highest ratings in surveys of customer loyalty. Loyalty occurs only when there is a personal, emotional attachment to someone in your firm, primarily your salespeople. By inducing turnover in your sales force with quotas, you will weaken these bonds of loyalty and make your clients vulnerable to competitive predation. Often, a firm takes the position that the clients are the property of the firm and not the salesperson. While it may be technically correct that there exists a client-company relationship, it is *incredibly misguided* to think in these terms. One relationship of several possible relationships is owned by the salesperson as we learned in Chapter 9 studying the Mirror Neuron System and Chapter 16 studying the Relationship emotional tonal algorithm. As noted in Chapter 9, prospects must figure out and synch with a salesperson via the Mirror Neuron System. Until this happens, the salesperson's effectiveness will be reduced because the prospect or client will have higher confusion and uncertainty as to what the salesperson is trying to convey, which begets distrust. By constantly changing sales staff due to turnover, you create distrust among your clients, which will cost your firm sales because your clients will never move beyond the acceptance emotional stage in the Relationship emotional tonal algorithm.

The best way to create an incentive is to remove the threat. Dump the quota. You will still have sales information which will allow you to track sales staff performance. You'll still be free to remove nonperforming sales staff. Do you still have to threaten the rest of your sales staff? There are many ways a sales manager can predict sales, including the methodology used to develop the quotas in the first place. What about the large number of sales staff that are threat/quota driven? You can control their performance with positive reinforcement. Joy is far more effective than any results you could achieve with negative, fear based, methods, and it will remove the fear induced turnover and other complications. In humans, nature uses positive reinforcement, joy, to achieve adaptation and results. Why aren't you?

A properly constructed incentive to accomplish these aims is one that pays little for the initial, low-hanging-fruit sales but ramps up steeply for each progressive sale. The incentive system should approximate the exponential effort to bring in the next sale. Some sales firms make the mistake of creating straight-line sales incentive systems that reward all sales equally. This is not in compliance with the Law of Diminishing Marginal Returns, which will force salespeople to find equilibrium between effort and incentive. A progressive incentive drives people to maximize sales with the resources they have available, rather than seeking equilibrium in fairness in pay for their efforts. A hybrid of this system is a tiered system of progression. This is usually driven by the ability of the sales firm's internal accounting systems to track pay scales for many individuals. While better than straight line pay scales, tiered systems suffer an interesting phenomenon. The bad news is the tiered system suffers the violations of the Law of Diminishing Marginal Returns, but to a lesser degree. Clumping of salespeople tends to be seen on these scales at the bottom end of the tiers because salespeople intuitively determine that going after that next sale being paid at the same scale as the last one on the tier they're occupying is not worth the additional effort, especially as they approach the limits of their skills and resources. The good news is that it gets closer to a salesperson maximizing his efforts before the equity/fairness issue kicks in.

COMPETITION VERSUS CHALLENGE

One of the age-old tools of sales management has been the sales contest as a way of spurring sales. This can be good or bad, depending upon how it's done; most of the time, it's done badly. A typical contest starts with a singular prize to be competed for amongst all or groups of salespeople. This sets the sales manager up for failure. Initially, it may boost sales as everyone gives it their best shot. But soon, a leader emerges and others will abandon the competition as they figure out they're not in the running to win. Those that will continue do so because they believe they can unseat the leader and win. Except for the eventual winner, what was learned here? Those that competed but lost will feel pain due to failure. The term "agony of defeat" just isn't a popular catch phrase; it recognizes that Paradaptive Intelligence Network will create psychic pain because losing evokes a corrective signal of anger, loss, or disgust, as discussed earlier in this section. All that competed and lost will feel the slight of having made an extra effort without receiving any reward for their efforts. Next time, they won't be so eager to join in the sales reindeer games. This is why cooperation, not competition, is the mode of operation for human beings. Otherwise, we would learn negative lessons that teach us not to get involved with anything until paralysis sets in. Again, the greater question is why do you want to introduce more negatives into the workplace? Sales has enough negatives in dealing with customers and prospects. Of what benefit to the entire sales force does the introduction of the pain and fear of losing bring? All that is accomplished with this sort of contest is that your sales staff learns to avoid them and not participate. Again, there is a better way to use the competitive spirit of the human reactor.

But first, why do humans compete? When does competition occur? Understanding the answers to these questions and the mechanisms of the Paradaptive Intelligence Network will help you use this information to wring extra performance from your sales staff.

In Chapter 2 we discussed the various gatekeepers of the Paradaptive Intelligence Network. One of them was the ego. The ego's job is to find opportunities for learning by identifying and pursuing growth opportunities that are close to and potentially in reach of our skill level. The key words there are "potentially in reach." Competition only occurs when there is someone, a competitor, you perceive to be within potential reach of your skill set. So setting a long time salesperson with a long list of established clients against a new hire whose only opportunity is with cold calling, or a client list that they barely know isn't a fair fight, and the new hire knows it. Do you think that he would jump into a competition wholeheartedly knowing that he was at such a disadvantage? It is hoped that you are hiring smarter salespeople than that. If you think back to any rival that you had at any point in time, whether in sports, in business, or for the opposite sex, you viewed that rival the way you did because you perceived him or her to be near or equal to your own level of skill or in whatever qualities upon which you were competing. So the only time that you will get full participation in a sales contest is when all your salespeople perceive that they all possess equal abilities, and that's never going to happen.

In nature, there are always going to be scarce resources, so you are geared for competition. But this is not blind competition. Competition derives from the reactor, whose mission is to protect the body. Subconsciously, the reactor accesses the skills, talent, beauty, etc. of a potential rival. If the advantage is too great to the rival, your ego will agitate you to move away and not waste energy and risk potential harm in a competition you can't win. Again, people may try and goad, guilt, or shame you into a competition by attempting to manipulate you with false emotion feedback so that you override what your subconscious is directing and enter into competition. Knowing this, one option is to handicap your contests so that everyone from beginner to veteran feels they have the potential to win. But this is fraught with pitfalls. Handicapping is arbitrary, and if done incorrectly, salespeople might feel you rigged the contest in favor of someone, triggering anger as a corrective signal because you put an obstacle to winning in their path with an unfair, uncooperative handicap.

The other option is not to pit sales staff against one another, but to pit them against themselves. Who is more closely matched to their talent level than themselves? So a well-constructed competition has your sales staff competing against themselves, which allows them to still work cooperatively with each other without penalty. But if there is a quota still in the picture, they can harm themselves with quota creep and all its attendant problems. A single prize guaranteeing losers and negative lessons can also be problematic. The best way to use the competitive element in our subconscious is to challenge it, not force competition. A competition has the potential for harm. A challenge is a growth opportunity with the absence of harm from failure coupled with joy potential, which will agitate the salesperson to repeat the experience.

The bad news to this approach is that if everyone can be a winner, then you'd better be able to afford all the prizes and spiffs. But, most sales managers would gladly lose incentive dollars for increased sales volume. Additionally, challenges of this type allow a sales manager the ability to measure his sales staff's skills for strengths and weaknesses for mentoring sessions in the future.

FOUR TYPES OF SALESPEOPLE

Sales is a talent driven profession, with many skills needed to make a salesperson successful. But, as noted previously, there are two main elements that drive this profession. These elements are relationship building and problem solving which also are high indicators of the other subsets of skills needed for a successful salesperson. Both of these are controlled by the Paradaptive Intelligence Network. Figure 19.2 is a new version of this classic graph updated to include Paradaptive Intelligence and problem solving, covering both emotional and analytic abilities. The graph has been broken into four quadrants based on skill level of the x and y axis values of Paradaptive Intelligence and problem solving. The quadrants have been labeled to identify those types of salespeople that occupy them, Low Performers, Nurturers, Problem Solvers and Top Performers.

Top Performers

This category, by virtue of arbitrary delineation, represents the top 25% of your sales force. This is somewhat misleading because, depending on your selection process, you may not have obtained the top 25% of the candidate pool. It only represents the top 25% of what you have on hand. This group tends to be joy driven, looking to maximize earnings. Of all the groups, this group also has the most equal ratio of both relationship/six basic needs driven approach and analytical problem-solving skills, which they apply in equal measure to prospects. Quotas are of no importance to this group unless they are unjustifiably high, representing an obstacle to obtaining incentive money. Because of the equal measure of relationship/six basic needs driven approach and problem solving, they feel they have two fronts or approaches to every sales problem and will find a way to succeed.

Top performers are the most mobile of the four types and the least likely to put up with quota creep. As top performers, they know that other sales companies will easily recruit them if they make themselves available on the employment market. This is another reason to drop quotas because of their penchant to drive off your most valuable performers, leaving lesser performers to populate your sales force.

Figure 19.2

Engagement/Skill Distribution Quadrants

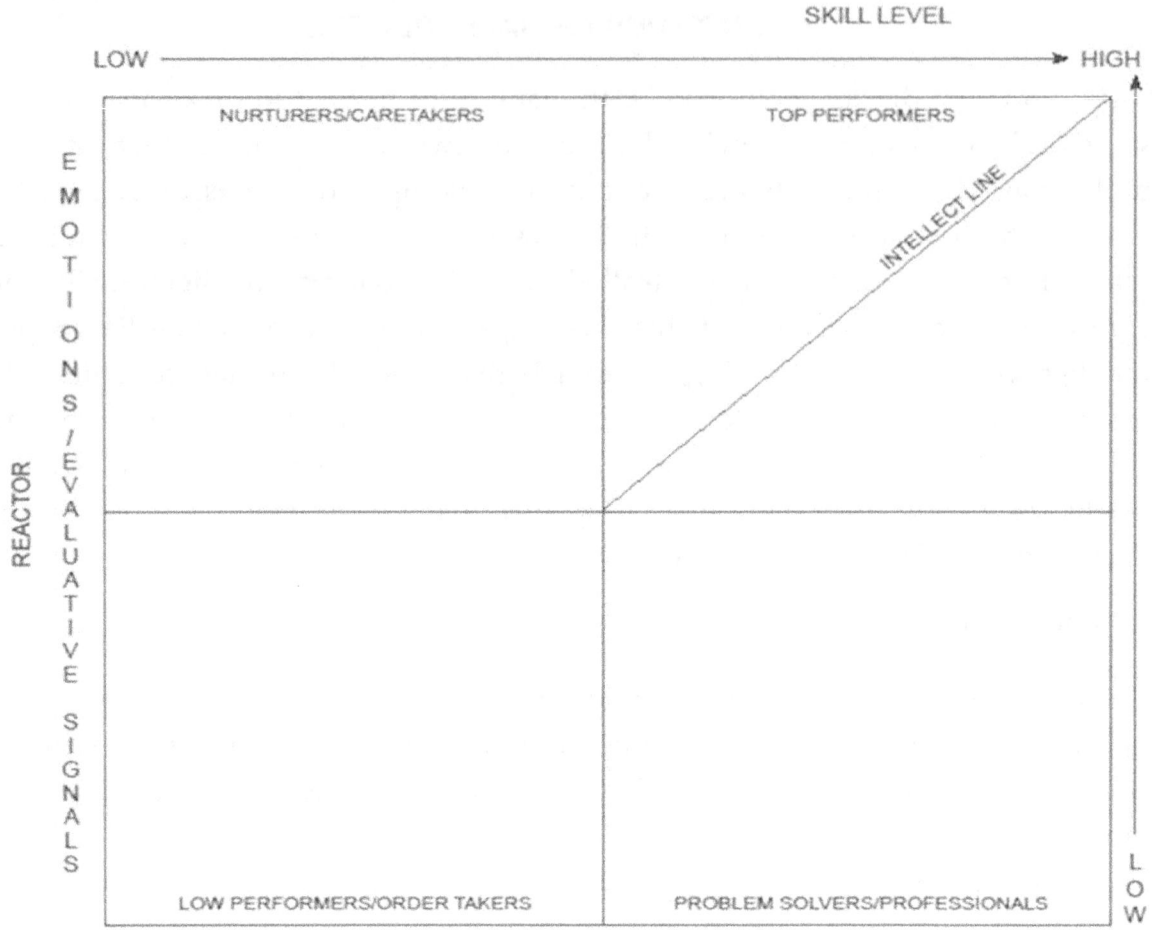

Because top performers use equal measures of relationship/six basic needs driven approach and analytic problem solving to solve sales problems presented by prospects, the limit of their performance will be their intellect. Because they are joy driven, their internal Paradaptive Intelligence Network will agitate them to maximize the amount of money their skill set will obtain. It is a likely presumption that a salesperson with a higher I.Q will perform better than those with a lower I.Q. because both are equally internally driven and possess equal skills, therefore, they are limited by their mental agility in applying their skills. This concept is represented by the Intellect Line that top performers will fall upon. (Figure 19.2)

Top Performers generally need no mentoring from sales management because of their well balanced approach of analytical problem solving and their understanding of the emotional needs of their clients. Their balanced approach of Relationship and Innovation algorithm use creates confidence, which makes them fully engaged in their joy-inducing job. This doesn't mean that their sales process could not be improved by the information of this book, though. By exposing them to the concepts of this book, you can allow them to focus more precisely on what they have been doing instinctually.

Nurturers

This quadrant of the graph represents salespeople who prefer to use and lead with their ability to emotionally connect with the clients and prospects using the Relationship algorithm. This gives them large connections and esteem needs satisfaction. This group prefers to nurture its clients by providing emotional support while prospects make their decisions. This group is typified by their desire not to inject themselves into the prospect's decision-making process by telling the prospect what to do, as it might endanger the relationship. They incorrectly believe that Relationship emotional tonal algorithm is more important than the Innovation emotional tonal algorithm. They prefer to give options as opposed to potential solutions rather than recommendations and adaptation plans. This group is more likely to use a features and benefits approach because of its indirect approach to sales, dovetailing with the salesperson's desire to nurture the relationship rather than manage the decision process. Salespeople in this group learned early in their sales careers that friendship, one of the 3 F's, can be instrumental in securing sales. This set up a confirmatory bias that, due to a few early successes using this methodology, set all sales as dependent upon this element of the sales process, solidifying in the salesperson's mind that their skills in relationship building are paramount for all sales.

They are also called nurturers because they derive satisfaction from nurturing a prospect while he or she makes difficult decisions, such as buying their product. Empathizing and sympathizing provide powerful stimuli to these individuals seeking to use their job to fulfill the need for connection. While this approach gives them powerful satisfaction of the need for connection, it limits the salesperson's need for esteem because this indirect approach is the least likely to generate sales. This all but blocks nurturers from achieving the remaining universal needs, creativity and meaning, because creativity comes in sales from problem solving and meaning comes from helping and improving the lot of others, which comes from selling products that nullify pain points.

This type of approach is biased towards women due to its emphasis on cooperation, but is not limited to women. Since studies show that 50% of the national sales force is comprised of females, you're more likely to find a concentration of females in this quadrant. Nurturing is especially effective in repetitive sales to the same customers or commodity sales where it can come down to friendship of the 3 F's.

From a mentoring standpoint for the sales manager, this quadrant is problematic. Problem solving is an inherited, latent ability that is not easily taught. A sales manager may challenge a salesperson to use more of their latent ability in problem solving ability, their Innovation algorithm, but cannot teach or mentor what the subject is not mentally receptive to or equipped with.

The problem-solving approach's downfall has always rested upon a salesperson's ability to identify the problem, which is not first nature to nurturers. But, Paradaptive Intelligence Selling can give these types of salespeople a framework with which to approach problem solving to the best of their organic skill set by identifying pain points focusing on nullifying them.

Because nurturers have a limited skill set to obtain sales with, they will see quotas as a threat. Because the job contains elements that they do not like, such as problem solving and other direct approaches, something that they know they are not well suited for, their Paradaptive Intelligence Network will constantly be giving them corrective signals such as fear. This feedback will agitate them vaguely to move away and not fully engage in their job.

Problem Solvers

This quadrant of the graph represents salespeople who lead with logic and adaptability. Problem solvers focus on the technical issues of the prospect. They lead with the Innovation algorithm, albeit a limited understanding. They can quickly identify problems and develop solutions. They are mystified by prospects that seemingly fail to grasp the straightforward cause and effect approach in which they present problems and solutions. They have no way of breaching the gap between what they see as something so obvious that it needs little explanation and the inexplicable inability of a prospect to see it, too. The emotions customers present are an impenetrable barrier which they can't negotiate with, dodge, or understand. This makes prospects unpredictable, messy, disorderly, and creates great amounts of frustration in these salespeople. They lack the understanding that the prospects are most likely being driven by fear themselves and that their thought processes and reasoning are being compromised' so they can't think rationally like the salesperson, or see what he sees so clearly.

This type of salesperson relies upon systems, procedures, organization, and metrics to perform his job. Because clients and prospects are unpredictable, problem solvers rely on metrics to produce sales, with an acceptable number of misfires and lost sales as just part of the equation. As they gain experience, they shift from a features and benefits style of methodology to a quasi-pain nullification method as they find what works and what doesn't, incorporating these changes into their processes.

In terms of universal needs, the problem solver scores a little higher than nurturer. The problem solver connects to people through their problems, which is a limited communication channel. He or she will find connection with a limited number of prospects and clients, but not to the extent of a nurturer. He has a greater esteem fulfillment because his expertise is more directly involved in solving problems, and his creativity need is fulfilled with creative solutions to problems. But because he is process and procedure driven, it is unlikely that they obtain any sense of meaning from his job. He will have trouble fulfilling his six universal needs which can only occur through interaction with other people. A problem solver will look to six universal needs fulfillment through the constant relationships of his fellow workers and company mates rather than through relationships with their customers. This quadrant tends to see concentrations of men because of their hardwired bias to problem solving.

This quadrant has also been called the professionals. This goes to the perception of someone who studiously performs their job without emotional entanglements. This is a very apt description of the quadrant because this type of salesperson seeks to remove all emotion from his or her work environment, including displaying their own and dealing with it in others, because they don't understand it. This also goes to myths of the poker face discussed in Chapter 9. However, due to the new understanding of the Paradaptive Intelligence Network and the Mirror Neuron System, this salesperson is awash in emotions and continually wrestles for control of their own internal workings. Misguidedly, he seeks to eliminate what cannot be removed, ignores what cannot be silenced. The only way that he can manage this clash of natural imperatives and the chaos it brings to his world is to not fully engage in his job. Since he has a limited set of skills and a dependence on process and procedure, quotas are problematic because the only variable he can manage is the total number of calls he can make. The percentage of conversion to sales is a fixed base in his process. The only way to increase sales is to increase the volume of the number of calls, which means more time invested with work, leading eventually to a clash between values in work and personal life.

Because problem solvers are one-dimensional in their approach to work, they feel vulnerable and unprepared for their work. Because they are dealing with people's emotions, which they find distasteful and disquieting, they do not fully engage in their work. Despite being labeled as professionals, this quadrant is populated by salespeople that are every bit as unengaged in their jobs as nurturers. But because they receive connection needs from a few clients, obtain esteem by solving problems and enjoy some creativity in the solutions they come up with, they get more out of their jobs than nurturers and tend to be a little more durable to the constant threats in most sales environments that lead to "burn out."

For sales managers, the quadrant represents a bountiful opportunity for mentoring and performance improvement. This book systematically turns emotions into procedures and processes that can be easily understood and adopted by problem solvers. The chaotic world of emotions that causes problem solvers to limit engagement can now be made orderly and predictable. The process and procedures explained herein lay bare the inner workings of the human emotional system in a logical fashion. Logic and emotions are no longer mutually exclusive or an oxymoron when used together. While the problem solver may never achieve the same comfort level in dealing with emotions that a nurturer has, understanding the process and procedures is more than a suitable substitute and can get them extremely close to the nurturer in terms of empathy and Paradaptive Intelligence.

Low Performers

This quadrant of the graph is populated by salespeople that either lack talent or motivation, or both. This quadrant also contains salespeople that are in "burnout," having succumbed to continual bombardment of corrective signals generated by company policies and procedures that have created obstacles and threats to their desired outcome to sell. Or, they fear to a high degree their inability to perform their job due to their skill set, or their ability to innovate new job behaviors due to prior experiences. They don't like their jobs and are actively disengaged. If an order is called in or placed in front to him, he will take the order, hence the nickname of "order takers" because they will not expend the energy to actively pursue sales.

Occupants of this quadrant have also been called "searchers." This term was coined by Chuck Mache to signify that these people are searching for another job, in Chuck's words "…preferably in any career but sales." This is not wholly accurate because poor management practices and lack of understanding of how the human emotion system is structured leads to the "burnout" of otherwise good salespeople who have performed well in the past. But it is important to note that once burnout sets in, it is difficult to reverse because the "burned out" salesperson's expectations have been realigned negatively towards the company, and to salvage these salespeople, the company would have to reform the policies and practices that were perceived as obstacles and threats in the first place, plus mentor the salesperson to reshape his expectations.

The power of this phenomenon cannot be underestimated. The Paradaptive Intelligence Network has direct control of the human endocrine system. This is the system that internally controls and signals the effects of emotions through chemical messengers, called hormones, throughout the body. So once unchecked threats and obstacles created by company actions and policies accumulate causing a salesperson to reach the burnout point, you're not only fighting an attitudinal response, you're now battling a biological, hormonal response. Every company must decide what it considers acceptable losses to their sales force to obtain company goals, but the best companies attenuate their policies and procedures aspect to create the least threatening and thus lessen interference to the salespersons' mission for minimal losses.

This is the exit quadrant. It is from this quadrant that sales managers cull salespeople of their choice. World class sales forces have high degrees of customer loyalty. Loyalty can only be attached to people, not to inanimate objects. Inanimate objects can only produce satisfaction via the Innovation algorithm. Brand loyalty is a misnomer. So when a formerly well performing salesperson leaves your firm, he walks out the door with a large portion of your customers' loyalty, leaving you only with product performance to anchor that customer as one of your clients. This creates jeopardy for your firm to competitive predation. As this book has gone to great lengths to explain, a properly constructed sales division removes all threats, creates opportunity for joy motivation, has very little turnover, creates optimal sales and has significant customer loyalty which creates strong, steady cash flows and the opportunity to become a world-class sales force.

WORLD-CLASS SALES FORCES

In order to understand what a world class sales force looks like, one must understand how a typical sales force appears. A 2011 survey reported in the Gallup Management Journal of 170 sales forces covering over 250,000 sales people reported the typical sales force engagement as 26% Engaged, 55 % Not Engaged, and 19% Actively Disengaged. See Figure 19.3. That same survey found that world class sales force was proportioned as 36% Engagement, 55% Not Engaged, and 9% Actively Disengaged (See Figure 19.4) This mean that a shift of only 9% of the sales forces into

Figure 19.3

Engagement/Skill Distribution of a Typical Sales Force

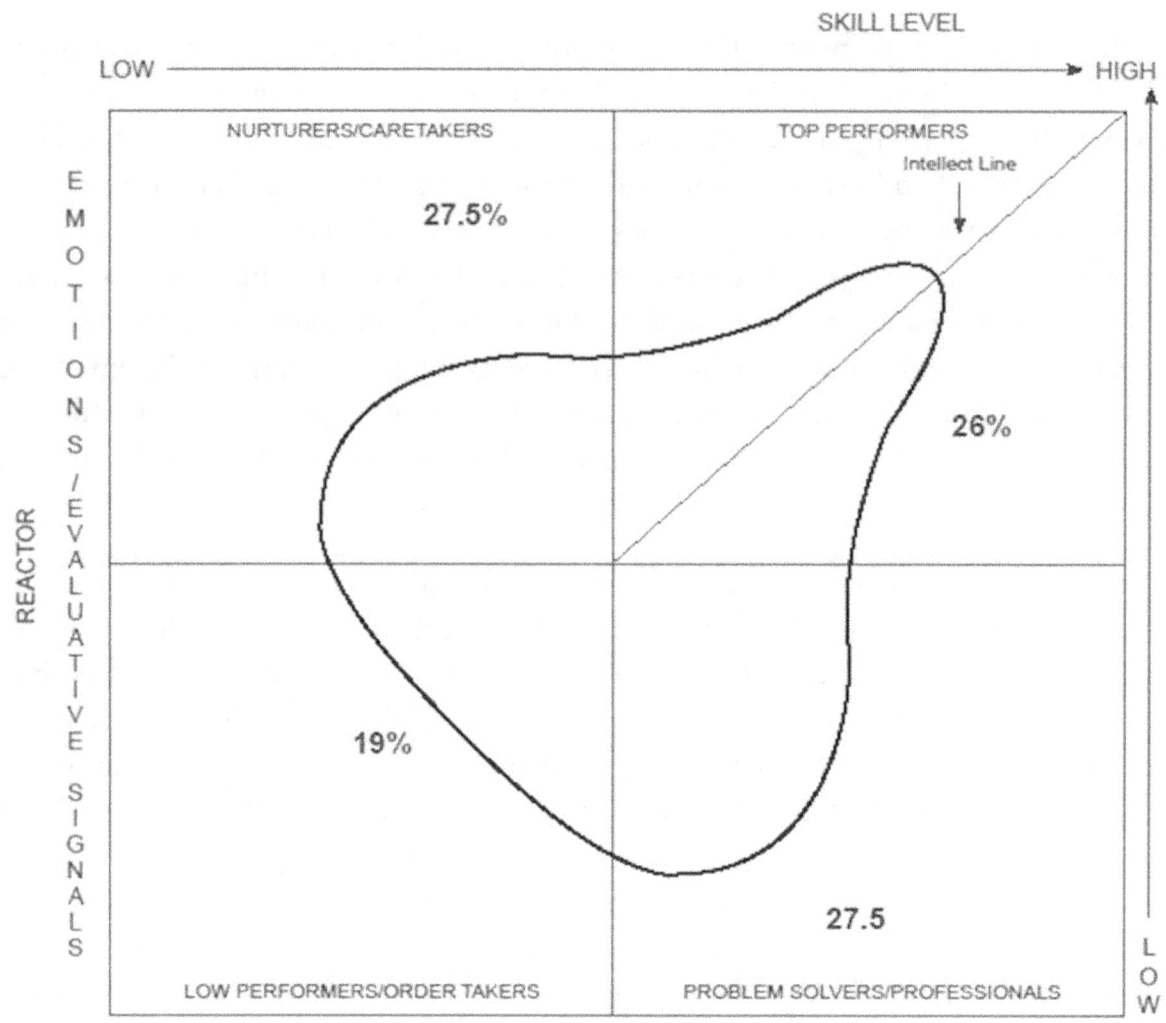

the Top Performers range will result in a world class sales force. This shift of 9% into the top performer category with a corresponding reduction in the low performers by 9% is certainly a reasonable goal and is obtainable by any sales manager willing to address structural defects in his or her operations and use the principals laid forth in this book.

The Engagement aspect of the Gallup poll is especially useful. The distribution of sales staff in terms of engagement is an identical mirror image of a typical firm's mix of Top Performers, Nurturers, Problems Solvers, and Low Performers. Engagement

— their emotional state — is a key factor in understanding and manipulating the performance of any sales force. It is the primary difference between a world class sale forces and yours. We can now accurately surmise that engagement of Gallup's survey was a measurement of the agitation express contained in each emotion. Of particular interest are the findings specifically portraying the negative/move away/avoid expression of a corrective signal most likely caused by a threat in the work environment.

In Chapter 10 - Fear and Innovation Adoption, we learned that the adoption of innovation is driven by prospects' fears about their skills sets relative to the innovations. The more diminished their skill sets are relative to marketplace innovations, the more fearful they are of pursuing innovations and new tools. The power of the Paradaptive Intelligence model applies to salespeople, too. Salespeople who do not innovate or are fearful of innovating new behaviors or obtaining tools in their sales repertoire are just like prospects; they are fearful, to varying degrees, of their skill set deficiencies to execute new strategies or tactics in sales. The Problem Solvers, also known as the "Professionals" are most likely to be centered on the corrective signal of growing pains. Clients' emotions are messy and a fact of life, a displeasure that must be dealt with as part of the sales process. They are fearful because their skill set in dealing with emotions is deficient. Nurturers are most likely to be centered on the corrective signal anxiety about innovating to become a better salesperson because they lack even more skills at persuasion than the Problem Solvers, and hope that by concentrating and developing relationships that will influence them to consummate a sale. Both of these are passive levels of fear towards innovating behaviors for sales improvements. Many of those in the Low Performers segment fears are to the left of the Line of Passivity in the anxiety or higher emotion state. They demonstrate the active aggressive/passive emotion anxiety due to their lack of skill in both persuasion and dealing with client's emotions. The Low Performers segment also contains personnel who are suffering "burnout," which is driven by a completely different process. There is a presumption that most of the Low Performers segment is composed of the "burnout" type. Most firms have reasonable hiring selection processes that identify sales traits before offering a position to an individual, so the possibilities of hiring a person who lacks either emotional connection or problem solving skills of sales is rare, but it does happen.

The Gallup survey measured three things: engagement, talent recruitment, and customer loyalty. The problem with the survey was that, at the time, the terms of measurement were understood but the causational relationship that produced the outcomes were not. This is another case of "black box" statistical relationship testing. But, now with our newfound understanding of the Paradaptive Intelligence

Network and its internal workings within the sales arena, this survey now comes into much sharper contrast and provides more meaningful information for the sales manager.

Figure 19.4

Engagement/Skill Distribution of World Class Sales Force

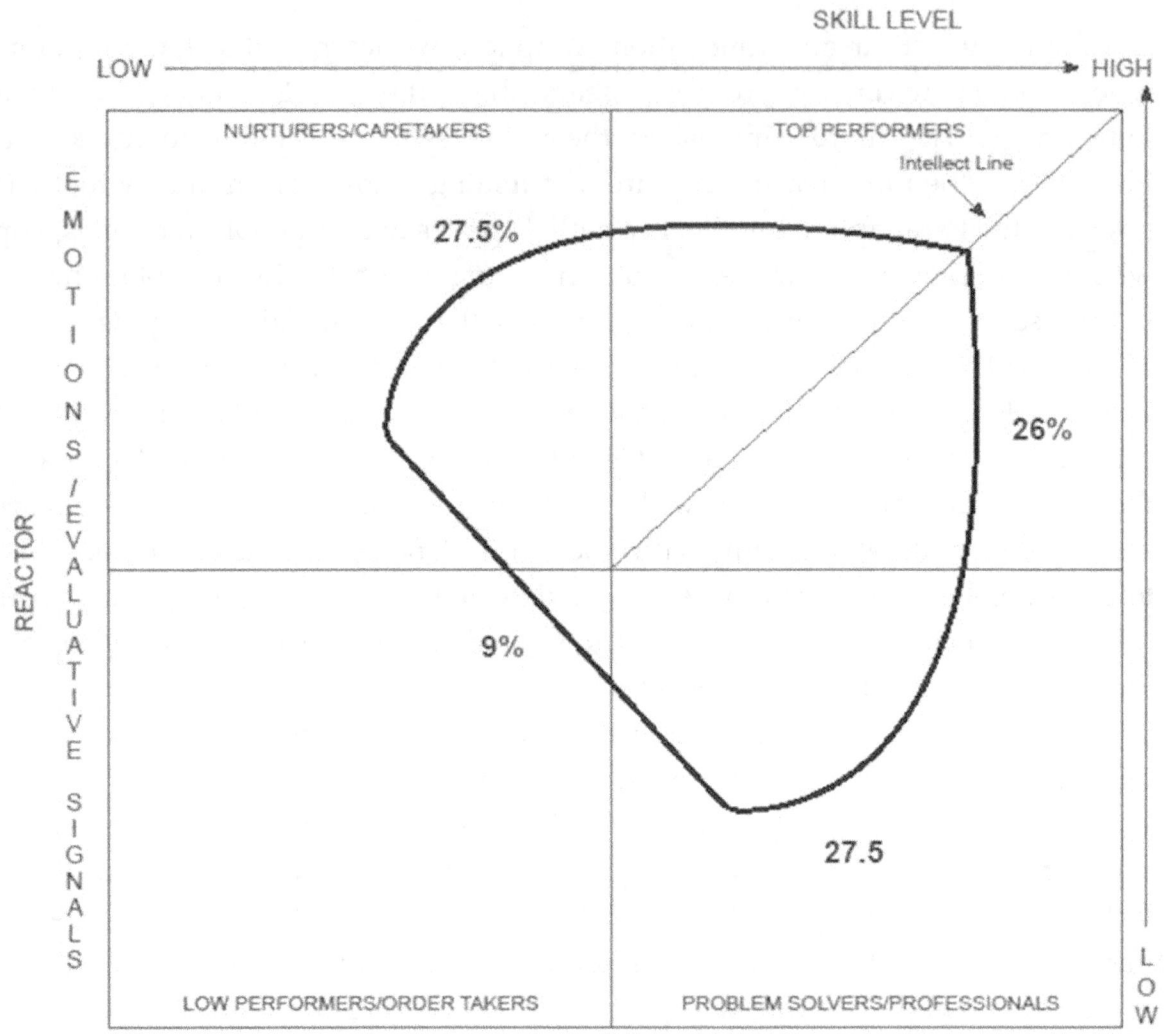

PROBLEM SOLVING/CORRECTIVE ACTIONS

ADAPTOR

The engagement/non-engagement issue of the Gallop survey comes into brilliant focus when you look at it in terms of a salesperson's HAC to be a good salesperson. Remember, the Innovation algorithm not only seeks, acquires, or builds tools but also controls behavioral innovation as well, and most certainly controls the HAC to change sales performance. Twenty-six percent of a typical sales force, the Top

Performers, are working in the present, on the growth signal/joy side of the Innovation algorithm. This allows them to focus on the task accomplishment of compiling the greatest amount of sales possible; they are motivated to maximize sales. They view quotas as an internal challenge, and thus a growth opportunity; this is play to them – it's fun. This is why studies consistently show that 25% of salespeople in any given firm are responsible for the vast majority of sales. Fifty-five percent of the sales force's emotional states towards behavioral innovation, the combined total of both Nurturers and Problem Solvers, are working in the corrective signal side in either growing pains or trepidations. Nurturers and Problem Solvers are to the right of the Line of Passivity, thus the passive non-engagement displayed in their jobs. Seekers, the nineteen percent that are actively disengaged, are operating to the left of the Line of Passivity in the anxiety emotion range, which is active aggressive/ passive. Low Performers, Nurturers, and Problems Solvers are motivated to nullify the threat/pain of a quota. Nurturers and Problem Solvers possess enough skill to make their pain go away by meeting quota and seek only to satisfy this pain nullification goal. They are not motivated to maximize sales, rather they are motivated by pain nullification.

As you recall, the defining element of the Line of Passivity was whether emotions driven by corrective signals were passive or active. So, what the Gallop poll was actually measuring was growth and corrective signals to become better salespeople by measuring passivity in non-engagement and active reactor responses in actively disengaged. Recalling what was described in Chapter 10 Fear and Innovation Adoption, the three levels of fear of why people won't adapt have to do with their skills set in managing, operating, and executing innovations. This perfectly describes Low Performers, Nurturers, and Problem Solvers who are being controlled by fear of their lack of skills. Using the Paradaptive Intelligence model, we can now precisely describe the findings of the Gallop poll findings and understand its underlying cause and effect relationship.

And just as important, as a manager, the path is now clear as to how to mentor the Nurturers, Problem Solvers, and Low Performers using the same exact formulas discussed earlier for prospects. It should now be abundantly clear why sales managers need to minimize the threat environment of their relationships with their sales staff. It would be impossible to mentor sales staff who are in the passive fear states of growing pains and trepidation if you represent an additional threat or are the source of the threat in the first place. Their reactors will be pushing them away from you and downgrading whatever you are trying to communicate to them via reactor interference of logic, reasoning, and the other functions of the adaptor. If you represent a threat to them, their minds will only work to placate you for no other reason than to make the pain go away, and you will not affect real change in your sales force. You will only create short-term behavior the mind fabricates to eliminate pain. When the pain subsides, the behavior is abandoned. Thus, we can explain our new understanding of the cause and effect mechanism of internal salesperson drive for improvement.

While all sales force quadrant residents will benefit from Paradaptive Intelligence sales training, the quadrants of Problem Solvers, Nurturers, and Low Performers will experience the greatest benefits. Top Performers, working on the growth signal side of the Innovation algorithm, need nothing more from managers beyond that of removal of obstacles to sales and some Paradaptive Intelligence refinements to their techniques for behavioral improvement. This can include removal of unnecessary, unneeded, or counterproductive internal policies, procedures, or processes to consummate a sale. Problem Solvers need you to not only teach and demonstrate Paradaptive Intelligence sales techniques to them, but also assure them and follow through that you will guide them through the implementation process in the field to make it easy for them. The Paradaptive Intelligence sales methodology already appeals to them since it is a process they can understand. They just need help with the implementation. Nurturers at the trepidation emotional state will have to be convinced by you that the disruption to their sales efforts to restructure their sale approach will be worth the interruption and that you will assist them at each step to minimize the period of disturbance to get them to the next emotional state of growing pains. There, you will show them how to easily implement it in the field (growing pains). Low Performers will need to talk to peers who have gone through the same process to be assured they have the capabilities to make the metamorphosis. Only peers can convince them they can do it. Your job as a sales manager is to have people on staff, success stories of salespeople who were Low Performers once, ready and willing to speak to these types of salespeople to convince them they can do it. And lastly, as a sales manager, you need to be able to jettison those salespeople who are in the paranoia emotional state. They just aren't worth your time as a recovery project no matter how invested you may be in them as people you were responsible for hiring or developed friendships with in the course of working together over a period of time. Their poor performance is not a temporary illness. Attitudes, fear and anger states, are generally long-term changes in the Paradaptive Intelligence Network. You've made a mistake in handling them in some way, leading to the inevitable emotional change within their Paradaptive Intelligence Network. Learn from the mistake, cut them loose so that they can find another application for their skills elsewhere without the burden of reactor disruption to their adaptor due to obstacles, boundary violations, or threats.

One of the simple beauties of understanding and working within the Paradaptive Intelligence sales model is that it becomes a common language between sales management and staff. If a staff member is anxious about making changes in the course of their work, whether it's a new product, change in management direction, new job tasks, or a shuffling in priorities, both manager and staff can work collaboratively to find out which portion of the Innovation or Friendship algorithm is at issue. Using the Paradaptive Intelligence model to sort out sales staff performance is yet another example of the unifying power of this model and its application to all human behavior, and especially those of business.

There are sales managers who, through tradition, corporate culture, or ignorance, believe that it is the responsibility of the salesperson to police and manage his or her emotions, not the sales manager. These belief systems are not rooted in nor tethered to the facts and findings of science as presented in this book. Every action you take as a sales manager will generate an emotion in the sales staff. And that emotion will do one of two things: agitate that individual to move away from the firm or move closer. If the company's actions agitate to drive your sales staff away, their emotion systems will bombard them with corrective impulses to leave your firm and disrupt their ability to do their job over time by interfering with and overriding thought, logic, and reasoning until the reactor's demands are met. It doesn't work any other way. The salesperson may be able to override and work through these interferences, but at best that salesperson's work product and effort will be compromised or worse due to your induced threat or anger state. If you recall Frederick F. Reichheld's words from his book, *The Loyalty Effect*, that started Chapter 16, "Loyalty is dead, the experts proclaim, and the statistics seem to bear them out. On average, U.S. corporations now lose half their customers in five years, half their employees in four, and half their investors in less than one..." the mechanism for the turnover in all these instances becomes very clear. In particular, we can see the impact of management actions upon sales force turnover.

The process of "burnout" is similar to the one explored in Chapter 9 where we learned that repeated affectation of an emotion leads to the adoption of that emotion via the Mirror Neuron System. Constant corrective signals caused by management's actions to your sales force will result in the adoption of moving away from the firm because they are seen as threats, boundary violations, or obstacles. If your firm becomes the threat by creating obstacles and boundary violations, then certainly the sales management team will not be viewed as a work partner. Any team cohesion, company loyalty, sense of tribalism, breed apart, or esprit de corps that you are trying to build will be totally undermined by a threat, obstacle, or boundary violation laden environment. The mind is not built for both — it can either move towards the company or move away. It does not average the agitation expressions it receives from the reactor and it certainly is incapable of eradicating a corrective signal from its awareness in the environment once identified. All it takes is one negative emotion generated by you or your firm's actions, policies, or procedures to create a perceived threat, and it becomes a corrective signal pain point.

The Gallup survey measured engagement, which we can now see as a measure of the threat, obstacles or boundary violations in the salespersons environment. Loyalty is a long-term measure of engagement in the sales force. Low engagement means high turnover. This creates another useful lesson as to why not dealing with or correcting issues in the sales force's environment has long term consequences besides sales that do not build market share. Low salesperson engagement = sales force turnover = low customer loyalty = loss of sales to competition.

If you want your firm to enjoy the benefits of customer loyalty, then you had better devise programs within your sales department to retain and keep your sales force happy, threat and obstacle free, because customer loyalty is attached to them on a personal basis. Secondly, to accelerate the development of customer loyalty, you need to devote time and resources to programs that will facilitate the bonding between your salesperson and the company's clients. This is accomplished by educating your sales staff how relationships work via the principles laid forth in this book on how, when, and where to use this knowledge.

Talent recruitment can be brought into sharper focus now that the importance of Paradaptive Intelligence has been linked to success and a better picture of what to select for now appears. The discounting of experience and the recognition of the value of Paradaptive Intelligence coupled with problem solving skills can result in a superior, world-class sales force. Unfortunately, these skills and talents generally can't be gauged in a typical job interview, the traditional method of selection for sales staff. Fortunately, there are tests that can augment the sales manager's regular process. After all, as a manager, you have to be comfortable with a candidate's communication capabilities, personal demeanor, and presentation, as well as other desirable attributes that can only be determined in a classic employment interview. At the SPAN Consulting Group, we can assist you in finding and implementing appropriate testing procedures to help in your selection process.

And finally, implementing Paradaptive Intelligence sales methodology will vastly help in creating a world- class sales force. Another recent survey of sales forces determined that additional product training does not help the bottom 50% of a sales force. This makes perfect sense, again, if we apply our knowledge of the Paradaptive Intelligence Network sales methodology. First, the presumption is that a lack of product knowledge is the root of performance problems. This points to a features and benefits mentality towards sales. This line of thinking holds that more product knowledge equals more sales. While salespeople's adaptors drive them to learn all they can about their products to increase their adaptability, this internal need does not necessarily translate into sales. In fact, it is not the lack of product knowledge that is holding this portion of the sales force back, but the lack of understanding of how the client is geared to think and the inability to provide an adaptation plan for clients in ways that relate to their pain points. While even in a world-class sales force there may be up to 9% actively disengaged sales people, there remains the other 41% in the bottom half that would not benefit from additional product training but would benefit from Paradaptive Intelligence based sales training. Additionally, there are the approximate 24% between the top performers and bottom 50% that will benefit the most from Paradaptive Intelligences sales training. This is where you will draw from and shift the 9% into the top performers segment of your sales force to become a world-class sales force. Paradaptive Intelligence sales methodology, when implemented by your sales force, will raise the performance of all engaged and non-engaged sales staff by giving them a more organic approach to sales in line with the way your prospects think, couched in the terminology of the exact emotions they are feeling about nullifying their business' pain points. This methodology is vastly superior to any other because it uses the emotions of your prospects and customers as the basis of communications rather than fighting them. It focuses on nullifying their pain points when their thinking is muddled so that they will benefit rather than be taken advantage of when they are vulnerable.

PARADAPTIVE INTELLIGENCE, THE INNOVATION ADOPTION MODEL & SALESPEOPLE

Having examined normal and world-class sales forces under the old paradigm of four quadrants of salespeople types — high performers, problem solvers, nurturers, and low performers — it is now time to supplant that with a new paradigm. This is possible because we now understand cause and effect relationships of emotions and innovation acquisition. The measure of engaged/not engaged/actively disengaged used as an early measure in studies cited worked fine for four quadrant modules, but lacked precision because engagement/non-engagement is vague and ill-defined. A much greater level of precision is possible if one applies the measures and examples used in the innovation adoption curve discussion to dissect the prospects a salesperson faces.

At first blush, making the comparison of prospects to a sales force seems to be counterintuitive. In actuality, the two are perfectly congruent. Prospects resist innovation due to fears of skill set deficiencies based upon past experiences stored in memory as exemplars. Salespeople resist innovations to improving their sales processes and activities for the same reasons. It really is universal. And because it's universal, the same definitions and methodology used on prospects can now be applied to dissecting a salesforce into its constituent elements. Rather than explaining the elements of a sales force through observed behavior, like sales styles such as problem solving and nurturing, or performance level such as high and low performers, we can combine that with the emotional foundations that drive the behavior. This opens a new world of mentoring for sales managers to address the root causes of individual sales staff through directed training specific to an individual's fear level, rather than trying to correct the situation by giving them more product training and hoping for the best in a performance change in that individual.

But, before entering discussion of treating a sales force as the same as prospects in the marketplace, it is important to note some of the vagaries of statistics that underlie the Innovation Adoption Curve model. As noted earlier, the Technology Adaptation Lifecycle developed by Joe M. Bohlen, George M. Beal, and Everett M. Rogers is based on some fundamental statistical principles. First and foremost are the principles of sample size and randomness. A large enough sample size to be statistically representative must be extracted randomly from a normal distribution, bell curve population. Through statistical techniques, a mean, or mathematically derived middle where half of the population is below this point and half the population is above it, can be fixed. At this point, Bohlen, et al., chose to divide the population through standard deviations. This is a mathematical device that describes the dispersion, the concentration, of the variability being measured. The bigger the spread, the greater the differential between population members. One standard deviation covers the middle sixty-eight percent of the curve, thirty-four percent of the curve to the low side of the middle, and thirty-four percent to the higher side of the middle. Two standard deviations adds another thirteen point five percent to each end of the high and low side of the first standard deviation. The third standard deviation adds two point five to each end. In this way, Bohlen, et al., statistically divided the graphs of people in the marketplace and their attitudes towards innovation into Laggards/Nonadopters, Late Majority, Early Majority, Early Adaptors, and Innovators. While these divisions are useful, they are also arbitrary to the mathematical formulas from which they are derived, while the Paradaptive Intelligence model works on a completely different base of measure, emotions. Even though these are vastly different, there is still enough commonality that these two units of measure can be related to each other. Now, add the measure of engaged/not engaged/actively disengaged to the mix and it seems to be an irreconcilable mix of measurements.

On the contrary, there appears to be some consistency across all these measures, albeit imperfect. The variances between these measures can be attributed to imprecise definitions in both researcher and participant, which lead to structural problems in the questions of the survey instruments/questionnaires. Both the Gallop Management Journal study and the Bohlen, et al., models were trying to measure attitude, which is a generalized term for an underlying emotional state, without understanding the nature of the Paradaptive Intelligence system. Even so, they got remarkably close measures. The Innovation Adoption Curve of Bohlen, et al., described Late and Early Majority combined as one standard deviation split into two by the mean. Early and Late Majorities adopters have high, discernible measures of fear drive the actions of these groups. The only difference is half of the standard deviation, the Early Majority, could control their fear because the adaptor was still dominant and in control, while in the other half of the standard deviation, the Late Majority, the reactor was dominant. In this way, both the statistical mean of the Innovation Adaptation Curve and the Line of Passivity are the center points, thus helping create a point of alignment for both models. The Gallop survey described this same group as Not Engaged which consisted of fifty-five percent of the respondents. The Innovation Adaption Curve model and the Gallop survey had relatively close numbers, sixteen and nineteen percent respectively, to describe the Paradaptive Intelligence model state of paranoia. Where the Innovation Adoption Curve and the Gallop survey really differ is in the measure of market and sales leaders. The Innovation Adoption curve model showed Innovators (two point five percent) and Early Adopters (thirteen point five percent) to combine for sixteen percent while the Gallop survey describes the corresponding groups labeled as Engaged at twenty-six percent of respondents. The discrepancy between these measures, ten percent, can be attributed to the emotion growing pain. While a person may have a very small amount of fear, it may not be enough to trigger the response of Not Engaged because the respondent was not fully aware of the mild state of agitation to move away and disengage from their company. For example, respondents probably accepted growing pains and even the leading edge of trepidations as a fact of life and not a point of disengagement which carries the connotation of quitting or losing one's job.

In the old paradigm of four quadrant sales types, the Top Performers were assigned as those individuals whose sales were in the top twenty-five percent. This is, again, an arbitrary demarcation. The Top Performers are actually comprised of Innovators (two point five percent) and the Early Adopters (thirteen point five percent). Understanding the source of high performers lets us understand the genesis of the old sales nugget that states five percent of the sales force produces sixty percent of the sales in a company. What they were looking at were the Innovators and the leading edge of the Early Adopters.

For further corroboration, the best way to model this behavior is to describe a typical sales force from a manager's perspective. In the Innovation Adoption Curve model, Innovators are described as the ones who are creating new solutions to problems, which we now recognize as individuals operating in the present and future in the Vetting and Application phases of the Innovation emotional tonal algorithm for the goal of innovating or improving sales behaviors. If you look at any sales force, your very top sales people are the ones who got there by pioneering new ways of solving sales problems and are constantly innovating new approaches. These are your Innovators. There is another group in the sales force whose sales are competitive to those of the Innovators, but don't quite compare. They watch who's innovating and quickly imitate when someone creates a new, breakout behavior. These are the early adopters. According to the Early Adopters description, this group has high contact levels with innovators, which in this example bears that out. Top performers are very competitive and watch closely what rivals are doing. They just wanted someone to figure out the next innovation and make it easy for them. This group is working on corrective signal side of fear at the growing pain level. They know they have the skill set to implement new ideas; they just don't have the wherewithal to figure out the puzzle, the innovation aspect. Then there is the middle of the pack, the Early Majority. Their actions are driven by the emotion trepidations, a passive fear still to the right of Line of Passivity. These people adapt new sales behaviors only when the company holds a sales conference. At the sales conference, the innovators and early adopters get up and explain how these new approaches work and the benefits they bring. Remember, the Early Majority segment is waiting for someone to show them how to make this change to keep up with the competition (other sales staff) in the least disruptive manner, and then assisting them with the change to make it easy. The Late Majority are the ones who will sit around after the sales conference waiting and watching. They are driven by the corrective signal of fear at anxiety. This is an aggressive/passive emotional state. They will sit around and grouse about all the changes that are occurring in the sales department and then turn around and try and walk those comments back by trying to find something nice to say about the same subject. By externalizing these fears in terms of complaints and other negative statements they are demonstrating, active aggression. Sooner or later, a marginal Late Majority sales staff member, someone fairly close to Early Majority boundary, will see someone close on the other side of that Early/ Late Majority boundary implement this change in behavior. Encouraged he gives it a try, and with the help of either an Innovator, Early Adapter, or Early Majority mentor, finds success. Others in the Late Majority that identify with this person will soon approach them to find out what it took to see if they can replicate the same process and success for themselves. They may even approach a sales management staff to get some help after they've convinced themselves through other peers' successes that they can do it. And then there are those who appear to be so stuck in their ways, that they make no attempt to try this new approach. These are the Laggards/Non-Adopters. They are driven by the corrective signal paranoia. They are not as stuck in their ways as they are afraid; afraid that their bad or mediocre performance is better than the disaster that awaits if they change their ways or innovate new sales behaviors. Their fear is visceral; it is obvious from the tone and the volume that they don't like change. There is one other component to this last group of Laggards/Non-Adopters. These are the salesperson suffering from burnout. Through an accumulation of insults and injuries to their sales activities and thus their careers, these people have developed an irrational level of anger towards the company. They do not adopt new sales behaviors because they are at the corrective signal state of rage towards the company which drives them to push back with aggression towards anything that has to do with your company. In fact, any of your employees that are feeling any of the lesser emotional tones of anger — fury, frustration, and annoyance — towards the company will be disinclined to innovate new sales behaviors when they are being driven by anger to push back with aggression towards your firm. The way the Paradaptive Intelligence system is organized, it cannot both move towards the company and move away from the company due to boundary violations or obstacles. The corrective signal will always take precedents. So those in burnout are incapable of availing themselves to the opportunities for sales innovation of the sales conference.

The above little homily of a typical sales force should drive home several important facts. First is the importance of conferencing in sales if you want to advance the skill level of your sales staff, especially if they are geographically dispersed, and the type of communication that will occur there. It clearly demonstrates the necessity of communication among salespeople. There has been a management philosophy held by many sales managers that communications among their sales staff isn't germane to the function of selling, and technically this is true. Communication among sales staff is only important if you're trying to improve the quality and thus the performance of your sales staff. This also lends management some idea how to structure these events to create opportunities for Innovators to explain new sales behaviors. Early Adopters will follow up for quick imitation. Early Majority staffers will get the whole story, process, and line up assistance from those who have done it and figured out the simplest, least disruptive approach to making the change. Late Majority staffers will become aware of the changes coming and talk to other Late Majority staffers about the innovations presented at the last conference to see if they can duplicate the success of their Late Majority peers who may have successfully implemented innovation to their sales behaviors from the last sales rendezvous. The second point is that implantation of new sales behaviors will never happen all at once to your sales force. Although you may believe, as a manager, that everyone will jump on board, this unrealistic expectation (non-experienced-based, imagination derived action plan) runs counter to the processes of the mind. Improvement to a sales force is a cyclical process over a period of time, just like any market penetration of a new product. The third point is to understand the universality of the Paradaptive Intelligence model in helping you understand all business behavior and decision making, whether looking at an individual sales staff member, your entire staff as a group, or the markets you serve. To achieve optimal results in creating a world class sales force in the shortest amount of time you need to understand how the mind processes decisions and innovation and works within its parameters, rather than to fight it or disable your sales force staff with poorly considered practices and policies.

THE FIFTH EPOCH OF SALES

Building a world-lass sales force is not only about how a salesperson approaches his work, but how management perceives the role of the sales staff. In order to see the importance of this, one must understand the history of the sales force.

Sales is currently considered a sub-function of marketing. It is just one of several elements that go into marketing the goods and services of a company. In reality though, marketing grew out of sales. One of the most influential factors upon marketing has been production processes. The four previous marketing epochs were driven by developments in manufacturing technology. The first epoch started with the Industrial Revolution and lasted until the 1930's. This epoch was called the production epoch because it was driven by man's newfound ability to mass produce goods. Relatively few products were available to consumers, which allowed mass produced goods to flood the market with little competition. The salesman's focus during this epoch was product placement and distribution channels. Services, which are communications dependent, were localized with little or no reach due to the lack of mass communications to replicate identical service standards across large geographic markets.

The second epoch, the sales epoch, arose from competition and lasted until the beginning of the 1950's. Mass produced products had saturated the market and now instead of being the only brand on the shelf, there were competitors with similar products competing for placement. The salesman's role during this time was to outsell the competition with aggressive negotiations based on price and quantity. With the advent of commercial radio, services started to be offered on a national basis, but the lack of a communications infrastructure made it difficult to operate widespread standardized services industries. Services were more personalized, based upon personal interaction, which radio could not really replicate except in local markets.

This continued competitive pressure in goods resulted in the third epoch, called the marketing department epoch. The emphasis was still on mass produced products, which lasted until the 1970's, but this epoch differed in that it now took a coordinated effort of many individuals to present a singular message across a burgeoning spectrum of print, radio, and television to create demand for products. The salesperson's job was still about product placement and distribution, but there was now an added dimension to clients and prospects to demonstrate what they would do additionally to help a retailer resell their products via media, national advertising, and local promotions. National TV became widespread but was prohibitively expensive for localized services. It was during this epoch that franchising of services came into its own as a way for services to access mass media aided by improved communications infrastructure.

The fourth epoch, the marketing company epoch, represented a break from a focus on efficiency of mass produced goods. Now companies shifted their focus from "how can we make products more efficiently to lower our price and beat the competition" to "let's find out what the consumer wants and use our expertise in mass production to produce it in the most cost-effective way so that we can get the lowest price to appeal to the broadest set of consumers." The salesman's job was to exhibit a broad spectrum of the company's products and then determine which of the company's lines would be suitable for vendors. It was still a mass production approach, but with an emphasis on tailoring the product mix at the vendor level for specific markets. Salesman gave canned presentations on the different product lines, while services franchising reached into every aspect of commerce and consumerism. Brand name services became the dominant player to a mobile society that preferred consistency in service, regardless of location. This epoch lasted until the 1990's.

The fifth epoch is characterized by personalization of technology and was driven by cable/satellite TV, telephone, and the spread of the internet. Production technology now allows for a proliferation of products at nominal costs due to mass production with integration of just-in-time component delivery, allowing for personalized mass produced products that conform to the consumer's, not the vendor's specifications, or have the ability to be customized after the purchase. Your firm's clients and prospects are awash in a sea of specialized, customized TV settings with channels tailored to their specific interest. Smart phone apps allow total personalization of communications and mobile connectivity. This allows for direct dealings with merchants, auctions, global listing sites, both large and small, without the middleman in order to get just what they wanted, with the features they desire, at the price they demand.

As little as two decades ago, a salesperson could "show up and throw up" a presentation to obtain a sale. This was due to the fact, that at that time, the salesperson was the main source of product information. But with the advent of the internet, product information no longer holds the power it used to because of its widespread availability of information from manufacturers, suppliers, vendors, distributors, and the like. In this environment, the salesperson is likely to encounter a well-informed prospect. This has shifted the salesperson's power from product knowledge to the post sale, application/implementation side of the sale. The trend is for the salesperson's role to move away from emotional phases earlier in the Vetting phase to the post sale phase of Application. Because of the availability and rapidity with which information flows due to the internet and electronic communication, it is easier for business to accept they have business pain points and find solutions with a internet search engine. The trend is for the salesman to help prospects select from products already identified by the consumer and tailor the implementation. This comes back to the importance of adaptation plans. The power of salespeople is moving from customer education to customizing implementation and application.

As we've seen, the epochs of marketing have moved very rapidly in the last three-quarters of a century. Because sales managers are usually promoted from the sales force, they tend to bring and are influenced by the standards, methodologies, and concepts from when they were salespeople. Consequently, sales management always tends to be an epoch behind the times in what the salesperson is experiencing in the field. Prospects can order their personal space and world to fit their whims, so if you have not structured your sales philosophy and operations around customizing every transaction and empowered your sales staff to negotiate customized services or products sales to meet their needs, then you are fighting the market's expectations and trends. If your sales force is giving a standardized, canned, or scripted presentation, circa 1980, and the marketing company epoch, then you will not be working within the prospect's expectations of the world. If you are attempting to negotiate every deal by proxy through your salespeople, you will become inundated to the point of paralysis. Paradaptive Intelligence sales methodology allows for a totally customized approach to every sale. While your product or service may be pre-formed, the application to the customer will feel customized, and thus requiring less negotiation on the part of your sales staff and you. Using the Paradaptive Intelligence sales methodology shifts the consumer's expectation of customization from the sales terms to product specifications, creating the flexibility that both the sales manager and the sales staff need, thus reducing their workload.

SALESFORCE LOYALTY

The same mechanisms that prompt customer loyalty in prospects also works with managing a sales force. Companies are made of people, and people are imperfect. As a result, the products that companies produce are not perfect and thus no salesperson will ever have the "perfect product" to sell. Because of the independent nature of salespeople, they must be treated differently than the average employee, whether they are a contract salesperson, or an employee on the company payroll. Because they work in isolation, without the support and comfort of corporate culture to bask in, their internal, emotional state, which sustains and guides them in isolation, is critical to their success and the company's success. If they feel negatively towards the company due to policies and practices that they feel are unjust, unfair, obstructive, or threatening, it will be impossible for them not to communicate this to prospects in one form or another, whether by a lack of motivation to see one more client in a day or a lack of enthusiasm in presenting the company's products because discussion of the company forces them to revisit the source of negative emotion. If a significant number of salespeople in your sales force have attitudes — emotional states — in the Enemy phase of the Relationship emotional tonal algorithm, then your company is in serious trouble.

Not only will your company not experience optimum sales, but it will incur more costs in training, sick days, turnover, empty sales territories, and all the other attendant ills of a sales force in varying stages of burnout. But the biggest problem that can be fatal to the company, and thus your longevity in sales management, will come when the inevitable "bump in the road" occurs.

Management is also made up of imperfect people. At some point, management will make a blunder in the marketplace. If you think you're immune from this potential, all you need to do is refresh your memory with the Coke – New Coke incident, IBM's relationship with desktop computers, or Microsoft's Vista operating system, to name just a few company blunders. Janet Robinson states, "Repeat business or behavior can be bribed. LOYALTY has to be earned." While this book has demystified the "earning" loyalty concept, the rest of her statement stands. If you have been getting by as a sales manager by getting repetitive behavior from your sales force via bribes of an incentive, bonus, or paycheck and not banking any loyalty, then you've jeopardized your career. When the inevitable product or market blunder occurs and those bribes diminish or dry up, the only reason for their attachment to your company is severed, and your sales force will leave you, likely in the middle of a disaster, the worst possible time for a regrouping management team. Since customer loyalty is attached to your salespeople, unless you've been diligent in banking loyalty with your sales people, you've just given away your best chance to recover from a crisis situation. There is no substitute for smoothing and covering over business imperfections like loyalty, whether it's from your customers or your sales force.

Any additional cost of business that is incurred in garnering sales force loyalty is offset by their greater productivity. Wide ranging studies described earlier in this chapter have borne this out. But the one thing those studies didn't measure was sales force loyalty. However, a secondary, indirect measure of loyalty is possible by measuring salesperson longevity with the company, which world-class sales forces abound in.

Sales managers are in the business of managing people who cultivate client relationships. If you, as business and sales managers, from the top on down to the territory manager, are not interested in cultivating strong, positive relationships and loyalty with your sales force, then you are cheating your owners, stockholders, or partners. One of the biggest assets you have is the relationship with your clients. Your competitors don't have the advantage of having the access you have to decision makers in your client base. If you are not building relationships with clients, if your corporate culture is to isolate and ignore relationships, to eschew loyalty, ESPECIALLY with your sales force, then you are not practicing defensive sales, leaving your company wide open for your competitors to expose your imperfections without the benefit of loyalty to offset them.

Sales force loyalty, is easy to achieve and is an intangible benefit beyond measure as a business asset, and doesn't appear on the company's balance sheets, especially with executives not arising from the field of marketing. Salesperson loyalty in a world-class sales force is the source and force behind the numbers on the company's spreadsheet and stockholder statements. And salespeople are the measure of customer loyalty as well, indicating both the short- and long-term prospects of the company. Having a great product is important, but studies, simulations, and sales models have shown that superior sales and marketing will beat better products every time. EVERY TIME.

Isn't it high time you start banking sales force loyalty? If you've built your career upon the premise of managing sales mercenaries, motivated only by money, then you've overlooked the potential of what can be accomplished by dedicated people motivated by loyalty.

As a last note, the reactor's primary mission is to learn. The more you learn, the more adaptability you have. That is why sales managers as well as salespeople must always be learning. With markets constantly changing, sales managers must lead their sales force in demonstrating their ability to adapt to whatever the market throws them. You will only gain their trust by learning what your Paradaptive Intelligence Network is telling you and translate that into solutions for your sales force. Leadership is demonstrating adaptability. So you must understand how to read and manage not only your Paradaptive Intelligence Network, but also that of your sales force.

The only way to build loyalty with your sales staff is to build relationships via the six universal needs of the reactor: freedom, power, connection, esteem, creativity, and meaning. One of the most misbegotten concepts in business is the myth of not developing relationships with your employees, like salespeople, so that you can rationally evaluate them and fire them if needed. If this has been your operating principle, it is strongly recommended that you change your practices or seek new employment because you've jeopardized your career and your company's fortunes with this kind of practice. If you plan on having any control of salespeople who work remotely in isolation, one of the key factors of accomplishing this is building relationships. All company sales policies and procedures must be evaluated in the light of whether they help an autonomous salesperson in the field build relationships with management and the company that helps a salesperson sustain their efforts by satisfying the universal needs of not only themselves but those of your clients. These six needs are always in force and active in salespeople; it's the way they're hardwired. If you're not working within its parameters, then you're fighting Mother Nature.

A world-class sales force starts at the C-level of an organization. Chief Executive Officers create the environment for subordinates to maximize the six universal needs in the company's sales apparatus, which is arguably the most important business function within the multitude of firm activities, which is why this book is must-reading for every C-level executive on down.

MANAGING THE PARADAPTIVE INTELLIGENCE NETWORK
AT A PERSONNEL LEVEL

Having looked at the reasons necessary for managing the greater parameters of the Paradaptive Intelligence Network within a sales force, it is now time to look at how that is accomplished on the micro level. First and foremost, a sales manager must always keep in their mind that their sales force is controlled entirely by internal feedback. This feedback system within their salespeople draws all its information from external cues. This means that the sales manager can play a critical and decisive role in controlling what feedback goes into their salespeople's Paradaptive Intelligence Network by providing the right type of feedback to extract optimal performance. This feedback will come in two forms: sales policies and personal interactions.

Now let's look at how sales polices provide feedback to your salespeople. Again, first and foremost, sales managers must concede and understand that every salesperson has two well established objectives controlling their entire work efforts. The first motivation is to maximize their income and the second motivation is to enjoy their personal life. The relationship between salespeople and their companies is contractual. Salespeople sell their time to their companies to nullify pain points in the personal lives because that is where pleasure is pursued. Of the salespeople's two main motivations, the prime objective is to maximize their personal live. Again, remember humans are designed to seek pleasure and avoid pain, such as corrective signal emotions. Now they may have a whole host of other motivations such as to be the best at everything they do (professionalism) or to perform their work in the most efficient manner (do only what is necessary and no more). These tend to be modifiers to the two prime motivations of maximize their personal pleasure and maximize their income. All feedback derived from their external world will be translated by their Paradaptive Intelligence Networks into emotions to indicate how well they are doing at the main objectives and modifiers. All sales policies will be viewed by whether it helps them further their primary objectives. Every time you add a constraining sales policy, it will be inspected by the Paradaptive Intelligence Network as to whether it will help them achieve their primary motivations of maximizing their income and personal life. If this new policy interferes and acts as an impediment to maximizing their income by reducing the set of potential sales deals by disqualifying certain classes of customers, then their Paradaptive Intelligence will signal anger as a feedback to this new external stimulus. If the new policy will make them work harder or longer to find more sales within the reduced pool of sales candidates and thus act as an impediment to maximizing their personal life and pleasure, they again are biologically program to react with anger. If you change a long existing agreement to the way they've conducted their job, you will be violating a boundary. Salespeople are biologically programmed to respond with the feedback emotion of anger. Anger is designed to engage in violence to push back boundary violators. While most sales professionals are capable of suppressing the urge to do violence to others, this biological drive to push back is usually expressed verbally. If you have angered your sales staff, you need to understand which of the two violations you just perpetrated upon those who you count on to perform so that you keep your job. If the contractual violation is really outrageous, then you can expect to disgust. They see your behavior as unwholesome and loathsome. If the contractual violation is so great that it irrevocably destroys the fabric of your relationship, you will see the emotion of loss. These are all corrective signals which internally signal the salesperson to move away from you, the sales manager, or the company. This is not a matter of choice for your salespeople. They cannot control or change this internal feedback, it's biology. The best they can do is to try and hide it from you as they fight to not externalize this internal feedback. And as we've learned, corrective signally is designed to disrupt higher order thought processes so not only have you triggered internal feedback to move away from you, but you've mentally handicapped your sales force to figure out a way to work around the new pain point you just handed them.

At this point, I know there are many managers screaming at this book saying "I've got to manage and direct the company's business, I don't have time to worry about the sales forces' feelings. They need to get over it. That's why I pay them incentives." If you're one of these, you may be right on one point and one point alone. On the rest of the points you are utterly wrong. Yes, you do have the job of managing and directing the company's business. If you are doing it in a way that is invoking corrective signals within your sales force, you're just not being smart about the way you conduct the company's business. By invoking these biologically pre-programmed responses of corrective signal you're working at cross purposes to achieve your management goals and sustain your career. The science is overwhelming clear: when negative stimulus is paired with even the most powerful positive stimulus, the negative stimulus will always be the dominant stimulus. This is the reactor seeking known danger, unwholesomeness, obstacles, boundary violations and things or events that could cause loss in the environment. So yes, you do pay your salespeople incentives, a positive stimulus, but how long will this override the negative stimulus you're laying down? Do you know? Have you surveyed your team? The true results of such a survey will come to many sales managers as quite a shock. In those sales managers who cannot truthfully answer these questions it is because their egos are filtering non-confirmatory environmental cues from the incoming sensory arrays. The sales manager thinks that changes in sales policies are no big deal and everyone will just follow along. These sales managers are focused on their motivations so their dysfunctional egos are only allowing in that information which is confirmatory to those objectives while screening out cues that he is introducing corrective signals to his work force and disrupting their ability to perform their job. This is the equivalent in sales of the ladies' man example given earlier in the book. This may all appear to be an insurmountable objective, to manage a sales force without disrupting it through corrective signaling emotions. But because you are now knowledgeable in the operations of the human Paradaptive Intelligence Network, you have options, lots of good options.

The whole Paradaptive Intelligence Network works on feedback. You must change your outlook to understand that your primary function as a sales manager is to control the feedback within your sales department being imparted upon your sales force. Again, there are now managers shouting at this book saying "I have things to do. My superiors expect reports, updates, data and other things for me. I don't have time to manage the feedback to salespeople. They're paid professionals; I expect them to figure it out themselves." If this is your position, then, again, you are utterly wrong. Everyone, including professional salespeople, need direction. You control that direction by the feedback you supply them. If you need to change a sales policy, don't create a corrective signal by violating the existing contractual terms of the employee-employer relationship. Instead, create a new positive incentive to change their behavior. This is what spiffs are for. Give your sales force a new direction and provide a new positive reward for moving in that direction. On a basic level, this is no different from training dogs, horse, or killer whales at the oceanic park. That's because we all share many parts of the same adaptation circuitry. By programming changes in this way to your sales staff you will always be rewarding sales excellence, not violating boundaries or introducing obstacles. Receiving a spiff or new incentive is a positive, growth signal, which internally drives your salespeople to keep doing what earned them the reward and repeat that experience. And just like any other mammal training, you will ween them off the incentive by rewarding every other, every second, every fourth, etc…. event until the behavior is changed and set. This will take planning on your part as a sales manager and require flexibility, but the rewards will be enormous as you create change in your sales department without introducing disruption.

Those managers who believe that sales professionals should be self-motivated and those that require your attention are not up to professional standards and should be eliminated could not be in greater error. The top twenty-five percent of every sales force is described as top performers. These are the models for the assessment of salespeople who should not need attention or growth signal feedback from you. After all, the top tier performers are the ones who require your least attention. Typically, the top tier performers just want you to stay out of their way since you tended to introduce obstacles to their high functional sales processes, right? But this way of thinking is exactly bass-ackwards. Top tier performing salespeople don't need much external growth stimulus. They're achieving their goals. They frequently receive high amounts of internal joy as reward for achieving faith, exuberance, and job well-done satisfaction as they reach their objectives of obtaining sales. They've become self-sufficient and self-sustaining at internal rewards. But the other seventy-five percent of your sales staff are not yet to that stage of internal self-sufficiency and sustainment of internal shots of joy to sustain them. Lower tiers have yet to develop sales methodologies that bring top tier level internal rewards of joy. This is why you as the sales manager must develop an environment that re-enforces good behavior. Treating top-performers with the same methodology and positive re-enforcement builds a platform of shared, common experiences that then becomes the culture of your sales team. Conversely, not to do so will create classes or castes of salespeople which will create strife, which works against potential synergistic gains and cross-pollination of styles and talents.

If you're in the business of managing Paradaptive Intelligence Networks, as all sales managers should by now seeing as their role, then it's important to remember to include all your avenues of feedback. Humans have five sensory systems: hearing, smell, taste, touch, and sight. Use all of these to your advantage. How? Praise works well for hearing. Food works for taste, so how difficult is it to let some salesperson whose behavior you wish to modify pick the donut type for you next sales meeting whether its old-fashions, apple fritters, jellies…. whatever. Don't underestimate the power of food to change human behavior. Aromas work in rewarding the sense of smell. There is a whole industry of aroma therapy evolving. Why? Because the science is good that smells can unlock powerful memories that guide behavior. Fresh air, the outside, can be an aroma, too. The sense of touch may seem to be a tricky sense to reward given the legal culture of today's workplace, but that doesn't mean it is not at the sales manager's disposal. You need to think of things that do touch you employees like chairs, desks, clothes – like company-logoed jackets to keep them warm, or cooling garments like short-sleeve companied- logoed shirts. And lastly, there is the visual rewards. As children, good work in school was rewarded with things like colored stars on a paper. This part of the brain did not go away in adulthood. It's still there and functioning. Albeit, adulthood visual rewards require a lot more sophistication., but the power of visual displays of achievement never go away; the trophy industry is built on this fact of nature.

Rewards and incentives go beyond just your sales staff; they have families and loved ones, too. Incentives directed at them are even more powerful. Think of it this way, the salesperson is probably internally motivated to achieve sales anyway, but for just a little extra effort that can make someone important to them receive a perk and be a hero. What spouse wouldn't enjoy a day at a day spa, game tickets, weekend bed-and-breakfast get away, or some other tailored incentive. A great example of this type of reward for sales was a children's bike. This particular bike had all the buzzers and bells of its day. They were bought in bulk, so unit costs to the sales department was actually minimal compared to offering more incentive money to the sales staff, and the salespeople could easily afford to buy the bikes for children if they wanted. But because they were already trying to maximize their sales and a little extra effort made them a hero at home, sales skyrocketed. The point is, that a sales manager can never tell what small incentive will reap huge sales gains, but he must always be thinking and trying to find it as a way of using all the Paradaptive Intelligence Network to achieve his goals.

All these sensory rewards for sales achievement also serve as a secondary force multiplier for sales managers. As sensory rewards are accumulated by sales staff, they become status symbols of achievement. And in the course of most business environments, sales staff families often have contact with other sales staff families. Visual. They talk. Let that talk turn to sales incentive achievement and welcome the help of others in sphere of sales staff influence help you achieve your sales goals through positive re-enforcement of sales achievement at home.

CONCLUSION

All businesses are dependent upon sales. They are built to initiate transactions of the particular type for which the business is built to conduct and will soon perish without them. While the multitude of business types produces a myriad of sales approaches, this has yielded a belief, held as an article of faith, that no two transactions are the same. Yet, management consistently forces their sales wing of their business to create uniformity in this process for predictability and ease of management. This has led to an industry of support services to sales management known as customer retention marketing and sales tracking. The first for continued business with clients that have already transacted business with a firm at least once, and the latter for the development of new clients. There have been two approaches to these two types of directed assistance: customized services and products for a specific market, or generalized products and services that attempt to capture what was believed to be universal steps in a sales process. Neither of these two approaches were anchored in any science of brain processing or functionality, but rather are tethered to the lore of sales that is the product of philosophies developed as people tried to grapple with their intuition of what was occurring. This has led to a classic case of "when you can't quantify what's important, make important what you can quantify." This in turn has forced the sales industry down a path of enlightened ignorance with copious quantities of data and information of secondary or tertiary elements of their sales process, but no direct measure of the precise elements of the process itself. However, using the Paradaptive Intelligence model now allows direct access for business managers to not only create uniformity for predictability and ease of management, but to have that tied by a good scientific foundation into the actual processes and programing of the brain.

20

"CLOSING" ARGUMENTS

"Viva la revolución!"
Anonymous

There are two types of improvements that occur in our understanding of the world. The first is called an incremental improvement. This is an *evolutionary* change because its nature is to improve or tweak the current model or paradigm, thus evolving it. These improvements can be explained within the language and constructs of the current paradigm. The second type of improvement occurs when a new paradigm is inserted into the folds of understanding. This occurs when the old paradigm has too many anomalies, unexplainable observed facts, special circumstances, or allowances to remain workable. When a new model of understanding emerges, it is called a *revolutionary* improvement because a revolution is not founded on the previous model, but instead sweeps aside all the old principles and conventions to create new terminology and constructs that unite observed fact and behavior into an understandable, systematic, and cohesive set of rules. Paradaptive Intelligence Network selling is a revolutionary improvement.

But just because the old model is patched-up and held together by bailing wire doesn't mean that somebody is in charge of going to the theory closet and pulling out a new one at random from the shelves within. While researching this book, at least a half-dozen competing theories of consumer behavior were examined and found wanting. All had excellent qualities, and all were fatally flawed. The primary fatal flaw was that all the models were not built on, nor referenced to, workable psychology models. None were tied to the emotional system, which is understandable because, until now, psychology had no accepted, bulletproof model of emotions. The Emotional Feedback System model developed by Katherine Peil is an emergent model and has not yet become the paradigm of the science. But those in science know that new paradigm shifts often take more than a lifetime before acceptance develops a majority stake and the process can be extremely political. Einstein knew this. He spent several years crisscrossing the country and globe selling and promoting his new theory of physics, Special Theory of Relativity, to gain acceptance. Scientists spend lifetimes attempting to improve the current model and are devilishly skeptical and resistant to altering their belief systems, despite their flaws, for they have invested a lifetime in development of these beliefs.

Overarching, grand unifying theories like Paradaptive Intelligence which models adaptation, consumer behavior, and sales, and Peil's science of peer-reviewed and published Emotional Feedback System, upon which it is built, are risky propositions in science. They are risky because they state a new set of guiding principles, laws, and relationships between elements of the discipline and are generally not as fully vetted compared to existing models. They're made usually with limited proof based on the science of the old model and then scientists spend lifetimes either proving or disproving them. Revolutionary models in science always emerge based on the research developed pursuant to the old model and not a large body of research developed specifically for the revolutionary model. Because initial proof for all encompassing theories are usually light on verification, it often comes down to a beauty contest of how well respected the author is or how their reputation is regarded. That's all well and good for the scientist. This book was written for business professionals, salespeople, and sales managers who can't wait for any beauty contest within the sciences. This book was written for people who want to understand what they are doing in sales and want to improve their performance now.

While the Emotional Feedback System has not yet found widespread acceptance within psychology because it was published just months prior to the publication of this book, this does not mean that it is wrong. Contrarily, the purpose of this book was to practically and methodically demonstrate the application of the Emotional Feedback System through a broader model of Paradaptive Intelligence Network to the real world. This, hitherto, has never been done, in any form, for any previous or current model within the psychology field. And it will never happen again because the other competing models within psychology cannot and do not adequately explain observed behavior like the Paradaptive Intelligence Network model. The Emotional Feedback System model of emotion, upon which the broader Paradaptive Intelligence Network model is based, is incredibly robust and will serve well all those wishing to accept its foundational brilliance. Those who accept the model for what it can do for them now, while scientists wrangle over it for the next few decades, will be able to explain and understand consumer behavior until evolution or God modifies the mind of man.

Welcome to the revolution!

ANTHROPOLOGY, ECONOMICS, BUSINESS SCIENCES...

Now that mechanism of adaptation, the human emotion system, has been laid bare in this book, we can see that many different sciences such as anthropology, economics, psychology, the business sciences, political science, artificial intelligence and the like have all been studying the same aspect, the adaptation role of the emotion system in man. Economics studies this relationship through the Paradaptive Intelligence lens of the emotions learning anticipation, excitement, and courage, and how individuals in societies examine cost and benefits; anthropology studies the Paleolithic application of Paradaptive Intelligence through the technology of stone tools, clothes, weaponry, shelters, etc.; the business sciences, marketing, management, finance, study Paradaptive Intelligence through the lenses of sales, relationship, and money, respectively. Psychology seeks to define, quantify, and organize our understanding of the emotional machinery as well as its maladaptation. Even political science is a study of societal organization through the Paradaptive Intelligence lens of the six basic needs of the reactor, and more primarily the need for freedom and power. All these sciences are peas in the same pod, studying human responses of the Paradaptive Intelligence Network's adaptation mechanism to specific stimuli. These are just a few examples, of which there surely are more, of the convergence of sciences all studying the emotional machinery of adaptation put forth in this book. Scientists studying man in any way, shape, or form now have a medium for cross-pollination and multidisciplinary study through the Paradaptive Intelligence Network's mechanisms.

Likewise, any book having ever been written on self-help in business must now be reinterpreted through the contents of this book. Countless scores of books have been written by legions of writers, all hoping to polish some facet(s) of sales, marketing, or management or update them for their times. Now we can see that those "facets" being polished relate to one or more specific emotions in the motional tonal algorithms outlined in this book. And all future works in the business self-help genre will have to reference the mechanisms laid out in this book or risk being irrelevant. It is also now easy to see why non-emotion specific topic books produced erratic results. Failing to understand at what stage to apply the advice of authors caused salespeople to forget the other required emotional steps in moving a prospect to a sale, and conversely, why the author's advice was occasionally successful if the emotional progression randomly fell in place.

INTUITION

In business, the word "intuitive" is often bandied about as a positive attribute of product or service. But, like most things discussed in this book, there remained a substantive absence of the true understanding of what was being described. Intuition is the Paradaptive Intelligence Network's algorithms operating in an unguided manner free of logic, reasoning, and imagination of the HAC mechanism of the adaptor. Animals, and our forbearer hominids, have a basic adaptation mechanism that lacks reasoning, logic, and imagination which was added only in the most recent additions to the homo genus, and a few other tool makers scatter around the animal kingdom. In this manner, it draws upon common, basic exemplars from memory rather than the adaptor's directed searches of memory. These common, basic exemplars are also the root of the concept of common sense. However, not everyone has the same exemplar catalog, including the common, basic exemplars presumed to be held by every individual. So when a product or process is described as intuitive, its features and operations are drawing upon the most basic, common exemplars held in the collective target market, thus appealing and relatable to the largest swathe of prospects.

The ability for the Innovation algorithm to run in an automated fashion without guidance from adaptor is now understood. This automated process is not as precise as an adaptor-directed process. We know that the reactor will impede and disrupt the functions of the adaptor as it executes its function to adapt the ever-changing environment when it detects a threat to the body or self. Yet, despite this interference, decisions do get made. And often enough, not the best decisions. Like the game show contestant that can't decide which door to pick, hems and haws, then blurts out a choice. Or the carnival huckster who tries to build up the suspense as a way of making you lose. Then there's the person who benefits from you making the wrong decision so they try to apply pressure (threat or other corrective signal) that will agitate the reactor to disrupt your rational thinking. In all these instances, decisions get made, providing insight into the basic operating mode of the Innovation algorithm. And this mode of operation can produce good results. Expertise in subject matter is largely about having a better developed exemplar library on a specific topic. So drawing from a well-stocked exemplar library on a specific topic in the automated mode of adaptation and decision making often produces excellent results. This is why an expert's guess is often more accurate. There is even a statistical process that averages experts' opinions (guesses) to come up with a specific finding. All this goes to illustrate the power of the Paradaptive Intelligence model in explaining human behavior in business matters.

PARDAPTIVE INTELLLIGENCE SELLING LIMITATIONS

Having extolled the virtues of Paradaptive Intelligence based selling, it's now time to understand its limitations. While Paradaptive Intelligence based selling techniques are vastly superior to any other, it can never achieve 100% sales efficacy. The reason is simple and one that you already suspect, the prospect's Paradaptive Intelligence Network. Because corrective signals create basic emotions that are disruptive to logic, reasoning, imagination, and thought, there will be clients that may be incapable of hearing or seeing the utility of the adaptation plans you're presenting. Additionally, humans have the ability to ignore the emotional signals coming from the reactor and override them. This can lead to a prospect concluding that acceptance of pain in business is the norm. This notion of pain acceptance has been romanticized in literature as "the human condition" or "man's suffering," leading to the misbegotten belief that it's just normal to have business pain and inefficiency. This is totally contrary to everything that is known about the Paradaptive Intelligence Network. Its whole purpose and function is the nullification of pain to increase survivability through adaptation, not acceptance of psychic pain. The only reason for man's suffering is the lack of an adaptation plan. So, as long as the pain threshold of a prospect is not totally disruptive and is in the range where he may still be functional, albeit at a reduced level, he may be able to, if only partially, ignore what his internal mechanism is shouting to nullify pain points.

When a prospect is pushed on the spectrum of pain intensity to where all logic, reasoning, and thought are completely disrupted, he is no longer in a position to evaluate any adaptation plan you are offering. He may grasp onto one variable, such as "how much" or "how quickly" and base his decision on this one aspect. Conversely, he may not like the crease in your pants and totally reject you for no other reason. Such is the havoc that a corrective signal from the reactor can have on the purchasing process. Another permutation of this phenomenon is the prospect being so disrupted that he can't hear what you are saying regarding the attributes of your adaptation plan or the terms of sale. Since he didn't hear what you've said, his expectations created by his imagination remain intact, and all of a sudden, a "miscommunication" erupts when you, your product, the terms of sale, or the implementation plan don't conform to those he imagined. Accusations fly and the salesperson becomes the bad guy for supposedly changing or misrepresenting some aspect of the "agreement." This has been off-handedly covered by the notion that the prospect was "distracted." Distraction has nothing to do with it. The prospect's brain functions have been compromised and disrupted by this reactor by design. All this demonstrates the necessity to move those prospects at or below the emotion anxiety to acceptance. Only those whose emotion level is at paranoia will make a sale impossible. Unfortunately, those whose Paradaptive Intelligence Network are at the paranoia emotion stage will be prevented of any adaptation. This group experiencing paranoia is of considerable size and removes a significant portion of the marketplace from the salesperson's potential market.

These are the prospects that don't seem to be in control or in charge of their business and are totally reactive to it. The business is running them rather than the reverse. His or her entire business perspective will be given over to the fear or anger generated by his reactor and, as a matter of course, everything will be seen through the lens of past failures, problems, insurmountable obstacles, and costs incurred by past adaptations, thus increasing the intensity of his pain point load rather than reducing it. This prospect is not living, business-wise, in the present. If he was, he would understand that in order to stop today's business pain he must change his ways, expending energy, time, and resources to do so. This client is looking for someone to waive a magic wand over his operations to make the pain points go away without him having to change anything he is doing.

Salespeople can manage, but never control, a prospect's Paradaptive Intelligence Network. The only way to override someone who is under control of the reactor is to manipulate the reactor by creating a bigger threat whose fear reaction dwarfs the one he is presently experiencing. What this describes is a business intervention. It is not the salesperson's place to decide where, on who, or when to perform a "business intervention," which by definition expresses use of force. Using force, i.e. manipulation, has long-term ethical problems, relationship problems, and possibly legal issues. This is the domain of the con man and it is not recommended for the professional salesperson. Salespeople, do not fall in the trap where the client believes that you are *the* answer. At best, you are *part* of the answer. The best adaptation plan for this business person looking for a business intervention is to look within themselves, guided by a trusted relationship. As your product or service eventually helps the client gain control of their business, and perhaps with a few other helpful changes, the client will regain their own footing and reassume control of their business.

THE LOGIC OF EMOTIONS OXYMORON

The purpose of this book was to explain emotions in consumer behavior in a logical fashion. While this was accomplished by allowing the reader to understand the causational relationship, structure, rules, and flow of emotions of consumer behavior, there is further application to all joy based decision making. Previous to this book, the epitome of opposites were logic and emotion. Logical emotion - a classic oxymoron. Emotions were perceived to be random, incoherent, and messy with no practical value. It was tied correctly, in part, to our mammalian brethren and thus viewed as not being uniquely human but rather a linkage to our baser animal. In fact, it is emotions, in particular the Paradaptive Intelligence Network that is our most defining human characteristic. Yes, humans have higher brain functions than animals, and it is the prevailing wisdom that intelligence is the defining human characteristic. If you look behind the curtain of the definition and described function of intelligence you will see the mechanisms of intelligence are one and the same as the Paradaptive Intelligence Network. Emotions are the hand on the tiller of that intelligence, guiding its usage, compelling us to use our intelligence to either change our behavior or our environment. And as noted at the beginning of this book, the Paradaptive Intelligence Network was responsible for our ascendancy among all hominids. The number and complexity of human emotions is vastly expanded over even our closest relation in the animal kingdom, granting humans an unprecedented level of command and control of intellect for adaptability. Emotions allowed us to adapt more readily and are the primary mechanism through which salespeople execute their jobs. Because it controls and directs the expanded reasoning of man, it therefore must be considered the defining human characteristic and the reason why we now understand consumer behavior in prospects and clients.

Two of the greatest fictional proponents of logic in the last two centuries were Sir Arthur Conan Doyle's Sherlock Holmes and Star Trek's Vulcan Mr. Spock. Both espoused the ascendency of logic as a refinement to mankind. While this may be true from a philosophical point, from a factual perspective, the progression of ...acceptance, learning anticipation, confidence, courage, etc., appears to be a logical sequence when in fact it is a string of pearls of emotions designed to internally signal to an individual just what to do next in adapting to changing environments and situations to achieve their goals. How ironic it is that logic is entirely dependent upon the emotions of adaptation to determine when logic has been properly deduced and applied.

Logic is an outgrowth of the mental adaptation machinery. It is a comparative engine to project efficacy and other aspects in acceptance, learning anticipation, confidence, excitement, courage, faith, exuberance, and satisfaction/self-actualization, as well as corrective signals. Logic is inductive and deductive reasoning utilizing known exemplars available from memory. Logic compares bits, pieces, or whole experiences of known information to current circumstances. The partner of logic is imagination, which is a rational extension of logic tethered neither to reality and its rules, nor known exemplars of memory. Imagination starts within the prospect at the starting point of "what would something look like if it were to fulfill this function or have these attributes" when there is no known exemplar available to the adaptor. Logic and imagination work so closely together and interchangeably, that it is often very difficult to determine which one is in operation at any one time. Logic and imagination working together is called intuition. The discipline of logic is the pursuit of learning to exclude imagination and the ego's confirmatory bias in problem solving and working solely from inductive and deductive reasoning. The irony deepens even greater when one realizes that logic is necessary and foundational to human emotions. The need to project attributes of problems and efficacy of solutions is elemental to the formation of an emotion. Mr. Spock and Mr. Holmes must truly be spinning in their fictional graves.

With the Paradaptive Intelligence Network and its practical application of SPAN selling in sales, commerce and the decision-making process is now an orderly and well understood process that is repeatable anywhere in the world, it is measurable in the intensity that can be determined, and it provides predictability because emotions follow in a universal progression. Measurability, repeatability, and predictability are the requirements of an all-encompassing theory and, hitherto, were not able to be used in the same sentence as emotions. Now, using Paradaptive Intelligence and SPAN selling techniques, the salesperson can move from being reactive and pinballing off of prospect's emotions to being an agent of adaptation able to anticipate, predict, and direct the proceedings of a prospect's buying and decision-making process with a large degree of control.

Ansel Adams once said, "There is nothing worse than a sharp image of a fuzzy concept." This sentiment brilliantly captures the sales scene prior to the entrance of Sales Psychology 101. The field of sales was dominated by statistical analysis of variables that was able to bring into exquisite focus a statistical relationship between those variables selected. But, because the actual causational relationship was not known or understood, often variables that were measured and compared against one another were actually derivatives of other variables already in the equation and not truly independent variables that good statistical analysis requires, such as multiple regression analysis. This muddled environ of unknown relationships between variables, though measurable, has presented the salesperson and sales managers with a fuzzy concept of what was occurring in the sales work sphere and was brought into sharp focus by statistical analysis. Now that the actual mechanisms of emotional progression and its role in sales have been laid bare, realignment can commence, starting with reinterpretation of existing studies. This will also lead to the abandonment of previous question based selling techniques that were both unfocused and fuzzy in concept.

And, as a last organizing notion, we can graphically look at the relationship of the reactor, adaptor, and conductor in Figure 20.1, and see how the concepts of Paradaptive Intelligence overlay and align with well-known models of salesperson types. This allows us to develop a transitional understanding from the known, old paradigm models to the new paradigms put forth in this book. The fuzzy concepts of old can be brought into much sharper focus and knowledge of how the mind actually processes information in the sales cycles and understand why misaligned salespeople perform the way they do.

THE ART OF PERSUASION

There have been numerous books written on the art of persuasion. But, by this time you've no doubt come to the conclusion that the art of persuasion and sales are one and the same, which is the correct assessment. Persuasion is nothing more than moving someone along the same emotional pathways of a sale for purposes of obtaining something other than making a purchase. Usually, it is to gain agreement on a point of interest to both parties. The key element in this process is really the emotion of acceptance and confidence. Getting both parties to agree on the definition and parameters of the problem may take critical analysis to tease the problem's elements into its constituent parcels and negotiation skills to determine which elements are critical and will need to be addressed in a solution. After the problem is defined at acceptance, the emotional pathway to resolution is the same as other sales issues. The only difference is that persuasion is a collective, external journey of two or more down the same emotional pathway of innovation rather than a singular, internal pursuit. In fact, the Acquisition phase of the Innovation emotion tonal algorithm graph can be quite helpful in allowing both parties to understand the assumptions and experiences that shape their opinion of how he or she sees the problem. This understanding of the past can be quite valuable in determining which potential solution will have the highest level of confidence.

REVIEW OF FEATURES AND BENEFITS SELLING

Throughout this book, the concept of features and benefits selling has been berated and discouraged. It's now time to take a little closer look at why. A features and benefits selling approach is a mash-up of two concepts, features and benefits. Each one of these has different emotional content. Features are logical interpretations and projections of physical characteristics of a product or service. This is the basis of pain point nullification projection. Benefits refer to the process of emotional satisfaction of various emotions in the innovation and relationship algorithms. Diving into features and benefits puts a salesperson starting in the middle of the innovation or a relationship algorithm without having first covered and established the initial emotions in order of appearance. This is why features and benefits selling is such a haphazard approach. In just as many instances the customer may be able

Figure 20.1

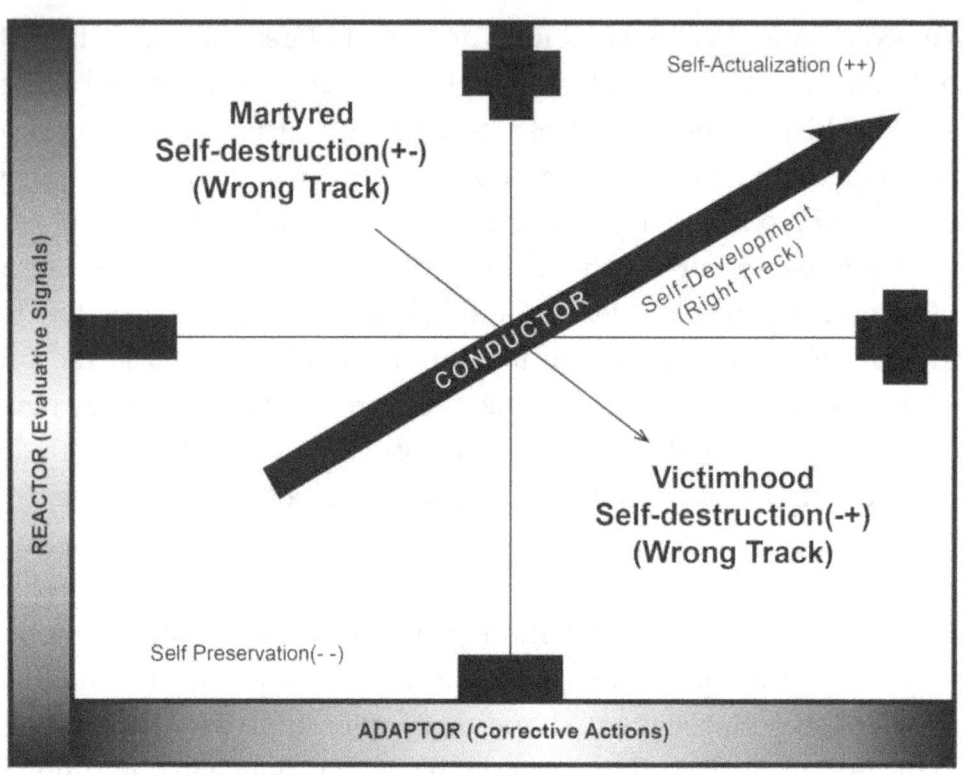

The Tri-Valent Self-Regulatory Logic

to go back and correctly satisfy their emotions in the adaptation sequence to align with your product or service, and in just as many instances they won't. In all probability, your product or service can't solve all of every prospect's pain points, having been designed for a specific set of pain point nullifications. So by jumping into the middle of an innovation algorithm with a features and benefits approach, you will automatically leave some sales on the table that your product of service was designed to address because the prospect won't be able to go back and make the alignment of acceptance, learning anticipation, and confidence. Do the groundwork required of every sale. Don't skimp or jump ahead because the prospect's internal circuitry can't and won't let them.

ACCRETIVE NATURE OF EMOTIONS

Emotions, as we've come to know Paradaptive Intelligence, are accretive. This means that layers are added to existing layers, building up a composition of feelings. Whether doing innovation or entering into a relationship, once one emotion is attained, you continue to hold that emotion even while the mind's hardwired circuitry is trying to achieve the next emotion beyond it in the sequence via the feedback process of the Human Action Cycle (Figure 20.2). For example, if you're trying to nullify a pain point and you're trying to satisfy excitement, you will have feelings of acceptance, learning anticipation, and confidence towards the particular solution option you're pursuing. In an Institutional relationship, it you're trying to satisfy kinship, you will have feelings of acceptance, curiosity, camaraderie, and attachment towards a person or institution.

While you may only be trying to satisfy one emotion at a time, you will have all previous satisfied emotions to that object until a negative event occurs to nullify these previous emotions (20.3). This means adding emotions towards solutions or persons and institutions as the Human Action Cycle achieves them, just like a pearl adds layer of nacre to create a depth of iridescent mother-of-pearl. This is why you feel many things towards solutions, people, and institutions that you've worked towards. It is why you're constantly curious about what's going on with friends, companies, brands, governments, etc. once you achieved the emotion of curiosity with them. Is it any wonder, now that you know curiosity is one of the lowest intensities of emotions that you obtain in starting relationships, that standard greetings such as "How are you?", "What's up?", "What's happening?", "How is everything?", "How's your family? Business?", "How's life treating you?" or any one of a couple dozen other greetings are all interrogatories of curiosity. Or that when you introduce a client or friend to someone else you say "…this is my friend (client) Joe…" instead of just saying "…this is Joe…" This is a statement of the emotion attachment. When you hear of a bad outcome or experience of a very, very close friend your first thoughts are "That's horrible – I wonder how Joe is feeling?" This is an action driven by having obtained the emotion compassion in that relationship. These are all indications of the accretive nature of the relationship you're in with that particular person or institution, or pain point nullification HAC.

Conversely, you may not have these feelings if your relationship has not reached that stage and you may internally berate yourself for not feeling these emotions towards people you don't know. You shouldn't be hard on yourself because you're only following nature's dictates hard-wired into your DNA. Or, if you have a solution you obtain courage for and implement, yet it turns out to not be able to nullify the pain points you wanted to the level you wanted, you'll scratch your head

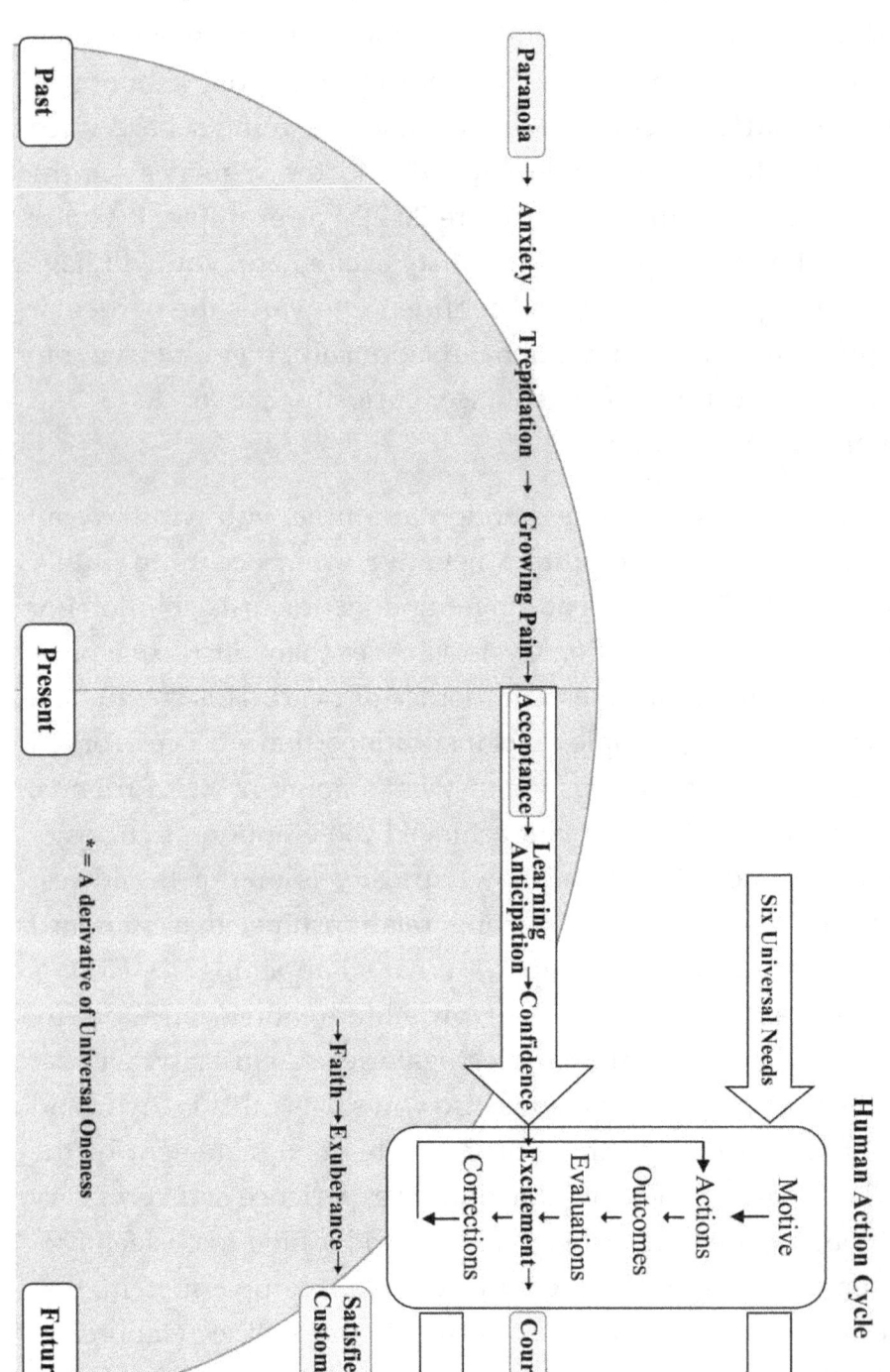

FIGURE 20.2

Human Action Cycle Feed Forward
and Accretive Emotions Accumulation™

and say to yourself, "I thought for sure it would work," all the while still feeling it was a viable solution (learning anticipation), it was the right choice based on what information was available (confidence), oddly, you're still excited about it even though it didn't pan out (excitement) and, if you had to do it all over again, you would (courage). These are but just a few examples of how the accretive nature of emotions creates differing depths of feelings towards innovations, people, and institutions. As a salesperson looking to learn from your experiences, it is vital to understand how and why you feel about a sales effort in a post-mortem examination so that you can set aside these feelings as being natural and right, rather than seeing them as validations that you were correct, and everything else was wrong. This is just an artifact of how the Paradaptive Intelligence Network operates. Engineers are especially vulnerable to this pattern of thought after spending countless hours designing fabulous flops.

It is also invaluable to understand this attribute of the Paradaptive Intelligence Network if you need to reorganize and redirect a sales team after failing to achieve an objective. For example, in the course of business, sometimes unforeseeable things happen after a deal is finalized but before the installation or the purchased product or service can be implemented. The customer has achieved courage and is in the faith stage. They are still committed to the sale. As a salesperson, knowing this will allow you to skip the common mistake of salespeople who go back and redirect the dialogue to convince the client that the product and price are still right, and that the risk is acceptable. Instead, knowing that the emotions are accretive and all the emotions that were necessary to accomplish the sale are still in place, you can focus on creating a new motivation of tailoring an installation process for a new Human Action Cycle using the Innovation algorithm to create a new implementation plan.

All these emotions happen so fast and feel so natural that we take absolutely no notice of our Paradaptive Intelligence Network at work the hundreds of times a day it influences our actions as it attempts to help us achieve our goals and build relationships to increase our survivability.

NEW ERA OF SALES MANAGEMENT

In the past, sales managers and professionals tracked and projected sales and sales force production by collecting such variables as cold calls, appointments, presentations made, follow-up calls, phone calls made, and other events that described salespeople's' activities. There is even a whole ancillary industry that provides internet based services to help track salespeople's' activities by providing formats of the abovementioned tracking variables for management to manage their sales force. At the end of the month, a salesperson would sit down with their

Figure 20.3
Accretive Nature of Emotion Tonal Algorithms

SOLUTION A

Paranoia → Anxiety → Trepidation → Growing Pain → Acceptance → Learning Anticipation → Confidence → Excitement → Courage → Faith → Exuberance → Satisfied Customer

SOLUTION B

Paranoia → Anxiety → Trepidation → Growing Pain → Acceptance → Learning Anticipation → Confidence → Excitement → Courage → Faith → Exuberance → Satisfied Customer

SOLUTION C

Paranoia → Anxiety → Trepidation → Growing Pain → Acceptance → Learning Anticipation → Confidence → Excitement → Courage → Faith → Exuberance → Satisfied Customer

CUSTOMER A'S EMOTIONAL STATE UPON SALES ENGAGEMENT

Paranoia → Anxiety → Trepidation → Growing Pain → Acceptance → Learning Anticipation → Confidence → Excitement → Courage → Faith → Exuberance → Satisfied Customer

CUSTOMER B'S EMOTIONAL STATE UPON SALES ENGAGEMENT

Paranoia → Anxiety → Trepidation → Growing Pain → Acceptance → Learning Anticipation → Confidence → Excitement → Courage → Faith → Exuberance → Satisfied Customer

RELATIONSHIP TO PERSON A (HORIZONTAL)

Rage → Fury → Frustration → Tolerance → Acceptance → Curiosity → Camaraderie → Attachment → Friendship → Compassion → Grace → Universal Oneness

RELATIONSHIP TO PERSON B (HORIZONTAL)

Rage → Fury → Frustration → Tolerance → Acceptance → Curiosity → Camaraderie → Attachment → Friendship → Compassion → Grace → Universal Oneness

RELATIONSHIP TO PERSON C (HORIZONTAL)

Rage → Fury → Frustration → Tolerance → Acceptance → Curiosity → Camaraderie → Attachment → Friendship → Compassion → Grace → Universal Oneness

RELATIONSHIP TO PERSON D (HORIZONTAL)

Rage → Fury → Frustration → Tolerance → Acceptance → Curiosity → Camaraderie → Attachment → Friendship → Compassion → Grace → Universal Oneness manager or submit a numeric estimate as to the chances of a sale occurring for those sales still in the "pipeline" or sales that were in progress at the end of the accounting period. This is an extremely haphazard way of estimating sales, not only because it tracks salespeople's activities, which are secondary indicators of sales occurrence, but also because the required translation into a numeric probability introduces inaccuracy. This process asks salespeople to translate their internal interpretation of the prospect's Paradaptive Intelligence Network and the emotional state they are currently experiencing into a numeric figure. Really?! This book has illuminated a new way of managing sales by tracking emotional states, which is the only true indicator for the potential of a sale. In addition, it doesn't add or create translation errors by attempting to convert emotions to numbers. Metrics will develop as sales managers learn that X% of sales in the excitement phase will convert to sales by salespeople who at Y stage, courage on the Relationship algorithm, and so on for the other emotions of the Innovation algorithm. It provides better metrics on two fronts. First, translation error is eliminated because you can directly ask prospects about their emotional state. Do you see our product as being a viable solution? Are you confident about our product's potential to fix your problems? Are you excited about the deal? Not only will this tell you more precisely where the prospect and your sale are at, it will also tell you why you didn't get the sale. If the prospect had achieved excitement but went with another vendor, you now know that there was something in the risk envelope that prevented a sale. So instead of asking the prospect for feedback in an open-ended question such as "What caused you to go with another vender?", you can specifically enquire what made the risk intolerable.

It also allows for sales tracking with precision relationships with your clients. Since relationships are cooperative and synchronous, what your salesperson is feeling about the relationship will be very accurate as to what the client is feeling towards them. Using this methodology, when you, as a sales manager, call on accounts you can ask the clients about the relationship with your company and get precise feedback. The marketing department can get stronger information with marketing research from clients about how they feel about the brands you sell. This will give sales managers invaluable information about their salesmen, company, and its products in the marketplace and will show patterns of failure. If your salespeople are unable to form strong connections, then perhaps they need to try outside events and activities to create better opportunities to satisfy the six universal needs of their clients. If justification is needed for sales budgets and entertaining fees, the sales manager will now have empirical data to justify the expense by being able to directly measure what their expenditures are garnering in the market place by tracking relationship improvements. Not only that, this methodology can also be used to measure your competition's presence in the market place by tracking their relationships with their customers or jointly shared accounts. This gives sales managers and sales professionals precision heretofore unknown. This will allow sales managers more precise information to adjust their pricing, product, distribution channels, and policies as patterns of failed sales start to develop. All this precision provided by the Innovation and Relationship algorithms can lead to mathematical probability equations that can easily be set up in any spreadsheet program, which are a whole lot better than your salespeople's SWAGs (Scientific Wild-Ass Guesses). The question is what do you want to stake your career to, your salespeople's SWAG or mathematically supported and proven equations of probability? These are just a few of potential uses of your new understanding of the Paradaptive Intelligence Network.

The future of sales management and the ancillary sales management tools industry will be geared towards utilizing Paradaptive Intelligence Network tracking due to its precision in charting prime factors of sales occurrence potential. Sales, as currently pursued, is an anecdotal practice based solely on conjecture. There has been no science, until now, to direct its growth as a profession. While many of its practices are correct and in line with what science has substantiated, far more of its practices are based on misguided interpretations, lore, and myth. In order to move forward as a profession, the sales profession must learn how the human mind makes decisions and work within that framework in order to remove the stigma of the huckster salesperson that uses illegitimate persuasion and manipulation to obtain sales. This means that the sales profession must become fluent in the human psyche and its adaptational mechanisms, of which emotions play a large and foundational role. This is already occurring in sales, albeit in a fraction of its salespeople — these are the sales eagles, the sales leaders. They are already intuitively doing much, if not most, of what has been outlined in this book. No doubt, at this point in the book, the reader has validated every point made in the book in their own lives and experiences. The beauty of what has been presented herein is that it does not need validation from some unseen scientist in a lab somewhere performing experiments. You are able to validate everything in this book yourself in your daily lives and daily pursuits as a sales professional. The truths contained between this book's covers are truly self-evident.

So, why are you waiting? Greater precision and performance have now been placed within the reach of the sales industry and sales professionals through understanding the Paradaptive Intelligence Network. Paradaptive Intelligence is the future of the sales profession and all business endeavors and will be until the human mind is altered as a species, even at which point, our current understanding will allow us to map those changes when they occur in a couple of millennia or so.

DEATH OF THE RATIONAL MAN MODEL

As has been thoroughly demonstrated, all human actions concerning buying and selling are controlled by emotions. It has long been held as one of the central precepts of business that humans make rational choices about money. It is this organization around this now defunct principle that lead to the United States of America's second economic depression starting in 2008. The financial models used on Wall Street were based on this precept and worked well within certain parameters, but when economic bubbles burst, first in housing and then rippled through financial markets selling housing contracts, great gouts of irrationality were introduced to the market place which could not be predicted nor understood at the magnitudes experienced under the old paradigm. But now, as students of Paradaptive Intelligence, we can clearly see that this was predictable through the model presented herein. Small amounts of fear can be tolerated and overridden by the adaptor when the reactor senses a threat. But as the threat increases, more and more irrationality is injected into human behavior, principally in the form to flee — the model's standard response to threats. This also explains why the current models used in financial markets work within certain parameters, the passive area of threat where the adaptor retains majority and thus primacy over the reactor. After the Line of Passivity, irrationality dominates because majority control of human behavior is passed to the reactor which is focusing solely on its prime directive to save the body and self.

The rational man model was not without basis as a model, but like most things discussed in this book, our foundational precepts were based on misunderstood observations. The formulation of a motive is entirely rationally driven or, put another way, forming the intent was rational. And this is what led to the assumption that the rest of the process was rationally driven. But all human actions are controlled by emotions; this means the acts of buying, holding, and selling stocks, or other financial instruments are totally under control of the Paradaptive Intelligence Network which controls the amount of rationality in human behavior. The greater the fear, the less rationality there will be.

Fear is a pack animal. It drives humans to seek strength and protection in numbers of those equally under the thrall of fear's spell. Again, this explains why panic spreads and individual actions of independent investors morphs into blind stampedes as rationality is encumbered in the market by threat due to the constructs of Paradaptive Intelligence. So, financial markets will be imperiled until the precept of the rational man model is removed and replaced with the Paradaptive Intelligence Network paradigm. All the world's greatest marketplaces of unadulterated consumer behavior and sales, the exchanges and commodities markets, will continue to risk unforeseeable meltdowns and wild gyrations because the opaque lens of the rational man model does not let them see fully the true nature of human adaptation as it manifests itself as consumer behavior and sales.

THE 98% SOLUTION

The range of the Paradaptive Intelligence model application is stated to be one hundred percent accurate across ninety-eight percent of the earth's population. The model is neither language nor culturally dependent because it is DNA encoded, so it will be applicable to ninety-eight percent of all humans regardless of any other ethnic, gender, or societal factors. But, because the Paradaptive Intelligence Network is an amalgam of several stand-alone systems that work in concert to increase survivability; there will be variability from individual to individual in efficacy and emphasis as no two systems will have the same exact DNA or learned exemplars upon which Paradaptive Intelligence is reliant.

But how was the ninety-eight percent application rate derived? The answer is as simple as its ramifications are large. With the new model of Paradaptive Intelligence, and its foundational component of Peil's Emotional Feedback System, we can now understand the feedback mechanisms of Type II Adaptation which manifests itself in modern societies, in part as consumer behavior and sales methodology. The Theory of Paradaptive Intelligence defines psychopathy as a genetic defect in one or more of the mechanisms of the Paradaptive Intelligence Network. In short, psychopaths have defective and partially functional Type II Adaptation systems. Two percent of the population has been estimated to have psychopathy. One well discussed theory of psychopathy has proposed it as an alternative mating strategy because observed behavior of psychopaths has them effectively being able to seduce mates, but having impaired pair-bonding circuitry designed for long-term relationships and parenting. Thus, psychopaths have been noted to have many more partners and therefore greater opportunity for progeny. The Theory of Paradaptive Intelligence sees psychopaths not as an alternative mating strategy, but as a parasitic mutation. Because psychopaths have impaired adaptational abilities, they are dependent upon those with fully functional Type II adaptation systems to achieve goals and adaptation which they convince or manipulate to share the bounty. This inability of psychopaths to accomplish goals has been documented in the work of Canadian researcher Dr. Robert D. Hare, one of the leading authorities in the area of psychopathy. He is also responsible for developing the 12-point test to determine the presence of psychopathy which is the current standard in psychiatry and psychology.

However, current research in the field of psychopathy has been mainly focused on clinical psychopaths. There are two classes of psychopaths: clinical and subclinical. Clinical psychopaths are the axe-murderer, crime spree, violent serial murderer, Ponzi scheme criminal types that often grab the headlines. Subclinical psychopaths have the same DNA deficiencies but, due to environmental factors in growing up that moderate their DNA imbedded tendencies, they never achieve the level of violence or lawlessness of their more famous brethren. Subclinical psychopaths live among us in our neighborhoods and work with us, usually causing a lot of drama due to their dysfunctional adaptive abilities seeking nonviolent ways to co-opt the functionals' goal achievements. It is very difficult to identify subclinical in situ, therefore very little is known about their numbers in the general population. It is therefore likely, as more is learned about subclinical psychopathy, the percentage of two percent of psychopaths in the general population may change. Perhaps the best way to summarize the information of this section is to say that all the principles, rules, and operating conventions presented in this book concerning Paradaptive Intelligence will apply one-hundred percent of the time to ninety-eight percent of the population.

THE LOST FUNCTION OF SALES

"A customer will buy an inferior product at a higher price from someone they like." This nugget of sales wisdom has been known to sales eagles since the beginning of sales as a profession. As written, it misses the factual basis, but comes close enough to illustrate the relationship between the two elements – the *someone* and the *something*. The inaccuracy comes in the use of the work "like," which is imprecise. Stated throughout this book, these two emotional algorithms, *someone* and *something*, happen concurrently in a transaction to influence and mediate each other. Additionally, it has noted that salesforces are among the most expensive forms of marketing, but also the most effective when managed properly. The reason for this is that a salesforce can bring an added dimension that no other form of business activity can obtain. Only face to face interactions can achieve emotions in relationship algorithms above a specific point. That demarcation point is the emotions in the emotion algorithms that satisfy the needs creativity and meaning of the Six Universal Needs. Advertising can't do it. Promotions can't do it, nor anything else one cares to proffer.

Actually, a customer will buy an inferior product at a higher price from someone who satisfies their higher order emotional needs. This was discussed in the sections of Acquaintance and Friendship Phases in Chapter 17. Emotions in relationship algorithms that satisfy the needs of creativity and meaning are all higher end growth signals which deliver higher doses of joy into the Paradaptive Intelligence Network. The word "like" in the original version of the nugget's imprecision stems from its failure to describe which type of relationship algorithm is supplying the joy. Conversely, we could take to understand that we "like" anyone who we're in a relationship of any type that satisfies the higher needs of creativity and meaning. It is these higher needs emotional satisfaction that has been lost to the marketplace. Unfortunately, due to current governmental interference via regulation in the free market, these higher emotional functions have been all but stripped from the marketplace. But before delving into this misguided governmental blundering, a quick review of the history of professional sales would be helpful as a foundation for further discussion.

In the Chapter 19's Fifth Epoch Section this book delineated the different epochs of professional sales driven by the advent of mass production of the Industrial Revolution. As recalled, in the first epoch, sales were driven by the lack of products available to consumers and the sales focus was on distribution network development. In the second epoch, initial consumer thirsts for product were slacked and competition among producers forced salesforces to focus on relationships for competitive edges. This competition drove producers to develop new product lines to find untended market veins to create competitive edges and increase volumes. This proliferation in product lines forced the development of new element, the marketing department in the third epoch which coordinated the sales efforts across product lines. The focus of a salesforce was to maximize sales volume by matching their firm's corresponding product lines, in the right proportions, for a specific distribution outlet's clients. In order to do this, salesforces had to have more than a passing knowledge of each point of their distribution channels which forced further focus upon relationships. In the fourth epoch of the marketing company, increased competition in a more global marketplace saw a shift from salesforce distribution channel reliance to management of up-channel, end-user consumer relationships. Marketing departments now superseded salesforces which managed the consumer relationships through media. The proliferation of product lines forced manufacturers to re-assess their relationship with the end consumer and this noted the first shift away from mass production to specified production tailored to consumer preferences. The fourth epoch of sales saw the start of the shift away from salesforces to media dominated relationship building with consumers as the primary sales driver. In the fifth epoch, the re-alignment of manufacturers' focus was completed as salesforces were further diminished as they tried to totally remove dependence on distribution channels by direct marketing to consumers with products designed to be customized to the individual wants and desires of the consumer.

There were several societal shifts that also corresponded with these realignments in sales efforts that must also be considered. During the second, third and most of the fourth epoch, client entertainment was considered a mandatory function of the position of a salesperson. This was work – salesmen were not at home with their families doing what they wanted with their time, often traveling excessively. They needed ways to entice clients away from their time with their families, too. Food, drink, and entertainment opportunities were sought and supported by manufactures' generous expense accounts for their salesforce. This was also an era when drinking was considered a much more socially acceptable American pastime – an echo of prohibition no doubt. Manufactures understood that relationships could not be built within their distribution channels, whom they were dependent upon, to their fullest extent in the constrained settings of an office environment. As manufactures started to shift their focus to consumer relationship building and away from dependence on distribution channel relationships, marketing dollars were shifted from sales' entertainment expense accounts into media advertising for consumer relationship building. Concurrent to these business shifts, societal and governmental views also shifted. While attitudes towards drinking in and of itself did not change, societal views on inebriation did. Inebriation and the actions of an individual while inebriated became less tolerated by society. In addition, governmental views, particularly in the tax code, changed their position on writing off client entertainment as a necessary business expense. This was in response to business excesses and abuses as executives used business entertainment as a method to finance their lifestyles free of taxes under the guise of business necessity. This resulted in more restrictive codes as to what constituted business entertainment and that which remained required substantially more documentation and paper work to claim. When more effort is required to claim a relief in the tax code, inevitably, you'll see less of those claims; and, so too, did this further diminish the use of client entertainment for the purposes of relationship building for the Six Universal Needs emotional satisfaction of creativity and meaning. In its infinite wisdom, when government decreed that business entertainment wasn't all that necessary and needed to be greatly restricted, they threw the "baby out with the bathwater" with this backlash against business entertainment. The government in its blunderings has determined that all business should be decided on the merits of the Innovation Algorithm alone with minimal interference from the component of the relationship algorithms. This removes another sector of competitiveness from the marketplace – who is better at building relationships.

These shifts in business, government, and society have resulted in a current attitude within business that if a salesperson wants to entertain a client, it's not necessary, but nice. So, if a salesperson wants to do it, they're free to do so, but will do it without company support. The salesperson should use their pocket money and write it off on their tax return. This nicely removes business enterprises from dealing with the regulatory burdens of business entertainment. This has further engendered the business attitude norm of "if a salesperson wants to do business entertainment, he's the one who will ultimately benefit through sales commissions, therefore, the burdens of business entertainment are theirs alone."

Now let's go back to the beginning of Chapter 16 where Frederick F. Reichheld is quoted in his book, *The Loyalty Effect:*

> "Loyalty is dead, the experts proclaim, and the statistics seem to bear them out. On average, U.S. corporations now lose half their customers in five years, half their employees in four, and half their investors in less than one. We seem to face a future in which the only business relationships will be opportunistic transactions between virtual strangers."

Business, in this particular case sales and marketing management, have abandoned the only tool capable of satisfying the Six Universal Needs of creativity and meaning in the Friendship Phase of relationships. Instead, business has hitched its wagon to media as its relationship building tool of choice and thus accepted its built-in limitation in which of the Six Universal Needs this type of relationship building tool can deliver. Is it any wonder that business statics of client loss within a five-year period and random transactions decried by Frederick F. Reichheld are the current norm?

Prior to this book and the Paradaptive Intelligence Theory, there was no understanding based in hard science that could be used to not only explain the mechanisms of relationships building to business, government and science, but also explain the malaise of customer infidelity that has beset modern marketing. The law of unexpected consequence is alive and well when we examine government tax code designed to curtail business relationship building. When these governmental restrictions were invoked, the biological underpinnings of relationships within business were not understood. By severely curtailing the involvement of relationship building within business by restrictive tax codes, the government edicts are now working directly against behavior DNA encoded into every human. Humans are driven to seek creativity and meaning. When laws are enacted that work against the most basic nature and needs of humans, the result is what we see now, a crippled marketplace functioning erratically as expressed by the statistics of client and consumer loyalty unanchored.

Distribution chain management, and their prime agents, the salesforce, as well as end-user direct-marketing salesforces can now be realigned using the model of Paradaptive Intelligence to bring back the lost science of relationship building to combat competitive loss and customer fecklessness. There is a historical reason why salespersons, when managed well, have always been the prime marketing tool, and now, thanks to the Paradaptive Intelligence Theory, we can explain the reasons on a solid scientific foundation.

MARKETPLACE EVOLUTIONARY FORCES OF CONSUMER BEHAVIOR

We have now seen the Paradaptive Intelligence Network's structure, function and operating principles described as well as examples of it in operation with real world scenarios. But to put it in greater context, you must now understand how this is the driving force behind marketplace selection for top performers. In preparation for this book, countless interviews of top performer salesperson from a wide swath of industries and sales venues were conducted and a pattern emerged. Those salespeople that were the most proficient at facilitating the buyers' Innovation Emotional Tonal Algorithm were selected by the marketplace as top sales performers. Those salespeople that could move buyers through the five emotions of the Vetting Phase of the Innovation Emotional Tonal Algorithm in the most proficient manner obtained the greatest portions of orders. Of those high order takers, those that were the most proficient at facilitating the consumer's path through three emotions of the Application Phase Innovation Emotional Tonal Algorithm kept the highest number of sales on the books and received among the highest remunerations. Those high achieving sales leaders that not only facilitated the Innovation Emotional Tonal Algorithm but were also the most proficient at facilitating the Horizontal Professional Relationship algorithm were able to make sales across the greatest swath of customers and these were the sales professionals that were the elite handful in every organization. Intuitively, they understood what the prospects were biologically compelled to do and helped facilitate the process to nullify their pain points in the most efficient manner. And their customers loved them for it. This is the source of concept of consultive selling. The biological imperative of pain point nullification is called consumer behavior. Understanding the biological imperative of consumer behavior, whether intuitively, as has been the case prior to the publication of this book, or now in a comprehensive, rational, quantifiable, and predictable manner, gives us a much greater insight into the stimulus and response of transactions and thus the protocols of the sales industry. We can now see how question based sales techniques indirectly are able to facilitate the customers' focus upon their pain nullification process. And we can now see how proper cultivation of the Horizontal Professional Relationship algorithm acts as a force multiplier by improving facilitation through directed, specific, and improved communication between buyer and seller in the Innovation/Technology Acquisition algorithm. In the end, it is biological imperatives that control what and how the marketplace selects for in adaption and the Paradaptive Intelligence model details this biology.

Now that the biological imperative mechanisms are laid bare, this should act as the basis for organizations to form the most expensive marketing program within every company, the sales force. Prior to this book, companies took their best guesses, some better than others', at hiring the right salespeople and making sales policies. This was usually done through the approximation of "experience." The belief was that "experience" was end-all to be-all. Whereas' in fact, what we can now see is that "experience" actually consist more or less of collection of Horizontal Professional relationships where there is greater communication. But greater communication cannot overcome products that do not nullify pain points. If relationships are used in this manner, they will soon degrade because relationships are dynamic and are constantly re-evaluated based on every communication transaction, which is the currency of all relationships. So firms would hire salespeople based on a set of hiring criteria that at best were assumptions and at worst opinions without proper foundation. They had an intuitive idea of what they needed in a salesperson, but did not understand how to identify or quantify the manifestation of the attributes for which they were looking. The elite sales firms not only have well developed criteria for sales candidate selection but training programs that teach reasonably useful indirect sales techniques that moved a salesperson closer than their competitors sales training programs to the point where a newly hired salesperson's internal Paradaptive Intelligence Network could develop a reasonably successful sales routine. By using the criteria in this book, organizations now have a template upon which to build recruitment and training programs. If the science is good, well defined, and verified, it will solve problems encountered in the field. This is the case with the science of Paradaptive Intelligence. These concepts have already been applied in the real world and the outcomes were predictably excellent. In the past, organizations would hope that through refined selection and proper training that their new hires would have to "wing it" for shorter times until they figured out that company's marketplace and became productive. By using Paradaptive Intelligence principles, selection and training no longer becomes a practice of "getting close enough" but becomes a system of on target delivery and instant productivity. As discussed in Chapter 19, a firm only has to shift nine percent of its sales force from the middle tier of performers to top performers to become a world class sales organization. Using Paradaptive Intelligence to understand a market's biological imperatives to the pain points encountered in that market segment promises to move every salesperson to their personal potential in sales limited by only their biological intellect and not by the unfounded sales folklore that has cluttered the sales industry and misled salespeople away from their highest possible productivity.

The DNA encoded process of adaption described in the Paradaptive Intelligence model was placed there by evolutionary forces to select for greater behavioral adaptation. So at the root of the marketplace, the most basic of all activities - the transaction – is a byproduct of evolution and its relentless pursuit for adaptation, both Type I (physical) and Type II (behavioral). A transaction is driven by the adaptation circuitry establishing a direct line of cause and effect of how transactions occur, or why they fail to occur. At its most basic level, the Paradaptive Intelligence Network is a feedback system to accomplish adaptive behavior by either changing one's actions to suit the environment or the environment to suit their behavior. The entire system is predicated on a motivation/objective and feedback received by various biological sensory systems to assure accomplishment of the objective. This is key to understanding all sales activities. If you, as a salesperson, are not setting your objectives and controlling your Paradaptive Intelligence Network to set or influence buyers' internal feedback to facilitate their Paradaptive Intelligence Network, then you are not performing in the most efficient manner. Not only are you not being efficient and less productive, you are working against Mother Nature and billions of years of behavioral adaptation evolution.

PRINCIPLES VERSUS SPECIFICS

Salespeople, as a breed, are looking for the easiest path through problems with the least amount of effort. All humans are. In the past, books on sales were purchased by salespeople with the idea that there would be useful elements contained therein that could be copied with little effort. This is not that book, nor can it be. The sales kingdom is just too vast for this book to create specific verbiage for every situation in every industry or selling situation. Instead, this book has striven to teach the principles of working within the Paradaptive Intelligence Network of your clients and prospects, and understand the science underlying it. By understanding the relationship and operating mechanisms of the components of the brain, you will be in a much better position to adapt this methodology into your business routines as you sell.

Understanding the Paradaptive Intelligence principles, rather than parroting prepared questions of other question-based selling methodology, will allow you much more flexibility to adapt when some new situation occurs for which you were not specifically prepped. And that always happens. By adopting Paradaptive Intelligence selling principles and internalizing them, as well as utilizing your own Paradaptive Intelligence Network, you will always have a guide to help you make the right decision, which will reduce the stress and confusion that you will experience in life while increasing your sales performance.

PUTTING IT ALL TOGETHER – AN OVERVIEW

We learned that there are three phases to sales. The first phase of the Innovation algorithm is based in the past and is called the Acquisition, the second phase is called Vetting and deals with predicting adaptation into the future, and the third phase, called Application, dealing with the actual implementation, costs, and benefits of the adaption (See Figure 20.4).

These three phases cover twelve emotional stages. The only guaranteed emotion and phase that a prospect will cover with a salesman is courage in the Vetting phase. All others are situational. And each one of the emotional phases has its own aim and criteria that must be met in order for the feed-forward feedback cycle of the Human Action Cycle to progress to the next emotional stage of Paradaptive Intelligence Network's algorithm. When you step back and look at the three phases and the twelve emotions of emotional tonal algorithm, some structure starts to emerge. The Acquisition phase is comprised of a corrective signal – fear, that ramps down to lower intensities as the HAC feeds forward - right. In Peil's EFS Model, this phase represents the self-protection circuitry of our adaptation system. The Vetting and Application phases are ones of growth signals – joy. The two growth signal phases ramp up from low intensity joy to emotions that provoke the strongest joy agitation in our Paradaptive Intelligence Network. In the EFS Model, the Vetting phase represents the self-development of circuitry of our adaptation system. The Application phase represents the self-actualization portion of the adaptation circuitry of the human species and is evaluative in programming. The stronger a signal becomes, whether corrective or growth, the closer it moves to becoming a pure basic emotion, with little or no differentiation between complex and basic emotion. The most pure forms of basic emotions are terminal signals, the highest intensities of the basic emotion, which is why all terminal emotions are enclosed in boxes in the graphs of emotional tonal algorithms. The emotional tonal algorithms show two

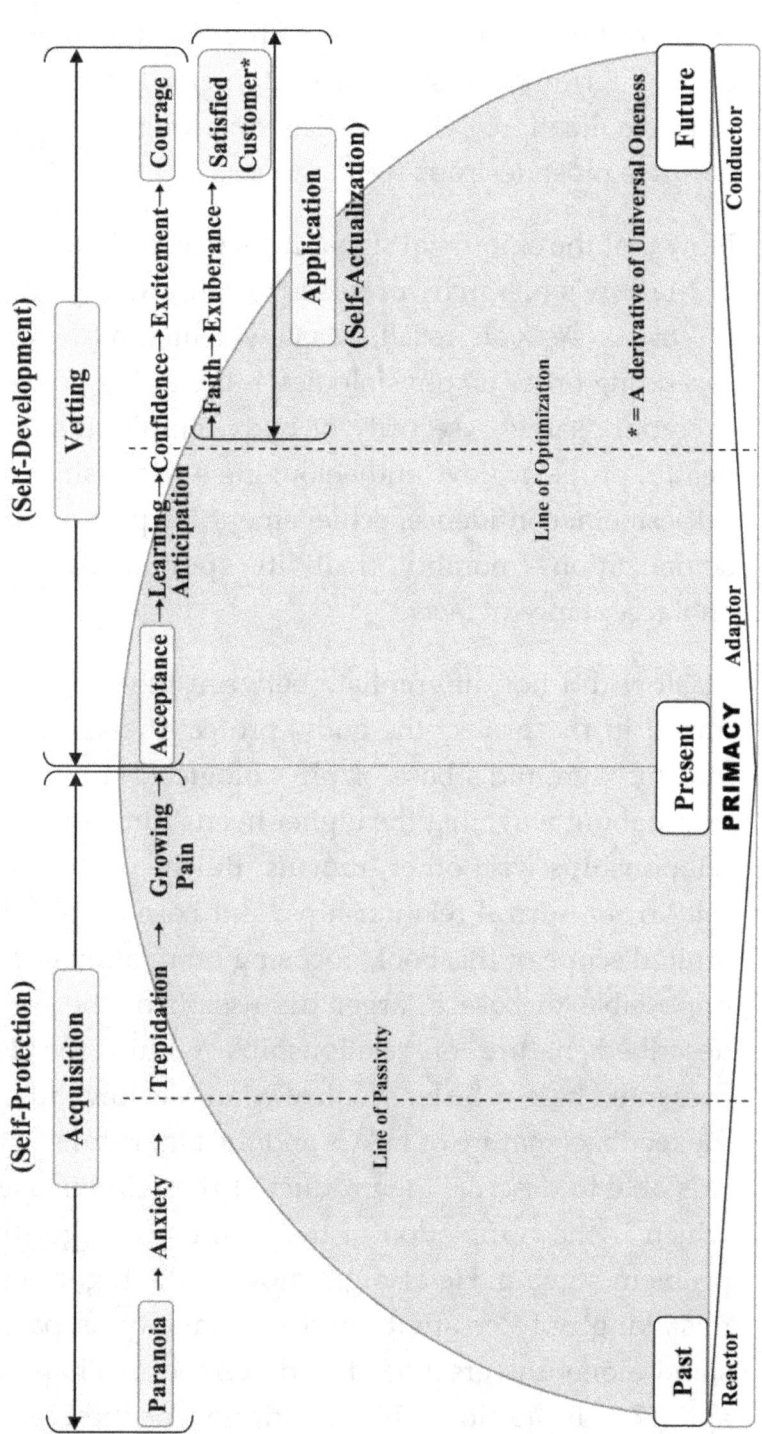

FIGURE 20.4

**Three Phases of the
Innovation Emotional Tonal Flow**

distinct growth signal paths separated on two different lines. This is done to show that even though these emotions are all part of the same twelve emotion The emotional tonal algorithms show two distinct growth signal paths separated on two different lines. This is done to show that even though these emotions are all part of the same twelve emotion progressions, after the terminal emotion courage, the intensity of joy in the following progression dips back to complex emotions which is close to the terminal emotion of the first line, but weaker signaling ramping up to another terminal joy signal in customer satisfaction that this book equates with Peil's self-actualization. Self-actualization along with courage are listed in Figure 8.1 as nature's most desirous feeling tones.

Now that the emotional signaling is mapped out, it's time to take a look at the classic of Maslow's hierarchy of needs to re-evaluate what he got right and where he got off track. As you recall, Maslow's hierarchy of needs was an organization in ascending order of: physiological – breathing, food, water, sex, sleep, homoeostasis, excretion; safety – security of body, employment, resources, morality, the family, health, property; love and belonging – friendship, family, sexual intimacy; esteem – self-esteem, confidence, achievement, respect of others, respect by others; and self-actualization – morality, creativity, spontaneity, problem solving, lack of prejudice, and acceptance of facts.

Maslow did not differentiate between the subconscious and conscious minds and mixed in the protect-the-body/protect-the-self mission of the subconscious mind into his pyramid's base of physiological. He was able to differentiate, albeit in a roundabout way, that the higher needs functions can only be filled in the context of relationships with other humans. But he didn't differentiate between "protect the self" from hurtful relationships; and based it solely on physical needs. Due to the limited scope of this book, focusing on relationships as it pertains only to sales, it is impossible to base a larger discussion of the errors of Maslow on the partially described nature of relationships within the Paradaptive Intelligence model presented herein. So let's look at what Maslow did get right. Without knowing about the feedback nature of HACs and the algorithms of adaptation and relationships, he was able to describe the product of these in his use of the feelings of achievement, which is the completion of the adaptation algorithm, which he also described as problem solving. He also got most of the higher order six universal needs correct, mistaking only creativity and spontaneity as part of self-actualization and not a stand-alone universal need as described in Chapter 17 and depicted in Graph 17.2 and 17.3. In addition, his description of these emotions alluded to a process by naming the product or outcomes of what we now know as algorithms. Graph 20.4 can also be used to tie in the concepts of the three phases of self-protection, self-development, and self-actualization into a universal construct when equating the universal need for power, corrective signals, and self-protection together; the Vetting phase, the universal needs of connection and esteem, and self-development together; the Application phase, the universal needs of creativity and meaning, and self-actualization together. All in all, Maslow's first forays into this realm resulted in a mash-up of a lot of the major pieces, but without any order nor statement of the processes that produced the emotions he categorized.

The simple graphs of Figures 20.4 and 17.3 are now able to describe a comprehensive, robust understanding of the Paradaptive Intelligence Network in sales that can remind the readers at a glance what they need to accomplish as they go about their business.

And lastly, we can now look at sales in a completely new light. Sales is a function of free markets, and only free markets. Sales is a voluntary activity, freely entered into by two people or groups. Central market planners of progressive utopianism eliminate choice from individuals via dictates and regulation of their central organization and thus eliminate not only the need, but also the opportunity, for cooperation. Centrally planned or highly regulated markets are compliance based, which is a one-way transaction. Cooperation is a two-way transaction where both parties mutually and voluntarily assist each other. We now understand that the adaptor is the main mechanism responsible for adaptation, which means its bias, cooperation, is the primary driver of all transactions, hence commerce. Economists describe the free market as a place of competition. That is only half right. What is selected for in the marketplace via sales is cooperation. Firms seek out products and services that deliver the greatest cooperation. The competition claimed by economists is actually competition among firms as to who can be and deliver the most cooperation. Providing pleasure by taking away someone's pain point is cooperation, which in turn engenders the need to reciprocate with remuneration to obtain it. The firms whose products relieve the greatest amount of pain points or provide the greatest pleasure/joy are seen as the most cooperative by consumers' Paradaptive Intelligence Networks. Those companies whose transaction policies, i.e. sales terms, are the most flexible, thus the most cooperative, will also be selected by the marketplace. Take a good long minute to fully understand this; it's foundational. All commerce, all transactions, originate from cooperation, which is central to the mechanisms of adaptation, the adaptor. This explains the poor performance of the sales industry as a whole whose focus is "Sell. Sell! SELL!!!" which has it on a path contrary to the central functionality of consumer behavior under the Paradaptive Intelligence Network's adaptor. This also helps explains the dichotomy between world-class sales forces and the rest of the pack. World-class sales organizations focus on providing cooperation to the greatest extent possible while the rest of the marketplace focuses on implementing rigid, uncooperative sales policies that appear to have short-term benefits to them, coupled with products and services that deliver lesser degrees of cooperation. These apparent benefits are illusionary because capitulation to impediments that force rigid transaction policies, rather than removing them, restricts your firm's flexibility, and thus its ability to cooperate, only leaving you vulnerable to other firms, your competitors, who will find a way to be flexible and cooperative where you won't. Understanding that you're in the cooperation business and that your mission is to become the most cooperative agent of change in the marketplace will drastically improve your performance. Once you understand the market is cooperative, not competitive, you will have a great start to becoming a world-class salesperson or sales organization.

And lastly, it's time now to take a comprehensive look visually at all the elements of the Paradaptive Intelligence Network as they work together controlling all human adaptation and business behavior, particularly consumer behavior and the actions that govern the sales cycle. The following, Figures 20.5, 20.6, and 20.7, represent the three algorithms that this book focused on: Innovation, Horizontal Professional, and Institutions. These graphs combine all the elements discussed in this book from beginning to end. At first glance, these graphs may look daunting to the un-initiated, but having come this far in the book, these graphs represent now familiar elements to reader who should have no problem understanding the mechanisms and their interactions.

THE NEXT CHALLENGE – LETTING GO

By now, you've started experimenting in implementing Paradaptive Intelligence selling into your day-to-day sales activities or recognized its foundation in every decision you make. The difficulty of letting go of practices and habits that have sustained your professional career is normal and understandable. Many of you have been educated or indoctrinated in sales methodologies which are more mythology, taught in seminars, training programs, and business schools that have the backing of tradition and prevailing wisdom. It might be helpful to remember that once the prevailing wisdom was that the earth was flat. The thing that changed this notion was the discovery of facts that when organized led to new perspectives. The new perspective allowed people to "discover" truths that had been hiding in plain sight, needing only a new lens of perception to come into focus. The history of science and man is littered with these new perspectives.

FIGURE 20.5

Comprehensive Innovation Emotional Tonal Algorithm™

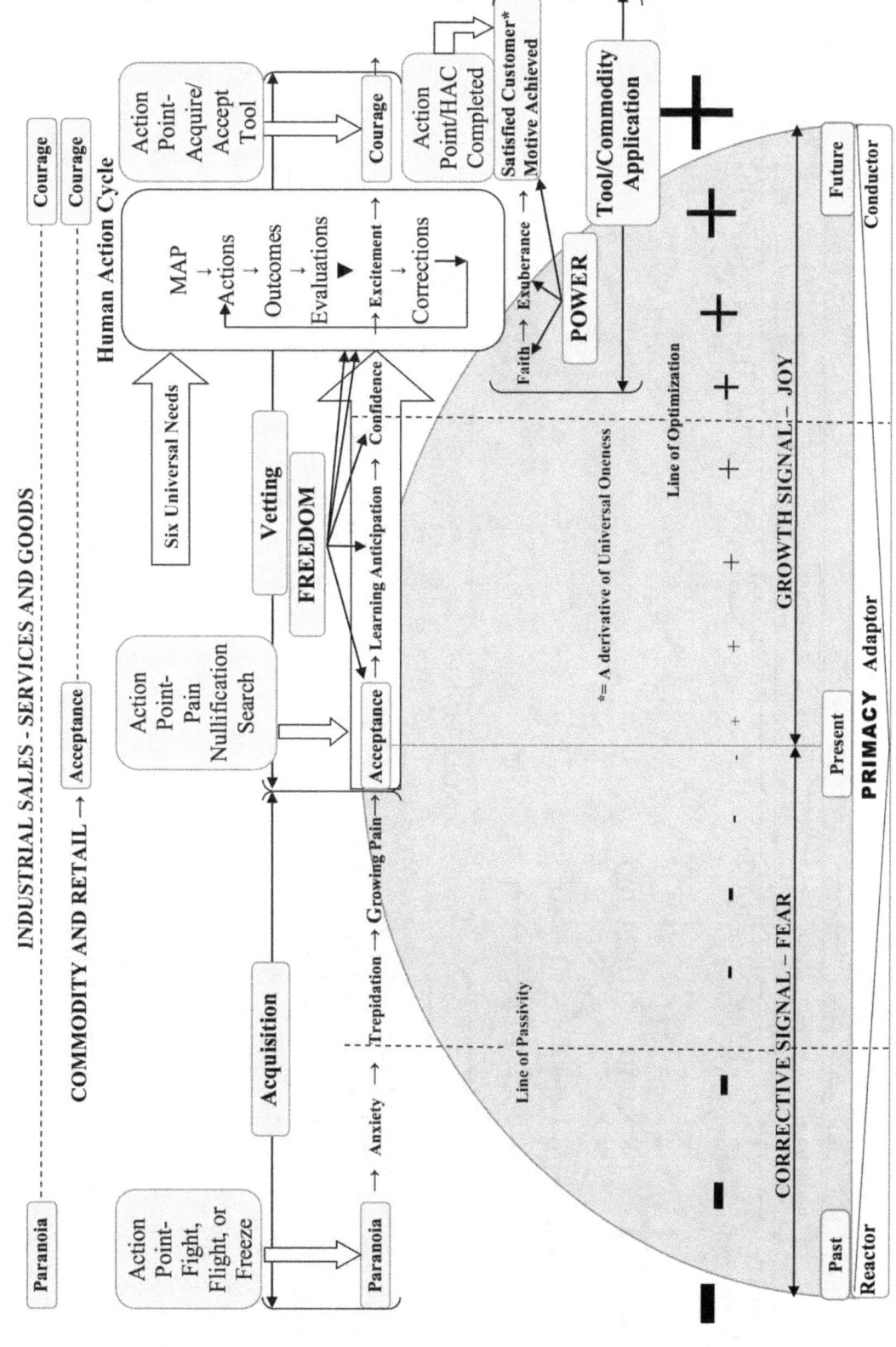

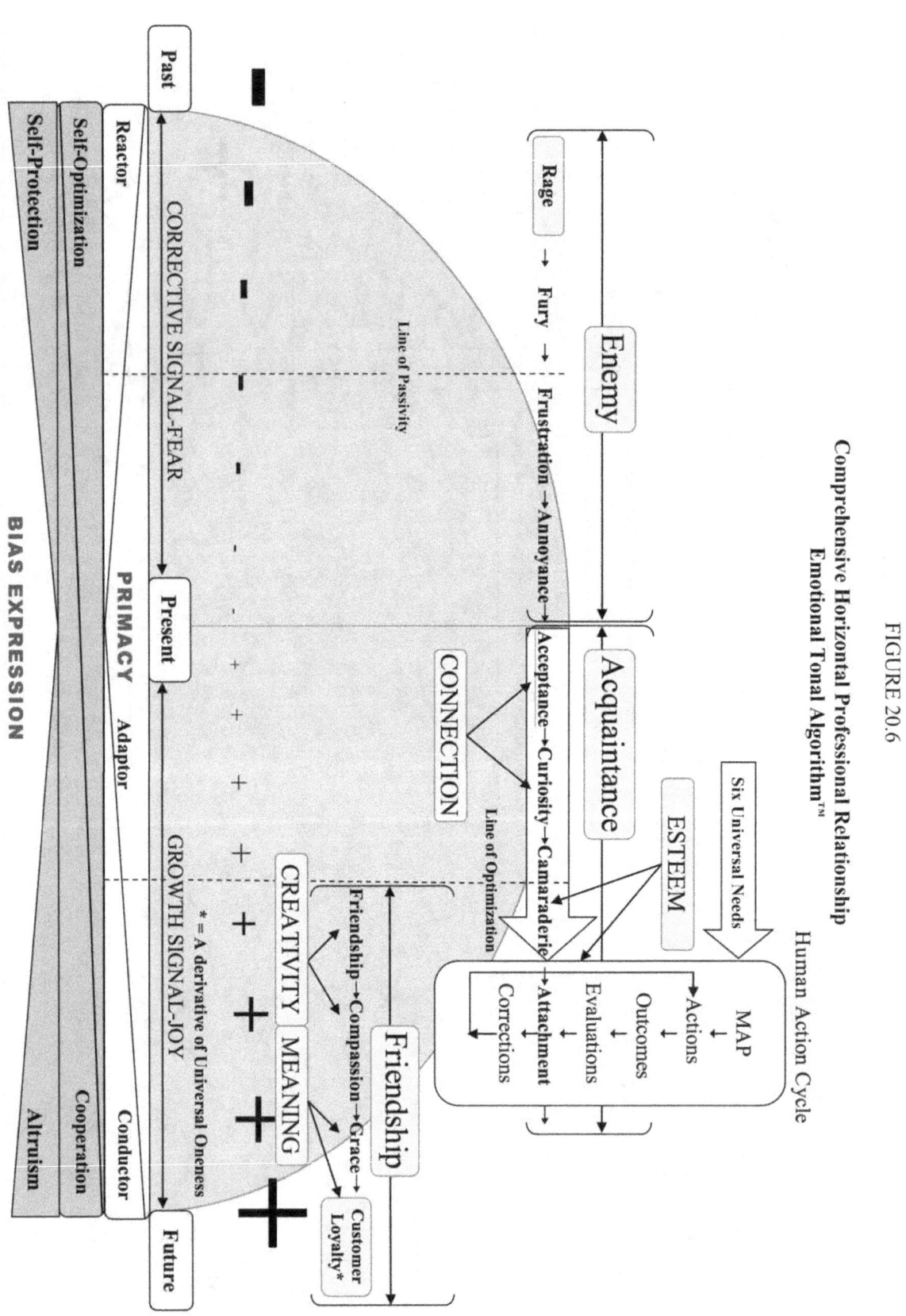

FIGURE 20.6

Comprehensive Horizontal Professional Relationship
Emotional Tonal Algorithm™

FIGURE 20.7

Comprehensive Institutional Relationship
Emotional Tonal Algorithm™

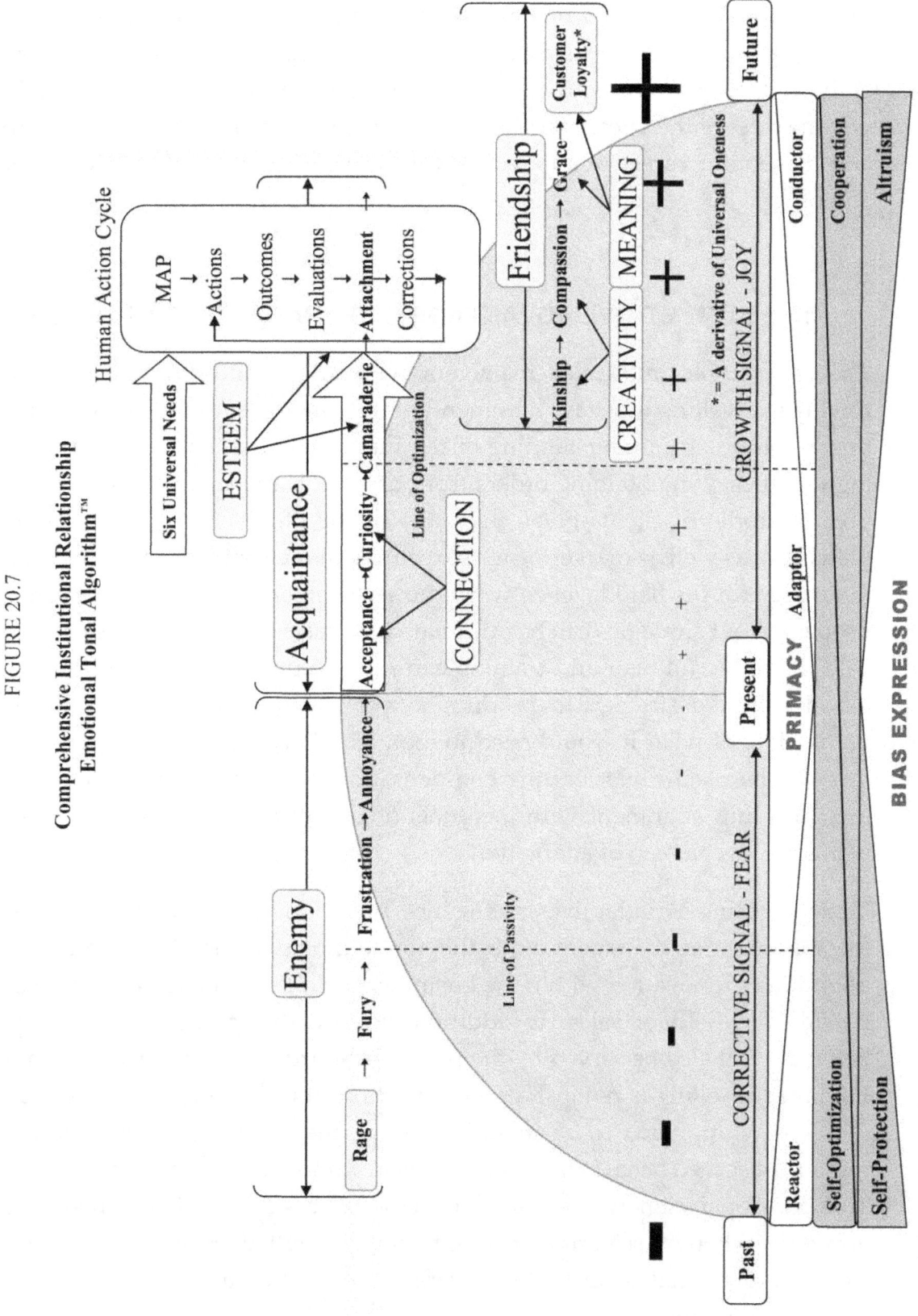

Don't let your old lens, your old paradigm of sales derived from unguided experience, statistical analysis of semi-random variables, and professorial indoctrination by those who've never had to sell for a living, stand in the way of turning your sales career in a new, better direction. In order to do that, you need to embrace the new paradigm of Paradaptive Intelligence selling. This book has given you the rules of the salesperson's road, but you will still need to get behind the wheel and drive your career in a new direction. Now, the most difficult task you face is accepting what you already know.

THE COMPETITIVE ADVANTAGE OF PARADAPTIVE INTELLIGENCE

The salespeople and sales managers who adopt and implement Paradaptive Intelligence selling will have a tremendous advantage over their competitors. Using this revolutionary understanding of the human adaptation mechanism will create higher efficacy in obtaining orders from prospects and directing salespeople to the proper profile of clients given the stage of the life cycle of their products. Sales managers, as well as marketing and executive managers, can now understand what must occur at the field level between the salesperson and prospect or client, so that proper rollout strategies can be formulated for sales force assemblage and activities. Sales force recruitment and training can now be understood within the context of broad cohesive strategy to produce a world-class sales force and provide the parameters of what it would need to look like. Paradaptive Intelligence principles can also be used in structuring compensation and incentives to drive sales force activities into alignment with the goals of becoming a world-class sales team by using the mechanism of adaptation.

Understanding Paradaptive Intelligence methodologies and principles will give salespeople and managers alike the foundational principles of adaptation and adoption of innovation within the business world that will serve them in capacities outside the field of sales. In addition, science disciplines that observe human behavior will also be served by the principles introduced in this book. Paradaptive Intelligence selling is not just a set of questions, but is used as a term to describe a whole new approach to business by linking the emotion/adaptive engine of the mind to observed behavior, business practices, and any applicable science discipline. This book opens a new era in the business sciences by creating a cross-disciplinary approach whereby scientific developments are pulled from the labs and journals from various fields and "engineered" for field application in commerce, politics… and life.

And a final point to close this book upon. By understanding how emotions work, via Peil's work with the Emotional Feedback System which is expanded by the Paradaptive Intelligence paradigm, of which only a limited portion was presented in these pages, you will be able to bring greater control of your mind and fuller appreciation of others. Understanding and using the guidance of Paradaptive Intelligence will have a profound impact upon the lives of its practitioners, allowing them to gain more control by understanding the internal guidance system we call emotions.

"Emotion has taught mankind to reason."

-Vauvenargues

This book covered quite a few topics within the realm of sales, introducing a myriad of concepts. It is understandable that quickly and accurately adapting these new operating principles may present a challenge to firms given the amount of misinformation and unsupported conjecture present in the marketplace which has become the foundation to modern business practices. The SPAN Consulting Group stands ready to assist in creating a world-class sales force or developing any other phase of your sales operations, from sales training to applicant testing and identification. In addition, the SPAN Consulting Group stands ready to help your firm implement sound business processes and training based on Paradaptive Intelligence principals in all phases of management, marketing, and political science. Information on contacting The SPAN Consulting Group can be found at the following website:

www.spanconsultinggroup.com

Appendix

Katherine Peil's Emotional Feedback System Theory was published in three languages by the international medical journal Global Advances in Health and Medicine.

Peil, K.T., Emotion: The Self-Regulatory Sense. Global Advances in Health and Medicine, March, 2014; 3(2):80-108.

www.ingramcontent.com/pod-product-compliance
Lightning Source LLC
Chambersburg PA
CBHW081522050726

47503CB00017B/2761